Loves Me,
Loves Me Not

Loves Me, Loves Me Not

Libby Malin

**RED
DRESS
INK**
™

LOVES ME, LOVES ME NOT

A Red Dress Ink novel

ISBN 0-373-89534-8

© 2005 by Elizabeth Sternberg.

www.RedDressInk.com

Printed in U.S.A.

ACKNOWLEDGMENTS

I'm extremely grateful to Red Dress Ink, but especially
to my editor, Kathryn Lye, for her keen insights and skillful
suggestions.

Thanks, too, to my writer friends Jerri Corgiat and
Karen Brichoux, whose support is available 24/7 even
when I sink into Amy-like neurotic paranoia. And...
to my friend Bruce Bortz for his faith in me.

Finally, I'm thankful to all my family for their encouragement,
particularly to my sister, Mary Ann, who suggested I
write fiction, knowing I'd always wanted to do so, and for
remarking one day that a florist who fills regular orders for a
man she's never met might make a good start for a story.

To Matthew

Sentir l'amour devant tout ce qui passe. Ne point passer!
—Sully Prudhomme

chapter 1

Red carnation: Alas for my poor heart!

Before I knew what flowers meant, I'd planned a bridal bouquet of mixed blooms. I didn't know then that ivy, which means fidelity, was a traditional bouquet ingredient. I was thinking merely of color—splashes of red and blue and pink against my ivory satin gown. The white roses and the blue cornflowers I selected were no problem. But when I lit on tiny red carnations, the florist raised her eyebrows, a gesture I interpreted at the time as one of haughty contempt for young brides who didn't really appreciate the nuances of color and texture. Now I wonder if she, like the flower, was trying to tell me something.

My goal in life is to own an in-ground pool. A cool rectangle of clean, safe recreation—just like the one my high school best friend, Sheila Vleznevchik, had installed in her yard our freshman year, setting up what was, in retrospect, the best summer of my life. All play and no worries—no job, no school and, best of all, no boyfriend. The calm before the storm, so to speak.

But my goal for today is to get rid of my migraine. This Friday afternoon, my mouth tastes of ash from the fire above my eyes. I have a scraping, yammering headache, and I'm trying to get rid of it without resorting to taking one of my "magic pills," the pain reliever my doctor prescribed six months ago with perhaps too much giddy enthusiasm. *A new product,* he assured me. *Does wonders for other women.* The way he said it, I half expected to see the lights dim, smoke rise from the floor and a voice cackle in the background.

I'm convinced my pills will eventually show up in some *Dateline*-like exposé ten years from now. You know the kind—*Drug's Hidden Side Effect: Insanity.*

No thank you, I'm crazy enough as it is.

Crazy or not, it's hard to save up enough money for an in-ground pool when you're just the manager of a slow-moving flower shop in the middle of Baltimore's business district.

Maybe if I take four Motrin, drink a Coke and eat a Hostess cupcake my headache will go away. I reach for my purse under the counter and pull out the plastic pill bottle. Grabbing a Coke—my third for the day—from the college-dorm fridge behind me, I swig the pills back.

I hold my breath and feel no pain. Exhaling, the throb begins.

Breathing always makes migraines worse.

The vise tightens around my forehead and squeezes in on my temples. If the Coke and Motrin don't work in an hour, I'm reaching for the magic pills. Damn the side effects. Already my sister thinks I'm nuts. And my parents tend to agree. My sister married well, whereas I, well, I managed to kill my fiancé.

I tie a green ribbon around yellow roses and pull out a note.

It's Henry Castle's order. He orders flowers nearly every week, at least once a month—different girls but always the same flowers. If Henry Castle has a heart, I've decided it is somewhere east of the moon, with his pulse beamed in from a satellite signal.

Scrunching up my eyelids, I try to remember his order. I should have written it down, dammit. But he called right before lunch, when my head was screaming at me, and it was hard to hear him over the din. I remember thinking, "Oh yeah, her again," but I didn't write it down because the pen was on the other side of the counter, which would have meant, well, moving. And moving, like breathing, is to migraines what lightning is to a forest fire. No good ever comes of it.

Note to self: do not trust memory when in throes of migraine.

It doesn't seem fair to get migraines on this job. After all, one of its attractions was its lack of pressure, its lack of decisions. The customer phones in the order and I fill it. What could be simpler?

I've always been artistic, and the shop's former owner was kind enough to give me a few days' training on arranging flowers and filling orders. He also left me a couple of handy guidebooks to ease the transition. One of them, *The Victorian's Hidden Language of Flowers,* has become my slow-period reading. I can tell you what every flower in the shop means, and why the yellow lily is a bad choice for a husband eager to make amends with a wife. It means falsehood.

But this brings me back to Henry and his dozen roses. Filling orders might not be rocket science, but it does require remembering to whom the orders go. Think, Amy, think.

An image dances across my mind's screen: "Thanking you for an incomparable night. Yours, Henry." But what about the "To…" part? Who gave him the incomparable night?

Yawning, I shake my head to clear it as I tuck in a stray fern around the sweet buds. The names of previous "incomparable night" givers parade through my addled brain in singsong fashion to the tune of the alphabet song. *Anne, Bea, Bess, Blanche, Cele, Di, Des, Fran, Kate, Mare, Ren, Carol, Maude, Tess…*

Tess. Yes, that was it. The memory floods back, temporarily displacing my headache. If only I could continually think, *really* think, with no annoying pauses, no blank moments, a constant stream of thought, disconnected words and images, pineapple ice cream followed by dog-running-after-boy, that sort of thing. Thinking stops the pain.

It had to be Tess. *It had to be Tess, it had to be Tess, beautiful Tess….*

It's nearly closing time. Sunlight blazes through the front window like flame. I'll deliver the flowers myself.

Pulling off my gloves and smock I run a hand through my hair, and look at my reflection in a dime-store mirror over the sink in back of me. My hair is short, sandy-brown and curly. Not very stylish. I'm short, too. And also not very stylish.

Minutes later, I am on the road in my ten-year-old Pontiac peering at addresses along upper Charles Street looking for the 3900 block. There it is—an old apartment house near Johns Hopkins University.

The university is the demilitarized zone of northern Baltimore. To the south and west of it are crumbling neighborhoods that saw their best days during a time when workers tramped off to Bethlehem Steel in the wee hours. To the north is old Baltimore, where they had gated communities before gated communities were cool.

After circling the block two times, I give up and double-park outside the door of a three-story building that exudes old charm. While juggling the unwieldy flower box in my left arm and pushing my sunglasses back with my right, I buzz the lobby with my elbow.

I want to see exactly what kind of woman gets suckered in by the promiscuous-flower-giver Henry Castle. I have conjured up an image—very fat and very silly. Surely he doesn't snare the good-looking ones week after week. There must be some kind of good-looking-women's club where his wanted poster adorns sea-foam-green walls.

The doorman opens up.

"I'll take those," he says huffily, eyeing my jeans and T-shirt as if they are a personal affront to him.

"Uh, I was supposed to deliver these in person. Mr. Castle insisted."

"I am authorized to sign for them, I assure you." He speaks with an exaggerated punctiliousness, as if he just graduated from elocution class the night before.

Across the lobby an elevator door opens and a long cool woman in a black dress glides across the floor. Her three-inch-heel sandals beat out a distant tattoo on the black-and-white tiles. She has shoulder-length brunette hair in one of those iron-straight ragged styles concocted by gorgeous women to make other women who try them look bad.

When the doorman catches her in his peripheral vision, he straightens, grabs the box from me and holds it out like an offering to a goddess.

"Miss Wintergarten," he simpers. "These just arrived."

So this is Tess. Not fat and silly at all. In fact, I'm feeling pretty fat and silly myself and I'm not even fat. She must have magical powers.

"Why, thank you, Ralph," she coos in an accent dripping with mint julep. As she takes the box I catch a whiff of her perfume and I know it's expensive because I always spritz myself with it whenever I'm in a department store. While she heads to a lobby chair and unwraps the note, Ralph turns back to me. His silent face says I should leave now since my work is done. No need for me to be around here and what am I staring at, anyway.

Ralph shuts the glass door on my face, effectively muting the scene. When I turn around to get in my car I notice I did not escape unscathed. A ticket has miraculously appeared on the windshield. If Tess does have magical powers, they're obviously from the Dark Side.

"Shit!" I screech, ripping the paper from under the wiper blade. I stomp my foot, but this does nothing.

It's this headache. It's ruining my life. Pineapple ice cream dog running after boy. Pineapple ice cream boy smacking dog. Pineapple ice cream all over dog and boy. Pineapple boy running into dog!

I slam the car door shut behind me and the window handle drops off. With an exasperated sigh, I stick it back in place, then turn the ignition and head out of town.

I make my way north of the city. The rolling farmland usually fills me with a sense of peace—an elusive emotion ever since the car crash that ended my engagement—but peace skitters ahead of me and I never quite catch up.

Maybe I need a change? Maybe I should look into that storefront in Craftsbury, Pennsylvania, that my sister, Gina, told me about?

Gina, bless her overprotective heart, is always trying to get me to focus on The Future, always trying to reignite my pilot flame of ambition.

Since I've moved to the country, her plans for me have moved there as well, settling on quaint little Craftsbury with its musty antique stores and picturesque Amish. Gina really likes visiting Craftsbury, and I suspect that her suggestions for me stem from her own unrealized dreams as much as from a desire to help me. She's suffering from Dream Trans-ference, dropping me into her secret desires. If I follow through and do as she suggests, she would be able to live vi-cariously through my success.

But Craftsbury—man, it's a one-horse town. Who in the hell would be buying flowers there? Well, let's see—people with deaths in the family, weddings. Hmm, that's nice. Pin your business start to a high mortality and divorce rate (with the subsequent remarriages.) Perhaps plot out some ideas to help along the natural flow.

"Take a memo, Brad," I say out loud, talking to my imag-inary secretary. "Investigate Pennsylvania mortality rates and ways to hasten same…."

Sometimes when Chuck, my delivery boy, messes up, or I let something slip, I blame it on "Brad." "That Brad," I say, "all looks and no brains. But hey, what can I do? Good help is hard to find."

Just that afternoon, a customer had been in the store ask-ing about tuberoses. My shop specializes in flowers that other florists overlook. In addition to the usual roses, carnations, daisies and dried-flower arrangements, I carry sprigs of lavender, passion flowers, pussy willows, rare irises and ex-otic orchids. If a customer wants it, I find it. I should have had some tuberoses, but the shipment had not arrived.

So I'd blamed it on Brad, and much to my surprise, the customer had said, "Oh, is Brad your boss?"

"Why, no," I had replied indignantly. "Brad works for me!" Damn straight he does, all muscles and chiseled face and surfer-boy hair. And he works for *me!* You got a prob-lem with that?

Even my secretary can't take my mind off my headache tonight, so I give up the game and spend the remainder of the drive in silence, letting the cool air rush through the win-dow, creating a wall of white noise.

I pull off the highway at Route 439 and drive for five miles until I come to a dirt road that leads back through a corn field.

Bumping and sputtering, my car delivers me to my house, an old farm home with peeling yellow paint, a wraparound front porch and windows that are long since overdue for reglazing. Trixie purrs from the front step then saunters away as I stop.

"Trix, you old devil, what did you fix for dinner tonight?" At the door, I reach down to pet the old calico as she meows saucily under my hand before slinking away. After I unlock the front door, I look straight back, past the messy living room, into the kitchen. A twenty-dollar bill lies undisturbed on its countertop.

"You should keep a twenty on your counter," my sister told me last week, "and if you come home and it's not there, leave immediately. It means you might be coming in on a thief."

And I said, "Why, Gina, what a great idea. I normally just keep a bloody dagger out, but this will be so much tidier."

I have no doubt I'll spend that twenty soon. Like tonight, in fact. No cash on me, no food worth making and I couldn't make anything, anyway, when this headache is like Kryptonite zapping out my energy source.

After ordering pizza, I pop open a beer and sit on the front porch. Smelling of Friskies salmon dinner, Trixie sidles up and not so subtly slips her head against my arm. I nuzzle her behind the ear.

"Maybe it's not the Coke that does it," I tell her as my headache starts to ease away. Trixie is always interested in my headache cures. "Maybe the headache goes away on its own by the end of the day and I think it's the Coke and the Motrin and the chocolate."

I am an expatriate from the city. I left last year and only

intend to return if my current abode is threatened by war. Looking around at the wide skies and windblown fields, I'm reassured that no tanks lumber over the horizon.

When Rick and I were together, we shared a flat on Calvert Street in a renovated row home on a quiet but trendy block. Three flights up, only windows on the back, very little sunshine. But then again, we created our own light and heat.

The beer tastes good even though I know I'm tempting another headache by going for the alcohol on the heels of a head-blaster day. I don't care. It clears the cobwebs and eases a different kind of pain.

"Come on, Trix, let's go look at the lower forty." Trix likes to walk our land together.

Actually, it's not my land. I rent the place for a pittance. Who but a city expat would rent a house in the middle of nowhere? But after Rick and I ceased being a couple, I needed to reduce expenses, especially since I was out of work for a while.

My head begins to throb again. Thinking. That's the ticket.

Or maybe not? Maybe *some* thinking—thinking about the accident that took place on this very date two years ago— is what makes it worse.

chapter 2

Goldenrod: Encouragement or precaution

*For our reception, Rick and I had chosen a restaurant in Du-
laney Valley—quiet, away from the city and very expensive.
We chose it partly for sentimental reasons because it was on
a date to that restaurant, Rick told me later, that he realized
he wanted to marry me. I remember that date but not because
of any special simpatico feelings between us. If anything, I was
distracted during dinner because Rick was sneezing a lot, and
I was worried he was coming down with something. It was
only when we left the restaurant that I noticed a field of
blooming goldenrod beyond the parking lot. "Make sure you
take an antihistamine the next time we come here," I told
Rick. He smiled and joked, "Maybe I'm allergic to you."*

Surely keeping my house scrupulously clean will convince
my landlord how pool-worthy I am. Cleanliness is next to
godliness, after all.

So I spend Saturday morning cleaning, the kind of spring

cleaning my mother used to do when I was a kid. She'd wash the walls. Who washes walls these days? Only nuts, and since I'm doomed by my headache pills, anyway, might as well get a taste of the white-jacket life now.

I beat the dust out of rugs, sort through clothes, polish silver and even take a mop with water and bleach to the porch ceiling that is encrusted with mildew. The landlord should be paying me I'm doing such a good job on his property. A pool would just be a down payment.

In the late afternoon, constant downpours replace the sun fading from view. Dagnabit, I think as I lean against my doorjamb peering into the dark clouds as if they'd searched me out specially.

The steady rain refuses to surrender to my mean-spirited stares. Giving up, I go into the kitchen and microwave some leftover pizza.

Forget opening a store in Craftsbury. I should just retire at the grand old age of twenty-six. Note to self: buy lottery tickets.

I reach for the phone and dial Wendy's number. Wendy and I met when I worked at an ad agency, where she still slaves away. I left when things came crashing down on me. Or rather into me. We shared the special bond of the downtrodden: low women on the totem pole trying to prove how clever and bright and creative we were, all the while afraid someone would find out we might be none of the above. And after the accident, Wendy was a rock, visiting me in the hospital and at Gina's, gently nudging me back into the world again and always careful to help me move at my own pace.

Not back yet from a visit to her folks' new home in Connecticut, she's left her chipper voice mail message on.

"Hey, Wen, give me a call when you…"

A vicious crack of thunder breaks the constant beat of

rain. Then the lights go out. And the phone goes dead. Guess I'm not godly enough.

A half hour later, I'm still mostly in the dark and sitting in my living room trying to read a murder mystery by the waning light of day. This isn't going to work. A watched pot never boils. A waiting house never…has the electricity go on when you're thinking you'd like it to.

After grabbing my keys and purse, I'm on the road not really headed anywhere except away. That song about driving in a fast car comes on the radio and I turn it up loud and sing along. I'm a nanosecond behind the singer as I struggle to remember the words.

As if by instinct, my car heads into town. I let it take me there, the late daylight gray as my heart. Everything's wet and grumpy and I fit right in.

On Saturdays, I can park on the street, so I do, and head into my little shop. The blue neon sign in the window crackles to life when I hit the switch inside.

Because it's in the heart of the business district, we're only open Mondays through Fridays, so I'll take this opportunity to catch up on some work. I flip on the computer and head to the bookkeeping program, sifting through some old invoices. While I wait for the machine to fire up, I try Wendy again.

Wendy, like my sister, has been ragging on me lately about getting "into the swing of things again." Dating is like riding a bicycle, they tell me. You don't forget how to do it once you've learned.

No, dating—after you had a fiancé—is more like having your BMW *replaced* with a bicycle. You might *remember* how to ride it, but do you really want to?

Wendy has even fixed me up a couple of times with some very randy fellows. She thinks some sex will make me feel better. I can't get angry with her after all she's done for me.

Besides, I admire her spunk. After following a medical student to Baltimore after graduation, she dumped him when she realized she was only sticking it out because her parents expected her to marry a doctor. Her father is a retired surgeon.

I reach for the phone and try her again. Eureka! On the last ring before the voice mail message clicks in, she answers.

"Hello?"

"Hey, Wendy, you sound out of breath!"

"Oh, hi, Ame. Just got in. What's up?"

As I talk, I hear her walking around her apartment, then the sound of water, and then a toilet flushing. Didn't I tell you we were close?

"Nothing's up. I was wondering if you'd like to go grab a beer or a coffee or something. I'm in town. Catching up on some work."

"Oh, Ame, I'm beat. Just drove six hours. Traffic on 95 was a bitch. And then my parents. You'd have thought they just got married the way they were squabbling. Put the couch here, hang that picture there. It was a nightmare."

"Guess you don't want to talk about it," I say.

"No. Yeah. I don't know. I haven't even had a chance to check my messages."

Aha. She wants to see if her boyfriend, Sam, has called. My guess is she'll opt for a beer with him even if she's struggling to remain upright. In fact, my guess is she'd prefer not to be upright with him, but might prefer to struggle.

"Do you want to call me back?" I ask. "I'm at the shop."

"Okay."

"I'm not going anywhere."

I stand and meander to the window, looking out on the rain-soaked street. The smell of wet concrete drifts into the store. It reminds me of when my sister and I were kids and we used to sit in a tent on the front lawn during a storm, oblivious to the fact that the camouflage-patterned cloth was not waterproof.

Not too many cars go by. Downtown Baltimore on a Saturday evening is like downtown Baltimore on a Sunday. Dead, except at Harborplace, where tourists scurry around soaking up all the atmosphere, sucking it clean from the rest of the city.

Ten minutes go by. Then another ten. I spend them pretending to do things, brightening up the flowers in the display refrigerator, checking for messages, cleaning up the counter and the shelf beneath it, starting a list of items that need to be ordered.

Soon I won't have any excuse to linger. Maybe my electricity and phone will be back on by now. Wendy's not going to call. She probably reached Sam, and is at this moment changing into her leopard-print thong.

I turn off the computer, tidy up the papers, look around the store one last time and flip off the blue neon sign.

"Omigod!" I jump when I see a dark figure standing at the front door. My heart starts thudding, my hands break out in a sweat.

He knocks. Bam, bam, bam.

"Hey, open up!"

"I'm closed!" I shout back.

"Come on!"

"I'm leaving!" I turn to get my purse. I'll head out the back way. Ugh. That alley always scares me even when I'm only putting out trash.

"I want to talk to you!" he yells. The flowery decoration of the store's window masks his face.

"I'm closed, I tell you." I will not be bullied into being robbed. Grabbing my purse and keys, I go into the back room to wait it out. I even turn on the light for a second, then turn it out again, hoping he'll see the flash and assume

I left. After a few seconds, I don't hear any more banging. But I do hear some ringing. The phone. Probably Wendy finally calling back. Dammit, I feel like talking. He has to be gone by now.

Staying close to the wall and out of vision of the door, I skulk to the counter and pick up the phone.

"Hello?" I whisper.

"Amy?" Wendy's voice.

"Yeah."

"You okay? You sound like you have a cold or something."

"No, no. Just being quiet, that's all."

Bam, bam. The irate robber is back, pounding away. "Hey, I thought you were closed!"

"What's that noise?" Wendy asks.

"Someone wants to come into the shop."

"Why don't you let him in? You could make a sale."

"I'm closed."

"That's no way to run a business. The customer is always right, remember?" Wendy is working on her MBA part-time.

The thudding increases, then stops as the man puts his hands in his pockets and peers through the glass. Dark complexion, dark hair, gold chain around his neck, bright white shirt open at the collar, gray slacks.

Well-dressed thief.

"Go ahead, answer it. I'll wait."

"Okay, okay. But if I have a problem, I'll say a code word and you hang up and call the police."

"What's the code word?"

"Pineapple."

"Amy, how in the world would you work the word *pineapple* into a conversation?"

"All right, something else. Tuberoses," I say, remembering the missed order from the other day. "They're flowers. This is a flower shop." The man starts pounding again.

"Just go get the door. Who knows, he might be some millionaire with a standing order for a dozen roses."

I put the phone down on the counter where Wendy will be able to hear the conversation. Then I casually walk to the door, not wanting to give this irate thief any satisfaction, regardless what Wendy says. After turning the key and cracking open the door, I smile.

"How can I help you?"

The man's jaw muscle works in fury and a vein in his temple bulges like some alien implant. "You can help me by telling me what imbecile fills the flower orders around here."

"Uh, that would be Brad."

He rolls his eyes and takes a deep breath. "May I come in? I would like to discuss an order."

Without a word, I gesture to the interior and he walks by, leaving a whiff of Tommy Hilfiger cologne in his wake. Rick used to wear that.

I saunter back to the counter, which I figure will provide some sort of protection. Plus, the phone is over there. Tuberoses. Tuberoses.

He follows and stands with his hands, balled into fists, on the counter in front of him. He's just my height, maybe even a half inch shorter, and I'm no tower.

"I would like a refund, a new order of flowers and a letter of apology," he announces, staring me in the eyes.

"Excuse me?" I say, staring right back.

"Yesterday, I called in an order. One dozen yellow roses. To be sent to a Miss Diana Malvani. Miss Malvani received no roses. But Miss Tess Wintergarten did. It caused me a great deal of distress."

So this is Henry Castle. Despite myself, I giggle. An image teases my brain. Tess Wintergarten luring Henry Castle with

her syrupy voice to her apartment, then bludgeoning him
with the roses.

"What kind of distress?" I ask innocently. I must know.

"I don't think that's any of your business."

"You said you want a note of apology. I should at least
know what I'm apologizing for."

"You're apologizing for screwing up my weekend, goddammit."

"I see. You had to make restitution."

"What?"

"My guess is you had to take her out, buy her dinner,
maybe take her to a club, spend some money on her." I look
him over. After-shave. He must have seen her today. I can't
help it. I laugh again. "My God. You had to spend all day
with her. You were just with her." I sniff. Maybe I can de-
tect just the faintest hint of her perfume? Naw, too hard to
do with that Hilfiger thing going on.

"It's none of your business."

"She made you spend all day with her." I am in awe. Tess
Wintergarten *does* have magic powers and they *are* from the
Dark Side. Getting a gigolo to give up his entire Saturday
just because he sent her flowers when he wasn't supposed
to? That is akin to levitation. I wonder if she offers lessons.

His dark face darkens even more. "It's none…of…
your…fucking…business!"

He reaches into his pocket and now I'm thinking, "Gun!"
He's going to exact revenge. He's not a thief. He's a maniac!
Tomorrow's headlines flash through my brain: Angry Cus-
tomer Shoots Florist. No—Angry Customer Shoots Beloved
Florist. Lovely Florist. Well-Regarded Florist. Whole City
Mourns Loss of Adored Florist….

"Tuberoses!" I shout. "Tuberoses!"

"What?" He pulls out…his wallet. I sigh with relief as he
opens it and throws his card on the counter.

"Nothing. I was just thinking how I didn't get my tuberoses order. That Brad." I smile sweetly while I peruse his card. Henry Castle, attorney-at-law. My heart goes cold. Downs, Macklin, Peterson and Squires is his firm. Rick was a Squires. Henry Castle works for Rick's father's firm. Gulping, my eyes as big as saucers, I push the card aside.

"So, what can I do? Who should I send the new flowers to?"

"Credit my account for the old ones. Send a dozen to Diana. And a dozen to Tess."

"Thanking her for an incomparable night."

"An incomparable *weekend,*" he says, his lip curling.

"An incomparable weekend," I repeat.

"Charge it as usual?" I ask, blustery business attitude showing. Wendy would be so proud of me.

Uh-oh. Wendy! She is still on the phone. And I'd said the code word—tuberoses.

Grabbing the phone to my ear, I scream, "Wendy, Wendy, are you there? It's all right. Don't do anything!"

But the phone is dead. She's hung up. Henry Castle is looking at me like I'm nuts. Nuts is fast becoming my natural state of mind.

"Is there a problem?" he asks me.

Funny he should say that because that's exactly what the police say about thirty seconds later when two of Baltimore's finest wander into my store.

One's tall and skinny, with strange bushy red eyebrows. The other's a "regular guy"—average height, average hair, average everything. I wouldn't be able to pick him out of a lineup five minutes from now.

"Is there a problem here?" the tall one asks.

Henry bristles before I have a chance to answer. "Why do you think there's a problem? Just because a Latino is in a store alone, you think I'm up to something?"

"Well, are you?" the average one asks, and he sounds as if he enjoys asking those kinds of questions.

"What I'm up to is no damn business of yours," Henry says. Spoken like a true lawyer.

The tall officer moves to the right side of Henry while the average one stays on his left. The tall one looks at me.

"Everything all right here, ma'am?"

I've become a "ma'am"? When did this happen?

"Uh, yes, sir. Fine. Everything is A-OK." I sound as phony as a cubic zirconia scraping glass. The tall one looks at Henry, then at his partner, and nods.

"Maybe we should talk to you outside, sir," the tall one says.

"I'm not finished in here," Henry seethes.

"I think you are," the average cop says, looking at me.

Now, there are times in life when clear choices present themselves. There are times when the lines to good and bad are as straight as highways in Kansas. And this was one of those times.

If I speak up for Henry, all is well. If I stay silent, he gets hassled by two cops who've decided racial profiling of young male Latinos is kosher. It should be easy, right?

And yet…I look at Henry—smug, dozen-flowers-a-month, thanking-you-for-an-incomparable-night Henry. And I think "Who am I to stand in the way of some cosmic karma too complicated for me to adequately comprehend?"

Henry looks at the cops, then at me. His eyes widen, his jaw works again. He is either mentally cursing me, or frantically issuing a telepathic command for me to tell the truth.

"I was just straightening out an order," he says more quietly now, in an altar-boy voice, obedient and small. He does not look at them. He does not look at me. "Right?"

"Right. Straightening out an order. No problem." But I'm

a little too enthusiastic, which makes the cops even more suspicious, so I have to throw in something extra to leaven the moment. "And we were making plans to go grab a beer. Right, honey?" I wink at Henry, who is beginning to look like Ricky Ricardo after Lucy tells him she accidentally burned their life savings.

The tall one backs off. "Okay, ma'am. We'll be cruising around the block. Just give us a holler if you need help."

The phone rings after they leave. It's Wendy.

"Jesus Christ, girl, are you okay? I called the police, but I kept thinking you were being held hostage or something. I was afraid if I called it would send him over the edge—the phone ringing, I mean—so I didn't call. But then Sam suggested I try in case he wanted to send a message to the cops."

So Sam is there already, helping my best friend plot my escape from a mad customer between orgasms. How thoughtful.

"I'm fine. In fact, he and I are going out for a beer." I wink at Henry again, and this time, he smiles back.

A flash of remembered hopefulness tingles my toes and prickles the back of my neck. It's an emotional déjà vu rippling through me, lifting my heart a half inch off the earth. For one hairbreadth of a second, I'm back in the Summer of Sheila V's pool, where every burst of sunshine was a guaranteed promise of good things to come and every jump into the crystal-blue water an affirmation of life itself.

I look at Henry, and I dive into the deep end.

chapter 3

Yarrow: Cure for heartache

Rick and I never argued. The closest we came to fighting was when, three months before the wedding, he developed a throbbing toothache. He hated dentists—but he was blessed with perfect teeth that would have made any dental hygienist proud. He tried everything to avoid going to "the man with the drill"—analgesics of all shapes and colors, and herbal treatments like yarrow, but nothing worked. Finally, I snapped at him and told him I'd call off the wedding if he didn't take care of the problem. I remember he sat at the kitchen table and mournfully stared at me, his chin in hand. He didn't say anything, and for a fleeting second his silence scared me. But he went to the dentist all the same.

So this is how I start dating Henry Castle.

Mission accomplished at my store, his mood changes from irate customer to roving wolf. He suggests a bar in Fell's Point that's full of atmosphere and noise and smoke. So I head there, half expecting him to stand me up and half wondering what the hell I'm doing anyway.

Then, I hear the voices in my head—didn't I tell you I was crazy? The voices are Wendy's and my sister's and they're both saying the same thing—"give love a chance"—except they're really kind of singing it in some weird sixties-type girl-group harmony. They're singing so loud that I can't argue with them that this is not about looking for love, but going out for a beer, and it's really more about curiosity than anything else. Or maybe it's about guilt for almost getting Henry in trouble with the law.

After I park my car, I sit quietly for a moment coming up with a good excuse for leaving if the date doesn't go well, but as soon as I think the word *date,* I get very happy and proud of myself. Yes, a date. A date I've managed to snag on my own, not some fix-up from well-meaning friends and relatives. Not bad, Ame. Everyone will be so proud. So whatever this little meeting started as, it's turning out to be a notch in my dating belt that I can brag about later. It will come in handy the next time Wendy tries to tell me I'm not trying hard enough.

I'm so fixated on this feel-good attitude that I eventually settle on the feeble "my cat has been unwell" excuse if I need to leave in a hurry. Once I'm in the bar and seated with Henry, however, I don't want to leave. Maybe because my expectations are so low, I actually manage to have fun.

"I wasn't sure you'd find it," he says when I come to the table. He stands and pulls out my chair for me.

You read that right—he pulled out my chair. No wonder he's able to seduce women by the multitudes. He's loaded up with Old World charm.

After we order some brewskies, he asks me if I'm hungry, which I am, so we order a pizza, both agreeing on mushrooms and peppers, even though Henry is willing to go with pepperoni if I really want it.

The business of ordering out of the way, I look into his chocolate-brown eyes and could swear they are twinkling.

"You were pretty mad at me," I say as I look away. I'm afraid if I look into his eyes too long, he'll cast a spell on me. Maybe he and Tess have some sort of coven thing going on.

"Well, you messed up," he says matter-of-factly, the ire completely removed from his voice now. "And it cost me."

"Cost you what?"

"Time."

I wonder how much time he's allotted to me. I change the subject.

"Do you often get hassled like that—by the police?"

Our beers arrive and he remains silent while the miniskirted waitress plops down paper napkins and bottles and glasses. Henry smiles at her appreciatively.

"Sometimes." He sips at his beer. "It's only happened in the car, though. Driving around town."

"Racial profiling?"

He shrugs. "Who knows? It's annoying. And it got me riled up. I probably shouldn't have cursed at that cop, but…" He takes a long swig of beer this time and licks some foam off his upper lip with a slow movement that is both erotic and sweet. Now that I can take the time to study him, I notice his well-muscled arms, his expensive Rolex watch, his strong jaw. Henry's a good-looking man, not in the Ken-doll sense, but in the sleek-leopard sense.

"You own the flower shop long?" he asks.

"Nope. Don't own it at all." And I proceed to tell him how I used to be in communications work but moved out of the fast lane after a car in the fast lane moved into me. I don't talk about Rick. Rule Number One of the new dating scene, embroidered on my heart by both my sister and Wendy, is: do not talk of dead fiancés. It's a real date-dampener. So instead, I just casually mention the accident without mentioning Rick, although I do show him the five-inch scar on my leg from the screws that had held the bone in place. He is suitably impressed.

"You're lucky," he says when the pizza arrives. "I represented a man last year who's a paraplegic now because of an accident."

When he sees my pained face, he immediately rephrases. "Not that I think anyone in an accident is lucky."

I mumble in agreement with a mouth full of pizza. So far, we've managed to talk about racial profiling and my accident. Terrific.

After an awkward pause, I move on to safer subjects. I mention a movie I just saw, and he saw it, too, so we're good for a half hour on that topic alone. And it breaks the ice. By the end of thirty minutes I feel like he's an old friend. Turns out, we agree on the movie—that it was a stinker—and the lead actress—that she's a mannequin who talks—and we manage to share some genuine laughs. Henry's eyes do twinkle when he laughs. He touches my arm when he makes a point, just gently, just enough to make the peach-fuzz hairs there stand up from the static electricity. Or some kind of electricity.

I swallow hard and try to think of something unsexy, but instead, the only thoughts that go through my mind are of the NC-17 variety. And then—I am not making this up—someone puts Marvin Gaye's "Sexual Healing" on the jukebox and I'm beginning to think that perhaps this is how heavenly signs manifest themselves in modern times. Forget burning bushes. Think Muzak.

A half hour after this, the pizza is gone, our beer glasses are empty, and we're still sitting there chatting away. We've moved from favorite movies, to favorite restaurants, all the way through to favorite books. We've talked about our pasts—up to a point. I still don't discuss Rick and I don't ask about the flower recipients and Henry doesn't volunteer info on them. He seems genuinely interested in my work in communications, though, and asks me a lot of insightful questions. I do most of the talking and it feels good. Except for an occasional conversation with Gina, or a quick gabfest with Wendy, my only contact of the verbal kind is with customers. Oh, yes, and with Trixie. But Henry is a better listener than Trixie.

Eventually, Henry asks for the check and insists on paying, even though I pull out my wallet faster than you can say "overdrawn checking account."

"Let me," he says, suavely placing his platinum Visa on the bill. "I'm sorry I scared you earlier."

Earlier? What's that? The entire episode is erased from my memory bank as I stare into those eyes. Henry insists on escorting me to my car like the flower-sending gentleman that he is. "Not a good neighborhood for a young woman to be walking alone in," he says, placing his hand on my elbow. I shiver.

When we stroll to my car, it's twilight—when the jewel-blue sky laughs at you, saying, "Hah, you thought you wouldn't make it through another twenty-four and yet, here you are." I'm feeling good. I'd come into town just to get away from the country and I'd landed myself with a date of sorts, a date with a real ladies' man to boot, which has to mean that I am, well, a lady. It's an affirmation.

Once at my car, he stands close.

"You have my numbers. Give me a call some time." Then he smoothly puts his left hand behind my neck and presses a kiss on my lips that makes it clear that any "incomparable nights" his litany of flower-recipients experienced were probably due in large part to his skill with his tongue.

We read the stories, like warning posts, about gigolos, yet we do not heed. I am in bed with a Don Juan.

Oh, yes, I go to bed with him! After that kiss, he asks me if I'd like a nightcap at his place, and I'm there and we've done it before you can say "Stupid is as stupid does."

Well, maybe not too stupid. I mean, after all, we'd actually had a good time, right? And Wendy would be proud, right? She thinks if you want a man, you should go after him—hey, as long as you're careful and safe about it.

But speaking of the sex part, maybe Marvin Gaye was right about sexual healing. Maybe Wendy was right, too, about needing sex to feel better, because I feel damn good after Henry Castle makes love to me. Sure, Henry might think of it as sex, but he does it as if it's love. I feel new and strangely clean, I feel rescued and deprogrammed. Henry is the kind of lover who makes a woman feel organic, he's the kind of lover the gamekeeper in *Lady Chatterley's Lover* must have been with all his talk of bodily functions as if they were sacred events. Henry is a natural lover. Henry *is* sex.

And he didn't need to ask to get me into bed. In fact, once at his place, after just a sip of cognac, he was asking me if I wanted to take it slower. I was the fast one. I wanted it bad. Or I wanted something and Henry would do.

The next morning, I am at Henry's condominium. His new two-story home on the harbor in Canton, one of those gentrified areas that fill the have-nots with envy and the haves with self-congratulation for reclaiming part of a decaying city.

Henry is out at a French bakery getting croissants and baguettes. But I'm giddy as a schoolgirl, so I phone Wendy, waking her up. It is, after all, only nine o'clock on a Sunday morning. I think I hear a man groaning in the background and I hope it's Sam.

"What is the meaning of tuberoses?" I ask her.

"Amy? What time is it?"

Holding the sheet to my chest I sit up in Henry's bed, which is a black-satin-sheeted platform thing in a room with teakwood furniture.

"Tuberoses. Don't you remember? *Tuberoses* was the code word. *Tuberoses* mean 'dangerous pleasures,'" I say triumphantly.

"Huh?"

"Henry Castle and me. I'm at his place."

She screams and asks all the right questions, and screams some more when I give her the right answers.

With promises to give her all the details later, I hang up and wander into Henry's shower. Here my newfound joy is dampened and not just by the warm water from the spigot. Some previous visitor has left her shampoo and soap, herbal and floral things that no man would buy, a reminder of Henry's past, or more accurately, a prophecy heralding his future.

Never Get Involved With a Philandering Man is my motto. I learned it early, at my mother's knee. My dad was a womanizer, who chased after everything in skirts until his organ gave out. He doesn't hear well now and doesn't read newspapers. We've all hid from him the news about the discovery of Viagra. Whenever he sees the ads on television, we tell him it's a hemorrhoid treatment.

So how did I end up in the bed of a bed-hopping Latino? I mean, can you get more stereotypical than this? What was I thinking—that if I met Don Juan he'd be Polish?

After I finish, I trundle out to the kitchen with his silk bathrobe around me, my head a mop of wet hair. This is a test I've devised for prospective relationships. Like me after a shower and there's hope. Henry, who has just returned from the bakery, does not flinch.

"Hey, you didn't put the coffee on!" he complains, then sets about doing it with some fancy-schmancy black machine that hisses and spits as soon as he flips the switch. I sit at the round table by a bay window overlooking the parking lot, and shyly take a croissant from the bag.

"You never told me how you got the job at Squires," I say. We've talked about his work—he mostly handles divorce cases—and we've talked about his loves, at least the material kind. He wants to buy a sailboat when he gets the money, and he hopes to trade his Beamer for a Porsche next year. But I've managed to stay away from asking him too much about his firm, which, after all, was Rick's firm.

"Something opened up there about a year or two ago, that's all."

I nearly gag. He took Rick's job.

"Yeah, but Squires. That's a very exclusive club. Did you know somebody?" I manage to squeak out.

"Nope. Not a soul." He pulls out a chair and sits next to me, grabs the bag and starts munching lustily on a piece of bread. He eats the way he makes love, with no inhibitions and his hungers on full display. There's something erotic about the way he paws at the bread, chomps on it, licks his lips. After downing nearly half a baguette, he turns and snatches a black mug from a mug tree on the corner of the counter. Thinking he's going to offer it to me, I pipe up.

"I take it with cream."

But instead, he pulls out the carafe, halfway through its brew cycle, and pours himself a cup.

"There's some in the fridge," he says, gesturing.

I get up to fetch my own coffee and cream.

"I think Squires was angling for some diversity," he says. "And they'd rather have a Latino than a black, *sí?*" He says

it with a cynical laugh. Eager to show off my multicultur-
alism I throw a few high-school Spanish phrases at him, but
he stares at me blankly.

"My father was Colombian," he says dryly, "but my
mother is American. They divorced when I was two and I
was raised in New Jersey. I took French in high school and
avoided languages in college."

"Castle? That's no Spanish name."

"Castellano," he ripples off his tongue. "Enrico Castellano.
My mother anglicized it when she moved back here."

Henry is on the second half of the baguette. If I want
any, I better say something soon. I decide to stick with the
croissants. They're more fattening anyway, and we can always
use more fat in our diets, right?

"Whitest law firm on the Atlantic seaboard," he continues, laughing again. "Big story in the *Law Journal*."

Ah, so that was it. Henry had traded on his heritage.

"You let them think you were some ghetto kid making good?"

"I let them think whatever they wanted to think. I'm a
damned good lawyer and I deserve a break just as much as
the next guy."

Maybe Henry Castle deserves a break, but the idea that
he snookered Rick's law firm into hiring him burns me. My
mouth puckers into irritation.

"Well, if you're so smart, buster, then you must know that
giving yellow roses to a woman signifies jealousy, not ardor."
There, take that.

"What?" His face changes from confusion to amusement.
"Oh. The flowers."

"Yeah. The flowers. If you plan on sending any to me,
you might want to be more creative."

"Like what?" He stares outside where a bank of red tulips
planted by some unseen landscaper blooms along the water's

edge. "Maybe I should just go out and pick a bunch of those."

"Red tulips? Declaration of love," I recite. I notice Henry does not jump out of his chair to go pick a few.

He sips slowly at his coffee. It's good stuff. He makes mean coffee and sweet love.

"Why do you send flowers anyway?" I twirl a piece of flaky croissant in my fingers. "Nobody expects flowers nowadays. Maybe a call the next day. But not flowers."

He leans back in his chair, the master sharing his secrets. "Ah, but that's the trick. The unexpected leaves no room for the expected."

"So the flowers take the place of the day-after-sex phone call? You send the flowers, they forget about wanting you to call. Or better yet—" I snap my fingers, getting it now "—they call you!"

"You are assuming facts not in evidence," he states. "Perhaps the flowers do not all go to women with whom I have had sex."

"All right, I'll bite. Which women on the list at my shop have you had sex with?" When he doesn't answer right away, I rephrase. "Maybe it would be easier for you to tell me which ones you *didn't* have sex with."

"Maybe it's better, my little *conchita,* if I don't tell you anything of the sort." He gets up and pats me on the head.

What the hell is "my little *conchita?*" Another lightbulb goes off in my feeble brain. Spanish-challenged "Enrico" makes up Spanish-sounding words when making love to his many *"conchitas."* He plays to the stereotype. I try to remember if anything south of the border slipped out during our tumultuous sessions, but I had been moaning so loudly I wouldn't have heard it anyway.

"So you used to work in an ad agency?" he asks, dredging up some info we'd gone over the night before.

"Gelman Agency, University Parkway."

"They handle a lot of movie openings, don't they?" His back is still toward me.

"That's the one. You know them well?"

"Not really. I wonder who handles their legal stuff."

"Schwartz and Mendle," I say, rattling off the name of another prominent law firm. In Baltimore, there are two kinds of law firms. Jewish firms. And old blue-blood firms.

"Schwartz retired. Maybe Gelman will want someone new?"

"What are you trying to be—a rainmaker for Squires?" I stand and walk behind him, putting my arms around his waist. He doesn't respond, so I back away. I'm feeling kind of used right now. "Maybe I should get going."

"You can use my shower," he says.

He thinks my hair looks like this all the time? Why do I bother?

"I already did."

By the time I gather my clothes together a few minutes later, Henry is on the phone with someone talking about "community property laws" and a headache nags at the outer edges of my brain. Maybe getting back to my country estate will cure that? Or maybe getting away from Henry will do the trick just as well?

At the top of the stairs leading down to his front door, he gives me a kiss hot enough to make me want more but cool enough to say goodbye.

"I'll be seeing you," I manage to croak out as I leave.

chapter 4

Flowering almond: Hope

Rick and I officially met on a blind date, but we'd actually met weeks before at a St. Patrick's Day party a coworker of mine had hosted at his new digs—a converted warehouse apartment with one of those huge, spacious layouts where no walls divide the rooms. Except for Wendy, I still hadn't developed a post-college social circle after moving back home from the University of Richmond. So I had looked forward to the party. Even so, I had to leave early because the music had pounded a headache off the walls into my brain that was synchronized to the beat. Sickly sweet amaretto— which the host had in rich supply after a misguided delivery landed on the "warehouse's" door—didn't help. Rick arrived late and alone, just as I was leaving. He was lanky, with straight blond hair in a preppy cut, blue striped oxford shirt, khakis, deck shoes with no socks and a big open smile. He looked so bright and honest and neatly pressed that I almost stayed. He looked kind. When a mutual friend set us up the next week, I remember thinking "This could be the one."

How does a girl go from almost marrying Mr. "Perfect" Fiancé to screwing Don Juan? Huh? How does that happen? Not only had Rick been All-American and a little shy, he loved his parents and even went to church on Sundays.

Rick's parents don't speak to me now. I can't blame them. It's so much easier to think I could have avoided the drunk instead of thinking that the drunk was some gun loaded and pointed in Rick's direction from the dawn of time.

At home, I feed poor Trixie and play back my messages. One's from Wendy, wanting more details. One's from my sister, wanting to know if I would like to come to dinner. One's from my mother inviting me over for dinner at their place. And one's a hang-up—probably a telemarketer.

In the kitchen, I reach for the Motrin and swallow two. Sometimes catching the headache early is enough to keep it completely at bay.

After letting the Motrin ease its way into my system, I lounge on the couch trying not to feel like Henry Castle's chump. He probably bedded me just to get more info on a potential client—my old ad agency. The phone rings and when Trixie doesn't answer it right away, I grab for the receiver.

"Well?" It's Wendy again, sounding more awake. Either she's had a chance to have some coffee or she had some Sam.

"Well what?" I walk into the kitchen and open my refrigerator, take out a carton of milk and smell it.

She groans. "Well, you know what I mean well. I want more, lots more. And what are you doing home so early, anyway?"

I pour myself a glass of milk, then I take the phone out

front and sit on the porch step. Trixie does her nuzzling routine again. "If you didn't think I'd be home now, why'd you call?"

"I was going to leave a message. Sam and I are going out for a drive so I was going to tell you we might stop by."

When you live in the country you become the destination of any acquaintance, coworker, family member or friend who wants to "take a drive."

"That's great. Stop on by," I say, and swig back the rest of the milk except for a few tablespoons. These I pour into a cracked dish by one of the porch posts for Trixie to lap up. "And as to Henry, there's not much else to tell. Great sex. Great time. But he had to get into the office to do some work."

Amazing how easily one lies to protect one's pride. The only work Henry had to do was done—get the scoop on the Gelman Agency.

"When are you seeing him again?"

"Not sure. I'm supposed to call him." Yup, that's Henry's modus operandi—get the girls to call him. And I don't want to flaunt the rules when I am so new to the game.

"You don't sound too enthusiastic. Are you sure everything is all right?"

"Everything is fine!" I say with some exasperation in my voice. I have a hair trigger for that question. After the accident, I couldn't go an hour without someone asking me if I was all right, and after two years, my patience has worn thin. "Henry and I had a terrific time and plan on having many more. In fact, he already told me he loves me and wants me to go meet his mother tomorrow, but I told him I couldn't because I'm having dinner with mine."

Wendy brushes aside my sarcasm and tries to ply out of me things I do not know. Did I sense he's looking for a relationship? Will the Orioles win the pennant?

I inhale a deep, cleansing breath of country air. Pollen catches in my throat and I cough.

"You okay?" Wendy interrupts her gushing to ask.

"Yup. Just hay fever. When do you think you and Sam will be here?"

"I don't know. Maybe noonish. One or so."

"Okay." That means lunch. Trip to store. If I hurry I can get in some supplies before they show.

The shopping takes me an hour, tidying up takes another hour, and making sure I look casual but presentable takes all of ten minutes. It's just as well I'm busy with these tasks. It keeps me from thinking too hard about why I jumped into bed with Henry Castle.

I didn't even sleep with Rick on our first date. And I can't remember now any unsettling feelings after making love to Rick for the first time. All I remember was the natural flow of our relationship from lover to fiancé. That's the problem with steady relationships. You forget the unsteady parts and only remember the early hope and then the constancy. Now I'm left without a map.

Don't other women do this—jump into bed with a hunky guy just because he looks like he'd be a good lay? Isn't this the new millennium when a gal goes after what she wants? I'm just getting with the program, right?

By the time Wendy and Sam drive up in Sam's red VW Beetle, I'm tired and cranky from too much thinking. I need a nap. I didn't get much sleep last night.

Wendy is a great friend—a shoulder to cry on, a cheerleader, a helper. Without her, I don't know how long it would have taken me to start living again. One thing she can never do for me, though, is stay in the background. She is the sun and I am some dinky little shadow. She has a centerfold body, sultry face and perfect hair. And she's smart, too.

For many months after I announced my engagement, I wrestled with whether or not to invite Wendy to be part of the wedding party. I was too afraid the photographer would use up all his film snapping pix of her instead of me.

Lucky for me I didn't need to sort out that problem, huh?

Sam is certainly no Frankenstein, but he's no candidate for male-model school, either. Tall and skinny, he always reminds me of a self-confident Woody Allen. He tries to deflect attention from a fast-receding hairline by letting his hair grow to his shoulders, but it's the kind of wispy brown hair you see on college professors, which is what he is. He teaches English at Johns Hopkins. Wendy met him when she got involved in a pro bono charity promotion. They've been together for a year and I keep expecting her to tell me they've been secretly married for the past few months but she didn't want to share it with me for fear of churning up my own aborted-marriage memories. It's the only explanation I can come up with for why he hasn't popped the question to her yet.

I mean, come on—where is this guy ever going to meet a Wendy Jackson again, a woman with brains and bod? He should start each day kowtowing in the direction of her apartment and repeating "I am not worthy" three times.

"Welcome to my country manor!" I quip as they come inside. Sam carries a bag and hands it to me.

"Sam got some strawberries at the market yesterday!" Wendy gushes. Wendy does a lot of gushing. It's her favorite emotion.

Inhaling the rich, decaying aroma of the strawberries, I place them on the counter next to the sink. Irony strikes me. I live in the country, but the best place to get fresh anything is in the city at Lexington Market. I begin to miss said city.

Figuring Wendy brought the fruit to have with our lunch, I start to clean and hull the berries. Sam wanders to the back door and looks out over the barren field that leads to the main road. He's never been here before, not that I haven't invited him. He and Wendy always seem to have something else "on tap" whenever I extend an invitation. So her self-invite today is a kind of makeup for all those turndowns.

"Wendy said you had a pool," he remarks.

"I said she is going to get a pool," Wendy corrects him. She stands next to me and helps with the berries. Today, she wears white shorts and a black T, and her hair is pulled slickly back into a funky spiky thing on the top of her head.

"You own this place?" Sam asks.

"Nope. I'm just a serf."

"What? You surf?"

Wendy stifles a laugh.

"No. I said I'm a peasant, not the lord of this manor." The strawberries are ready, so I place them on my tiny square of a table. "You know, we can eat outside. I'll put some things on the table and we can take them with us." This is my way of saying I'll set up a buffet. But after the serf mix-up, I'm staying away from complicated concepts.

"Sounds great!" Wendy helps me put out cutlery and plates, and the platter of cold cuts I'd bought at the store. Sam, however, has turned into a vegetarian since last we met, so he only takes lettuce, unripened tomatoes, cheese, bread and berries on his plate. I'm angry that he went vegetarian. It seems traitorous to his carnivore legacy, like being born Catholic and converting to atheism.

I have no lawn chairs, so we drag out kitchen chairs and sit around like a bunch of hillbillies with a couch on their porch. It's an awkward meal. Sam doesn't talk much around me and I get the impression he doesn't like me. I can't figure out what I've ever done or said to warrant this disaffection, so the only conclusion I'm left with is a bad one for Wendy. He doesn't like me because he knows I like Wendy and wouldn't want to see her hurt, and he must be planning on some hurt somewhere down the road. The schmuck.

Wendy, however, is oblivious to this sad state of affairs. She prattles on about how she and Sam are going to the Hopkins fair next week and Center Stage tonight and out to dinner tomorrow. She's giving me the Litany of Love—all the reasons she should stay with Sam. Dating Sam is an act of defiance for Wendy. Not only did she leave her parent-approved doctor wannabe, she got involved with a beatnik college prof. Wendy's a rebel. And Sam…Sam is shy. Shy of marriage, that is. Feeling particularly cruel after my night with Henry, I decide to strike to the bone.

"So, Sam, what's up with you?" I ask innocently, then jab a piece of rare beef and stuff it in my mouth. Between chews, I try to start, "I mean, we never talk about your plans. Tenure on the table?"

Talking about tenure actually perks Sam up. Turns out he *is* in line for tenure and his prospects are good, so he spends ten minutes graciously offering me a minilecture on how hard it is to get tenure in his field because it's so "fucking competitive," and how unusual it is for someone his age to be in line for it at a university of Hopkins's prestige. When he's finished, I go for the bull's-eye.

"That's terrific. I guess that means you'll be settling down since you don't need to worry about looking for a job at another college." After I say it, I get up to take my plate inside as if it's the kind of comment one is used to hearing around young men. Maybe in 1950, but not today. I'm hoping the anachronism doesn't penetrate.

When I step back outside, Sam is standing, awkwardly holding out his plate as if he expects me to take it. I don't. Instead, I position my hand above my eyes, shading them from the glaring sun. It's getting warm.

"I'll be staying in Baltimore. Good city," he mumbles.

Wendy's no slouch in the brains department, so I know she got the message. I just gave Sam the opportunity to say something really sweet, something like "Yup, now that my future's settled, I'll be able to make some plans," at which point he should have looked at Wendy and winked, or at least winked at me.

No wink, no sweet something. Sam's a schmuck.

Wendy stands and takes Sam's plate. She's not smiling and she looks a little defeated, and I feel like squeezing her hand and telling her it'll be all right, just the way she did with me when I was in the hospital. But she recovers on her own, without my help. By the time she comes back outside, she's plastered a smile on her face. Her hands in her pockets, she announces she'd like to take a walk.

So we all tramp off down the road, talking about everything but the subject that's on all our minds—why Sam is such a schmuck and won't ask Wendy to marry him. We talk about the weather, we talk about Wendy's job, we talk about whether I'll go back into communications work or not. We work ourselves into a sweat, we're trying so hard to avoid the Big Topic.

Wendy's smile is about to crack when we finally head back to the house, and she makes some remark about being awfully tired, wanting to take a nap before they go out. Sam picks up on the cue and says he'll drive her home, then run some errands himself. He seems really good at picking up on the cues about the right time to leave a woman.

I'm strangely disappointed. Although tired myself, I have a question I need to ask Wendy and I don't want to ask it around Sam. I want to know how many times she went out with him before sex. Maybe I don't understand the program. I need to know. I'm in the game now and I want to be sure I play by the rules. Looking at Sam, though, I realize he probably didn't have any rules. And whereas Henry had asked me if I wasn't rushing things, Sam probably insisted on doing so. Poor Wendy. Knowing her, she might have thought that kind of eagerness charming.

On my porch when we return, I find a surprise. A big white box with fancy gold ribbon. Flowers!

"Didn't see the delivery truck go by," I say as I open the card. "Must have come from York Road instead of the interstate."

"Who are they from?" Wendy asks, her natural cheer returning.

"Henry." The note reads, "Thanking you for a really incomparable night." Laughing, I pull out the flowers. Not roses—he learned his lesson there. A lavender plant instead, its pungent fragrance igniting a smile. "Mmm... lovely. I can plant it." The florist, I notice, is one in Towson and open on Sundays, and I wonder if Henry uses several floral shops with which to conduct his serial flower-sending.

"So what does lavender mean?" Wendy asks, admiring the potted plant.

Remembering, I redden.

"Purity," I lie. "Isn't that funny?" But it's not funny at all because one of lavender's meanings is *distrust,* according to the Victorians. Either Henry didn't bother to look it up, or he has a wicked sense of humor.

Sam is eager to go now. Maybe it's the flowers—is he afraid Wendy will expect him to send some? So I make a big to-do over bringing the plant into the house and looking for a clay pot in which to set the plastic container, and spritzing the leaves with water and reading the care instructions, even though I know already what they say. Take that, Sam. Get Wendy some flowers. It doesn't take much and look at the reaction.

Sam ignores these silent messages and says something about having to grade papers before going out this evening.

He doesn't even thank me for lunch, but Wendy does. With a bright smile that breaks my heart because I know Sam doesn't appreciate it, she tells me she'll "catch up" with me later, and gives me a wink.

Sam and Wendy are gone soon in a flurry of road dust, and I am left with a sink of dirty dishes and a potted plant from Henry Castle. I sit the lavender on the table so that I can smell its melancholy scent while I wash up. No dishwashers in old farmhouses. One more reason why returning to the city might not be a bad idea. Even my old apartment with Rick had a small dishwasher.

Henry is a devil, I decide. He knew I knew what his cards always say, so he adds the word "really" to imply our night was different from the other "incomparable" ones he's racked up over the years. But he is thoughtful enough to send me, a florist, different flowers—not just different from the roses he usually sends, but different in general. A potted plant instead of cut blooms. He might be a devil, but at least he's not Sam.

Maybe lavender means something else in some other book of flowers, maybe it means "the past is over" or even "great days ahead." Or maybe it just means, "Yes, Amy Sheldon, you'll get an in-ground pool."

chapter 5

Foxglove: Insincerity

*Twenty years ago Rick's father suffered a heart attack. Al-
though digitalis and diet forestalled any fresh problems, Rick
had grown used to a quiet household, developing ways of hiding irritation at his parents' home, of smiling when he was
angry about something, or serenely staring into the distance
when his mother was difficult. He was often silent when we
left their home, and it quickly became clear that if I wanted to
get my way with Mrs. Squires on wedding preparations, I'd
have to meet with her privately, away from Rick and, most of
all, away from Rick's father.*

I'm getting my pool. Unfortunately, I won't be able to
enjoy it.

Remember that hangup recorded on my voice mail?
Turns out it was my landlord, Pete Swilton, calling to say
he sold the house I live in without actually showing it to
anyone because the new owner isn't interested in the house

but only in the property, and Pete had showed that to him one day when I was at work. The buyer got some sort of zoning break and is putting in a swimming and tennis club. My house will be razed to make way for the new place. In fact, I think my house is exactly where they're situating the swimming pool. So much for being in the right place at the right time.

As luck would have it, my lease is up at the end of the month. I could force Pete to let me have more time, but I figure I shouldn't screw him over because he's been a good landlord, letting me pay my rent late a couple of times when I was strapped for cash because of car repairs.

Besides, Pete tells me that bulldozers will start moving earth around the property as soon as next week. Bulldozers and me—I just don't see it.

After Wendy and Sam leave, I spend the rest of Sunday afternoon eating microwaved popcorn, watching the Nazi Channel (all right, it's really the History Channel, but they broadcast a suspiciously large amount of stuff about Hitler), and pretending I'm not waiting for Henry to call.

Who does call is my sister, Gina. I tell her I went on a date. Major excitement. I tell her I have to move and she is practically hysterical with joy. She wants me to move back in with her and her husband. Then Mom calls about a half hour after this—probably because Gina's called her—and Mom thinks I should move back home. But first she thinks I should come over for Sunday dinner at five, and since I have to eat dinner anyway, I agree. Not caring if Sam is still there, I call Wendy after this to complain about my family and moan about my potential homelessness, but Wendy only half-heartedly offers me her couch, which I know is merely pro forma just so I can gratefully decline. Wendy doesn't sound too happy, but I don't pry. I suspect she and Sam had a spat on the way home related to my previous prying questions.

When I trundle over to my folks' house, Mom issues another invite to move back home. Every month, I try to have
dinner at least once with my parents in their split level in
Parkville, a homey little suburb in the northeast corner of
the county that should have Simon and Garfunkel songs
piped over a loudspeaker along the streets. The lyrics seem
to just trip off the tongue at the sight of those asbestos-shin-
gled ranchers and duplexes.

You would think that coming of age in the sixties would
have made my mother and father pretty cool folks with
"tales of the revolution" that I could use to impress my
friends. Instead, my Dad avoided the draft by going to college, then got a job with the phone company, and my mom
worked for a bank after college, then stayed home when
Gina and I were born.

When I was ten, my father started spending a little too
much time at the office. Eventually I was able to put two
and two together and came up with three—mom, dad and
whomever he was boinking at the time. Gina figured it out,
too, but she and I didn't actually talk about it until after she
got married and I got engaged.

My mother makes tuna-noodle casserole and meat loaf
and roast chicken dinners. After a trip to Europe with my
Dad, she also makes flans and pastry-encrusted chicken in
cream sauce. Today, she makes pork roast, sweet potatoes and
corn.

"Your room is still like you left it," she encourages me
when I tell her I need to find a new place to stay.

Just what I want—purple dust ruffles and photos of high
school friends I never see anymore.

"Besides, if you move back here, you can save money.
Didn't you say you want a place with a pool?"

My father eats silently. If he wants me to move back
home, he shows it by a healthy appetite. If he didn't want

me to move back home, he'd obviously be too sick at heart to eat well.

"An in-ground pool."

"Those are expensive," my father says, reaching for the salt.

"Not if she gets one of those garden apartments, Frank. They have pools. But the rent is usually higher. There are some in Timonium, I think. Or Lutherville," she says, mentioning sections north of the city.

"I was thinking of moving back into town," I say, peering through the darkness looking for butter for my potato. My parents' dining room is always dim, even though it has a large sliding glass door that leads to a deck. They keep the curtains drawn so that the room won't heat up and the air-conditioning won't be overtaxed. It's unseasonably warm today and they've turned on the AC.

"What do you want to do that for? You can't get a pool there," my mother states.

"I miss city life."

"Gina says you have a boyfriend." That traitor Gina. I mentioned Henry once and she already told Mom.

"I'm seeing someone. Nothing serious."

"You should bring him by."

"Maybe."

After dinner, I help Mom clean up, sit on the deck with her a little while, then tell her I want to get home before dark, which she likes to hear. She doesn't like the idea of people driving after dark, especially since my accident.

All the way home, I keep telling myself I won't call Henry. It's a mantra—do not call him, do not call him, do not call him. But that damned lavender plant is screaming its own mantra back at me across the miles—he wants you to phone, he wants you to phone, he wants you to phone. It's a test of wills.

I lose.

As soon as I enter my lavender-scented home, I am pulling out the card he gave me yesterday. Since he expects me to call and he knows I know he expects it, this call isn't really a capitulation, I rationalize. It's the acknowledgment of a joke.

Laughter in my heart, I punch in his number and am half surprised when he answers the phone. His voice is husky, though, which immediately makes me suspicious. Looking at the lavender, I remember its meaning: distrust.

"Hey! Just thought I'd call and say thanks for the plant. Even though I expected it, it was nice. Cute."

"No problem," he says in that noncommittal voice people use when they're trying to figure out who they're talking to. Then, "I dozed off watching the news."

Dozing off—or screwing another broad? The lavender plant appears to pulse and glow. I close my eyes and shake my head.

"Sorry, didn't mean to disturb you. I can call back later." Call back later? Why?

"No, no, that's okay. What are you doing?"

What I am doing is nothing but feeling sorry for myself, which I have perfected to a high art—I have an exhibit at the Baltimore Museum next month, did I mention it?

Henry coaxes me out of my gloom by telling me about a boat he looked at, and then by asking if I'm doing anything special and would I like to have dinner with him at his place?

Before you can shout "Warning! Warning!" I am throwing some clothes into a duffel bag, putting out extra food for Trixie and trying to find my leopard-print thong. It's hidden in the back corner of the linen closet.

By this time, I've given myself the Millennium Woman speech about five times. It's a cross between a Virginia Slims ad and a feminist manifesto. It goes something like this:

Henry is good for me, in the physical sense. I am mistress of my own destiny. If I want good sex, I should get it, as long as I'm careful. Nothing ventured, nothing gained. A stitch in time…

No, wait a minute. Those aren't Millennium Woman words of wisdom.

So you see the problem—every time I start thinking New Woman, I end up back at Old World. And then my Inner Feminista morphs into some babushka-covered grandmother shaking a clawlike finger at me and croaking out, "A man doesn't buy the cow if he can get the milk for free," except she says it with this thick accent that sounds all guttural and flu-like. And then a debate ensues between New Woman and Babushka Crone with New Woman howling that if she wants to give away her milk and keep the cow to herself, that's her decision, and Babushka Crone retorts with some curse where all the words end in sneezes.

Let's face it. I'm a mess. But one thing's for sure—I'm not going to get any more straightened out by living like a nun, right? Right. Even Babushka Crone would agree to that. (Surely she would.) Besides, I've put both her and her sparring partner back in their boxes for the night. The night belongs to Henry.

Henry does not disappoint. His coffee-making skills are matched by other cooking talents. When I arrive at his condo, the smell of something with lemons and garlic fills the air, soft music is on the CD player, the lights are low, candles glow in every room, and two glasses of ruby-red wine sit waiting on the coffee table in front of his black leather sofa.

Do I tell him I already ate? Hell no. I'll just do a Scarlett O'Hara routine, right? Stuffing myself before the big party so I can eat daintily in front of the boys.

But the food's too damned good for that tomfoolery, so

I decide to test Scarlett's technique a different day. Besides, I didn't eat much at Mom's—it was too early for dinner. Henry has prepared some pan-fried chicken thing with a capers and lemon sauce, risotto, fresh asparagus, and berries and cream spiked with brandy for dessert.

"You get these at the market?" I ask as we polish off the berries.

"Yeah. Yesterday."

Hmm…so Henry and Sam were wandering around Lexington Market this weekend and they didn't even know it.

If Henry uses his culinary skills to entice women into bed, well, it works. After that seductive dinner, I am in his bed faster than you can say "plants don't lie." Actually, we don't make it to the bed. At least not at first. We make it on the sofa, and in the shower. And *eventually,* in the bed.

I was wondering if my recollection of his skills in that regard had been skewed by my own long fast. But no, he really is an incomparable lover. I'm thinking I should be the one sending *him* flowers.

It's nearly midnight by now and his bedroom is lit only by the wan light cast from the parking lot lamps outside. His breathing tells me he's falling asleep. With my head on his shoulder, I listen to his heart thudding away in his chest. He has not said a word about staying the night, and since tomorrow is a workday, I figure I should go home. Sure, I packed a bag, but I'm not going to force myself on the guy. I have *some* standards.

Creeping out of bed, I grab my T-shirt from the floor and pull it on without my bra. Henry wakes up and eyes me.

"Where you going?"

I see him staring at the outline of my breasts in the snug shirt. His eyes glisten like some sexy wolf's.

"Home. Gotta work tomorrow."

Reaching out his hand, he gently pulls me back to bed

and kisses my neck. Then he reaches up and fondles my breasts, sending electric shocks down my spine.

"Don't go," he murmurs, nipping my ear. "Stay all night, *conchita.*"

Do I need a second invitation?

I slip back under the sheets and he is, amazingly, aroused again already. While he fumbles in the bedside table for protection, I close my eyes. I feel like Trixie. I feel like purring and nuzzling my head against his arm. In a few seconds, he's doing enough nuzzling for the both of us.

The next day, I am left wandering around his condo after he vamooses off to work at seven-thirty. While he is Mr. Get-Ahead, my shop doesn't open until nine-thirty-five. Sure, it's supposed to open at nine-thirty, but I always manage to rush in about five minutes late each day.

Over coffee, he asked me if I'd like to go sailing some time. Of course I would, I said. But I really don't like sailboats or planes or anything but terra firma. However, I also don't want to encourage Henry to look elsewhere for companionship.

I know, I know—I remember what my Inner Feminista said about getting good sex and to hell with the rest. But that damn Babushka Woman has a hold on me. I can't seem to relinquish the idea that this might be a prelude to a relationship. Some kind of relationship. As I stared at Henry over my coffee, I did the tally. He's a good listener. He's a good cook. He's good in bed. Is there a down side here?

As soon as he leaves the condo, I am faced with an ethical challenge. Do I rack up thousands of dollars on his telephone, trash his apartment, or should I just look through his personal things?

Being a good girl at heart I opt to just look through his personal things.

It's a futile search. Henry's condo is as empty as Henry's heart. He doesn't own anything personal enough to count. In fact, I'm beginning to wonder if he's camping out in the model condo without the Realtor's knowledge.

His clothes are folded with fascist precision. The only photos he keeps are two old pictures of what appears to be his mother and him on his various graduation days. His bills are paid, and his kitchen cabinets would have Martha Stewart filling out adoption papers for him.

The only clue to a personal life is in his refrigerator, which is stocked with the instruments of last night's seduction—bulbs of garlic, white wine, lemons, butter, shallots. I open the freezer, expecting it to be empty, but my heart turns as cold as its insides.

Häagen Dazs ice cream. A new quart. Coffee-flavored. I open it up and notice only one portion is missing. Henry hates coffee ice cream. He told me Sunday morning. I didn't believe him because he loves coffee itself. Since I love coffee ice cream, I'd joked that he was probably hiding some to keep it all to himself. So he had opened his freezer and shown me that it was bare except for ice cube trays and two bags of frozen broccoli.

Now there is Häagen Dazs in his freezer. Someone must like coffee ice cream. Someone for whom Henry bought this coffee ice cream. Someone for whom he bought it some time between when I left Sunday morning and when I arrived Sunday night.

The man's a dynamo is my first thought. The way he and I did it I can't imagine him having any energy left for someone else. But maybe this someone else doesn't put out. Maybe it's some version of Tess Wintergarten. Someone he really wants, someone who listens to her Inner Babushka, and when he can't have her, he opts for Door Number Two, Amy Sheldon, who's so desperate for a good lay she reaches for the most-likely-to-sting brand from the shelf.

I am tempted to finish the ice cream and place the empty carton back in the freezer. That will show him. Next time he has Ms. Dazs over and she goes to get her coffee ice cream, won't she be surprised.

Before grabbing a spoon, I stop myself. This is ridiculous. Two nights together and I'm already a green-eyed monster? And if I eat this ice cream, I'll be a *fat* green-eyed monster.

Better to replace these negative vibes with constructive ones. Maybe leave notes hidden throughout his condo for the next woman to find? Beware, these notes will say, you are in the home of a philandering misogynist. Turn back, before it is too late.

Listen to the flowers!

chapter 6

Chinese chrysanthemum: Cheerfulness under adversity

Dealing with Rick's mother was like negotiating with an inscrutable foreign power. We'd meet, we'd talk, we'd go over seating arrangements, color schemes, flowers, and I'd walk away from the rendezvous happily assuming we were of the same mind. Invariably, she'd call Rick shortly after our meeting and tell him her true wishes, which were usually at odds with mine. Poor Rick became the messenger of these thwarted plans, and he was so apologetic about it that I usually ended up feeling sorry for him and compromising away my own desires for the perfect wedding. It was more important, after all, to have the perfect marriage.

When you work in a flower shop, you usually don't get flowers delivered to your office.

So I'm pretty surprised when a Floral Garden truck double-parks out front and a confused deliveryman races in with another one of those white boxes. After I sign for it,

I put it aside and finish an order for a customer standing in front of me.

Then, I take a few phone sales. Then, I fill some orders.

It's a good hour before I actually turn to the box and rip open the tiny note. Yeah, yeah, it takes enormous self-control, but it makes me feel so damn good to ignore it, as if I'm ignoring Henry himself, making him wait for my attention and affection.

I get through the hour of delay by imagining instructing "Brad" to open the note for me—"Take care of that, will you, Brad?" And then while I focus on some other task, imaginary Brad fumbles the card out of the envelope and reads it aloud.

What a satisfying fantasy—me, all ambivalent and desired, and Brad, all hunky and jealous.

But that Brad—he isn't very good at reading aloud, so this daydream falls a little short and I have to read the note myself.

This time, the note says, "Words cannot express… All my love, Henry."

All my love? Henry Castle, gigolo judge of gigolo contests, is confessing his love for me? I don't think so.

"All my love," is a euphemism for "Cordially." For about six months during my senior year in high school, I had a British pen pal. He always signed his letters "All my love," which had me mentally calculating how long it would take to get homesick after I married him and we moved to the English countryside. The way I figured it, a good five years would roll by before I'd be hankering for my homeland. My calculations were brought to an abrupt halt, though, when I discovered my pal Sheila was getting letters from him, too, as was our English teacher, Mrs. Beckwith, who, come to think of it, looked a lot like the Babushka Crone of my recent imaginings. Our British friend from "across the pond" signed all our letters the same way—"All my love."

The flowers themselves don't speak of love. This time it's an oleander plant. Oleander means "beware."

At least he's honest, I think with narrowed eyes. Honest but cryptic. Why send hidden messages? Why not just come out and say: "I'm a philandering playboy and as long as you want to play, I'm game."

My hand reaches for the phone and I hear myself thanking Henry and asking him outright why he doesn't just say things to me instead of hiding them in flowers. And then I remember that I am not after a relationship. Ah, yes. Not after a relationship. Uh-huh. Is that Babushka Crone I hear laughing in the background?

Now I'm the one hiding things. From myself. I pull my hand back from the phone. Better that I should try to get in touch with my own feelings before raking over his. Luckily for me, I have to hurry to finish several bouquets—one for a funeral—before the delivery boy comes in. No time for moping, psychoanalyzing or rash phone calling.

Every time I think of calling Henry, I force myself to remember what I felt when I discovered the Häagen-Dazs. Betrayed by ice cream. Would I ever eat it again?

Actually, I think so.

But will I trust Henry? No. He's obviously sending me messages that let me know up front what kind of relationship we'll have. Good sex. But batten down the hatches on your heart, matie, there's a bad one blowin' in. Why buy the boat when you can sail for free?

Between flower orders and other work that afternoon, I scan apartment listings and even make a few calls about them. Despite my bluster about moving back into the city I've decided I'm better off in the country, so I peruse the listings in my neighborhood and in Carroll County.

Nothing opens up, though. Two places I call have already rented. And one had their phone disconnected.

I'm drumming my fingers on the countertop thinking, when the phone rings late in the day.

It's Henry.

"Well? Did you get my flowers?"

"Yes," I say, trying to sound cold. But there's something about his dark voice that reminds me of how he sounds when he's in ecstasy. And besides, he's breaking his rule. He's calling me, instead of waiting for me to call him. Despite myself, I melt a little inside, and I think that I should try to be less judgmental, and more open. "Do you know what oleander means?"

"No. What?" he asks, and I can't tell if he's pretending.

"Beware."

He laughs heartily. "How appropriate."

"At least you didn't say 'thanking you for an incomparable night' again."

"Now wait a minute. I said 'thanking you for a *really* incomparable night' the other day."

"I'm kind of busy," I say, even though the shop is dead and empty. I want to sound cool and hip. I want my Inner Feminista to come out. Where is she when I need her? "What's up?"

"I have to go to a banquet on Thursday. Baltimore Legal Defense Fund. At the Hyatt. Want to go?"

I die inside. I've been to that gala, but with Rick. What if his father is there? What if my memories are still there? Yet Henry asking me means, well, something. And it would feel so good to go out on his arm, any man's arm, to a big party and to show everyone—anyone, strangers even—that I have a guy. Even if he's just a good roll-in-the-hay guy.

"I...I don't know. I don't have anything to wear," I lie. I have a blue silk dress that I've never worn. I'd bought it for the rehearsal dinner. I wonder if it still fits.

"Buy something new," he says, the laugh still in his voice.

"That's expensive!" I say, indignation in my voice.

"You must have something, Amy." His voice is softer, even a little pleading. Or maybe just exasperated.

I don't know what to say. Of course I have something. If not the blue silk, then some black evening trousers. When I don't respond, I hear him sigh quickly and a voice in the background tells him someone is on the phone.

His tone changes to ice. "Okay. Whatever. I have to go. I'll see ya."

I'll see you? What happened to "all my love"? My hand lingers on the receiver and I have an irresistible urge to call him back and say in a rush that I want to go with him but I can't because, you see, you took my fiancé's job, and his father isn't too keen on seeing me anymore because of the accident, and oh yes, did I mention that I was driving, but I'd really like you to see me in the blue silk dress because I know it would make your eyes shine the way they did last night and what I want most of all in life right now, besides an in-ground pool, is to make a man's eyes shine with desire. And you're a man. My man. And boy does it feel good to say "my man." Even if it's just for the time being at least.

I feel like sobbing.

Instead, I look up as the bell jangles on my shop door. And I see a mottled-face Wendy clutching a tissue doing enough sobbing for both of us.

"Honey, what's the matter?" I ask her, immediately going over to her and putting my arm around her shoulders.

"He's married!" she shrieks.

My heart goes into my stomach. Henry married. He's not just a gigolo. He's an adulterer. Stupid, stupid Amy. Giving your heart to the first guy who runs his finger down your spine the right way. Who was I trying to kid? It was my heart, sister, in that bed, encased in a red-hot libido, but my heart all the same. My God, Wendy's a good friend, sobbing her sympathy out on my shoulder.

I hold her tight and bite my lower lip to keep myself from crying, too. And I remind myself that it's better to get the pain over with quick, up front. The flowers should have told me, but I refused to listen. It was too soon to start a serious relationship anyway. Sure, it's been two years, but at least one of them was consumed with physical therapy. It's really only been a year since I've been feeling myself again, and only half of that where I've had enough energy for anything. I can't really be too disappointed. Hey, it's not so bad. I'll get over it. My first breakup since Rick. One day, I'll look back and think, that was tough but it's a good thing I started seeing guys again.

"Married? How'd you find that out?" My voice trembles as I ask her.

"I went to his office to meet him for lunch," she sniffles.

"Huh? What for?" I hand her a tissue from a box on the counter. Wendy met Henry for lunch. What a friend. Trying to check him out for me. I'm touched, despite my anger and my pain.

"I wanted to surprise him," she says, sounding annoyed. "But he wasn't there. Instead, a student comes in and asks me if I'm his wife."

Rewind. A student? In Henry's office? A law office?

Wait a minute. Another image supplants the one of Henry sitting behind his desk with a picture of his wife and kids for Wendy to see. This new scenario takes place in Sam's office. Sam the professor. Sam the schmuck.

And—forgive me, Lord—I'm relieved. My face reddens with shame. Yes, I admit it. I'm glad Henry's not the adulterer even though it means Sam is, and Wendy's shaken to the core. All that matters is it's not my Henry. *My* unmarried Henry. I've been spared, while the Angel of Heartbreak has darkened Wendy's door.

"Wendy, that's hardly evidence," I manage to sputter out, but inside a little voice is screaming for joy. I pat Wendy's shoulder and usher her to a stool behind the counter. From the fridge I retrieve the last of my Cokes. Note to self: re-stock Cokes before another migraine hits.

"No, that's not all." She thanks me for the Coke and takes a deep gulp. "A professor came in to leave some papers for Sam. So I said kind of nonchalantly that I was waiting for him to go out to lunch. And he says, 'So you're Sam's wife.'"

She starts to cry again. I get another tissue while she continues to talk. "He must have overheard the student and assumed…"

"Still not enough." But it is enough. I know it. And now my shame is fading away, replaced by gut-wrenching sad-ness for my friend, who doesn't deserve this, who deserves fidelity and kindness, which is what she offered to the un-grateful Sam.

"He starts talking to me about all these things—things that Sam must have told him about his wife. He asks me when I got in, how was the weather in California, anyway, and when did I think I'd be able to move East."

"What did you say?"

"Nothing! I just kind of mumbled 'Don't know' and eventually he went away and so did I!"

So Sam will return to his office and some friendly pro-fessor will compliment him on his wife's looks. Life is good.

Eyeing Wendy, I decide life is not good. She's invested nearly a year in this guy. Who would have thought that a college professor would lie like that? A college professor who looks like Sam?

"So you haven't actually talked to Sam yet?" I don't know what to say. I certainly can't say that everything will be okay and maybe she's mistaken and maybe Sam is really as faithful as Fido. I can't say that. And I certainly can't say "Thank God you didn't mean Henry."

"Sam's a schmuck," I finally manage to blurt out, thinking somehow that this will comfort her.

"What?"

"Sam's a schmuck. I always felt he was a schmuck. He never looks me in the eye."

Wendy stops her sniffling and straightens on the stool. "You always felt that way?"

"Yup. Always. There was always something about him that kind of, I don't know, smelled wrong."

"Why didn't you say anything?"

"You seemed happy. I didn't think it was my place."

"Why not? You're my best friend." Her eyes are wide and watery, and her stare cuts me. I am now the betrayer, not Sam.

"I...I don't know. I just thought..." What does anyone think under those circumstances? I didn't want to sound like her mother, who thought dating a college professor was akin to going out with a Communist. "I didn't want to judge."

"But you did judge. You just kept it to yourself. That's not fair, Amy. I wouldn't do that to you." Her wounded look makes my mouth go dry. She's right. I should have said something. I was being selfish. I was afraid if I said something, I'd ruin our friendship, and I needed her friendship.

"I'm sorry."

"Did you know he was married right away?"

"No, but I guess I suspected something was up."

"You suspected he was married and you didn't say anything at all?" Wendy looks at her watch and shakes her head. "Damn! I have a four o'clock."

"What have you been doing since lunch?"

"Walking around. Thinking." She's stopped crying and just looks angry now, but her anger is directed at me.

"Do you want me to call your office and say you'll be late? I offer. "Or why don't I tell them you won't be back today? You should go home. Relax. Put your feet up. Watch a movie." I want to do anything to help her now.

She stares at me as if I have two heads. Which I do if you think about it—the two women inside me are starting to wage a battle over what they have just learned. No, not that Henry's not the adulterer. They just learned that I care about Henry. Or at least want to care about him.

"If you had told me you suspected Sam was married, I would have listened," she says in a low, tired voice.

"I tried to warn you once," I say feebly, the memory coming back to me.

"When?"

"When Sam couldn't get together with you at Christmas. Remember? I said 'That doesn't sound good.'"

Wendy leans her head to one side and her lip twists upward. "That was a warning? Why didn't you just write it in Swahili and send a telegram?"

"Well, I figured you'd get the message—when a guy can't be with you at the holidays it can only mean one thing."

"He has parents he needs to visit, just like I had parents I needed to visit except they were in Mexico last year." She has stopped crying. My therapy has worked.

"Well, okay. It was just a hunch. That he was up to something. I didn't know. I was like you. In the dark."

She glares at me, her eyes thin slits of anger. "You're not like me. You're not dating a married man." She shakes her head in frustration. "I have to leave or I'll be late."

With a flick of her head, she turns and departs. So I have now become the enemy and Sam is safe. That crafty Sam. How'd he do that?

Another headache nips at my brow. Too much to think about. Philandering boyfriends, angry friends. I can't compute it all. I'll call Wendy later after she's had a chance to have a good cry. The only thing I can do to soothe the blow is offer a shoulder and a box of chocolates.

No, a box of flowers. I tear off an order sheet and write Wendy's address. Chuck will be in soon for the afternoon deliveries. I choose an oak-leaved geranium for true friendship and a white chrysanthemum for truth. Wendy won't get the message, of course, but it's enough that I know what I'm saying—that I stand by her as a friend during this time when she learns a hard truth. On the card, I write, "Hoping to cheer you. Ame."

When Chuck comes in a little while later, I explain the deliveries to him slowly and carefully, enunciating very clearly and even showing him on a map where some of the folks live. In particular, I point out Wendy's apartment and instruct him to leave her delivery in front of her apartment door, and not in the lobby.

Chuck asks me about working part-time during the summer, in the shop itself instead of just on the road.

"I'll let you know," I say. "But Brad has first dibs on the job. Let me see what he wants to do." Chuck doesn't know there is no Brad.

For months now, I've been shorthanded. A part-time employee, Danielle, quit to go to Florida with her boyfriend. If I ever get sick or want to go on vacation, the shop is just shut for those days. But since I don't own the place, I need to clear any new hires with my brother-in-law Fred, who deals with the owner, his client.

After turning the closed sign over and locking the door, I decide not to head home right away but to trek over to Gina's. I can spend some quality time with her, mooch some dinner, then talk to Fred about the new hire idea. Trixie has enough cat food to last her through a nuclear winter so I'm good to go.

During my short drive north of town, I pass Tess Wintergarten's apartment complex. Damn, that woman's good! As soon as I drive by the building, my car starts to growl like a bear with an empty stomach. Tess doesn't even need to give you the Evil Eye for her dirty work to be accomplished.

By the time I arrive at Gina's stately home, my car sounds like a souped-up motorcycle. Gina must have heard me coming because she stands on the side porch with her arms crossed over her chest. She's staring at me.

"My God, what's the matter with that thing?" she asks when I tramp into her house. It's cool inside. Gina has the AC cranked up to do battle with the spring heatwave.

"Don't know. Just started."

"You better get that checked. Is it going to be okay?"

"Yeah. It'll be fine. I'm sure." She ushers me into the kitchen and I sit on a stool at the counter while she whips up something from a gourmet cookbook, chopping shallots, garlic and chicken and throwing them in a pan. The dish is similar enough to the one Henry cooked for me that I start to get the hots.

"Wendy's boyfriend is married," I offer as conversation.

"Sam? I never liked him."

"Same here. She's pretty broken up about it."

"She's dumping him, right?"

"Sure," I say, but I'm not quite sure at all. In married-person's world, the land my sister lives in, it is only logical that one would break up with a married boyfriend. In unmarried-person's world, it's not so clear. I rub my forehead with my fingers.

"You have another headache?" Gina asks. "I've got some aspirin."

"Any Motrin?"

"Nope. Some Excedrin. And Extra Strength Tylenol."

"No, thanks. I'll take something when I get home."

We chat about our parents for a while and Gina tells me about a new store she's discovered that sells discount designer clothes, and a new show on HGTV that she loves. Three years older than I am, Gina was an art history major in college, which is how she met Fred. He was taking an art history class to fulfill a liberal arts requirement. They married right after they graduated, which was seven years ago. I know that Gina wants to have kids, but Fred has been a little slow coming around, which is one more reason I'm not too fond of Fred. He likes to take vacations all over the world and go out a lot.

Speaking of Fred, in about an hour he arrives home hot and weary. After a quick kiss on Gina's cheek, he looks over at me and smiles. Fred looks a little like a clean-cut version of Sam. Same receding hairline and wispy hair, same skinny figure and long face, but he wears Brooks Brothers clothes and is appropriately shaved and shorn for the workaday world.

"How's it going, Ame?" he asks me while he pours himself a Scotch. When he holds up the bottle in my direction, I shake my head no at the invitation.

"Pretty good," I say. Then I remember the part-time job I need to talk with him about, so I launch into my spiel. While I talk, he looks down, swirls his drink, grimaces, twists his mouth to one side—not good signs. I wonder if I've done something wrong.

"Business has been slow," I offer, "but I expect it to pick up soon. Wedding season."

"Well, yeah," he says noncommittally.

Gina empties a steaming pot of pasta into a colander.

"You should tell her, Fred."

"Tell me what?"

Fred looks sharply at Gina. "It's not official."

"What's not official?"

Gina stacks plates and cutlery on a tray to take outside. We'll eat on the patio. "She needs to make plans."

"What plans?" I open the sliding door to the flagstone patio to let Gina walk through. After she places the tray on the umbrella-shaded table, she starts setting out plates and cutlery. I go out to help.

"What plans?" I ask again, more insistent.

"Fred," Gina says, exasperated, "either you tell her or I will."

Fred steps over to the door. "Macgregor is thinking of liquidating his assets."

This is accountant-speak for "you're out of a job." Macgregor is the man who owns "Flowers by Amy," a shop he bought for his own daughter Amy to run. She ran all right— all the way to Madrid with some matador wannabe. But the name of the place made it seem like Karma when Fred originally told me about the job.

"He's going to sell the store?"

"Sort of." Fred takes a slow gulp of Scotch. "He's going to sell the building. Has a good lead on it and it will probably be final by the end of the week."

"I didn't know he owned the building."

"He owns several buildings downtown," Fred says seriously, as if I'm a dummkopf for not knowing. "But this is not information to be bandying about." He glares at Gina, who just shrugs her shoulders.

I swallow hard. "If he sells the building by the end of the week, how much longer before I have to leave? I mean, how long do I have a job?"

Fred does not answer right away. Instead, he pours himself another Scotch and offers one to Gina, who grabs it on her way back into the kitchen.

"I don't really know. Depends on how quickly the new owner acts."

"Who is the new owner?"

"I shouldn't say."

"Some Japanese firm," my sister blurts. She empties the pasta into an earthenware dish, then pours the chicken over the top. "Dinner's ready. Grab the glasses, Ame." I notice she does not ask Fred to grab the glasses. Fred is an old-school kind of guy. Me work. You cook and clean. That sort of thing.

A Japanese firm? Ouch. Chances are they're not going to keep a money-losing flower shop going for long. Chances are they'll close me down before you can say "a sushi bar would work well here."

"So I guess this is a bad time to think about hiring new people, huh?" I say and grab wine glasses, a bottle of pinot grigio and the corkscrew.

chapter 7

White clover: Think of me

A month before the accident, Rick and I had dinner at my parents' house. It was a warm night, and, at my insistence, my mother had set the table outside. She didn't want to serve al fresco—she warned of insects and rain. But I thought their deck was far more elegant than the dining room. At least we'd be able to stare at the dusky blue sky with its bashful early stars, instead of at a mass-produced painting of a sea at sunset. Knowing Rick's mother was an excellent cook, Mom knocked herself out and made a shrimp and pasta dish worthy of any gourmand. After dinner, I strolled barefoot with Rick around the back lawn, showing him my mother's recently planted vegetables. Hidden in the cheerful clover, a bee attached itself to my foot and stung me! I'd made it to adulthood without once being stung by a bee or wasp, so this was more than a physical pain. It was an affront—on my home turf, to be felled by a lowly bumblebee.

The foot was still a little sore four weeks later, and I almost used it as an excuse to beg off our commitment that night, the night it all ended.

To drown my sorrow I have too much to drink at dinner. I polish off three huge glasses of vino while my sister and Fred sip daintily on one apiece. Because of the wine and the fact that my car sounds like a Mack truck on steroids, my sister insists I spend the night. I don't protest and it feels good to sink into a bed with a new mattress and expensive Duvet. She puts me in one of her house's four bedrooms—the one farthest from the master suite, on the front corner of the house.

Damn front corners. Gina and Fred might live in an expensive part of town, but their house is near the corner of Roland Avenue where buses start roaring down the road at 5:00 a.m. as people head off to jobs in the city. When the noise wakes me up, I feel like putting the time to good use by spray-painting sheets and hanging them out the window to warn passersby: "Badlands ahead. Tess Wintergarten."

Instead, I wander downstairs and start the coffee, then take a shower. By now I have a headache that has all the makings of a migraine. Shouldn't have had that wine last night when I already felt a headache coming on. To make matters worse, I left my magic pills at my house and the shop. None in my purse. Way to go, Amy.

Fred is showered and dressed by the time I come downstairs again. He's drinking coffee at the kitchen table, reading the business section of the *Sun* and poking at some whole-grain cereal that probably tastes like cardboard. He has set out no bowl for me even though I arranged three mugs next to the coffeemaker when I awoke.

"Morning," I mumble.

Fred does not respond until he's finished reading his article. Then he closes the paper and looks up at me. "Sleep okay?"

"Fine. Just a little noisy this morning."

Standing, he reaches for the coffee carafe and pours himself another cup. "Well, you have to get up eventually."

"Ain't that the truth."

Gina shuffles in, yawning, in a silky robe of deep blue. "Thanks for putting the coffee on, Ame." I notice she doesn't assume Fred did it. "Anybody want pancakes?"

"Not me. Had some cereal. Maybe tomorrow. I have to get going." He smiles at her, his "little woman," then gives her a peck on the cheek. When he leaves the house a few minutes later, he doesn't say goodbye.

"You have a headache still?" Gina asks, popping in some toast.

"Yeah. I need to get to my house. Feed Trixie." I need my drugs. Fast. I need to get away from here. Fast.

"You can borrow my car."

"My car will be fine. I'll get it checked on the way back into town."

"Is your cell phone charged up?"

"I don't know. Probably." Not. I don't have a cell phone, but I have kept this from my sister. After the accident, a week didn't go by that Gina didn't bug me about getting a cell phone, as if having one would have made a difference.

I had every intention of getting one, too, but then her pestering triggered a case of *spitenfreude,* which is a German word I've made up to mean the joy you feel when you are doing something secret to spite someone else. It seemed kind of fun to give her a phony number and pretend I never turn the phone on.

But then procrastination kicked in and I never bothered to get the actual phone.

"Well, give me a call if you need help." She sits opposite me with her toast and coffee. "I'm worried about you, Ame," she says.

Ah, yes. The old "I'm worried about you" talk. She's nipped at the edges of it for the past few months. Looking at her worried eyes I'm grateful it took her this long. She managed to restrain herself from giving the speech when I got out of the hospital and when I decided not to go back to my job, even when I moved to the country.

"You've been kind of drifting for the past two years, which is understandable," she begins to say, slowly. "But now you have a chance to stop the drift. The shop being sold is really an opportunity for you to reevaluate where you are and where you want to go." She leans back. "I was reading an article the other day about realizing your dreams. This doctor—I think he's a behavioral psychologist—suggests you sit down and write an essay, nothing long, describing what your life would be like if you could have everything you want. Maybe you should consider doing that. It might help get you back on track."

Because Gina has been such a good sport about not bugging me to "get on with my life," I respond with good cheer. "You're right. I should try that." Phony good cheer. "When I get home this morning, I'll do it." I take my now-empty mug to the sink. "I think I should get going, though."

"Call me when you get home," she says.

"Okeydoke."

Before leaving I help her unload and reload the dishwasher and listen to her talk some more about recipes and decorating ideas. By the time I hit the road at eight my head is throbbing to the rhythm of my car's engine—a ragged roar of sound and pain.

I'm hurting so much that I actually cry my way home. Bursting into tears, I hit I-83 and weep my way up the interstate and onto Route 439.

Maybe it's the fact that my car is clearly giving up the ghost and I don't want to see her die? Maybe it's the fact that

I'm losing my home and my job in short order? Maybe it's the fact that when I think of writing that stupid "what I want out of life" essay I imagine a whole list of things that I don't ever envision getting?

An in-ground pool. A good job. A nice house. My old fiancé.

And, oh yes, no more migraines. Wiping my face with the back of my hand I mutter a hello to Trixie at the door, but she ignores me and runs for the bushes. Inside, I tear open a headache pill and pop it in my mouth, then check my messages. The house smells rotten—even the lavender can't cut the scent of old strawberry hulls in the kitchen trash. My messages play while I set the trash can outside.

"Hi, this is Wendy. Thanks for the flowers. That was really sweet of you. Give me a call when you have a chance." She sounds better. Not happy, but definitely calmer. And no longer angry with me.

"*Conchita,* when you make up your mind about the banquet, let me know." Hmm…he's called me twice now.

"Pete Swilton here." Pete's tentative voice cuts into the room. "Uh…give me a call."

After opening up all my windows to let the fresh air in and the rotten-berry smell out, I call Pete back. He owns a farm in Pennsylvania and one of his sons answers, but tells me to hold while he gets his dad.

By the time Pete comes to the phone, I've managed to pour myself a Coke and find a Little Debbie chocolate cake to eat.

"Miss Sheldon, I'm glad you called back. I've got a deal to offer you." Turns out Pete's buyer wants to get a jump start on the construction season. He's willing to offer me the equivalent of a month's rent if I move out right away.

"What's right away?" I ask, pouring myself some more Coke.

"Uh…by the end of the week."

I nearly spit the Coke out across the room. Looking around my small place, I imagine packing up my belongings and heading out in a week. Impossible. Not with a job and…

A job? A job? I won't have a job soon! *Take the money,* my inner mercenary child whispers. Screw the job.

"Okay," I say evenly. "You pay my moving expenses, too, and you've got a deal." Pete agrees in a heartbeat, which makes me realize I could have asked for much more.

After hanging up, I give myself an hour to let the headache pill work, and when it finally does, I'm calmer and more energized. I start making a list—not the list of things that would make me happy. This list is more practical—what I need to do in order to be moved and financially secure in a week's time.

First order of business: find a place to live.

But I procrastinate with that and instead ring up a moving van and self-storage place to make arrangements for the move. Since I didn't specify how much money Pete would need to fork over for moving expenses, I order the priciest package—the movers will pack up everything for me, down to the rotting-berry trash if I happen to leave it out for them.

"No point in going into work today," I tell Trixie, who meows at the front door. "In fact, I think I'll take off all week."

All week—vacation. I deserve a vacation. I return Wendy's phone call and reach her at the office before she heads into a meeting. She is repentant even though she doesn't say so.

"I talked to Sam," she whispers. Her office is big and open and she has a nice cubicle by the windows, but it gives her little privacy.

"And?"

"And he says they're getting a divorce."

Oh, no. The old "getting a divorce" line. Surely Wendy won't fall for—

"He wants to go to Jamaica with me!" Her voice is excited and I'm ready to throw the phone at the wall.

"Uh, do you think that's wise?" I ask, treading softly.

"I haven't said yes yet," she says. "Let him sweat for a while."

Let him sweat? What does the guy have to lose? So he can't have sex with Wendy in Jamaica. Big deal. He can go have sex with his wife in California. And if that professor friend of his mistook Wendy for Sam's wife, the "little woman" must be a pretty good-looking package, too. How does he do it?

Since Hopkins is so close to 3900 Charles Street I'm beginning to think that Tess Wintergarten and Sam are in cahoots. I can see Sam and Tess jumping and dancing in a circle on the lacrosse field shouting spooky chants that turn rational women into idiots and old Pontiacs into rusted wrecks.

"How are things going with you?" Wendy asks. "Were you at Henry's again last night?"

"No. Stayed with my sister. But I have to call him. He left a message for me."

"That's great, Ame. This could be the start of something really good for you. It's about time you got on with your life."

"Gina said the same thing."

"And Henry seems like a nice fellow."

"You've never met him."

"He sends you flowers. How many guys do that?"

I want to tell her that if not many guys do it, it's because Henry has cornered the market. He sends enough flowers to make up for the rest of his fellow men. For all I know, he's worked out some designated-flower-sender deal with the rest of the male race. For all I know, he could be sending flowers to someone else at this very moment.

"Yeah. It's nice." I'm about to tell her that I'm losing my job but she has to run to her meeting.

"On Friday, a bunch of us are getting together. Want to come? Women's Work at seven," she says, naming a new female-only athletic club.

"Sure. Sounds good."

Now that I've returned two of my three messages I can't put the last one off any longer. I reach for my purse to pull out Henry's card. Who am I trying to kid? I have his phone number memorized. I have his fax number memorized. And his e-mail address for that matter. If I knew his social security number I'd probably have that committed to memory as well.

"Squires Law Firm," a new receptionist answers, and out of habit I start to say "Could I speak with Rick, please," but stop myself before I get to his name, quickly changing it to Henry's.

After a detour through Henry's personal secretary, another new woman I don't know, he's on the line. But I'm still rattled by my near mix-up and my voice shakes a little when I say hello.

"Anything the matter?" he asks.

"No," I lie. Then I start crying again. Another good way to test a relationship—begin it with a crying jag. Here I thought I'd cried myself out for the day, but damned if new tears don't start staining my blue jeans. "I'm losing my job," I add at last.

"Oh, man. That's a bummer," he offers as consolation. "I have a few minutes. What happened?"

So I explain about the Japanese firm and my house and my accelerated moving plans. "Look, I have a client coming in," he says after my monologue. "But I can come see you after work if you want."

I'm touched. He seems genuinely interested in making me feel better. Looking around, I can't imagine suave, career-climbing Henry comfortable here. He comes to this place and he'll know instantly that I'm a fraud. I'm no savvy urbane sex kitten. I'm just a kitten. Maybe not even that.

"Sure. Let me give you directions." I have a dating death wish, I guess.

"I'll bring something to eat," he says before hanging up.

Henry and food. Two primal needs taken care of.

But it gives me something to look forward to, and throughout the day, I feel like a swimmer who's just set a record—tired, with puffy eyes, but happy. I spend the day sorting through my things. There isn't much. Even though this is a three-bedroom house, I only have furniture in the living room, kitchen and one bedroom. The dining room is empty except for a few old chairs and sideboard. The other bedrooms hold some boxes.

When I moved here from my apartment with Rick I didn't have enough to fill the space. I thought it would be fun to decorate, slowly accumulating what I needed. But I never found the time or money to do it right.

A few of the boxes contain remnants of my past with Rick. The scheduling book from the wedding planner. Folders with information on various banquet rooms. Brochures on potential honeymoon spots. I'd saved them for several reasons. Obviously, they were a connection to happier times. But I guess I also thought that maybe I'd need them again, that maybe I'd find another Rick and I could start planning all over again. Like for a job vacancy that needed to be filled.

"This is the reason I break down in tears on the Interstate," I say to Trixie, who follows me around. After I look at the contents near the top of one box I lug it downstairs and put it outside with the trash. No need to dig further.

As the heat of the late spring day settles on the house, I nap, serene at last on my country-quilted bed. That was the one purchase I made to spruce up my new digs when I moved. A new quilt. It made the bed feel fresh and blanched of old associations.

Showered and changed by evening, I feel like someone in a Wyeth painting. I've put on a blue sundress and smeared honeysuckle-scented body cream on my shoulders. Even though Henry says he's bringing food, I feel like I should put something out. So I find some crackers and an unopened square of cheese. Cheese keeps forever, right? I'm slicing up the cheese and putting it on a plate when I hear wheels crunching on the dirt road.

I can't help it—my heart starts thudding in anticipation. When I open the front door, I see Henry scowling as he stares at the dust on his Beamer. In one hand is a large plastic bag obviously filled with carryout boxes and tins. In the other hand is his jacket, slung over his shoulder, Frank Sinatra-style. Oh baby.

"You made it!" I cry out.

He looks up, takes in my dress with his eyes and stops grimacing. It's not a smile, but it will have to do.

"Just barely. Traffic was a bitch. I can't believe you commute this every day."

"Mmm…smells good. What did you get?" I take the bag from him and turn to go in the house. But he stops me and kisses me, pushing me into the doorjamb. The sun warms my shoulders. Henry warms my insides.

"Chinese," he whispers. "It can keep."

I decide to give him a tour of the house starting with the bedroom.

A half hour later, we're lying intertwined under my quilt with the sound of bees whirring near my rhododendron outside. Its brilliant purple-and-rose-colored blossoms could open any day.

I trace a line down Henry's nose to his chin to his chest and he smiles with his eyes closed. "I guess we should eat," he says.

"Yeah. I'm hungry." I sit up and crawl over him to get to

the floor. But he grabs my butt and kneads it with his hand in such a way that other hungers start to resurface. "You're wicked, Henry," I purr.

After I kiss him, he lets go. Even a sex machine has other needs and we can both smell the sesame oil and garlic of our Chinese feast.

Downstairs, he helps me set out the cartons and I grab some plates from a cabinet.

"Tell me about your job," he says as he dives into the rice and lamb two flavors, forgoing the chopsticks and opting for a fork. I'm a fork person, too. Never could grasp the chopstick allure.

"There's not much more to tell. The building will be sold. And it's unlikely that the shop will stay open."

"Is that what you want to do—retail?"

"Not really. I kind of landed there. After the accident."

"What about going back to Gelman?"

I shake my head. "No openings. Plus, I don't think I want to go back there. I don't have happy memories of that place." Part of the reason for that, of course, is because I associate my time with Rick with Gelman's. But I'd also grown tired of the agency with its too-hip, too-cool approach to promotions. I'd even started looking around for other jobs before I left there.

"You're not interested in communications work at all?" He looks around the kitchen. "You have any beer?"

"As a matter of fact," I announce cheerfully, "I don't. I do have some Coke."

"Water's fine."

I fill two glasses. Once again, he eats as if it's his last meal, and if I want my fair share of the dumplings, rice and lamb, I better plow in or they'll be gone. "I'm not sure what I want to do," I say after scooping what I consider to be my portions onto my plate.

"Have you thought of going to a career counselor?"

"You mean one of those people who gives you tests that they pull out of *Cosmo* magazine?"

Henry does not laugh. "They do good work. I know one. Has an office on Pratt Street."

"I don't have the money for that right now, especially when I'm facing unemployment. I'll find something."

"It's not as expensive as you think. You can buy different kinds of services. You don't need to get the whole enchilada."

"Oh, Henry, I love it when you talk Spanish," I coo.

Again he does not laugh. "If you're serious about getting something, I can help. But if you just want to screw around…"

Curious choice of words, that. "Screw around." Does he mean "If you just want to screw around with me, but you don't want anything more serious, I'll back off?" Or does he mean "If you just want to screw around with your career…" I look into his eyes searching for an answer, but none rotates into view.

After dinner, we sit on the front porch and watch Trixie chasing flies.

"What are these?" he asks, pointing to the rhododendron's flat waxy leaves and full buds.

When I tell him, he pulls a branch closer to inspect it.

"And what do they mean?"

I twist my mouth and close my eyes, thinking. "Beware. Danger."

He laughs. "Do all flowers mean 'beware'?"

"No. Only a few."

"Just the ones I like."

"You like yellow roses. They mean 'jealousy.'"

"I'll have to get a flower book so I don't accidentally say something that will get me into trouble."

"Have you been sending a lot of flowers lately?"

He smiles but gives no quarter. "I sent some to you."

Some. Hmm…does that mean he sent others?

"You use several florists?"

"You can't always get good service at some. Better to spread the business around."

I blush, remembering my mix-up with the order to Tess Wintergarten.

"That reminds me," I say. "You never did tell me what you had to do to make it up to Tess Wintergarten. And why'd you have to make up for sending her flowers, anyway? Usually you have to make it up when you don't send flowers."

Picking up a stone, he throws it into the field. "I had to go antique shopping with her. But that was on Saturday. On Friday night, I had to change my plans and take her dancing."

"What? You were originally planning on taking Diana Malvani dancing?"

He stays silent, which is my answer.

Now I'm getting mad. Mad at myself. Just because Henry has taken an interest in me lately doesn't mean he's left his ways behind. When will he take Diana dancing again? When he gets tired of me?

"Your car is leaking something," he says after a while.

"Huh?" I stand, staring over at the old Pontiac as if it has just betrayed me.

"I noticed it when I drove up. There's a trail of something from the road down to the house." He points over at the car as I walk toward it. Following me, he sniffs the air.

"Gasoline," he says.

"You know something about cars?"

He laughs. "I know nothing about cars except I like to drive them. Wrong Latino type, *conchita*."

Conchita, schmonchita. Henry's beginning to annoy me with this phony Spanish routine. I smell the gasoline, too, and lean over to peer under the body of the car. Oddly, no signs announcing the problem and its potential cost greet my eyes. In fact, I don't even see the leak. But the smell is definitely stronger. "I thought it was just my muffler," I say.

"You shouldn't drive it if it's leaking gasoline."

"Right, I shouldn't."

So I'm starting my week with no job, no house, and now no car.

The essay Gina suggested I write is suddenly crammed with stark necessities. Forget whimsical touches like figuring out what I want out of life. Now my needs are desperate and simple.

In a strange way, this makes me feel better. I'll be too busy now to worry about what to do with the rest of my life.

Nobody can blame me if I don't get on that right away.

chapter 8

Mushroom: Suspicion

*Because Rick was a good-looking man, he was a prime tar-
get for hungry, good-looking women. Despite the fact that I
never saw evidence of infidelity, I was sometimes unsettled by
the attention his model-perfect looks would garner when we
went out together. He knew it bothered me and he was sympathetic, telling me I was "cute enough" to make men's heads
turn. Cute enough? That hardly mollified me. And when his
firm hired a gorgeous lawyer fresh out of Yale, all blond hair
and blue eyes and slim figure, I began to morph into a green-
eyed monster, irritated and grumpy when he worked late, hy-
persensitive to the slightest slight. One night, I was near tears
by the time he came home close to eleven, envisioning he'd
begun a torrid affair on the conference room table. Not knowing he'd be working late, I'd slaved over a special steak dinner. With exotic mushrooms and expensive herbs, it was a
brilliant, but lonely, success. He brought home a peace offering—ironically, a dozen yellow roses! Sure, I knew they were*

*really a gift a grateful client had given him, but they dried my
tears, especially when he told me that the new blond lawyer
was unhappy and jumping ship to another firm.*

Before Henry leaves for the night, he asks me again about
the banquet, but now I have a reason to refuse.

"I'm sorry. I checked my schedule and I promised some
friends I'd get together with them." This is a half lie. I am
getting together with Wendy and her friends on Friday, not
on Thursday, and I hadn't even made that plan when he
asked me the first time.

Henry accepts my excuse with no comment. He kind of
shrugs, kisses me and tells me he'll call me.

As I throw away the empty Chinese cartons I reflect on
the fact that we only made love once during this visit, instead of the marathon number of times on the two previous occasions we'd gotten together. At first, I interpret this
as a good sign. It indicates that there's more to our relationship than sex, right? But then, as I lean against a porch
post admiring my rhododendron, I realize there is danger
in this fact. Perhaps he is already tiring of me and is ready
to move on to another blossom, another Di, another Tess,
another Amy.

It shouldn't matter. I don't want involvement, right? I
want a dating relationship. I want to play the field. Now I
want my inner voices to speak, to give me direction. I want
clear maps, not cloudy views.

Where is that damn list? I want an in-ground pool, a new
home, a new job and now a new car! That's what I want.

Remembering the car, I inspect it again, hoping that it
fixed itself.

It hasn't. If anything, the smell is even stronger.

"Good thing I'm taking off this week," I tell Trixie, who
brushes against my bare ankles.

I pack some more that evening, mostly my clothes in two huge suitcases. I really need to spruce up my wardrobe, but I can't afford to go clothes-shopping now that my money spigot is about to be turned off.

Maybe Gina and Henry are right. Maybe I need to start thinking about a career choice again.

Even though I'm only in my twenties, I feel too old to be taking tests and writing essays. I settle in front of the television with Sunday's classifieds on my lap and a red felt pen in my hand.

I'll read every single one and circle those that appeal to me, even the ones for which I'm completely unqualified. Perhaps this little exercise will prime the pump and get the juices flowing.

I am halfway through the *C*'s—and yes, I circled "chemist" after deciding maybe I need to think about returning to school—when I get caught up in a cooking show. Chicken with grapes and feta cheese. Maybe I should write the recipe down and try it on Henry one night. As the ingredients scroll by, I frantically scribble them in the margin of the newspaper.

When I'm finished, I rip off that edge, taking with it a large chunk of the *D*'s and *E*'s. There are a lot of good jobs in the *E*'s, too, I notice as I copy the recipe onto a note card in the kitchen a few moments later. Editor, executive director, education paraprofessional.

Because I rose so early, my eyelids are heavy by the time the show is over. I've only made it halfway through the alphabet, but this leaves me feeling satisfied and happy. Something to look forward to tomorrow—finishing my job hunt.

After neatly folding the paper and leaving it on the kitchen table, I close up shop, coax Trixie in for the night and clean up for bed. When I finally put my head on the pillow, I smell Tommy Hilfiger, Henry's scent.

I sleep better than I have in years.

★ ★ ★

And I awake, early and grumpy in the morning.

Pete has wasted no time. Now that I've agreed to sign on the dotted line and get out early, he must have given the new property owners a thumbs-up to getting started with construction. Instead of waiting until next week as Pete had originally suggested they would, bulldozers are rumbling and coughing onto my estate at first light.

Grabbing a terry robe and tying it around my waist I run to the door. Trixie leaps out and dives away from the huge machines.

A helmeted man stares down at me.

"Did you know you have a gasoline leak in your car?" he hollers.

"Yeah. Thanks!" I scream up to him. After that good-morning greeting, I tramp back inside and make myself a cup of java. There isn't much in my house for breakfast since I haven't had a chance to shop, and since I'm leaving by the end of the week I didn't want to stock up.

How am I going to stock up, anyway? Can't drive the Pontiac.

A panic attack starts to take shape, curling up through my toes and into my fingertips, buzzing into my chest and giving my heart a little jolt. No Place to Live flashes the neon sign in my brain. No place to live! No place to live! Homeless!

With perspiring hands I see myself pushing a shopping cart full of rags and old soda cans through downtown Baltimore. It's come to this—my trip out of the fast lane has landed me in the gutter. What the hell was I thinking? Who can save me?

I reach for the phone and call Gina. It won't be so bad, I rationalize. Just for a few days or a week or a month. Then

I'll find something—an apartment, a condo, a forest ranger's shack.

Gina's perky voice greets me after two rings.

"You're up early," she says after the hello's are out of the way.

"Well, that's why I'm calling you," I say, and proceed to tell her about the bulldozers that dropped in for morning coffee. "So I was wondering if I could camp out with you guys after all. Just for a little while. A week or so, maybe." Please make it just a week, Lord. Let me win the lottery.

"Honey, that would be grand," she announces, but there's a certain lack of enthusiasm in her voice. Wasn't she just trying to convince me to move in with her a few days ago? Was that all a show—an offer I was meant to refuse? I chalk up her reaction to the early hour. Her sisterly instincts haven't kicked in yet.

"Fred's going to be out of town at the end of the week. Some conference in Colorado. So this is perfect timing!" she says, this time with suitable excitement. Ah, so that's it—Fred and me in the same house for extended stay. Does not compute.

"Great!" I return. "We can rent some movies." Better to think of it as a sleepover than temporary shelter. It seems so much more fun that way.

"Oh, yeah," I mention casually before getting off the phone, "I think I'll need to get a new car."

"You can borrow mine while you're here!" Now that the sleepover mentality is affecting us both she is vivacious. She starts planning. She tells me that she will fill the tank and give me Fred's keys. She asks me what I want for dinner when I come. She asks me if the room I stayed in was comfortable. She gives me her schedule for the next few days that includes a hair appointment and a club meeting and a get-together with some friends. Then she tells me not to worry,

I won't be an imposition at all. I get the impression she's thinking out loud—convincing herself how neatly I'll fit into her world. By the time I get off the phone I'm tired. It's as if I just lived through her schedule with her. All those appointments and meetings do wear a girl out.

I spend my morning packing up my few fragile belongings, and cleaning. I find a rhythm that keeps me moving forward without thinking too much and it feels good to be occupied with meaningful tasks. I call the movers again and ask them if they can come earlier, and the only time they have open is tomorrow, Thursday morning, so that lights the fire under me even stronger.

Although I don't have much and I am having the movers pack it all up for storage, I find other things I have to do. Disconnect the phone and electricity, change my post office address, cancel my insurance on the car, find a job.

It is midafternoon before I can sit down and tackle that last task. And even then it takes me a good half hour before I'm really able to focus.

First, I can't find a pen. All right, so I have a ballpoint right there on the kitchen table. But it's some cheapo thing with a clicker top and some business name on the side. Note to business owners: ballpoint pens are not good promo items unless you can afford expensive versions with huge lettering. Anyway, this one puts out a weak blue trail. Surely I would miss some good ads if I circled them with this puny thing.

So I ransack my purse, my kitchen "junk drawer," my dresser top, and finally the sofa cushions, where I find yesterday's red Sharpie. I will feel very productive circling ads with its elegant crimson flair.

Speaking of ads, I then have to go on a treasure hunt for the newspaper. In my rush to clean up, I must have put it out with other recyclables. After pawing through a stack of

old papers, I finally locate the right strata—this week's edi-
tions—and pull it out with maestro-like assurance.

And then I remember I'd ripped out a section in order to
write the recipe on it. Another search, this one fruitless. That
scrap of paper must have been swept into the trash can
when I was scouring the kitchen.

No matter. There are plenty of ads left, right? But the
thought of those lost ads nags at me and I have trouble con-
centrating. I remember some good ones on that scrap, ones
that matched my skills. I'll have to get a new newspaper.
Meantime, I can look through the ads in this one. But wait,
if I do that and then buy a new one, I'll have two papers,
both the same, but with different ads circled. It could get
confusing. Better to give up the hunt until I get the new
paper.

Before I reach this conclusion, though, I do manage to
make my way through the *S*'s, and the Sunday section's a sea
of red ovals. The ink bleeding through the thin paper to the
underside makes it look as if I've found many more prospective jobs than I really have. And half of those jobs are in the
"chemist" category, if you know what I mean.

Even though the job-hunt part of my day only occupies
about two hours, it tires me out the most. I have an early
dinner of leftovers and try not to wonder if Henry will call.
I do try to remember what it was like to be in the early part
of a relationship where the will-he-call-me-tonight question lurks in the corner of your mind.

Uh-oh. This unleashes the dueling voices, one carping
about how I shouldn't even be thinking "relationship" while
the other shouts her disdain. I'm tired. Too tired for debates.
So I turn on the TV and watch reruns of the *Donna Reed
Show,* feeling all cozy as I start to live in that world where
doctors actually made house calls and a wife wore pearls to
breakfast.

Henry doesn't call, but I've managed to convince myself that I don't care if he does. And I feel better by the time I go to bed. Tomorrow, I'll greet the movers and trundle off to my sister's for an open-ended sleepover, then I'll move on with my life.

Right?

It's 5:30 a.m. and I'm dressed in my Tweetie Bird night-shirt rummaging around one of the trash bags to reclaim all my prewedding memorabilia.

I tell myself I might need the stuff. Not for my sake, mind you. No, no, it's for Wendy. Wendy will get married some day (once she's free of Sam, of course) and I don't want to be sitting around with her as she plans the wedding, slapping myself on the forehead wishing I'd kept the catalogs, the tip sheets, the lists. My God, the lists alone are worth their weight in gold.

So in the cool hush of dawn, I manage to drag all that stuff from oblivion and place it back into a box where it will rest safely rotting for another thousand years. Great junk for an archaeologist to discover some day. Yes, saving it is a public service, no matter which way you view it. Either Wendy will profit from it, or some anonymous sleuth in a British field hat and Bermuda shorts will uncover it as a relic of the Wedding Planning Epoch.

"Come over here, chap," I hear him saying to an identically dressed colleague with a fusty-smelling pipe in his mouth. "Have you ever seen anything as organized as this, old boy? Why, it's a veritable treasure trove. Whoever saved this material was most assuredly a public-spirited citizen, I'd say, a true patriot of the first class, a demmed good sport, what ho, jolly good, cheerio and all that."

All right, so maybe they won't talk like that in the future, but in the predawn hours my fantasies all read like old B movies. I can't think straight, let alone fantasize imaginatively.

The point is—and this is really important—I'm not saving the stuff for myself. It's for Posterity. Or Wendy. Or maybe even for Gina's as-yet-to-be-conceived daughter. I just know I can't give it up and throw it all away. It seems cruel that anyone would expect me to do that. Who is that "anyone," anyway? And why are they doing this to me?

I don't go back to sleep after rescuing my wedding things from the cliff of nothingness. I change and drink coffee and putter and worry. Will the movers arrive on time, and if they do will they get everything safely in the truck?

Eventually, they do arrive and I offer them coffee and make awkward small talk and the move begins.

I hate watching furniture being moved. I'm always afraid that the movers are going to drop something on their toes and blame me. I think they're blaming me for how heavy the furniture is, as if I've loaded it up with lead weights just to make their job harder. So I'm cringing a lot, which makes my head start to ache a little. Dammit.

Complicating the movers' task is the bulldozer parked right at my front door. Thursday must be some national earth-moving holiday, because the bulldozer operator and his pals haven't arrived. This means the moving van can only park at the end of the dirt road instead of next to the house, causing the movers to walk everything a good ten yards before they get to the ramp of their truck.

They're so happy at the end of this job that I imagine they'll be taking *really* good care of my things.

Gina is coming at noon to pick me and Trixie up. By the time she arrives I'm sitting, frazzled and hot, on the porch trying to hold on to the cat, who wants nothing more than to scamper away. She senses something is up.

At exactly 11:59, Gina pulls up in her silver Volvo. Pushing her sunglasses onto her head, she gets out and grins.

"Nice dress," she quips. I'm wearing the same sundress I wore the other night when Henry, who still hasn't called (But am I paying attention? Hell no!) was here. Then she looks at the cat and her smile fades. "Oh, I forgot you had a cat."

"Is that a problem?" I ask, picking up one suitcase while Gina gets the other.

"Fred doesn't like cats." She clicks open her trunk and we scoot the luggage in. "And don't you have a pet carrying case or something?"

"I think I accidentally let the movers take it."

"I was hoping we could stop at the mall on the way home," she says, eyeing Trixie.

"We can take Trix to your place, grab some lunch, and then go shopping," I suggest.

Flipping her sunglasses back on her face, she slides behind the wheel. "Okay. Fred's not going to be home until Tuesday anyway."

Fred not being home until Tuesday has nothing to do with going to the mall and everything to do with Trixie. Looking over at my sister I wonder if she plans to hire some canine version of a goodfella so she doesn't have to deal with this problem. Or maybe she figures she can talk me out of keeping the cat. Hugging Trixie close I buckle myself in and we take off down the road. I send secret telepathic messages to Trix assuring her that wherever I go, she goes.

Whatever my apprehensions about moving in with my sister, they are kept at bay for this one afternoon as we take a trip back to our childhood. At least back to the time when you didn't need to worry about what you were going to eat, where you were going to live and who was going to pay for everything.

With a happy abandon I'd not experienced since my mother took me into Hecht's department store and told me I could buy any dress I wanted for my senior prom, I shopped away the afternoon. Towson Town Center is a multistory temple of consumerism filled with specialty shops and boutiques, as well as the grand dames of the Baltimore retail trade, including good ol' Hecht's.

Gina tells me she's treating me since my birthday is coming up, and any time my eye lights on something, she asks me if I want it. At the end of the day she's bought me another sundress, two pairs of slacks, a designer wraparound sleeveless top, some Victoria's Secret lingerie, and a pair of strappy sandals that I can only imagine wearing *with* the lingerie in Henry Castle's bedroom.

Speaking of Henry, I think of him from time to time during the day, which only heightens my sense of being a teen again. It's as if I'm back in the days when thoughts of a high school crush float through your mind like the words to a favorite song.

To cap off our youthful afternoon, Gina takes me out to an early-bird dinner at a trendy bar off of York Road, where we order fattening burgers only a giant could fit in his mouth, and ice cream sundaes for dessert.

"It's a good thing we wore expandable clothes," she laughs, loosening the top snap on her designer jeans. Gina is a good-looking woman, with perfectly frosted short hair and manicured fingers. Away from Fred she's as gay as a spring day, and it occurs to me that she has made some trade-off that she is more than happy with.

"Did you do that exercise?" she asks me as we slurp up the last of our ice cream.

For a minute I think she's referring to physical exercise since we just snarfed down a diet-busting meal, then I remember—the "essay" on my "perfect life."

"Yes," I lie. Lying has become too easy lately, and I wonder if I'll have to go through some twelve-step program to give it up.

"Was it helpful?"

"Yes," I lie again. And more: "I came up with a few things. In fact, I was going through the paper and circled a bunch." There, no lie.

"Great!" She reaches over and actually pats my hand. "Mom and Dad have been worried about you, too."

"They shouldn't. I'm probably doing better than they are."

"Ain't that the truth. I was over there two weeks ago," Gina confesses, "and Mom was screaming at Dad about messing up her kitchen."

"Payback time."

"In spades."

Our eyes meet in that way that communicates a thousand unvoiced thoughts. Poor Mom. Poor Dad. They've got what they deserve. We love them anyway. And to think we used to hate them.

All in a flash, these thoughts jump from my eyes to hers and back again.

"We can rent a video tonight if you want," she says after paying the check with her credit card.

"That's okay. I'm kind of tired." This is true. I woke up early to get ready for the movers, then ended up sitting around waiting for them for two hours.

We leave the restaurant with a sense of regret, somehow knowing we won't recapture this feeling for a long time.

At home, I am chagrined to find that Trixie has left us little "gifts" on the kitchen floor and on my bed. Before Gina can notice, I quickly scoop them up and toss them, and spray the air with room deodorizer. Gina is outside, watering plants, but wrinkles her nose when she comes back in.

She looks at Trixie who bounds for the door, but says nothing. That crafty Trix.

I retreat to my room where I spend a half hour washing the Trixie stain from the white duvet, and another half hour trying on the clothes we bought. When I get to the sandals and the lingerie I think of where Henry is tonight. At the gala.

From downstairs, I hear the television blaring. HGTV is airing a home-design special. I know I should offer to watch it with Gina, but I'm restless. Now another feeling comes churning up from my past—that same sense of fidgety impatience to get on with life that I used to get sitting in my purple-skirted bed as a kid at home.

What did I do when I felt that way? I'd grab the keys to the car and tell my mother I was going for a drive. Then I'd bop around my friends' neighborhoods, just cruising slowly past other ranchers and split levels. Sometimes, I'd catch a glimpse of a girlfriend out on the lawn. Once I caught a boy two-timing his steady with another girl.

Henry. Henry is at the gala. Is he alone?

I rush downstairs and I breeze into the small den where Gina's watching TV.

"Can I borrow your car?"

"What? Sure. Keys are in my purse in the kitchen. Did you forget something?"

"No. Just want to take a drive. I might go see Wendy."

"Okay." She laughs. "Don't be out late, or I'll worry."

"Sure thing, Ma."

In a few minutes I'm on the road. This time I've decided to avoid Tess Wintergarten's evil rays by taking an alternative route into the heart of the city. It's nearly seven-thirty now, and chances are Henry and crew are already in the Hyatt doing the pretend-laugh routine with colleagues and friends.

But I feel like a kid and I'm enjoying it, bopping down the road, looking for friendly faces.

Late-day light is cutting across the city creating a glare that makes me squint. The air is fresh and cool now, and with the windows open I catch the scent of other people's dinners wafting along the streets. I'm happy.

I let the Volvo take me way into town, to the harbor where the water glimmers in the early evening sun and where cheery tourists and shoppers stroll. I convince myself that this is my real destination, that I'll park the car, take a walk, listen to the soothing caw-caw of the seagulls and catch a little of the soothing peace that lapping water seems to offer.

But then I pass the Hyatt. Nothing unusual there. The party's inside. Good thing, I realize. It would be silly to think I'd catch a glimpse of Henry. That's taking this teenage trip down memory lane a little too far, doncha think? Cruising around to see if you can "accidentally" run into your boyfriend? (Not that Henry's my boyfriend, mind you.)

But then I see someone exit the big front doors and I stop, even though it's a green light and the car behind me is honking.

Tess Wintergarten stands shimmering in gray silk, smoking a cigarette as long as her svelte figure.

Dammit.

I should have known she was a smoker.

chapter 9

Purple violets: You occupy my thoughts

After my first date with Rick, I told myself I'd wait two days and then call him. My dating history had taught me that it was folly to wait for the guy to call you—it didn't always signify disinterest. I figured if Rick didn't seem pleased to hear from me when I called, I'd let the matter drop and move on. But I needn't have worried. The very next morning after our first dinner together, Rick called me. He told me he couldn't remember when he'd had a better time, and wanted to get together again soon. He promised to call me midweek to make plans, and he was true to his word. Rick always, always called when he said he would.

Phhhhhtt. My self-delusion rips away like a partially filled balloon suddenly released. False hopes. So, Henry is not true to me ("And why should he be?" the Inner Feminista screams, "that isn't what you wanted in the first place." And the Babushka Crone doesn't even answer because the Inner Feminista has spiked her Metamucil with sleeping pills.)

What's more, I drove all the way into the city just to see if he *would* be true. Like I said, I'm a mess.

I drive back to my sister's and the sun's slanting rays are now just annoying, not cheerful. And the open windows let in a wasp who scares me half to death and I have to pull over to let him out, then close the windows and turn on the fan.

When I get back to my sister's house, she is fixing herself some hot tea, pouring it into a delicate porcelain cup decorated with hand-painted violets.

"I was going to take a bath, then read in bed," she summarizes. "How's Wendy?"

"Wendy's fine," I lie. "I think I'll go up early, too." I don't go up right away. I wait for Gina to finish her tea, then I grab the cordless phone from the kitchen and sneak upstairs with it.

It's too early to call Henry. He won't be home from the gala until at least ten o'clock, if that. And I will call him. I'll stay up all night if I have to, but I'll call him. After all, I want to find out how the gala went. I want to show him I'm interested even though I couldn't go. Just a friendly call, a warm, how'd-it-go kind of thing. Uh-huh. Sure.

After my sister heads upstairs to her whirlpool bath, I settle into the den and watch television, peripatetically flipping through the channels like a hurricane blowing through with the remote. I'm hardly aware of the time passing.

Actually, it's been thirty-seven minutes since I got home.

At ten, I finally punch in his numbers. What a shock, I get his voice mail.

In the next hour, I try his number again twice (but who's counting?) Now I'm transported back to that part of high school I hated—the aching hell of wondering if your boyfriend is out with someone else.

At eleven-thirty, I have this devilish idea of trying Tess

Wintergarten's number and then Henry's. If Tess answers, I'll just mumble "wrong number."

After I find Tess's number in the phone book, I dial and wait. Five rings. Then her voice mail with that mesmerizing drawl. It must be the accent that lures them in. It's hypnotic.

Quickly, I try Henry. Still no answer. At least if the two of them are out together, they're not in bed.

Or maybe they are, I think, and he's not answering the phone. I try to remember if the phone rang while he and I were otherwise engaged. I can't even remember if he has a phone in his bedroom. Surely he has a phone in his bedroom. But then again, he and I didn't always do it in the bedroom. He could be in the shower with her.

This is ridiculous, I mentally scream. THIS IS EXACTLY WHY IT WAS A MISTAKE TO GET INVOLVED WITH HIM. There is no such thing as sex without involvement. No such thing! Who made up that rule—a man?

I am ashamed to admit it but I try his condo two more times, five minutes apart so in case he is home, and in bed with Tess, he'll think it's an emergency and pick it up. And then I'll say, "What? No, this is the first I've called you all evening." And hope to God he doesn't have caller ID.

By twelve-thirty, I've convinced myself that I'd be doing him a favor by driving down to his condo just to make sure he hasn't been murdered by some *Basic Instinct* copycat. But I stop myself, take a few deep breaths, drink a finger of Scotch, count to ten, think about soaking in the tub, and go back upstairs.

My new clothes are strewn around the room as if someone emptied a treasure chest there. They don't seem so happy anymore, and I have this gnawing feeling in the pit of my stomach that I've made a mistake. Whether that mistake was going to bed with Henry or not going to the gala with him, I can't decide.

After washing up and changing, I climb into bed but don't sleep well. Visions of Tess and Henry dance through my head.

When I wake up I'm cross and sick at heart, but reasonably normal again. In fact, when I think back to the lunacy of my stalking routine the night before, my face flushes with embarrassment. I might be nuts but I can't be that nuts. Unless, of course, it's my pills. That's it—my migraine pills. "May cause sleeplessness, palpitations and overwhelming urges to stalk boyfriends"—surely that's in the pamphlet that comes with them.

Because of the traffic noise, I'm up before Gina again and I put on the coffee for us both, being careful to set out mugs, cereal bowls, plates and other things so that when she comes down for breakfast she'll have someone taking care of her for a change.

My gesture has the desired effect. When I walk into the kitchen twenty minutes later after my shower, my sister smiles broadly while sipping at her Colombian roast. What I would give to sip on my own Colombian.

"I love having you here," Gina says. She puts the paper down and goes to the freezer where she pulls out frozen waffles. "Want one?"

"Naw. I'm not that hungry." My lunacy has left no room for hunger. Sitting down, I stare at the headlines but they don't give me any information I need. None scream Job for Amy Here, or Amy, Great Apartment Waiting. Or even, Forget About Henry.

Remembering his flower-sending habit, I realize I can find out if he was with Tess last night at his condo by calling every single florist in a twenty-mile radius and asking if they're placing an order for Henry Castle today. I mentally add it to my to-do list.

"What's on your agenda today?" Gina asks while she stands in front of the toaster oven waiting for her waffles.

"Job hunting."

"That's good." When the toaster dings, she pops the waffles onto a plate, licking her burned fingers after the maneuver. "Want to go out tonight?"

"Can't. I promised Wendy I'd meet up with her and some friends."

"Not going out with Henry, huh?"

"Nope." I know she wants me to say more but my heart isn't in it. I can't even think of a good lie. It's his night at the soup kitchen, perhaps? Or he's masterminding a special spy mission to Cuba?

After breakfast, I borrow her car and head into the city. It's the darnedest thing—every car I'm in seems to head downtown. This one takes me to my flower shop. When I go inside, the air seems musty with the sickly sweet overtones of a funeral parlor. A couple days away and already it feels like a closed-up tomb.

Speaking of closed, I don't bother to turn the sign over to "open." I have no intention of doing flower business today except, perhaps, beginning an inventory and closing out the books for the owner as he gets ready to sell.

No, my intentions are to...well, sit around and mope. I don't even realize this is my goal until I'm behind the counter, with the lights off and the closed sign on the door. Leaning my elbows on the counter I listen to the phone ring a couple of times but I ignore it. I've forgotten to bring the want ads with me, so I can't even do some proper job hunting.

Job hunting. Maybe I need to go to an employment agency.

Nix that. I see myself sitting across from some blue-suited office-manager type asking me what I want to do and then I open my mouth and say "Own an in-ground pool" and start sobbing. No future in that.

Among the stacks of mail I find the morning paper, but the classifieds in the daily are but a shadow of the copious entries in Sunday's paper so I only take a quick gander at the paltry pages. Their lack of promise seems to reflect my own dead-end future. I'm about to call Wendy for a girlfriend sympathy-fest when I remember her own need for pity. Making a mental note to call her later, I give myself a pep talk. It goes something like this:

"Think of all the neat clothes you could buy if you had another job."

"Think of all the nice dinners out you could afford if you had a better job."

"Think of the great places you could live if you had a decent, steady income."

"For God's sake, Amy, think of the in-ground pool!"

While the daily paper is a washout, the on-line version would have complete classified listings. Not only would the *Sun's* want ads be on the Internet, the whole world's want ads would be there, too. With a too-quick movement that knocks a plastic vase filled with silk flowers to the floor, I turn to the shop computer and fire it up.

For an hour I browse Monster.com and CareerBuilders and Jobsinc—anything that says anything about jobs. If I want to live in Desert Rose, Arizona, there are some terrific upper-level public relations jobs. If I want to move to Candlewood, Alaska, I can become an executive of a snowmobilers' organization. If I don't mind relocating to Marshland, Florida, I can head up the nonprofit organization Save Our Alligators. Deserts, tundra or marshes—not my idea of prime real estate, so I pass.

Throughout this search, the phone rings several times. Aching from sitting slump-shouldered in front of the machine for so long, I eventually check messages.

Five potential flower orders that will find other florists

when I don't return their calls. One call from Wendy. And one from my sister.

"Ame, are you there?" Gina's voice says. "Wendy was trying to reach you. And I'd like to talk to you if you have a moment." Her voice sounds a little high and strained, so I call her back first and catch her on the third ring.

"Are you still at the shop?" she asks.

"Yeah. Cleaning up some stuff and searching some job databases."

"You could have done that here. On Fred's computer." She sounds hurt that I didn't ask.

"You said Wendy called. Is it important?"

"I don't now. Didn't sound that way." She hesitates a second and I know something is on her mind. I wonder if Trixie has left any more gifts recently, but I remember letting her out before I left and I can't imagine Gina letting her back in. Then I think maybe Gina's found out she's pregnant and I start to get excited. But no, it's not that.

"Fred called," she begins. "He was pretty upset. Turns out the Japanese firm that was going to buy your building? Someone is trying to interest them in another property. His client is pretty mad."

Uh-oh. I can imagine the call now. Fred blustering and blubbering. "You never should have said anything in front of Amy. Who knows who she talked to? Didn't you say she has a new boyfriend?"

"Sorry to hear that," I say. "Does he know who the someone is?"

"Squires Financial."

Ah, the Squires family—their tentacles are in Baltimore's law, financial and shipping businesses. Squires Financial is owned by Rick's uncle. I warm from guilt. The dots aren't that hard to connect. I mention to Henry that my building is about to be sold to a Japanese firm. Henry mentions it to

Squires. Squires mentions it to his brother. His brother does some nosing around and lures the Japanese to one of his many real estate holdings.

Hmm…at least this means my job might not go.

"Fred says if the building doesn't sell in the next month, the owner goes into bankruptcy."

Scratch that idea about still having a job.

"The owner doesn't blame Fred, does he?" I ask, and my voice sounds like a guilty thief. I clear my throat. "I mean Fred can't control the market."

"I'm not sure what the owner is saying. I just know poor Fred feels pretty bad."

Poor Fred probably made Gina feel pretty bad, too. I'm wondering what she wants me to do, or even why she bothered to call me about this, but then again, it's probably because she expected me to say I didn't mention the potential sale to a living soul. What the hell—I've been lying about so many things, what's one more?

"You know, I didn't mention the sale to another living soul," I say nonchalantly. "I wonder if Fred has a leak in his office or something."

I hear Gina exhale. Just what she wants to hear. Some ammunition to lob at Fred when he starts getting huffy about the incident.

"Are you coming home for lunch?" she asks.

"No. Probably not. I was thinking of going to an employment agency."

"Don't those mostly do secretarial positions?"

"I guess I'll find out."

"Well, don't settle for just anything."

"I will definitely not settle for anything that doesn't pay."

Gina laughs. "If you're going to be out tonight, I might have some friends in for a drink and a movie."

"That's okay. You won't disturb me."

After I hang up with her, I dial Wendy's number, swallowing my disappointment that none of my phone calls to date have been from Henry. Because I've been so busy feeling sorry for myself about hunting for a job, I've managed not to feel sorry for myself for not getting a call from Henry. Or for stalking him.

Wendy answers her own phone on the second ring and gushes with sincere regret as soon as she hears my voice.

"I might not be able to go out with you tonight," she says.

"Why not?" My fingers tighten on the receiver and fear warms my face. I already know. Sam has sucked her into doing something. I swear there's a vortex of evil centered on North Charles Street. She's under some spell. I need to get her to a deprogramming center and fast.

"Sam wants to talk."

"Wen-dy," I whine.

"It's just to talk, okay? It's the least I can do."

"I thought the least he could do was take you to Jamaica."

"Well, that doesn't sound like it's going to work."

I can't help myself. I let out a snort of derision. "Of course it's not going to work—he had no intention of it working! He just said it to get back in with you—so you could have this little talk."

"That's not true. He couldn't help it. He was just asked to co-chair an important conference this summer. It means a lot for his career." Her voice is tired but not angry when I don't buy her explanations for Sam the Schmuck. Her ability to defend him is being worn down. I soften my own tone.

"So what are you going to talk about?"

"The divorce, I guess."

"No, Wendy," I say slowly, "what are *you* going to talk about? Not him. You."

She pauses and I visualize silent tears streaming down her

face. When she speaks again, her voice is congested. "I don't know. I was going to listen mostly."

Sighing, I press the phone into my ear, lean on the counter and begin to rip an old order sheet into tiny bits. "Wendy, you wanted me to be straight with you, so here goes. I'm worried about you and don't want you hurt any more. You should go into this talk as if it were a business meeting. What's your goal? What is it you want from Sam?"

When she doesn't answer, I answer for her. "You want him clean from other obligations. You can't be running around with a married man. You're not that kind of woman. You wouldn't do that to yourself or another woman. You need to tell Sam you won't see him until the divorce is final."

I hear her sniffle. "We've been together a long time," she says, and I can hardly hear her.

"Do you want me to come get you and take you…" I am about to say "to my place" when I realize I don't have a place. "We can go get a cup of tea or coffee or something."

"Thanks, Ame, but I have a project proposal due by the end of the day."

Remembering what a stickler our boss used to be about deadlines, I wince for her.

"Then how about this? You talk to Sam tonight and we get together afterward." That, at least, might keep her from caving too deeply to his "charms." If she knows she is going to see me and have to explain what happened, she might find enough spine to stand up to him.

"All right," she says a little reluctantly. "What time?"

"Ten?"

"He's not coming over until after eight."

"He's coming over to your place? Why not have him take you out to dinner?"

She says nothing, so I'm the one doing the caving. "Okay. I'll meet you at Zabo's," I say, mentioning a bar on Centre

Street. If she knows I'm waiting for her, surely she'll come. "Ten o'clock. Try not to be late. I haven't been sleeping well and will probably be tired."

Mistake. "Then maybe we shouldn't…"

"No, I'm fine. Ten o'clock. I want to talk with you. Really."

When she hangs up, I am not optimistic. If he's going to her place, I can envision what will happen. They won't talk. They'll just do. She'll get weepy. He'll be understanding. Hug hug, kiss kiss, why don't we take this to the bedroom, honey.

It's disconcerting to watch Wendy go through this. I'd always thought of her as strong and directed, not like me, not a swirling mass of indecisiveness. If even Wendy can be felled by an imperfect man, what chance do I have?

At least our ten o'clock meeting should keep her from doing anything too rash….

Off the phone, my life feels as empty as my shop. I want to call Henry and pour my heart out about Wendy's heart. I want to rant and scream because I can't do it to Wendy. My hand even hovers on the phone, gently touching it, as if this physical connection will be enough to satisfy me and I'll be able to stop myself from phoning him. I even turn it over and punch in his office number, but as soon as I hear the receptionist at Squires answer with her perky hello, I go zooming down into an abyss of depression as I feel the full weight of what has become of me, and I hang up before saying a word.

I used to be a fiancée. I used to call Squires and talk to Rick, kind, laughing Rick. Rick would always have a smile in his voice when he heard it was me. I never had to debate whether I should call him. I could call him five times a day and he'd listen to me. I could have talked to him about Wendy and I can imagine his clucking agreement, his quick assessment of how right I was to give Wendy the advice I did, his offer to talk to her himself. I start to choke up. With Rick, I didn't wonder if I was too needy or too aloof or too jealous of Tess Wintergarten.

And now…and now I live in early-relationship purgatory, suffering the torments of those who have not yet entered the kingdom, still poised to be thrown back into frigid hell.

I close my eyes. I take a deep breath. I have to stop this. It's Henry who deserves my ire, flower-giving Henry. Fixate on that thought. Henry took Tess out last night. Who knows what he'd be doing tonight? Besides, I've got plans for tonight anyway, so I shouldn't really expect him to nose around.

But, oh, yes, I can expect it. I do expect it. If he wants to see me this weekend, shouldn't he call to set it up today? And shouldn't he miss me—as much as I miss him?

Miss him? When did this happen? And when did other bad things happen—like men expecting women to be sexually available and women thinking it's what we should do? Why did I have to be born just as they changed the rules?

An image appears—me in ruffled apron, pearls, mock turtleneck and plaid skirt, welcoming Henry home from work as if we were characters in an old kitchen-appliance ad. Then I turn the page and see Henry, like my father, an adulterer, and me, like my mother, tolerating it because it's part of the deal.

I don't want that deal either.

I want my old deal back! The one where I get the house, the car, the honeymoon and the happily ever after! The one with the in-ground pool.

When Rick and I were engaged, we used to daydream together. He wanted a house in Roland Park, not far from his family. I wanted to stay in the city for a few years, then move way out to the country. Since we couldn't agree on the exact location of our ideal abode, we focused on other areas of concord. An in-ground pool. We both wanted an in-ground pool. He for the exercise and me for…well, the memory of that perfect carefree summer, where everything was kept safe from the hurly-burly of the world, away from the Sams and Freds and Henrys.

After the accident and the physical therapy, my sister convinced me to see a grief counselor for a while. He was an unconventional guy. I had trouble relating to him. He looked like Freud, for crying out loud, with the neatly clipped beard and the piercing eyes. When I first went into his office, I half expected him to say, *"Zo, vass ist deine problemen, meine susse liebchen?"* Instead, he'd offered me coffee in a Southern drawl. Wow, talk about a double take. Freud with a Southern accent. That knocked the grief out of me for at least one afternoon.

Dr. Freud—his real name was Waylon Witherspoon—didn't say much. He just sat there with a pen and paper on his knee listening to me ramble on about how my leg still hurt and I was afraid I wouldn't walk right again and it hardly seemed fair, and he would offer me tissues. Occasionally, he'd ask a question that usually had the same effect on me as the misfit accent. I can remember the questions clearly, there were so few. "Did Rick remind you of your father?" "Did you ever lose a pet when you were younger?" "Are both your parents still alive?"

These usually followed some outpouring completely unrelated to the question. And I'd stare at him, suddenly dry-eyed, wondering if he had been paying attention at all. And the absurdity of sitting in the office of a grief counselor whose failing was that he wasn't a good listener would hit me like a cold shower and I'd want to laugh. Pretty shrewd, that Dr. Waylon Freud. Throwing those non sequitur questions at me to put me off the grief scent. Very clever.

Funny, even though I told him a lot of stuff about my

struggle to get through the days after the accident, I never got around to telling him how much I wanted an in-ground pool. I didn't get to a lot of things with him. The insurance money ran out and I couldn't justify paying his fees out of my own pocket just for an occasional laugh.

With not much to do in the afternoon, I think of going home, to Gina's, but stop myself because I don't want to be in her way and I don't want her to think I'm not trying, even though I'm not. Trying, that is.

I do some more halfhearted job searches after I find a local business weekly among the mail. Mostly I read stories about who's moving into what jobs in the communications field in Baltimore. Once someone takes another job, it's like musical chairs—everyone else in the field scurries to try for the now-empty slot. I notice that a public relations assistant has just left her job at a local college and moved on to the Red Cross. Hmm…working on a college campus. That perks me up. I'd like that. I look for the phone book and call the college, asking for Human Resources. When I get a secretary, I ask about the job. It should be posted by the beginning of next week. Better to wait until then to send in an application, she tells me helpfully, because they might rewrite the job description.

Eureka! A job lead at last. This has been a productive day after all. My brief incursion into possible employment energizes me and I'm able to finish straightening the store and the inventory. By the time five o'clock rolls around, I feel like I've really done something.

The day is dying on me and I don't want to stick around to view its rotting corpse so I decide to leave. Scratch the women's night out if Wendy's not going. I don't know a number of her friends. I'll have dinner with my sister, then hightail it down to Zabo's at ten, and try to control my addict-like desire to call Henry. Maybe I'll take up smoking instead.

Outside, the day is warm again. It's one of those phony summer days that Baltimore throws at us in the spring—like the phony war, they precede the real thing. I hop into Gina's Volvo, shove my sunglasses on my head and crank up her stereo, pretending that I'm young and carefree. At least I have half of that equation right.

Becoming so engrossed in trying to feel cool I forget where I'm driving and head past the Tess Badlands. Frustration grows as I creep along Charles Street, caught in some jam due to a faulty light that I'm sure is just one more example of the reach of her powers. Damn that Tess—she does like to show off when I'm in the neighborhood.

At least I manage to keep the car safe. No grinding noises or oil leaks, no bumpers falling off or hood ornaments rotating while a gravel-toned voice murmurs "I want your soul."

When I reach Gina's, though, I'm chagrined to find she isn't home, and I have no key. Perhaps this is part of Tess's spell. If so, I mock her powers by sitting on Gina's patio, cool in the shade of umbrella and trees, while I pet a purring and contented Trixie.

"Don't get too comfortable, girl," I tell her. "We don't know how long we'll be here. I might be getting a job. A good job."

Gazing out at Gina's perfect pool-size lawn, I can't help but notice that it's looking a little ragged. The grass is in need of mowing and weeds sprout among her landscaped gardens.

At least sitting out on Gina's flagstone patio keeps me away from the phone. I hear it ring inside and smugly imagine it to be Henry until I realize that I don't think I've given him Gina's number. No wonder he hasn't called! Now I have a legitimate excuse to call him.

But Gina arrives in such a rush that I am saved from calling Henry. She's loaded down with groceries so I help her take them into the house.

"I thought you'd be out all day," she says, juggling bags as she unlocks the door. I can't tell if she's disappointed. Besides, I was out all day. What did she expect—that I'd stay at the store until midnight?

"Things quieted down. Hope you don't mind." I start unloading the bags in the kitchen while she goes for more in the trunk of Fred's Saab. She's bought what is called "comfort food" nowadays, and most of it's instant—boxed potatoes au gratin and a prepared roast beef, frozen French fries and Pepperidge Farm layer cake. This is not the way Gina normally cooks for Fred. For Fred, she makes *Silver Palate* recipes with ingredients we couldn't even pronounce growing up, let alone identify as vegetable, animal or mineral.

Seeing me eye the box of potatoes, she says, sheepishly, "I thought I'd try some of these things while Fred's out of town."

"Mom made this sometimes," I say, fingering a box of Rice-A-Roni, "with those frozen hamburgers."

Smiling, Gina pulls a box of said hamburgers from the grocery bag. "We can have some tonight."

For the first time all day, I laugh. "I'll help cook."

Maybe it's the fact that we're eating food from our childhood, but over dinner Gina and I bond by sharing memories of when we grew up. She rattles off names of girls she went to high school with and what she thought of them and I screech in happy agreement with her assessments, never realizing she felt the same way. We talk about Mom and Dad and she tells me things I didn't know—that Mom went to the parish priest for counseling at one time when she was upset about Dad and that she confided in Gina, which bothered her a great deal.

And here I'd always imagined my sister as not having any burdens, of breezing through life, an A student, meeting her fiancé and getting married after college, living the good life. She tells me that she hopes to work on a family soon, and that if Fred doesn't come around she might just forget to take her pills.

We have such a good time talking that I even manage to forget about trying to call Henry. After dinner, I offer to clean up so Gina can get ready for her friends. She invites me to join them, but they're going to watch *Pretty Woman* and *Thelma and Louise,* and frankly, both those movies leave me kind of cold. I just don't get the whole glamorizing a prostitute's lifestyle, and two women riding off a cliff isn't my idea of an affirmation of life either. Henry agrees with me. Those were some of the movies in our movie-discussion at the Fell's Point tavern.

I do help her set out glasses and popcorn bowls, and enjoy watching her flit around happy and carefree.

"How'd you manage to get married women together on a Friday night?" I ask, tossing some popcorn in my mouth while I sit on a stool and watch her mix up daiquiris.

"Two are divorced, and one's husband's out of town like Fred," she explains.

"Oh, that's too bad," I say. "I mean about the divorces." Unless, of course, one of them is Sam's wife.

"They did okay financially. And one of them has a steady boyfriend who's looking serious. He's a college professor."

Egads. I nearly choke. A college professor? Why do I instantly think of Sam as the only dating college professor around? But he's a schmuck and of course a schmuck could have more than one girlfriend even if he is married.

"Really? What does he teach?" I ask after gulping down some water.

"Economics."

Relief. The doorbell rings and I hang around so Gina can introduce me to her friends. There is an awkward moment when one of them, Penny Barton, remembers I was engaged to Rick Squires and offers her sympathy. I thank her and instantly recall how awful it felt to thank people for telling me how sorry they felt for me. I was about to leave, but now I feel compelled to stay for a few minutes to prove to her that she didn't upset me with her remarks.

Eventually, Gina ushers them into the family room and starts serving drinks, so I slink away into the dark and up to my room. Yes, I think of it as my room now, sort of the way I thought of my room at my parents' house as my room even though they owned the house.

With a couple of hours to kill, I try reading and napping but mostly end up thinking of Henry. I'll call him tomorrow. That keeps me from calling him tonight. But it doesn't keep me from moping. My energy level is low because it's the end of the day, so the floodgates open and I can't hold back the scenes—that he's already forgotten me and moved on to someone else.

At last it's close enough to ten that I can leave to meet Wendy. I change into black capris and a stonewashed sleeveless shirt. Gina knows I'm going out so I just waggle some fingers in the air at her as I creep by the door to the family room.

The night air is cool and good. I let it revive me on the way into town, only rolling up my windows when I cross the Badlands.

At Zabo's, I order a beer and fend off a buzzed Don Juan by saying I'm waiting for someone. Yeah, why should I settle for a fake Don when I can have the real thing, huh?

Wendy is late. Annoyed, I check my watch every five minutes and order a club soda after the beer is gone. I'm about to get up and call her when she finally walks in. With Sam.

She is beaming and my heart is a concrete block. Sinking

fast. When they sit at my table, their aura sends me psychic messages. First, they've had sex. Second, Sam has no intention of divorcing his wife. Third, Wendy does not know this. Why, why was I born with these telepathic powers?

Sam only glances at me when he says hello, and he doesn't order anything when he sits down while she orders a margarita. What does this tell me? It tells me their conversation before coming to Zabo's went something like this:

Wendy: Look at the time! I told Amy I'd meet her at Zabo's at ten.

Sam: Do you have to go?

Wendy: She's waiting for me. Hey—why don't you come with me?

Sam (inwardly groaning): That's okay. I'll head on home.

Wendy (knowing she can make him feel guilty since they just made love): Oh, c'mon, go with me, sweetie.

Sam (feeling guilty): Okay, just for a little while.

"Been waiting long?" Wendy asks.

"Well, since I got here on time, I've been waiting exactly thirty-eight minutes," I say, glaring at Sam. But my arrow misses the target and strikes Wendy instead.

"I'm awfully sorry, Ame. We were…detained." She titters, which confirms my had-sex theory.

Her laugh sends me over the edge. Squaring my shoulders, I look at Sam. When he won't stare me in the eyes, I confront him.

"Sam, what are your intentions?" I ask, straight out of an old movie.

"What?" One side of his mouth curls up in annoyance. Wendy's eyes widen with horror. Her drink arrives and she takes a big sip.

"I said, what are your intentions?" I repeat. "Wendy's my best friend. I don't want to see her hurt. Are you getting a divorce or not?"

"Amy!" Wendy nearly gags on her drink. She puts her hand on my arm. "Sam and I worked things out. You don't need to…"

"It's none of your fucking business," Sam says cordially. "What Wendy and I do is between us. No one else."

Wendy stares at him. Shock and disappointment register on her face. "What Sam is trying to say is that he's working on it and I need to be patient."

"Hah!" I say loud enough that folks at the next table look our way. "Do you put that sort of line in your Schmuck 101 syllabus?"

Sam stands and pushes his chair in. He looks at Wendy, not at me. "You want me to drop you home?" he asks her.

She reaches up and touches his arm. "I…I…"

"I'll take her home," I say defiantly. I hate the way that sounds—as if I'm her lover trying to keep her away from the Big Bad Boy, as if I can love her better.

Before leaving, Sam delivers a parting shot. "I hardly think you're qualified to pass judgment on me, Amy."

Why didn't he just bludgeon me to death? It would have been far less cruel than that cryptic, intended-to-inflict-maximum-damage missile. What did it mean—that since I was driving when Rick died, I was a lesser person than an adulterer? That I lived in some outer ring of goodness while the inner rings were reserved for folks like him? I wanted to jump up and challenge him to "take this outside." I wanted to fight. I wanted to hit, to hurt, to scream at someone. Damn him. Damn Rick. Damn Henry.

After he leaves, Wendy looks both apologetic and worried. "He knows about Henry," she says.

This still makes no sense to me, and I want to concentrate on her problem and getting her to stand up to him, but I can't help myself. I have to ask.

"Knows what about Henry?"

She waves her hand in the air as if it's nothing. "Oh, you know, about the other women, the flower thing." The flower thing. I curse myself for telling Wendy this bit of information during a girlfriend confess-all phone call.

And I don't know if she means he knows only what she has told him or he has some expanded knowledge of Henry through other circles. You know—the huge male club where men share all their women-snaring secrets. I resist at last, forcing myself to focus instead on her woes.

Leaning into the table, I rest my hand on her hand. "Wendy, I'm very disappointed in you. Sam has no intention of divorcing. Can't you see that?"

She pulls away and reddens. Even after one drink, her voice slurs. She'd probably been drinking at her apartment with Sam before coming to see me. Poor Wendy. She's hurt bad, and headed for worse.

"What do you know? Didn't you hear him? He said we're working things out!"

"You have nothing to work out!" I whisper at her. "He's the one with the working-out to do. Specifically working out of his marriage. There's no future in this relationship for you. None!"

She sits back and scrunches her mouth into a tight pucker, folds her arms over her chest and orders another drink when the waiter scoops up her empty glass.

If logic won't work, cruel bluntness will have to do. After all, Sam just showed me how effective it was as a weapon. And she had chastised me for not being up front with her before.

"Sam doesn't give a shit about you," I say, low and serious. "He's using you for the sex. You had sex before you came over here, didn't you? And as soon as he can, he leaves. He doesn't stay to hang out with your friend. Tell me, when you go out with Sam, do you ever *not* have sex?

And when you drove out to the country to visit me last week, I bet you went back to your apartment, had sex, and he left. As soon as he gets his payoff, he vamooses. Listen closely…he…does… not…love you." It does not escape my attention that I could be describing my relationship with Henry.

A fat tear rolls down Wendy's cheek and I feel pretty bad but still plunge forward. "And here's what your life will be like if you stay with him. You'll hang on for another year because Sam will keep telling you he's 'working things out' and maybe sometimes he'll even throw in a line about how 'fragile' his wife is. At the end of that year, you will give him an ultimatum in a fit of angry pique. And Sam will not give in. You will. You'll see him again and start the whole process over. Until eventually, he leaves you. But it won't be to go back to his wife. It will be because he's found another sucker to have sex with no strings attached."

Maybe the use of the word *sucker* is taking this lesson a little too far. I regret the word as soon as it spills out of my mouth. Wendy visibly flinches, closes her eyes and lets out a long, long sigh. When she speaks, her voice is tight.

"What do you know? You had the only decent guy on earth and you managed to…" She doesn't finish. Instead, she covers her mouth in dread. But she is looped enough not to offer an immediate apology.

And what can I do? Slap her? That will only add to our lesbian-lover act.

"Then I guess you won't want me taking you home," I say quietly, and pull some bills from my purse. "Here, you can take a taxi home. It's on me."

I throw some money on the table for my soda and stand to leave. Before I'm at the door, she's right behind me, hobbling on four-inch sandals she probably put on to get Sam all hot. I, meanwhile, am wearing flats. She touches my shoulder and I want to shake it off and yell to anyone who will listen that this is no lover's spat.

"Hey, Ame, wait up. I'm sorry," she says. Then hiccups. She's really gone. I can no more trust her to get in a taxi as I can trust myself not to call Henry as soon as I get home.

"C'mon," I say. "I'll take you home." Then, out of a perverse desire to fuel the fantasies of a couple of drooling fellows by the door, I wrap my arm around her shoulder and hug her close. Let them imagine what they want. Wendy's my friend and she needs me.

Her apartment is actually within walking distance, which is one more reason I'm glad I offered to take her home. If I had left her to walk it on her own, who knows where she would have turned up?

Even so, she is asleep almost as soon as she gets in my car. No more chance for heart-to-hearts about Sam or her own accurate aim at my soft spot. A few minutes later I help her toddle into her building, and even make sure she's safe in bed before leaving. And yes, I shed a tear or two myself because she finally said what has been welling up inside of me for two years and what I was never able to say to Dr. Waylon Freud: that I screwed up somehow. Even though none of it was my fault.

I drive off toward Gina's, not caring any more how close I come to Tess's spell.

Maybe Tess is asleep and her powers don't work because I make it home unscathed. Gina's party is still going strong when I come in, but I can't bear to face those ladies, especially the one who'd offered her sympathy earlier. I'm afraid she'll take one look at me and see I'm not worthy.

For the past two years, I've been constantly reexamining my "worthiness"—for sympathy, love, you name it—and how to protect it. It's as if I can prevent the next catastrophe with careful planning. I've started listening intently for "other shoes to drop" and visualizing bad omens in tea leaves, clouds, flower orders or women whose names rhyme with "Bess."

If I'm prepared, I can brace myself for any potential body blows and will be more likely to survive with my psyche intact.

All this is to say that I have no idea yet what kind of guy Henry really is. Just because he's not ordering flowers from my shop doesn't mean he's not ordering any flowers at all for other babes. So I am restless to get this disaster plan moving forward. I want to call him and say, "Stop procrastinating, you jerk, and break my heart now so I can get on with my life. I'm working a plan here."

I quietly let my sister know I'm home with a gentle tap on her shoulder and quickly head off to bed.

In the kitchen, I make a fast stop for a glass of milk and the phone taunts me. Then I remember—my voice mail will still be working. Phone's not officially cut off until Monday. Grabbing it, I quickly punch in the numbers. Four messages!

Two are hang-ups, one's a call from the movers informing me that if I want to check my shipment for breakage, I have thirty days to make a claim, and one, God bless him, is from Henry.

"Hey, *conchita,* what are you doing tonight?"

I don't care that it came in at 5:25. I don't care that he doesn't whisper sweet nothings or offer proposals of marriage or even promises of fidelity. He's called. That's enough for me tonight. Take that, Tess.

chapter 10

Lily of the valley: Return of happiness

*One area of cheerful agreement in the wedding-planning saga
was the selection of the men's boutonnieres. When I suggested
lilies of the valley instead of roses or carnations, Mrs. Squires
was delighted with this tasteful straying from conformity. My
mother was happy because I was happy, and I was filled with
a contented joy because lilies of the valley reminded me of that
no-worry summer spent around Sheila's pool. I'd discovered
a new perfume that year—the dime-store scent Muguets des
Bois. After an afternoon at Sheila's house, I would splash the
perfume on my wrists and behind my ears right out of the
shower, and it made me feel sophisticated and innocent all at
once. After selecting the boutonnieres with Mrs. Squires, I
stopped at a pharmacy on the way home and bought some of
that old perfume. It immediately transported me back to my
girlhood.*

In the morning, everything is different. The gloom of the
night before has lifted; I awaken rested and refreshed and

can't wait to get started on the day. In fact, I'm up an hour before Gina, who sleeps in due to what I believe is an overdose of daiquiris. When she finally comes downstairs at nine, I have baked Pillsbury cinnamon rolls and frozen hash browns, and I pour her a cup of coffee. I'm showered and dressed while she holds her head with one hand and pulls her robe close with the other.

"Try four Motrin and a Coke," I say, pulling a pill bottle from my purse, then placing it on the table.

"Coffee's fine. Thanks for fixing breakfast."

"You have fun last night with your friends?" I ask.

"Yeah. Lots. Too much." She laughs a little and stops when it becomes clear that laughing and headaches are like propane and a match.

Looking at her lush backyard through the sliding doors, I am imbued with a sense of reckless optimism.

"Who takes care of your lawn?" I ask.

"Some father and son company. Except the father died last month. I'm not sure if the son's going to keep up the business."

"Let me do it."

"What?"

"I don't like staying here without paying you back."

"Silly, you're family."

"Yeah, but I don't know how long I'll have to stay until I find a new job and a new place. Let me do your lawn. It'll save you some money and make me feel like I'm not a freeloader."

She's too tired to argue. "I don't even know if our mower still works. They used their own. Big rider things."

"I'll check on it. Where do you keep it?"

"In the garage."

"Okeydoke."

"Ame, really, you don't have to." Her spirit is willing but her flesh is weak and she doesn't sound all that adamant. And she looks pretty pathetic holding her head with one hand. Poor Gina. She's not used to tying one on.

Before she can protest further, I leave to look at the mower. Right—like I'll know if it's okay just by looking at it. This should give you an idea of the kind of slaphappy mood I'm in.

It sits in the corner, behind the Volvo, and I don't see anything obviously wrong—like a blade lying loose next to a wheel—and I know enough to be able to unscrew the cap and see it still has gasoline in it. It will do.

It's only nine-thirty, but in the distance I hear the whine of a fellow mower. I want to be part of this community of Saturday mowers, marching across lawns with mowing songs in our hearts. I want to feel the wind whip at my face as I push my machine over the fields, shearing away the tall weeds, soaking in the scents of just-cut grass, communing with nature. Why didn't I think of this earlier? This will kill so many birds with one stone—pay back Gina, plot out a new career in landscaping, keep me from calling Henry right away.

Because I am so needy, I've decided the best therapy is to try to make him needy, too.

My goal for the day is to wait until noon to call him. I figure if he sleeps in, that will give him ample time to get up and wonder why I'm not calling. Make him miss me. I've decided to check my voice mail before I call him just to see if he's tried me again. So it's with a light heart and a serene soul that I start the mowing routine.

When we were small, my father used to handle the mowing, only giving in to paying a neighbor's boy when he had to work overtime or see one of his girlfriends. For some reason, Gina and I never asked to do it, even though I'd look longingly at Jimmy Kamen as he cut neat swaths through our grass. It seemed like so much more fun than washing walls or vacuuming, which were jobs we got stuck with as Mom did the spring cleaning. I'm looking forward to re-capturing some of that youthful exuberance as I look over the mower.

Luckily for me, Fred is obsessive-compulsive and has hung the mower manual in a plastic bag from a hook in the garage above the machine. I spend five minutes figuring out spark plugs and starter switches, then roll the thing into the drive-way and up the slope to the front lawn.

Pulling the starter cord presents a problem as I struggle to find the right amount of strength to get her whirring, but when she finally purrs to life I feel like a kid with a hot rod, rarin' to go. Off I march into the wilderness of overgrown grass, coaxed into Alaskan-king-size by the chemicals Fred and Gina have dumped on it once a month. The mower struggles through the thick patches, causing me to pull back so the motor won't go out. I quickly become attuned to its rhythm, however, and merrily make my way in concentric squares around the front yard.

It doesn't take me long to realize that this would be great fun except for the fact that it's really hard work.

In ten minutes, I'm sweating so much I have to use the bottom of my T-shirt to wipe the perspiration from my eyes, and my thighs are screaming at me to stop tormenting them and let them sit down.

No matter. I'm on a mission. To hell with my discom-fort. This is man's work and I'm doing it. Grunt-grunt.

Still huffing and puffing twenty minutes later I'm only halfway done, and this is just the front. Maybe this is why the Kamen boy never looked happy when he mowed our lawn. And maybe this is why his abs were made of steel, I think, as I use my own to nudge the mower up a slight incline.

Oops, Gina didn't really like those irises. A patch of new stalks flies into the air in the far corner of the yard, their flat leaves falling like timber.

But I'll get better at this with time. How many lawns could I mow in one day—three, four, five? If I start early and mow until sunset. I wonder how much Gina paid her father-son team to do her yard. Probably a pretty penny. Nothing's cheap in this end of town. Maybe fifty bucks? Maybe seventy with trim work thrown in? That's at least two-fifty a Saturday if I manage to rope five clients. Not bad. I don't even need an office for that. How much does a lawn mower cost, anyway? If I get one of those rider ones…but no, I want the exercise, too. Maybe I can get both—a push mower and a riding mower—and alternate between them at jobs. If I mow on Sundays, that's another two-fifty and I'm only working weekends. I like this, I like it. With fifty-two weeks in a year, that means I'd make around 25 K just working Saturdays and Sundays!

Around a curved section, I carefully maneuver the machine to avoid a newly planted bed of annuals. I manage to miss most of them and make a mental note to rake up the fallen so Gina won't notice.

After I complete the front, I take a break and head in for a cool drink and a bite to eat. Gina is on the phone, obviously talking to Fred, so no danger of me giving in and calling Henry before my self-imposed noon time. But I linger, waiting for her to get off, and when she finally does, I've decided to do the rest after an early lunch when I have a new wave of energy.

'She's looking a little more chipper now, but still in her robe. Holding a coffee mug in hand, she leans against the counter as I microwave myself a hamburger. When I offer her one, she turns up her nose and shakes her head.

"Everything okay?" I ask.

"Yeah. I might lie down, though. You need anything?"

"Nope, I'm fine."

If she's going to nap, I shouldn't mow the back right away. It will disturb her peace. So I snarf down my burger and give in and call Henry. Hey—it's nearly eleven by now. Voice mail picks up. Inhaling, I get ready to leave a message with Gina's number but think better of it. I want to actually reach Henry, not have to wait for him to return my call.

To distract myself, I wander into the den and flip on the TV, which seems permanently set on HGTV. Switching to a cooking show, I watch as some French chef mutters what I'm sure are obscenities aimed at Americans as he prepares a dish whose artful arrangement on the plate requires him to touch the food at least 2,345 times. No thanks, I'll stick to my prefabricated burgers.

I try Henry again after the show, but still no go. As another cooking show scrolls into view, my eyelids become heavy. Napping seems like a damned good idea and I let myself meander down that happy path.

When I awake, it is nearly one. I've slept for more than an hour. But I don't feel lazy, I feel victorious. It feels so good to catch up on my sleep. I'm energized and ready to tackle that lawn again. Stretching, I turn off the latest cooking show—this one featuring a German who touches the food only twelve fewer times than the French chef—and head for the kitchen. Still no sign of Gina, but I figure she's had a good hour to doze it off and if I wake her up now, it won't be a tragedy. So I go back outside to the mower, which I'm beginning to view now as a trusty friend, like an old horse who's carried me through many a battle.

"Hello, Old Blue," I say to the machine, patting it on the handlebar. But it's red so that name doesn't really fit. "It's working time again," I drawl. She does not answer.

This time, I start her up with one deft pull and we're

chomping away at the heavy growth like a Gillette on a two-day-old beard. Since the backyard is bigger than the front, the sweat factor increases a hundredfold. It's also more difficult, with fewer straight edges and a steep hill at the end of the yard.

By the time I make my way around most of the lawn, it's nearly two and I'm heading to the trickier part of the job—the area near the flagstone patio with its curved and angled edges. A bunch of lilies of the valley nestles against the stones.

Here, I can't do the concentric-circle thing because it's too hard to get the mower's edge against the border. I have to push and pull it in and out as if I'm vacuuming, a time-eating process that tires my upper arms. But hey, it's better than push-ups. I never liked exercise, anyway. It seems so self-centered to spend all that time on yourself. At least here I'm doing something that helps someone, that gets something done, that...

Eeeyowza! Something flies into my face and slashes me across the eye. Godammit—the lawn is fighting back!

The mower sputters off as I reach up and touch the wounded spot. There's blood on my hand! What the hell is going on here? I wander to the patio door but am not reassured when my sister comes into view and drops her coffee cup as she catches sight of me through the glass.

"Amy, my God, what happened? Get in here! Let me call a doctor! Sit down, sit down!" She pulls me through the open door and I sit at the kitchen table, now beginning to feel a little woozy, but I'm not sure if it's from the gash or the fear generated by Gina's reaction.

"I don't know what happened," I say. "I was doing well and then, bingo, the grass threw something at me."

Gina soaks a clean dish towel in water and gently washes my face, but this does not stop the flow of blood, which is coming from what she describes as a wicked three-inch cut above my right eye. It hurts, too, and I can feel the headache starting to hiss and gasp to life at that spot. The throbbing intensifies.

"I'm getting dressed," Gina insists, "and taking you to the hospital."

"Gina, that's crazy. It's just a scrape." But part of me will be glad to have it taken care of if for no other reason than I don't want to be left with an ugly scar. And hell, I might meet a doctor, right? The lawyer circuit isn't working for me—one dead, one philandering. Maybe I'll be more successful on the doctor circuit.

Gina's back in a few minutes but not before the phone rings. She answers it in her bedroom and I assume it is Fred, but when she comes into the kitchen, she tells me it was Wendy and she told her about the accident and that I'd call her back. Gina's put on another pair of designer jeans with a peach silk camp shirt, and since she's still suffering from the night before, her ashen face doesn't look good next to its warm hues. Hiding her own aches, she takes charge.

"Do you think you can walk?" she asks, coming over to me and putting her arm around my shoulder to help me up.

"It hit my eye, not my leg," I say, and stand. But the room does spin a little, so I let her let me lean on her. I'm not willing to admit I'm dizzy from the accident, though. It could just be I'm not used to so much exercise all at once. I had been feeling a little light-headed on that last pass near the patio.

In the car, she does my seat belt up as if I were a child. While reaching across my blood-stained shirt, she plucks something from it and holds it up as evidence. "A hairpin!" she exclaims, letting me see the twisted piece of metal. "It must have fallen out of my hair one day!"

She hands it to me. I don't know what to do with it. Then

she hands me a damp wash-cloth she's brought along, scowling when it drips on her silk.

"Here, honey, hold this to your eye to stop the bleeding. I really don't like the way that's gushing. You could have hit an artery or something. Maybe I should call 911 instead." She hesitates before turning the key.

"No, I'm fine. Just go ahead."

"Okay. It's only a few minutes away." She backs out of the garage so recklessly that she dings a fender on the corner of the door. Fred will not be pleased. Gina winces but forges on nonetheless.

She manages to get us to Greater Baltimore Medical Center in under fifteen minutes, which has to be a record on well-trafficked roads on a Saturday afternoon. But then again, we are traveling in the opposite direction from Tess, so we are out of range of her evil spell.

Along the way, I recalculate the lawn-mowing business. I wouldn't be mowing each week of the year, I remember. There is that pesky thing called winter. So that would cut down on profits. With worker's comp insurance sure to be a bite, I'm thinking that this lawn-mowing gig is not a good career move. Better to find out now rather than after investing half your life in it, right?

By the time we arrive at the hospital, I don't care anymore why I'm feeling woozy or why I'm bleeding so much. I just want it to stop. A migraine has exploded near the site of the original damage and it is taking hostages in my brain. I might have to surrender soon. I try not breathing but that makes it worse.

Gina is all bluster and business when we walk in together after she stashes the car in a handicapped parking space near the door. "You're handicapped right now," she explains. I make her promise to move it.

We end up waiting nearly an hour to be seen by a doctor after the nurse evaluates me and places me at the end of the triage line, probably behind the fellow who looks like he's having a heart attack and the woman who is retching into a plastic bucket. Personally, I'm glad they took her before me.

By the time I get into the little curtained cubicle to be seen, all I want is a big fat juicy pill to make my headache go away. I curl up on the gurney and close my eyes and wait another half hour until a woman doctor comes in with a clipboard in her hand. She's attractive with an auburn pageboy and green eyes and lightly freckled face. Her name is Dr. Robin Wheeler.

After Gina explains what happened, Wheeler takes a good look at me, asks a few questions and tells me I'll need that gash closed up.

"Head wounds always bleed a lot," she tells Gina, even though I'm the patient. "We see a lot of kids whose parents get all excited about a bump to the head." Wheeler laughs a little at those silly parents. I wonder if Gina is making a mental note never to bring her kid here when she has an emergency. Who would want a patronizing doctor shaking her head over those excitable parents, huh? They see a bump on the head hemorrhaging like Niagara, and they overreact, those moms and dads. Better to let Johnny bleed to death than bother the good Dr. Wheeler.

Wheeler disappears and it's several years before she comes back. At least it feels that way to my throbbing head. Several times she passes our cubicle and Gina tries to get her attention, even calling out her name at one point. But Wheeler acts like she's deaf in that ear—whatever ear happens to be facing us at the moment.

Eventually, she comes back in, smiley face in place, glue gun in hand. Well, not a glue gun per se, but some sort of glue-y stuff that she uses instead of stitches to pull the gash together. When I ask for a pain pill, she looks at me suspiciously, as if I'm an addict who hurt herself just to get the free drugs. She gives me some souped-up Motrin, which I swig back before a nurse even has a chance to give me water, which I'm sure just reinforces their drug-addict image of me.

Closing my eyes again, I lay back down awaiting my discharge papers. Gina peppers the doctor with questions about whether or not I should see a plastic surgeon to make sure there won't be a permanent mark, but I drift away, trying hard not to think about my headache and think only of pleasanter things. Pineapple ice cream dog running after boy. Henry.

Henry.

I hear Henry's voice. I must be dreaming. Dr. Wheeler accidentally gave me a hallucinogen, right? It's a damn good hallucination, though, because I smell his Tommy Hilfiger cologne, too.

A nurse says, "Amy Sheldon? She's back here."

The curtain opens and there he is—in the flesh. Or at least, in the flesh in my dreams. I don't know anymore. How did he get here? How did he know where I was, that I'd hurt myself?

In this dream, he reads minds because he answers my questions before I have a chance to say them out loud.

"Your friend Wendy called me. She said your sister was bringing you here. Jesus Christ, Amy!" He looks at my scarred face with a mixture of concern and disgust. I'll take the former, thank you very much. "What did you do?" He comes to my side and stands with his hands on the edge of the gurney.

"She hurt herself mowing the lawn," my sister says, coming back into our cubicle. I introduce them, and Gina gives Henry the once-over, then looks at me and raises her eyebrows, but she does it so quickly that I can't make out the code words she's sending.

"Bobby pin to the brain," I say, smiling wanly. I've always wanted to smile wanly.

They stand awkwardly staring at me, both of them with concerned looks that seem to ask me how I could be so dumb as to kick up a hairpin with a lawn mower and create a not-so-neat three-inch gash above my eye. But I ignore their scorn and sit up.

Sitting up is a mistake. It intensifies my headache pain, which I can't hide.

"Something the matter?" Gina asks.

"This migraine. Started in the car," I manage to spit out between the threshing, slicing blades of pain that mow down my mind's fresh, green thoughts.

"Doctor!" Henry calls out to Wheeler who crosses our line of vision. Hah! Like she'll listen.

For Henry, she does listen. Dr. Wheeler stops and comes into our crowded stateroom immediately. Is it the drug or is Henry giving her the once-over? Is it my paranoia or is Dr. Wheeler using those green eyes to flirt with him?

"She has a migraine," he says, pointing to me as if I'm Babette, the pet poodle.

Woof, woof, I want to say, and hope that Henry pets me and nuzzles me behind the ears.

Wheeler comes closer. "You get these often?"

"Every week or so."

"Taking anything for them?"

The magic pills. I want one. I give her the drug name and dosage.

"Okay. I'll give you one."

"Can I take it with the Motrin?"

She smiles condescendingly and pats my hand the way they taught her back in Bedside Manner class. "Yes, you can.

And I think you're all set to go now. The nurse will have you sign a few papers and that's it!"

When she leaves, Henry's eyes go with her.

The nurse, a little tugboat of a woman, brings the papers and the migraine meds. These pills are so magic that they dissolve in your mouth without water. They taste like peppermint. Yum. As soon as it hits my tongue, I have a Pavlovian response and the pain recedes. The guy who invented them should be beatified.

As I scoot off the gurney, Henry helps me. Now that the pain is going away, I become aware of just how hideous I must look—blood-spattered shirt, grass-stained jeans, hair damp from sweat, grimy face decorated with Frankenstein wound, and I probably have b.o. to boot. What a catch.

Gina scurries ahead. "I parked illegally," she calls over her shoulder. "I'll meet you at the house."

So both Gina and Wendy have conspired to get me together with Henry today. I wonder when they thought of planting the hairpin in the lawn to set me up for this whole E.R. trip, too. No matter. Henry gently leads me to his BMW and doesn't even make a fuss about me dirtying his leather seats. Once I'm strapped in, he asks for directions to my sister's house and we glide back on to the road.

"I must look a mess," I say apologetically.

He smiles. "I didn't expect to see you in evening dress."

Wrong response. First, it conjures up images of Tess in evening dress. Not a good comparison. Secondly, he should have lied and said I look fine. Lying is the right answer here.

"I'll get cleaned up at Gina's."

"I tried to call you," he says as he smoothly maneuvers the car through heavy traffic. It is now late afternoon, well past the hour when I'd told myself I could call him. One more reason this hairpin setup was a neat little scheme.

"I know. I checked my voice mail. But I didn't get the message until today. Phone's being disconnected."

Henry chides me for not telling him I'd moved in with Gina and for not giving him the number. "If you expect a man to take you out, the first step, my little *conchita,* is to make sure he has the right phone number." I like hearing him call me *"conchita"* now, and I like the way his hand artfully shifts the gears as he intently studies the road. No wonder women fall for race-car drivers. A big machine under them, skillfully handled.

"Stay for supper," I say simply as we near Gina's house. "It's just us and Gina. Her husband's out of town." I don't know why I mention this. Henry doesn't know Fred.

"You're tired," he says. He pulls the car into the driveway, turns off the engine and sits. Gina has beat us home, and I see the light on in the kitchen up above.

"Not too tired. Those pills are great."

"I didn't know you had migraines." His brow creases as he says it. He actually looks concerned.

"There are lots of things you don't know about me," I say, trying to sound coy, but it's impossible to sound coy in a bloody T-shirt. It blocks coy rays. "Come on in. At least stay for a drink."

He doesn't protest and we head in together. He even takes my hand.

Gina brightens when she sees us. She's already pulling down cocktail glasses and doesn't waste a moment offering Henry a Scotch or gin or whatever he wants. He opts for a bourbon, neat, but I take nothing. Too many systemic anesthetics on a tour bus through my nerve cells as it is.

"You should stay for dinner," Gina says to Henry.

"Hear that? She'll be brokenhearted if you say no," I tease him.

Grinning, he sips his drink and nods. "Okay. Can I help?"

That's a charming gesture, I note—not only agreeing to stay, but offering to help. Maybe there's more to Henry than I give him credit for. He did come to the hospital and he hardly knows me. I mean, we're sex partners, but in today's world that doesn't signify anything deep, necessarily. Though looking at Henry now, with his gleaming eyes and happy grin, I wonder if it does mean something to him, despite the regular flower orders, despite the notes about "incomparable nights."

Gina refuses aid and shoos us into the living room while she cooks. I wonder what she'll make since her recent supplies aren't of the gourmet variety. Hearing her opening and closing cabinets, I know she's wondering the same thing.

In the cool blue living room, Henry sits on Gina's white sofa and looks admiringly around.

"Nice place," he says. "Squires doesn't live far from here."

Ah, yes. The Squires. Old money. Old Baltimore. Old Amy.

"I better take a shower," I say. "I'll be right back."

In the shower I try to pretend I'm diving into a clear warm pool and leaving everything behind, but nothing dulls the throbbing of the scar. Every time I duck my head under the spray, I spring back as the water hits the wound, so I have to bend my neck in a contorted way to shampoo my hair.

Not wanting Henry to wait too long, I rush through dressing, quickly fluffing my hair with the dryer and throwing on the sundress Gina bought for me, a red print number that floats around my ankles and makes me feel pretty the way Maria felt pretty in *West Side Story*. Lucky for me we went shopping or I'd have nothing to wear. I haven't done laundry yet and my "good clothes" repertoire is limited and stored away.

Earrings, a dusting of powder and smear of lipstick, as well as a spritz of a knockoff of a designer perfume, and I'm good to go.

When I reenter the living room, Gina sits perched on an ottoman listening to Henry talk about his work at Squires. For an ice-cold minute, I worry that she has told him about Rick, which I have yet to do. But I can tell from her stricken face that she's not let on. She looks at me with raised eyebrows as she makes an excuse to leave the room. This time, I catch the code. She is saying: you didn't tell me he worked for Rick's old firm.

Henry pats the seat beside him and for the twenty minutes while Gina finishes dinner, he and I are like two sparking teenagers. He draws a soft line around my cut, asks about my headache and kisses me on the forehead. Inside, a little voice (a good voice, my voice, not the Inner Feminista or the Babushka Crone) keeps saying in wonder, "You were hurt and he came to you" over and over again. And it didn't take much. Just a scratch on the forehead. Like Sally Fields, I feel like saying "You like me, you really like me."

By the time Gina calls us to the table, I'm ready to melt into his arms due to a whole different kind of painkiller.

For dinner, Gina has thrown together boneless pork chops, Betty Crocker potatoes au gratin and a salad. We eat at the kitchen table, and I see the Pepperidge Farm chocolate layer cake thawing on the counter. She's even uncorked a bottle of rosé, but I have only half a glass, Gina barely touches hers, and Henry limits himself to one because he's had the bourbon and he's risk-averse when it comes to drinking and driving.

"The cops like to pull me over," he says to Gina.

Gina manages to ask him all the questions I have not.

"So, Henry," she says nonchalantly as she passes the potatoes, "have you ever been married?"

I nearly do the gagging routine, expecting him to get all huffy about invading his privacy, remembering Sam's performance the night before. But Henry smiles, acknowledging what my sister is up to, and shakes his head no.

Note to self: send Gina a thank-you note.

She segues from that into his law work, and talks about various divorce lawyers she knows who represent friends. When she's finished with that chitchat, she casually asks if handling so many divorce cases turns him off to the idea of marriage. Now I'm feeling my veins pulse in my neck and my eyes are saucers but she ignores the death rays coming from them.

"Nope," Henry answers between mouthfuls. "Not at all. I'll get married one of these days." He says it like it's the same as buying a car. He'll get around to it eventually. He has so many to choose from, after all.

Gina then manages to get him talking about his goals, other than owning a boat and a Porsche. He wants to own his own law firm some day, to be the Squires of his own little empire, and he wants to live in the country.

"The city scene is important when you're young and hungry," he says, wiping his mouth. Even though we haven't offered gourmet cooking, his plate looks as if a canine licked it. Maybe Henry is part canine. Maybe he's part wolf. I try to remember if it was a full moon when we met.

"But it's crowded and noisy and it's hard to find parking spots," he complains.

"Wendy likes it," I say. I want to say that I liked it, too, but that would lead to a question about when I lived in the city, and then Gina would send me Morse Code messages with her eyebrows telling me to fess up about Rick.

"You'll have to introduce me to Wendy," he says, winking at me.

Note to self: do not introduce Henry to Wendy. He'll be sending her flowers in a heartbeat.

After dinner, Gina serves cake and coffee and won't accept our offer to help her clean up. Henry stretches and yawns like a cat, not like a canine, then taps me on the knee.

"I should be going."

Going where? It's only eight o'clock.

"We could sit outside for a while."

"You're exhausted. And I have to get up early tomorrow." He strokes my leg.

"Why?" I don't want him to leave. For the first time in a long time, I feel the same as I did when I was with Rick. Normal. Comfortable. Safe. The same way I used to feel diving into Sheila Vleznevchik's pool.

"I'm driving to the Eastern Shore." Standing, he walks to the glass door and looks out. Gina is running water and rinsing dishes, but I would like to talk to Henry alone to find out why he's going to the shore tomorrow and who he's going to meet there. I'm too embarrassed to carry out my interrogation in front of my sister. I haven't attended interrogation school the way she has and I'm afraid my questioning isn't up to her standards. And hey, I do have some pride.

Opening the door, I step outside so that he'll follow me, which he does.

"This is the scene of the crime." I point to the edge of the patio where the lilies of the valley smirk at us, and where Old Blue failed to protect me.

"Too bad Gina's your sister. You could sue. I'd represent you." He puts his arm around me and kisses my head. Oh, man, if Henry's not getting serious, he sure does a good imitation of it.

"Why are you going to the shore?" I ask, now that we're out of Gina's earshot.

"Prospective client. I was going to drive down tonight. I'm meeting her at ten tomorrow."

Meeting *her?* Dang. A near escape. Why does the client have to be a her? And why can't I just enjoy Henry for who he is? Why do I need to be constantly scouring his future for signs of Sam? For signs of heartbreak.

"Weather's supposed to be nice," I say, looking up at the clear sky. A faint moon is painted in the corner of the washed-out blue.

"Yeah. It won't be that bad." He draws me to him in a hot kiss, and by the time he's done, I feel gooey and normal and not normal all at once. Stay, Henry, I want to say. Or even, "Take me with you." Just don't leave me here on the verge of something.

"I really have to be going." Turning, he pops his head in the kitchen and thanks Gina for dinner, then comes back outside and we walk around the house to the driveway. At his car, I lean inside while he gets ready to leave.

"Thanks for coming today," I say, smiling. "It was really thoughtful."

"No problem." He looks at my white shoulders. "Next time you mow a lawn, you might want to wear a tank top."

I have a faint "tennis shoulder"—bare, white skin where my T kept the sun at bay. Now I realize that while I thought of myself as sexy and sweet in my new sundress all night, he'd seen those stupid shirt lines.

"Oh."

"I'll call you," he says and puts the car into gear.

"You have Gina's number now?" I don't remember giving it to him.

"I can look it up." He inches out of the driveway.

"What if it's unlisted?" I call after him.

"Is it?"

"No."

His teeth flash in a broad smile.

chapter 11

Calla lily: Panache

Rick and I chose a small band for our reception, but I was nervous about dancing. He had no fears—his private prep school had included dancing lessons in the curriculum. After I was through teasing him about how cute he must have looked in his short pants and bow tie waltzing with pig-tailed princesses from the all-girls' academy down the road, he suggested the way to alleviate my apprehension was to take a few dancing lessons together. He could use the brushup, he announced, and I would feel better after a class or two. He arranged for private lessons at Peabody Prep, and our teacher was a bohemian-looking woman whose age was masked by pancake makeup and Cleopatra eyeliner, and who wore a long-fringed shawl imprinted with a swirling calla lily design. Her body had lost the slenderness of youth but none of its dignified hauteur. Even the most regal model would have looked like a slump-shouldered teenybopper next to Madame Duarte's rod-straight posture.

The lessons helped—not so much because of what she taught me, but rather because of what I learned about Rick. He could dance, but not with any flair. We were perfectly matched, and would have fared competently, if not brilliantly, on the dance floor when the band struck up our favorite song.

Of course Henry sends me flowers. This time, it's a big spray of mixed varieties—yellow daffodils (regard), white lilies (youthful innocence) and some bachelor's buttons (celibacy.) Talk about mixed messages. You figure it out because I can't. The card reads, "Hoping you're feeling better. All my love, Henry." It's certainly better than getting flowers that signal "distrust" and "beware" and "unfaithful." Hell, it's better than getting no flowers at all.

And when they arrive on Sunday afternoon, it helps me forget that he's probably meeting with some Southern-accented, long-legged beauty on the Eastern Shore, giving her his lopsided grin and *"conchita"* look just to get her business. Henry knows his assets and uses them well.

Gina likes Henry. She told me after he drove off the night before, and she tells me again today. "Any man who would come to your side when you're hurt is a decent human being," she says seriously.

Wary as I am, I have to admit that Henry's riding to the rescue when I was in the hospital impresses me. It gives me a warm feeling, a contentment, a sense that I am loved.

I analyzed it all last night. Gina spent the evening watching *Designing for the Sexes* on HGTV and I sat up with her a little while to be companionable. During commercial breaks, she talked about the accident, looked at my scar with concern, and pronounced Henry's likeability. But I was tuckered out from the day and my eyelids were drooping fast, so I excused myself and went up to my room, where I sat on a window bench staring into the night sky, my legs curled under my dress, my chin resting on my arms.

The inner voices were all gone and there was only me, Amy Sheldon, left to figure things out on my own. Exactly a week ago, I had been dateless and clueless and sex-starved. Now, seven days later, I could lay claim to a real date of a guy, with whom I could have fantastic sex whenever he was in the mood (which seemed about any time I was). But I was still clueless.

What do you want? I whispered to myself. What about that life plan Gina urged you to write? What would it say now? What would it say about Henry and you?

The problem is I don't want to write a life plan. I want someone else to write it for me. If I could stare into a crystal ball and see happiness with Henry, even for a short time, I'd race toward it, no holds barred. But since no crystal ball is available, I'm left at sea with no rudder, nothing to guide me except my own fears of heartbreak. That's the trouble with heartbreak. Once you experience it like I did with Rick, the bruise never quite heals. Even that night I felt it throb and strain and issue its own warnings to beware.

I must have sat in the window seat for an hour because I heard Gina going to bed before I moved. By then, my legs were cramped from being under me so long. My right leg in particular, the one that had been injured, ached like hell. I forget I need to coddle it, like a difficult pet.

But my physical pain served as a reminder of what Henry did that day—come to me in a time of need. That counts for something. Doesn't it?

Neither of us has used the *L* word. Way too soon for that, and maybe we'll never get that far. After all, I keep reminding myself, this is all about getting on the bicycle again. It doesn't necessarily have to be about getting into the BMW. The allegorical BMW, that is.

Anyway, this languid Sunday afternoon Gina tells me that she thinks Henry is like me. Although, for the life of me, I can't figure out how she came to this conclusion after one evening's conversation. She says that the way he ate her prepackaged dinner, the way he was comfortable talking to his "girlfriend's" sister, the way he obviously didn't care how I looked (thanks, Gina, I really needed to be reminded how awful I must have looked)—all these make Henry Castle a "keeper" in her book.

The only thing she manages to chide me on is my behavior, not his.

"Why haven't you told him about Rick?" she asks as we sun ourselves on the patio. She's fixed wine spritzers for us and we're pretending to be pampered ladies of leisure. For dinner, she is making the prepared roast beef with the gravy in a plastic packet, and frozen fries, with Dove bars for dessert.

"I don't know," I say. "I guess because it's such a downer."

"Amy! He was part of your life!"

"Yeah, but when do you bring it up? Right after the introduction? Hello, I'm Amy Sheldon and my fiancé was killed in an accident two years ago? I might as well smack a Caution—Fragile label on my forehead."

At the mention of my forehead, Gina looks at my wound. "How are your stitches?"

"Just a little itchy and sore."

She takes another sip of her spritzer and slathers some sunblock on her chest. "You have to tell him sometime. He works for Squires. I would have thought that was a good time to bring it up—when you found that out."

I remember when I found out he worked at Rick's firm—the angry moment in the flower shop that seems like years ago now. A love affair is like a dog's life—multiply each day by twenty.

"I'll tell him. Maybe I'll tell him tonight." That shuts Gina up about my responsibilities, but she then talks about having Henry over to dinner when Fred gets home, and I don't care if Henry is up to that because I'm not.

"I need to talk with Fred about the shop," I say, veering off into another direction. "If it's closing regardless what happens, I should just start folding it up and looking for something else full-time." I don't tell her that I've been closing it up all week.

"That's not a bad idea. I'm glad you're getting out of that, anyway. You could always go back to school, you know."

"How would I do that?"

She rolls over. "At night. You could go to law school."

I have never, in my life, expressed an interest in becoming a lawyer. Does she think I should do it just to show an interest in Henry's work? Isn't that taking things a little too far? Hmm…an idea occurs to me.

"Is that something you've thought of?"

"Sometimes."

Aha. More Dream Transference. "Well, Gina, you should do it. Fred has enough money. And you're not working. I never knew you thought of going to law school!"

"Well, you know, Mom and Dad never thought of careers for us—just marriage."

Yup. Life in the burbs. Grow up and get married. Career? Raising kids is a career! Sit down and eat your peas!

"I say 'go for it!' I bet you could get into law school in a snap. You were always tops in your class."

"I don't know. I think that moment has passed, if you know what I mean."

Not at first, but then I figure it out. She wants kids now. Not law school. Kids. Kids *will* be her career.

Later, we gorge on the roast and fries and forget about the salad, which is one of those bagged things, anyway. Gina says she'll make chef's salad for lunch the next day. I insist on cleaning up and she spends nearly a half hour on the phone with Fred in the evening, her bedroom door closed. Who knows why, but she does seem to love the guy.

When she comes back into the kitchen, she is smiling like a Cheshire cat.

"Guess who called while I was on the phone?"

"Wendy?"

"Well, yeah. But Henry called, too."

I resist the urge to race through the house to grab the phone and return the calls. Instead, I wipe my hands, glance out back at the waning day, demurely pick up the cordless in the kitchen and set a leisurely pace up the stairs. Once out of sight, though, I skip to my room feeling like a teenager who knows she's getting asked to the prom.

I'll call Henry first, but only so I'll have some real news to share with Wendy when I call her. Not because I really want to talk with him. No. Not at all. Not. At. All.

He answers on the third ring and sounds tired. Not "just had sex with yet another babe" tired, but "worked hard today" tired. He asks me how I'm feeling. I ask him how his meeting went. Both of us answer "okay." He tells me about his week, which is very busy. I tell him about mine, which is not.

At the end of the conversation, I'm feeling that ache. It's the "I wish he would say he loves me" ache and I despise myself for needing that so early in the game. Riding a bike. This is all about getting on and riding the bike. Nothing more.

"Call me this week," I manage to say. "I'll be at the shop a few days. And doing some job hunting."

"I'll try. Maybe we can have lunch some day."

"Yeah. I'd like that."

"I liked your sister. Nice, down-to-earth lady."

"She wants you to come to dinner when her husband is home."

"To inspect me?"

"No," I laugh, thinking "yes, of course."

"Just tell me the time and the day, *conchita,* and I'll have my people talk to your people."

"Thanks, Henry. For coming to the hospital yesterday."

"No *problema.*"

I'm feeling so warm and cozy by the end of our conversation that I don't bring up the fact that I was engaged to Rick Squires. It seems like such a mood-killer. Why burden Henry with my problems.

I try calling Wendy, but get no answer.

As it is, I don't reach Wendy until the next day, Monday. I wake up all bright-eyed and bushy-tailed except for the dull pain above my eye, but at least I can shower without having to twist my head around funny. I'm feeling so good that I actually make a to-do list, even scheduling the whole day out into timed increments. Nine-thirty to eleven—job hunt. Eleven to noon—redo résumé. Noon to one—lunch. You get the picture.

When I arrive in the kitchen, Gina is already there popping toaster strudels onto a plate. This is the last day before Fred comes home, the last opportunity for prefab food. She glances at my shorts and T-shirt and looks confused.

"Is that what you're wearing into the shop?" she says as she squeezes gooey glaze over a cherry strudel.

"I was going to job hunt today—you know, look at ads." I walk behind her and pop my own strudel into the toaster oven, then grab a glass of OJ from the fridge. "Make some calls."

"Who's minding the store?"

I resist the urge to say "Brad" and finish my orange juice

before answering. "Nobody. But since it's going to close anyway, I thought I'd grab the opportunity to get a head start on my job search."

Gina frowns. "Ame, I don't know if that's a good idea. The owner probably expects you to be there every day, selling the stock, taking care of orders and that sort of thing."

"What's he going to do—fire me?" I laugh. "Give me a bad recommendation? It's not like I'll be looking for another flower shop job." And didn't Gina tell me just the other day that I could job hunt from home?

Gina takes her plate and mug and sits at the kitchen table. "I'm relieved to hear you say that—that you'll be looking outside of retail. I always thought of this job as a temporary thing. But that still doesn't allay my concerns about letting your current employer down."

Uh-oh. Anytime your sister throws the word *allay* at you, you know she's serious. As soon as I drizzle the glaze on my just-popped strudel, I join her at the table.

"I guess I never thought of the shop as anything but a tax write-off for Fred's client. I mean, I never see the owner. I always deal with Fred. And nobody seems to care if I do a good job or a lousy one. When I had the flu this year and didn't have anyone to cover for me, there wasn't a peep. That was an eye-opener."

"Actually, Fred wondered about that. But I told him you were sick and couldn't do anything about it." Red fruit filling leaks on her hand and she wipes it off with a paper napkin.

Ah, now I see. Gina's been talking to Fred.

"You should have said something. He should have said something." No coffee. I forgot my coffee. I get up to grab a mug and fill it. "Okay, I'll go in today. I can make some calls from there, anyway."

"I think that's a good idea." Gina's good mood returns,

her cheerful voice, the one that sounds like a mother asking little Johnny what he did in school today. "So tell me, what field are you looking in—communications again? Do you want Fred to nose around for you?"

"No. I'll be okay. I'm going to ask Wendy for some leads." I have to call her, anyway, to catch up. Wendy—I sure hope the reason I couldn't reach her wasn't because she'd been out with Sam. Something deep inside me growls at that prospect.

Gina's day consists of grocery shopping—probably to load in more Fred-friendly food—and an oil change. She heads out before I do since she's all dressed and ready, and I need to change. Damn responsibility.

I slip into khakis and keep my T on, then remember Henry suggesting we get together for lunch some time this week, and so I change instead into tight black pants and the fuchsia wrap blouse Gina bought me. I even put on those uncomfortable sandals we picked up. I can take them off in the store and throw on my loafers. I put my loafers in a bag and I'm off.

At the shop a few minutes later, I realize I drove into town without once thinking of Tess Wintergarten and her Circle of Doom.

Despite the fact that I told Gina I'd be opening the shop, I keep the closed sign turned over until I have a chance to reach Wendy. When I do, her voice is mellow and quiet, which she attributes to the fact that the office is mellow and quiet and she has to keep it down or everyone will hear her. But I suspect something is going on.

"I'm sorry if I snapped at you the other night," she says, and for a minute, I don't know what she's talking about. Then I remember our evening with Sam at Zabo's. It seems like an epoch away. Dog years. "How are you doing? What happened with your eye? How can you even drive?"

I imagine Gina telling her I'd poked my eye out when

Wendy called during the whole unfortunate business with the mower and the hairpin, so I allay her fears (*allay* can be a nice word) and give her the whole story. Including the part about Henry showing up and having dinner together and him calling me last night.

"Thanks for calling him," I tell her, knowing that she probably called him as a makeup for her bad behavior at Zabo's. "Where'd you get his number?"

"I looked it up," she says. "You and Henry—who would have guessed you'd find someone your first time out? You always were a lucky stiff."

I let that pass. I don't consider myself too lucky given the circumstances. "Don't go jumping to conclusions," I warn her, "Henry and I are just having fun together. Lots of fun." It feels good to make it sound light and easy. Maybe if I tell enough people, I'll start believing it, too.

"Besides," I add, "I'm not convinced Henry is looking for anything serious—either."

"Well, he sounded, I don't know, concerned when I called him about your accident. Like he cared." She herself sounds wistful, as if Henry's tone made her realize what she was lacking with Sam. "Like it was more than just fun."

I can't help myself. I have to know more. "What did he say? I mean, what did you say and what did he say?"

"The way Gina described it, it sounded like you were barely breathing," she says. "And, well, my car has been running kind of ragged and I couldn't come to see you—and…"

"So you called Henry for a ride?"

"Sort of. But I never got around to asking because he was asking me for lots of details that I didn't have. And he sounded in a rush—like he wanted to get to you as soon as possible, so he was off the phone before I had a chance to ask if he could pick me up."

I think Wendy is stretching the truth, but I don't care. My guess is, at first, she might have called Henry to get a ride, but once she sensed his concern, she let him run with it, as a gift to me. She would know how good it would make me feel to have him show up at my side, so she let me enjoy it. Wendy is such a good friend. I wish I could do more for her. I wish I could come to her aid the way she's come to mine, but I feel inadequate. My attempts at slaying her devotion to Sam failed, and only made her feel bad.

"I tried to call you a couple times," I tell her. "Where were you this weekend?"

"Just around."

Around with Sam. I sigh and slump against the counter. Now I have her to the point where she won't even confide in me. What a great friend I've turned out to be. "Look, Wen, if you were out with Sam you don't need to hide it from me. I know it must be hard."

"Well, he did come over. We just went to an art exhibit. We'd been planning it. Before." She doesn't sound happy, not the way she used to sound when she told me about what she and Sam did on weekends.

"Do you know anything more about his situation?" Oh, to hell with being reserved. "About his wife, I mean."

"She teaches at Berkeley."

"So there are two Professor Terrills out there."

"No. One Professor Terrill and another Professor Moroni. She kept her name."

So Sam ponied up more info on the wife. Did he do it to make Wendy feel a part of this problem? Or sympathetic to his wife?

"She hasn't been able to find a position on the East Coast and she's not sure she wants to," Wendy volunteers softly. "So they've been separated."

Separated? Sure, they have three thousand miles between

them. But that's not the same thing as a legal document. I suspect Sam did not include that nuance in his explanation, and I doubt Wendy pressed him on it. Far better to imagine some mean hag out in the Golden State taunting him and harassing him until he reaches for the Make-Your-Own-Divorce kit.

"What does she teach?"

"Political science."

Of course. She's a Marxist. No wonder Sam won't give her up. Marxists are de rigueur on college campuses. Why should he give up his own private stash?

"So what are you going to do?" I ask her.

"I don't know. Think about it. I need to use up some vacation. Maybe I'll go away somewhere by myself. The beach." Her voice is really sad and I know why. For months now she's been hoarding her vacation time so that she and Sam could go away together. Now she's facing the prospect of doing that alone. Wait a minute—she doesn't have to go alone.

"We could go together."

She laughs, a good sound. "Amy, how could you afford to go to the beach?"

"I have some money saved up. For emergencies." To be exact, I have $2,347.89 in the bank. It will be enough for a down payment on a car or the security deposit on a new place if I'm careful. But I need a job first.

"You shouldn't be using emergency money to go to the beach with me! Besides, you won't want to run off and leave Henry."

"If we get a place together, it won't be that expensive." No, it will only be half a kajillion dollars instead of a full kajillion. "And as to Henry—I told you, we're just having a good time." Yup, back to that one.

A week on the beach might be nice. Maybe a week of

sun and sand will bring some equilibrium back to my life, help me get some perspective on Henry. Does he really care—was his ride to the rescue sincere or just part of his whole seduction package? Surely the beach would provide the answers. After all, the ocean is like one huge in-ground pool, right?

"I might go see my parents next weekend," Wendy says.

Wow—this is bad. Wendy's parents are wealthy but cantankerous. She's the only friend I've ever had who wished her parents would have divorced when she was younger. Her mother, from the way she's described her, would fit right in with Tess and her crew. If Wendy's thinking of going to see her parents, especially after she just saw them, she must really be hurting. Or trying to keep herself from seeing Sam.

I try to keep myself from calling Henry and she tries to keep herself from seeing Sam. This is hopeless. There must be a support group for this.

Her mood makes me reluctant to go on about Henry, which disappoints me because I'm at that stage where I do want to talk and speculate with a buddy and I want to ask her advice on how to tell him about Rick. But the Sam situation has created a barrier between us, and I hold back. I don't want to inflict any more pain by giggling like a schoolgirl over my new "crush" while she's dying inside. She has to go back to work, anyway, so we leave it that I'll call her this evening.

"I wish you still lived in the city," she says mournfully. "We could grab a beer or something after work."

"That reminds me," I say, "do you know of any job openings—in public relations, communications?"

"Hey, I'm glad to hear you're getting back in the saddle. Nothing's open here. In fact, Gelman is making noises about cutting back again. But I'll look around!" Cheer has returned to her voice and we end the conversation on that note.

Getting back in the saddle, up on the bike—I guess I need to do all those things. I clean up some papers and rue the fact that I left the Sunday want ads at Gina's. This is becoming a habit—leaving the want ads anywhere except where I need them. Am I subconsciously sabotaging myself? Hell no. Nothing subconscious about it.

Refusing to be defeated by my inner evil twin, I pull up the *Sunpapers* Web page again and look online at the want ads. I actually copy down a few—a PR specialist at a local hospital, a director of communications for a trade organization, a PR chief of the local orchestra, "communications specialist" at Center Stage, and a few other nonprofits. Nothing in the corporate world, though, but maybe that's a good thing. Maybe I need to ride a slow-moving pony before I jump on a Triple Crown contender.

I'm feeling happy and upbeat for the first time in ages, and before I log off I decide to do a little Googling. First, I do Henry and come up with about a dozen entries. It's mostly his name popping up in charity events, a couple of alumni association gigs from his alma maters, and a *Sunpapers* story about a divorce of two prominent Baltimore attorneys in which Henry represented the wife. I don't know what I had expected to find, but I'm relieved not to have found it. Maybe I thought I'd see a list of his former lovers, complete with footnotes.

Before I put my cyber surfboard away, I impulsively type in "Professor Moroni."

I end up with a few hundred hits, but I quickly eliminate the Web sites where some girl named La Professora Alfonsa Moroni does things with barnyard animals, and find Berkeley, where I point and click my way into the political science department before you can say "break my friend's heart."

Moroni has a rap sheet as long as Henry's...well, you

know—conferences, papers, books, awards for teaching excellence, plus a sizable amount of community service work, as well as a soupçon of student protest leadership. Hey, what's a Marxist without some good old-fashioned student protesting? Her bio provides some convenient links to some of her rants, er, papers, so I zoom to a few of these, looking not for her philosophy but her photo. On the third try, I find it, and I slump back in my chair feeling as defeated as Wendy is.

For every woman, there is an archfiend, a woman who embodies all your crushed hopes about yourself, all your fears about your aspirations, the kind of woman you secretly wish you were and know you're not hardwired to be. The kind of woman most likely to cut your heart out if you lose your boyfriend to her.

Wendy could take losing Sam to a bimbo or a slut or even some jiggly co-ed. None of those kinds of women would assault Wendy's core beliefs about herself or her fears about her deficits. But losing Sam to a woman who is attractive in a dark, ethnic way, whose heavily lidded eyes seem to hide the secrets of harlots from days gone by, whose political beliefs are as passionate and intellectual as they are cockamamy and passé—that is a blow.

Rosa Moroni is an attractive woman with dark, shoulder-length hair, thick, serious lips, and large eyes. Although the photo is only a head shot, it's clear from the way her sweater tugs at her shoulders that she's probably stacked, too. From her bio, I know she's a first-generation immigrant. Her parents are Italian and Greek. She speaks three languages, including English and the languages of her parents.

Wendy is honey-topped whole wheat bread. Rosa Moroni is foccaccia with olive oil, peppers and hard-to-pronounce cheese.

And I know in my heart of hearts that Wendy knows this. Like I said, she's no slouch—she probably Googled her as soon as she got the name from Sam. She probably pried the name from Sam, in fact, just so she could Google it. And if she saw this, she knows Sam is not going to leave Rosa Moroni for a bright, sexy, but no-spaghetti-on-the-menu–part-of-town Wendy Jackson. Wendy might be willing to wait for Sam, but it's clear to me that the only woman Sam is willing to wait for is Rosa Moroni. She's a talisman, a good-luck charm to bring fortune in his climb up the ladders of academe. Wendy, on the other hand, is merely a knickknack with no mystical powers.

Wendy knows. No wonder she wants to go to her parents. She wants to curl up in her nest, no matter how uncomfortable it is, and lick her wounds. I ache for her. I feel like calling Sam and chewing him out. No, I feel like calling his boss, the dean of his department, and the president of the college, and making up a story about how Sam Terrill cheated on his SATs or lied on his résumé or sexually harassed students, both male and female. I want Sam to suffer.

Maybe I'll enroll in one of his classes.

chapter 12

Fig: Fecundity

On my first birthday with Rick, his parents sent me a basket of fruit! He explained that his mother didn't think it polite to choose personal gifts for people she didn't know well, but she had wanted to remember my special day in some way. I remember that day well—a cloud of worry hung over me because I thought I might be pregnant. As it turned out, I wasn't, and I never shared my worries with Rick. Our relationship was starting to deepen, and I didn't want to cloud it with troubling decisions. Because of my worries, I hardly appreciated Rick's gift, a small book of love poems.

Who needs Sam to make you feel bad when you can get anonymous prospective employers to do it with only a little more effort?

In the space of a week, I've received two rejection letters without even the courtesy of an interview.

After a marathon session at Fred's computer Monday

night, I had a résumé polished up that would occupy a shrine in a college career counselor's office. I've got snappy cover letters and promises of references. I hand deliver a couple of these puppies and put the rest in the mail.

My recent job-hunting efforts are but faint parries compared to the rigorous jab I make at the beginning of this week.

The hospital and the trade organization say "no, thanks" so fast I'm reeling. Neither's probably a good fit for me, anyway. A little too efficient for my freewheeling style. Application in. Rejection out. Ba-da-bing-ba-da-boom. At least I know where I stand.

Over dinner Thursday night—pork loin marinated in lime juice and tequila served with wild rice and asparagus—Fred tells me those places probably had internal candidates lined up and that between the flower shop job and the accident, it's as if I haven't been working for two years, anyway.

"You might want to look into a career-development seminar or something," he says, waving his fork at me. "You can sometimes make good contacts that way. Networking. It's all about networking."

I can't imagine making good contacts with other people looking for jobs unless he means contact in the physical sense. A group hug, perhaps? But I nod seriously as if Fred is giving me pearls of wisdom and I better take notes, while I'm trying very, very hard not to think of him naked.

You see, Fred and I have been on thin ice since he got home from his business trip Tuesday. First, he's not crazy about Trixie. He practically kicks her out of the house if he happens to spot her nosing into any room he's occupying. And she scratched a chair leg one night. So it was an antique chair. So it had sentimental value. So it was his favorite aunt's favorite chair.

Then there was the little naked incident just yesterday when I happened in on Fred and Gina—I can hardly think about it now—doing it.

With no kids around they must be used to having the house to themselves. I had stayed late at the shop last night so I could meet Wendy afterward for drinks, but Wendy was a no-show and I came home early.

At first, all I heard was a man's voice saying, "Oh, yeah, that's right." I just thought Gina had on some HGTV home-repair show. Too late—I realized it was Fred's voice. Too late because I'd already wandered into the den and there was Gina on top of Fred. Fred saw me first and said "Shit!" then Gina turned and grabbed an afghan while shrieking, "Oh, no," and when she moved off him, I saw him naked.

Whatever Fred's faults are, I now know why Gina thinks so highly of him.

It's an image burned into my retinas. But we pretend it didn't happen. At least Gina and I pretend. Fred, on the other hand, is a simmering mass of resentment that manifests itself in him telling me to be more mindful of my appearance or to get him the inventory records of the flower shop or even to be careful who I mention the sale of the building to.

The sale is back on since the Japanese bailed on the Squires Financial property. I think Fred is now convinced that I leaked the information to Squires. Initially, this made me indignant. Then I realized he was right. I had leaked it to Henry.

All of this is a long way of saying I have to move. I don't want to inhibit Gina's chance of having a baby, and I suspect Fred is a little sex-shy with me in the house since I caught him with his pants down.

Besides, Fred annoys me and I annoy him. He's been on my case this morning and now this evening because he knows I've been goofing off while looking for a job. He's given me a couple of lectures disguised as well-meaning advice that I think are really just more payback for seeing him naked. That mark will take a long time to erase and the best way to wipe the slate clean is to get out of Dodge.

Even Gina realizes it's time for me to vamoose. After Fred's most recent lecture on attending career-development seminars, I thank Fred, clear my throat and say I'm thinking of moving. Gina doesn't protest, which normally would be her automatic reaction, sincere or not—"Don't go, Ame, we're having so much fun!"

Instead, she says, "Where would you move to?"

"Wendy's," I blurt out.

"The food place?" Fred asks incredulously.

"No, her friend Wendy," Gina says, looking at Fred as if he's crazy. She doesn't get to do that very often. I'm glad I was here to witness it. "She lives downtown. Not that far from the shop, right?"

"Uh-huh," I say with a mouth full of rice and pork.

Fred thinks about this and decides it's a good thing. A really good thing. "Living downtown might look appealing on your résumé."

I nearly spit out my food. That has to be the most obvious line of bullshit I've heard since some guy in a bar tried to get me into the sack by telling me he was entering the seminary the next day. BS or not, the writing is on the wall. Gina might love me, but she'd love me more if I left her and Fred alone in their baby-making factory.

After helping Gina clean up I retreat with the cordless to my soon-to-be-former bedroom and call Wendy. She answers on the second ring and it's clear she's been crying.

"Hey, what's the matter?"

"The usual," she says morosely.

"I'll come see you. Hang on." Okay, so I have an ulterior

motive. I'm going to ask her if I can move in with her. But this will kill several birds once again with that multipurpose stone. I move in, get out of Gina and Fred's hair, and act as a control on Wendy's Sam urges. And she, meanwhile, can act on my Henry urges.

I've kept myself from calling Henry all week, but it's been a struggle. Sure, I could have just given him a breezy ring at his office, a "how are things" kind of call that leads to a "thought I'd update you on my crazy life" conversation where he's chuckling and happy and I'm joking and happy. But if I make that call, a line is crossed. I'm assuming things. I'm assuming we're past the "keeping track" stage of a relationship where the time of the call, the initiator of the call, the reason for the call and the tone of the call are all tallied up in a "contact assessment" calculation that tells each participant who cares more.

We're still in the stage where phone calls have meaning, where they are as significant as the first tentative cables from foreign emissaries after years of tension. One misstep and the future, as we hope to know it, is lost.

So I don't call.

And here it is Thursday and not once did he ring me up. The fact that he'd mentioned possibly getting together for lunch this week just makes it worse. I'd started looking forward to it. Now the weekend looms and I'm both disappointed and annoyed. He's waiting awfully late to make a date with me. Is he trying other babes first? Am I just his backup? What happened to wanting to have dinner with Gina and Fred? Maybe I should have Gina extend that invitation now. It would give me an excuse to call him.

Gina's watching the news with Fred, so I whisper that I'll be borrowing her car and that I'll call before heading back. That's just in case they want to go at it again while I'm gone.

The car is another reason I have to leave. Now that Fred

is back from his business trip, Gina and I share the Volvo. She tries too hard to be generous and I always feel I'm putting her out when I take the car. Even tonight. If she had a previous engagement, she wouldn't let me know. Then again, maybe she likes getting rid of me.

I mosey into town and find a parking spot near Wendy's apartment, which I take as my karma starting to kick in. Surely I'll find a job tomorrow.

But the karma shatters like a Ming vase in the hands of a two-year-old when Wendy lets me in. She is crying so hard she's practically hysterical. Wadded-up tissues litter her sofa in the living room at the end of the hall off the front foyer. And her curtains are closed, shutting out light and the view of the city from her wide picture window.

"Let me get you some water," I say, and put my purse down. I go into her small kitchenette that separates the foyer from the living room and pour her some water, and therein lies the tale. As I run the spigot, my gaze falls on a ripped bag from a local drugstore. The receipt is attached to the bag with a staple. Wendy bought three items today—a candy bar, a toothbrush and a pregnancy test.

"Here," I say, giving her the glass in the living room, struggling to keep my hand from shaking. I pat her on the shoulder as she huddles at the end of the sofa with the water and a tissue. "I'll be right back. Need to use your bathroom."

To the right of her living room is a short hallway with the bedroom on one side and the bath on the other. I slip in and don't even bother to close the door. There, on the edge of the sink, is the evidence. EPT with its unambiguous sign that Wendy is "with child." Crap. That shit Sam.

Taking a deep breath, reminding myself this is about Wendy and not about my anger, I step back into the living room and sit on the floor in front of her.

"Does Sam know?" I ask. But I already know the answer.

She just confirms it when she nods her head yes. Do I even need to ask her what his reaction was? The tissues tell me. They are the crumpled pieces of her heart leftover from the explosion.

"And he wants you to do something about it?" I ask. She nods again. Standing up, I lean over and give her a big bear hug. And dammit, I start to cry, too. Gone is my professional nurse's attitude. Gone is my strong and mature approach. I'm mad and sad and pissed and want to kick pigeons. Especially ones that look like Sam and men like him.

"That's why you want to go to your parents," I say at last, sitting on a chair diagonally across from her. "To tell them."

"No," she says. She blows her nose and wipes a strand of hair from her face. "I don't want to tell them. I do want to ask them for some money."

Wendy never asks her parents for money. In fact, it's a point of pride that Wendy lives by her own means instead of palming funds off Mom and Dad. She's afraid if she takes their help, they'll want to control her life. Lots of strings attached, the kind that don't break easily, like fishing wire.

"Money for what?" I swallow hard. Okay, okay, I know women are supposed to be in charge of their own bodies and have choices and control their destinies. And yes, I've always thought of abortion as an option if I found myself in Wendy's position. But the reality is it's a really bad way to fix a mistake, and I hope to God she doesn't want to fix this mistake this way. I think of Gina wanting a baby. I think of an unbelievable scenario—Gina adopting this child. I think of me adopting this child—I could raise it to despise college English professors. But I can't, for some reason, imagine Wendy "getting rid of it."

"Money to go away," she says, and I exhale. "And think. And…I don't know. I don't know." She shakes her head back and forth convincingly as if she doesn't know, so I put my arm around her and do the comfort thing again, hoping I'm giving her at least some of the warmth she gave me when I was the one who needed help. When she has control, she takes a deep breath.

"I thought I was pregnant once. As a teenager. By Donald Westcott. Class president of Choate." She smiles but there's no happiness in it. "And I thought if I was, I'd just run away to the beach and live there during the pregnancy and have the baby and raise it all by myself if I had to." She laughs and there's only cynicism in it. "Boy, was I ever stupid."

"Is that what you want to do—go to the beach?"

"Maybe. At least to get my head together. Will you go with me?" She looks at me with desperate eyes obscured by tears.

Even though I'm genuinely sorry for Wendy and want to help her, I have to admit that my selfish thoughts return— that is, if I go away with Wendy to help her get her head together, maybe I'll get mine together at the same time. I see myself diving into some beach hotel's pool, lying on the sand, staring at the waves, and feeling time stop while I work things out. Things like whatever happened to the pre-Rick Amy and how do I get her back. Things like how to loosen up and just have fun. Things like how to learn to trust again. Maybe there's an old manual of some kind buried in the sand. Since it's early in the season, the beach would not be crowded and I could find it.

"Sure. I would just need to make some arrangements." Like find another place to live and work. Simple, right?

Wendy calms down and wipes her eyes with a new tissue. She manages a weak laugh, a real one this time, a laugh at herself. "I'll probably call in sick tomorrow. I haven't been feeling well."

"Morning sickness?"

"Morning, noon and night sickness," she says, rubbing her stomach.

"Have you eaten anything?"

"No."

"What did you have for lunch?"

"Just some crackers."

I stand. "I'll fix you something. Let me see what you have." But in her kitchen a second later the only thing I can find safe to fix is a can of beef barley soup. I heat it up for her and make some tea, and serve her at her tiny table pressed up against the kitchen wall in the living room. Mothering is what Wendy needs, and some semblance of a good mood, or at least a calmer one, begins to return. It feels good to wait on her after all the nursing she did on my behalf.

"Have you seen a doctor yet?" I ask.

"Next week," she says. Daintily, she wipes some soup from her mouth. I can't imagine Rosa Moroni doing anything daintily.

"You need someone to take care of you." Okay, go ahead and cringe. You know where I'm headed with this. I want to move in with Wendy, which I can do and it'll still be a good deed, right? In fact, I *am* thinking of helping her, even if it does mean I get a place to stay in the deal. I'm not heartless.

"I wanted to talk to you, Wen, about possibly crashing here for a while. I could help you. Make sure you eat, take care of things."

"Did you have a fight with Fred?" she asks.

"No. It's just they need their privacy. They want to…" They want to have a baby! Stop! Do not say that! "They want to redecorate and I'd be in the way." Lying is too damn easy. No wonder you're taught not to do it at an early age. Once you figure out how painless it is, you're hooked.

"Sure. You can crash here." She smiles at me and pushes

away her bowl. She's eaten only about half of it, and it wasn't a huge serving to begin with.

To prove my worth I start to clean up immediately. I wash the dishes, I gather all the tissues into the trash, I even change the sheets on her bed and wipe down her bathroom. By this time, she's dozing on her couch so I pull an afghan around her shoulders and grab the cordless phone from the wall.

When I call Gina, she sounds a little breathless and I wonder if I managed to interrupt her again.

"I probably won't come home tonight," I say.

"Henry caught up with you?"

"What?"

"Henry called here. I just assumed…" She assumes I'm at his place.

"No, I'm still at Wendy's. She's not feeling well. So I thought I'd stay over and kind of help her out." I'm dying to confide in my sister and tell her that Wendy is pregnant, but I don't. Not because I'm afraid of violating Wendy's trust. No, I don't tell Gina because the contrast will make Gina feel bad. Unmarried woman pregnant by schmucko married boyfriend vs. married woman who wants to get pregnant by decent husband.

"Oh. Do you need to come home and get some stuff?"

"No." Then I remember. "I have your car!"

"If you come home to pack a bag, I'll run you back into town," she offers. Little did I realize just how eager she is to get rid of me.

"All right. I'll be there in about fifteen minutes." After hanging up the phone, I nudge Wendy awake and tell her I'm just going to pick up some things at home. Home. Gina's place had become home. When had that happened? So many things just creep up on me.

I take Wendy's key to let myself back in. Before I go, I tell her that I promise to take care of her.

★ ★ ★

Gina is practically waiting at the door with my bags packed. Sure, she seems genuinely wistful about all the great sisterly bonding we were able to do, but it's clear that those special moments are best appreciated in retrospect than in real time.

"Fred and I were thinking of going to a movie," she says, explaining her rush to throw clothes in a suitcase and head to Wendy's. Fred, however, is nowhere to be seen, and my guess is he's lying naked on their bed as we speak. Can't seem to get that naked image out of my mind.

In the car, I hug Trixie to my chest, feeling somehow strangely protected as we drive past Tess Wintergarten's apartment. Cats have their own secret powers, you know.

Although Gina offers to come up with me, there are no parking spots nearby so I grapple with my suitcase and the cat and wish Gina a quick goodbye, which she points out is not really a goodbye since we're still in the same city, still going to see each other, and by the way, when am I going to invite Henry over to meet Fred?

Henry. I still need to return his call. Man, do I feel triumphant having so many things get in the way of Henry.

When I let myself into Wendy's apartment, she's no longer on the couch, so I tiptoe into her bedroom to make sure she is all right. She's sleeping soundly, so I go back to the living room and settle on the sofa for a relaxing conversation with Henry, my reward for being kicked out of my sister's house and comforting an abandoned, pregnant friend.

I don't realize how much I want to talk to him until I actually hear his voice. I'd been expecting to get his voice mail, thinking he probably gave up and went out. Henry isn't the waiting kind.

"I'm at Wendy's," I tell him. Then I tell him about her pregnancy. Yeah, I know—I shouldn't have. It's private. But

I can't help it. I want to talk with someone, to have the Rant of Rants about Sam, to soak up the sympathy from Henry that Wendy really deserves.

The only problem is, you really can't rant about men with men the same way you can with women. Men have this irritating habit of taking up for their species. While Henry clearly feels sorry for Wendy, he also asks a few pointed questions—like had they been having unprotected sex, and why did she stay with him if she knew he was married? Call me crazy, but I suspect Henry thinks that Wendy is partly to blame here. Imagine that, a woman being in control of her own body means, well, a woman being in control of her own body. His comments deflate my all-consuming bubble of outrage against Sam. Outrage is sometimes my favorite emotion so I'm doubly disappointed.

"Is she going to be okay?" he asks at the end of another spiel about what a schmuck Sam is.

"She goes to the doctor next week."

"Then what?"

"I don't know. She might raise it on her own. Or put it up for adoption." It seems funny to call a baby "it."

"I'm glad to hear she's having it," he says, a surprising admission, and one I'd reached on my own just hours ago. So Henry likes babies. Very interesting.

"I could handle that for her," he adds. "Private adoption. I don't think we've done any of that in the past, but there's always a first time."

Good old Henry—jumping in to help my friend and making a few bucks while he's at it. Maybe that's why he likes babies.

We stay on the phone for nearly an hour. As we wind down I notice that darkness has covered the city and Trixie is meowing like crazy. She wants to go out. Damn. This is going to be tough. She'll have to get used to doing her thing inside now and I need to get a litter box because I've left her old one at Gina's.

Henry is getting ready to ask me out. I can tell because he starts off by complaining about how hard I am to get hold of.

"If you keep moving like this, how am I supposed to keep track of you?" he asks with that good-natured tone in his voice, that tone that says we've made love and enjoyed each other.

"Well, you've got me now, so what is it you wanted to talk to me about?"

"The weekend. I thought we could go away together."

Go away together? This is promising. "Where?"

"St. Michaels," he says.

St. Michaels. A quaint town on the Eastern shore. I'm seeing romantic bed-and-breakfast bedroom in my mind—chintz curtains, rose-scented bath water. Perfect place to tell Henry about Rick after a couple of glasses of wine and a leisurely stroll by the water, and maybe a leisurely stroll through our libidos, too.

"Sounds good." We make arrangements to meet. He'll pick me up at Wendy's—in the lobby, so he doesn't need to find a parking spot—around six the next evening.

Before he hangs up, he says something that hits me like an electric shock.

"I'm thinking about you a lot, Amy," he says. Then quickly, "Talk to you later."

"Thinking about you a lot?" Is that some windup to saying the *L* word? I try to remember how it was with Rick and me. Once I got used to feeling loved, I forgot what it felt like not to have it.

After I hang up the phone, I'm startled to see Wendy standing at the alcove by the kitchen.

"Do you need something?" I ask her.

"My throat's just dry. I was going to get some milk."

I rush to get it for her. After all, this is my job now, while I'm looking for another job.

"I didn't hear you come in," she admits, after swallowing a glass of milk. "Did you get your stuff in okay?"

"Yup." Just then Trixie purrs at Wendy's feet.

"Oh, Trixie! I forgot about you!" She picks up the cat and pets her while Trixie meows contentedly in her hands. Looking at Wendy with this small bit of life it occurs to me that she'll make a good mother. I can see her kissing some kid's scraped knee, or cooing over his homework assignment, or cheering her on at the school ball game. Wendy might dress up like a sophisticated woman but underneath she's a mom. Maybe we all are.

"Has my mother called?" she asks.

I scurry to retrieve the phone from the couch. "I don't know. I was using it."

After handing it to Wendy, I watch as she punches in the code to retrieve her voice mail. She shakes her head back and forth as she listens to an obviously long message.

"Yup," she says after she clicks off. "But it's too late to call her back. They go to bed at nine."

"Is it okay for you to go visit them this weekend?"

"Uh-huh. She just went through the menus she's fixing." Wendy grimaces and for a second it looks like she is going to burst into tears again. Or maybe throw up. "I don't know how I'll be able to eat. And then she'll start nagging me. It's going to be hard."

"Call the doctor."

"What?"

"Tomorrow, call the doctor you're going to see and explain you're pretty sure you're pregnant, and having morning sickness, and ask if she can recommend something."

"It's a he. But that's not a bad idea." She smiles. "I better get back to sleep. Let me get you some sheets."

"Don't! I'll be fine. Just point me in the right direction."

The linen closet is in the bathroom, so after Wendy tells me where to find things, I set up my own little bed on the couch, which isn't quite long enough for even my short body, so I end up spending most of the night in a quasi-fetal position, which has a lot of irony in it given the current circumstances.

My sleep is further interrupted by Trixie, who meows so much I'm afraid she'll awaken the entire apartment building. Poor Trix will have to get used to being a city cat. I'll get her litter box in the morning, or buy a new one. In the meantime, she can use the newspapered corner of the bathroom I've set up for her.

I finally fall into a deep sleep around three and am jolted upright by the sound of water running in the kitchen. In the space of five minutes, four hours have passed. It's nearly seven and Wendy's up, fixing coffee and determined to go into the office.

"I'm feeling much better," she says chirpily. "How about you? You sleep okay?"

"Great, just great," I lie. I try to focus on the room and remember where I am. Ah, yes. Wendy's. Pregnant Wendy's.

"It really made a difference you coming over, Ame. I can't thank you enough. I feel like I can face the world."

"Well, listen, you take it easy today. Don't overdo. When do you head out?" I yawn and hope I'm making sense. Did I say something or just think it?

"I'll head for Connecticut right after work." She sips at her coffee, warming her hands around the mug. "Mmm, that reminds me. I only have one key!" She holds up the key I left on the kitchen counter last night.

One key. She must have lost the other one. No, wait a minute, Sam probably has the other one. The schmuck.

"I guess we could agree to meet here at a certain time," I say.

"All right. I'm leaving right at five and I'll stop here to pick up a few things."

"Okay. I'll meet you here then."

"You going into the shop?"

"I was planning on it."

"Doing anything special this weekend?"

"Henry and I are going out."

She smiles weakly at me. It must hurt that I've got a boyfriend when she has a schmuck. But hey—things might work out for her. Henry could be a schmuck, too.

"There's coffee but I usually pick up a bun or something on my way to the office," she says, opening cabinets looking for food. In the refrigerator, she pulls out a carton of something and throws it in the trash can.

"That's okay. I'll buy something."

In a few minutes, she is ready to leave and she looks like the old Wendy—confident, attractive, in control. She wears a short sleeveless black dress and a loose silver chain around her hips, and black flats. She carries a thin attaché case and sunglasses.

"Don't forget to call your doctor," I remind her.

"Will do. Thanks again, Ame."

After she leaves, I take my time getting ready to go. Now that I'm living with Wendy, the pressure to get a job will be greater. Unlike my sister, Wendy doesn't seem to believe in food. If I want any, I'll have to buy it myself. That means I'll need money if I don't want to dip into my savings or starve to death.

I mentally calculate how many paychecks I can probably still count on before the shop closes for good. Enough to buy a week's worth of groceries. I'll be fine.

I shower, drink another cup of java and throw on a sundress. After Henry's call last night, I'm feeling pretty and sexy. As I finish putting in earrings, I hear the phone ringing. But

I can't find it! It's somewhere in the living room, muffled, under a pillow or something. I must have put it there after Wendy handed it back to me.

Too late, I locate it on the floor by the sofa. The beep-beep-beep of the voice mail signal taunts me. I don't know Wendy's code. I'll have to wait for her to retrieve the message. Damn. Maybe it's Henry. Or maybe it's Sam. Oh, to erase Sam-left messages.

Note to self: learn voice mail code.

chapter 13

Dahlia: Instability

I think I talked more to Mrs. Squires about wedding preparations than to my own mother. Rick was Emily Squires's only child and I suspected she longed for a daughter over whom she could fret and fuss. At first, her enthusiasm was charming, and I felt like I was bestowing a gift on her by letting her be such a large part of the planning. But it quickly became clear that involving her created complications and discord. I have always loved gladiolas with their straight, bold lines and tightly held flowers, and I'd wanted them as part of the arrangement at the church. But Mrs. Squires was adamant that gladiolas were "funeral flowers, dear" and steered me toward dahlias and zinnias instead, a compromise I made after Rick interceded on her behalf, promising me a honeymoon suite full of gladiolas to compensate. I wonder if she had gladiolas at his funeral. I couldn't go. I was still in the hospital then. Gladiolas can mean "you pierce my heart."

Not catching that phone call turns out to be a bad thing. But I don't discover that until nearly ten o'clock on this fine Friday night, nearly four hours after Henry is supposed to pick me up at Wendy's apartment. Four hours that I spend roaming around her building, looking up the street, tapping my foot, wondering if I should try to find a phone to call Henry, and cursing myself for not buying a cell phone.

Here's how it happens: Wendy meets me at her apartment a little after five. Buoyed by thoughts of going away with Henry, I've had a great day. I sent off some new résumés, even reaching new creative heights by actually penning a press release in lieu of a cover letter announcing I'm applying for a job at Center Stage.

I mean, I got to thinking about naked Fred's advice—that I've been out of the job force for two years—and I realize I need to show rather than tell folks I'm capable of working in a public relations office. So I cranked up the shop's computer and wrote, in perfect press release format, a phony one announcing my application for the job, including all my qualifications and even a pithy quote from me about how excited I'd be working in a premier arts organization in my native town.

When Wendy shows up a little late, it's still not enough to chip away at my good mood. She's nervous about going to her parents and feeling a little queasy, but she did manage to reach her doctor, who told her to drink ginger ale and eat crackers. She's late because she stopped to pick up some. While she throws up in the bathroom, I throw things in a bag, then she throws things in a bag and I jump in the shower. But she wants to get going because she's hoping to get there before it gets too dark since she doesn't like to drive to Connecticut in the dark. What is "too dark" anyway? If it's dark, it's dark. Anyway, I leave out plenty of food and water and litter-box stuff for Trixie, and Wendy and I race out the door together because Henry said he'd be by at six and it's already six-ten.

In all the confusion, Wendy forgets to give me her key. And she doesn't check her voice mail. At least not that I know of. If she did, she forgot to tell me about it.

And that was Henry who called this morning to tell me he'd be in depositions all day, including one scheduled at five-thirty, so could I meet him at his place at seven and we can leave from there and if I don't call back, he'll assume that's okay.

When I don't show up, he tries calling Wendy, gets no answer and starts to fume.

So he's fuming at his condo and I'm fuming at Wendy's apartment building. Our fuming is like twin smokestacks against the Baltimore skyline—decorative in a primitive sort of way but ultimately not good for us.

Now you're probably wondering why I waited four hours. Simple—what else was I going to do? I don't have a phone. I don't have a way of getting into Wendy's apartment. And I figure I'll at least wait until ten before calling Gina because that will give her and Fred a chance to do the horizontal mambo for a few hours.

At ten-o-five, I'm getting ready to walk to a nearby shop to use the phone when I see Henry's blue BMW come around the corner. He's honking the horn and looking annoyed. Grabbing my bag, I jump in before the light turns.

"Where were you?" we ask simultaneously. Unlike in comedic movies, however, we do not then laugh together uproariously. Instead, we throw accusations as fast as darts from a Ritalin-deprived teen.

"You said six…"

"I called…"

"Why didn't you try me again…"

"Weren't you worried…"

This fast-paced conversation lasts until we hit the outskirts of the city and is then followed by its natural opposite—stone-cold silence. Silence consumes the drive until we hit the highway but finally is replaced by snappy questions when he turns off near the Bay Bridge.

"Shouldn't you…" I point toward the big green sign reading Bay Bridge.

"We're staying in Annapolis tonight. Since we got going so late, we can't take the boat over until the morning. I'm not that good a sailor."

"The boat?"

"I wanted it to be a surprise," he says, with no good humor in his voice. "I have the keys to Squires's sailboat."

Beautiful Dreamer. I think the name of the boat as he says it. I've been on this sailboat with Rick. Clammy hands squeeze my heart and throat. I want to jump out of the car. This is not good.

More silence ensues until he pulls the car into quaint little Annapolis and drives up to a hotel in the center of town. It occurs to me that this is stupid—we could have stayed at his place for the night and left in the morning for the bay. But I keep this observation to myself. Somehow, I don't think Henry's in the mood for canny insights.

He registers us and we lug our stuff up to a fifth-floor standard-issue hotel room. After examining the bathroom to smell the little soaps and shampoos, I ask Henry if he's eaten yet. He hasn't.

"Want to go to a restaurant or order in?" I ask.

He looks me up and down. I'm still in my sundress and I'm feeling good the way it hugs my body. My forehead cut has healed to a thin ridge by now and I've figured out a way to camouflage it with makeup and hair. I might not be center-fold material like Wendy, but I'm not bad. I've got all the right curves in all the right places. Henry appears to be noticing.

"We can order in." He sits on the edge of the bed flipping through the room service menu. I crawl behind him and wrap my arms around his shoulders. He kisses my hand and places the call to room service, ordering a steak sandwich for himself and holding out the phone to me so I can place my own order. I ask for a burger and fries.

"Wait!" Henry shouts before I get off. He takes the phone from me and orders a couple of beers.

"Don't want to drink too much," he says after placing the phone back on the hook. "We should get going early tomorrow."

Speaking of getting going, Henry doesn't waste any time. With his eyes locked on me, he peels off his shirt, revealing his rock-hard pectorals and glistening shoulder muscles. Henry has the body of a street fighter. It oozes strength from every muscle. Bare-chested, he pulls me down on the bed and begins to untie the little string that keeps my sundress in place.

"Room service will be here soon. They said fifteen minutes." I am motionless, enjoying the feeling of him enjoying me.

He nuzzles at my neck and my insides have a meltdown.

"I can do a lot in fifteen minutes."

He's right. He *can* do a lot in fifteen minutes, and, with my help, he does. He slides off my dress with a deft hand, undoes his belt buckle with the other, and kisses my face, neck and breasts while I fumble to get his pants off.

Before I can say "yes, yes, yes," Henry is inside me and I am saying "yes, yes, yes!"

This man has talent.

I'm in the shower and Henry has his pants back on when the food and beer arrive. Both of us are in far better moods when we sit down to eat, so is it the perfect time to spring my former-fiancé story on him and ruin the whole thing?

No can do. Looking at Henry's happy face as he chews, I nix that idea. Another time will have to do. Maybe during sex. I'll just casually shout it out.

"How's Wendy?" he asks.

"As good as can be expected. She's going to see her folks this weekend. I think she's hitting them up for some money—maybe to go away somewhere."

"Didn't you tell me she's getting her MBA?"

"Yeah. Working on it. But she's dropping her summer classes. They were supposed to start in a couple weeks—end of May."

He shakes his head and I can't help but wonder what he thinks is worse—getting knocked up or having to drop the MBA program.

"It pays to be careful," he says, smiling. Henry is meticulously careful when we have sex.

His comment annoys me. Wendy's problem isn't about being careless with a condom, I want to scream. Her problem is about being careless with her heart! Sam's a schmuck! I wonder how much it would cost to place an ad with that message in the Hopkins newspaper.

After dinner, we take a leisurely walk along the waterfront and Henry locates the boat. Just seeing it makes my heart clutch a little.

I don't like boats that much anyway. I have a fear of heights, you see, and I think of a boat gliding across this deep, deep chasm and that the fall to the bottom is pretty steep— there's just water in the way. I prefer pools, with their known and graduated depths, where everything is neatly confined to a rectangle of shimmering aquamarine.

He holds my hand and talks about growing up in New Jersey. It's the most he's talked about his past. His mother got a good settlement from his dad, so they didn't want for anything. He went to a private high school, even learned to ride horses, and was given a Mustang convertible when he graduated in the top tenth of his class. His mother is active in local politics and actually has a law degree but doesn't practice any longer.

"How did she meet your father?" I ask.

"Her senior year in college on some exchange program. She was in Colombia studying Spanish literature."

Ah, the old college-meet. College, I've decided, is more about meeting your fiancé than about learning anything. Forget the whole liberal arts thing. It's not about liberating your mind. It's about hooking up with someone. If you don't meet your fiancé in college, you're hosed. Look at Wendy. Look at me. I was lucky to meet Rick after I graduated. And now I'm in that post-baccalaureate dating desert where only the strong survive and the bones of the lost litter the landscape for miles.

"I'm surprised she didn't teach you Spanish," I say as we make our way past an outdoor café where hushed late-night conversations and timid laughter scamper around the edges of the lane.

"Once she and my father split, she didn't want much to do with all that," he says, with no trace of bitterness. "His family was, well, less than reputable."

"You didn't know him at all?"

"Nope." We stand on the edge of the water where lights flicker on the lapping waves, and boats gently rock to the beat of wealth. "And don't cry for me, Argentina. I had a good life. Plenty of male role models. Some good uncles, great grandparents." He puts his arm around me, and I think the obvious Freudian question—does Henry Castle seek in the arms of women the affection he never received from his absent father? Looking up at his untroubled face, I scratch that theory. If Henry Castle likes his women, it's because he likes women. Period. End of story. Freud would find Henry

Castle's libido a straight line from desire to coitus with no pit stops for regrets.

"What's 'less than reputable' mean?" I ask. "From the wrong side of the tracks?" If blood lines are a prerequisite for dating Henry, might as well find out now. Mine are more along the mongrel variety.

"Wrong side of the law. My mother was naive enough to think that wealth in Colombia can come from sugar cane."

"Oh." So Henry's father was one of "those" Colombians. "You know, a lot of our flowers come from South America."

"That's how a lot of drugs get smuggled into the country. In flower shipments."

I don't want to know how Henry knows this.

Henry reciprocates my interest in family by asking me more about my own, so I end up telling him how Gina wants to have a baby and how my father had a thing for the ladies and how if he ever comes to dinner at my parents' house he'll be stepping back into the 1970s.

"No problem, *conchita*," he says, holding me tight. "I liked your sister. I'd probably like your parents." Then he kisses me deep and tender, and it's time to go back to the hotel room.

There's something about being in a hotel that ratchets up the sex drive. Maybe it's the fact that people use hotels for assignations, or that hotel rooms are where brides and grooms have their first night (as husband and wife at the very least). Whatever. Henry and I end up having a veritable sex fiesta. Forget the early start the next day. By the time morning rolls around, we've tasted each other more than we've drunk from Morpheus's cup, and we're damned tired. When we finally do open our eyes, it's nearly ten o'clock.

"Damn!" Henry says and gets out of bed quickly. "Come on. We should get going!"

I suggest showering together, but Henry wants to get on that boat now more than he wants me. Or at least, he knows he can get more of me later, but the boat won't wait all day. While he showers, I order breakfast, something light that won't slosh around in my stomach as we slosh around on the waves.

We're so efficient getting ready that we've both washed, dressed, packed and gulped down some toast, grapefruit and coffee in a little over half an hour. While I wait outside, Henry pays the bill. Henry never suggests I pay the bill. Even our first night at the bar—he paid. I don't know if this is his usual procedure or if he's sorry for me because I'll be out of a job soon.

It is one of those perfect spring days where the air is a touch of sweetness on your cheek, the sun winks behind cotton ball clouds, and tourists' smiles spread like fairy dust the anticipation of good things to come.

When we get to the boat, Henry gives me some rudimentary instructions on how to handle it. I remember some of it from when Rick took me sailing. Like Rick, Henry insists I wear a life vest, but he forgoes that equipment. Rick had worn one, though, and I can't help looking at Henry and thinking that he doesn't wear one not because he thinks he'll look silly in it but because he's so cocksure he would win any battle with the waves, and if he couldn't, he wouldn't want to be around to suffer the humiliation.

We have a few close calls throughout the day—once when we head straight for another sailboat and Henry can't get the rigging right, and once when we lodge on a sandbar for a quarter hour until we figure out how to use the wind and the motor to push us off. But even those moments are broken by laughter as we poke fun at our own lack of experience. Henry is happier than I've ever seen him, ever. He grins the entire time, even during the close shaves. And he takes my mistakes in stride, enjoying showing off to me his obviously studied knowledge of seafaring. For my part, I throw a few "ay-yay, maties" his way and beg to "trim the mains'l" since it's the only sea jargon I know.

By the time we reach St. Michaels, I'm surprised to realize that not once did I feel seasick and not once did I feel petrified. It's a far cry from my expedition with Rick two years ago. I'd been so afraid of breaking something or being lost at sea that it took two weeks for me to loosen up the fake smile I'd plastered on my face that day. And, oh, yes, I'd even retched once.

The bed-and-breakfast Henry's scouted out happens to be the one from my dreams. After we check in, we hug and kiss and there's something really sexy about the taste of sea-salted skin, but we resist the urge to fall into bed so that we can grab a bite to eat before the dining room closes in preparation for dinner. We're the only ones in the restaurant and we laugh and giggle over crab cakes while Henry tells me he'll order oysters later that night while winking at me. Oysters are sex food. I get it.

Whether it's the oysters or something else, Henry is in rare form that evening. After a late dinner and a walk along the waterfront, he does a slow-simmer routine on me in bed, until I begin to wonder if there's something slightly sadistic in his languid pace. Is he waiting for me to beg him for it? We make love only once, but it's good enough to last the whole night.

As we lay in each other's arms, Henry tells me more about himself.

"I never wanted to be a burden to anyone," he says, "so I worked damned hard in school to get scholarships. It became a habit—working hard."

"You've done well." I stroke his cheek in the moonlight. "And you're still young. Getting hired at Squires is a huge accomplishment." Perhaps now I'll tell him about Rick? But he's opening up to me and I don't want him to stop.

"I'm forcing myself to enjoy life more," he continues, "instead of just working. I don't want to turn fifty and wonder what the hell goes on outside a wood-paneled office."

Forcing himself to enjoy life? Is that what I am—a component of his new program?

"Didn't you—you know—get out a lot before? I mean, in school or after." What I really want to know is what his dating life has been. Here I'm not divulging my history with Rick but prying him on his history. But hey—the opening has provided itself and who am I to waste it?

"I was never a party animal. And I never got dragged into a long-term relationship. Just a date here and there."

This is a good news/bad news confession. On the one hand, I've just learned that Henry Castle has no "baggage," no ghost-of-girlfriends-past to haunt a new relationship. On the other hand, I've learned that Henry Castle could indeed be relationship-phobic.

I wrestle with how to ask him exactly what he means by "a date here and there," and also, does what we have fall into that category or does it fall into the "dragged into a long-term relationship" category, or does he plan to extricate himself before the dragging begins, Your Honor?

But his soft snoring tells me I'm too late. The witness has fallen asleep on the stand.

I fall asleep that night feeling oddly disappointed by Henry's nocturnal confession. It tells me nothing more than what I already know—that we have fun together, that he enjoys being with me. At the most, it tells me he considers me a good pal, a buddy, perhaps a dear friend. When he'd started talking, I'd begun to expect more.

As if to herald our impending departure from this paradise, the weather on Sunday is less cheerful. More clouds roll in and we both are afraid we'll be caught in a storm, so we hurry off after breakfast instead of antiquing as we'd planned.

Knowing the limits of our seamanship, we're a little nervous on the way back to Annapolis. Henry's grin leaves him when a soft rain starts, but we manage to pull into the marina before the winds whip up and the storm thunders in. Because we outran it, we feel like savvy sailors now, proud of our skills and proud of our luck.

To celebrate, Henry treats me to lunch at an outdoor café. We sit close to the wall, out of the breeze and damp, but enjoy smelling the water-laden air while we sip at a brandy.

When we finally get back in the car to head for Baltimore, I feel like I did on the way home from school field trips—tired and happy and sad at the same time, eager to preserve these memories in a scrapbook or with a friend who didn't go along.

A friend. But of course I can't share them with Wendy. The contrast factor would hurt her. Henry was great to me, while Sam…you know what Sam is.

As we pass Federal Hill, I call Wendy on Henry's cell but she doesn't answer so we go to his condo. We're both hungry and weary so I manage to cook some scrambled eggs—an omelet's beyond my skill level—and Henry opens a bottle of chardonnay.

He unlatches windows to let the spring air in, and we enjoy a quiet meal in his kitchen.

"Here's to your sailing ability," he says, toasting me.

I blush. "What ability? I just followed orders."

"You were a good sport. Not every woman I know would sail to St. Michaels when she hasn't sailed before."

Ouch. Two pinpricks here. One, "not every woman I know" is an allusion to all the other women he does know, the "dates here and there." And second, I have sailed before but I haven't told him. I hate this feeling. Maybe I should tell him a little.

"You know, I was engaged a couple years ago."

He does not stop eating. "Oh?"

"And he died. In the accident I told you about."

"I'm sorry." He looks up at me. Is he staring at my forehead, at the "fragile" tattoo there?

"That's when I broke my leg and arm."

"I remember you telling me." He pours himself more wine and offers me some. "That must have been very hard."

"Took a while to recuperate."

"I mean getting over your fiancé's death." He stares at me as if scouring my soul for remnants of Rick. He has stopped eating and so have I. It is as if time has stopped and whatever I say next will determine the fate of the world.

"It *was* hard," I say at last, "very hard. But my family and Wendy—they helped me a lot."

He pauses a moment, and I wonder if he's the one now trying to form the appropriate questions. Is he going to ask me if I'm over Rick? Is he going to ask me if I have fully recovered? The same panicky feeling that gripped me when I saw *Beautiful Dreamer* shining in the sun now grasps my throat, making swallowing difficult and obvious. I don't want Henry to know the answers to those questions—because, goddammit—I don't know them myself!

"I'm trying to do what you're doing," I say quickly, "enjoy life."

He reaches out and strokes the line of my jaw. Smiling sadly, he leans back. "Is the accident where you got the other scar on the back of your leg?"

Although I've shown him the jagged white line on my calf from my leg break, I have a very thin scar, hidden behind my left knee. Henry must have discovered it when he was discovering other things about my body.

Blushing, I nod. "Yes. I didn't know you noticed."

"I notice lots of things. I like to notice things." He stands and takes his empty plate to the sink where he runs water on it.

"Wendy's got a one-bedroom, right?" he asks with his back to me.

"Yup."

"That must be awfully tight."

"It's okay." I feel like a spy who's avoided detection, grateful that the subject has changed.

"I have more room. You should consider moving in with me."

chapter 14

Honeysuckle: Generous and devoted affection

When I first met Rick, he was living at home and searching for an apartment. On Saturdays, and sometimes after work, he'd take me with him on his flat-hunts. He looked both in and around the city and came closest to a deal on an apartment in Towson where the perfume of sweet honeysuckle bewitched you as you walked up its drive. Right before he put down the deposit, he confessed that he would prefer to live in the city but was tired of looking. That's when I suggested we live together, in my tiny apartment on Calvert Street. At first, he laughed and said his parents would hate the neighborhood, but then he quickly agreed and moved in the next weekend.

Sometimes when life presents me with questions, I wish I could think like a computer. Computers are based on the binary system, right? Which really comes down to breaking everything into "yes or no." So when you open a program and start typing away, the computer isn't thinking, "Oh, she wants this letter or that word or that sentence." The computer is thinking "*a* equals yes, every other letter in the alphabet equals no" for every single keystroke.

Everything comes down to a yes or a no.

I know we like to think that all of life's questions are more complicated than that, with a few juicy "maybe's" thrown in to spice things up. But I have this theory that even they can be turned into "yes" or "no's" if broken down into smaller questions.

So the question before me now really isn't the obvious one: should I move in with Henry? That question's answer is a clear-cut "maybe." No, the small questions behind that big one fall more along these lines:

Do I need a place to stay? Yes.

Would Henry's place be convenient? Yes.

Would Henry's place be comfortable? Yes.

Do I like Henry? Yes.

Will moving in with Henry change our relationship? Uh-oh, another maybe.

Every time I come up with "maybe," I deconstruct again. The smaller questions behind that one "maybe" are ones I don't want to even articulate right now. They deal with things like whether I care for Henry, whether I want to ratchet up the relationship, whether I think he does, etc., etc., etc. They're questions I just don't want to face. So my internal computer crashes and I'm left with no guidance, no electronic voice telling me yes or no and I can only kick and sputter and wish I knew more about computers.

As it turns out, it's a good thing Henry offers to take me in, at least for the night, because Wendy doesn't return until nearly midnight. I know because I phone her every half hour. I'm worried sick about her, envisioning her careering down the road, sobbing, her vision blurred, an accident waiting to happen. When she finally answers the phone, she apologizes right and left for not being there. Her parents had friends over for dinner and insisted she stay, which meant she wasn't on the road until nearly eight o'clock. Translation: she's getting money from her folks so she must do their bidding.

"Are you at Henry's?" she asks sleepily.

"Yeah. How are you feeling?"

"Not so bad. Only one queasy moment this weekend— when my mother insisted I taste-test her calamari appetizer. Blech. Still makes me gag."

"I think that would make me gag even without being pregnant." I'm not big on eating slimy fishlike things. *Slimy* to me means this creature was meant to slide on by and not be caught.

"So, this is great that you're with Henry," she says. But there's no girlfriend exuberance in her voice, just a placid good will.

Henry is in the bedroom sleeping. I am on the phone in his kitchen.

"He wants me to move in with him."

It's a measure of how much Sam has hurt her that she doesn't start shrieking for joy at this news. If anything, she is cautiously happy, as if she isn't really happy at all but knows that I am.

"Is that what you want?" she asks.

"I...I think so. I don't know. It's so sudden." I'm not sure what I think. All I know is Henry has two baths, two phones, and he cooks like Emeril. Oh, yeah, he has two keys, too. He already had me put one on my key ring. So lots of "yeses" there. "I can stay with you, though. I promised I'd help you."

She laughs softly—a positive sign. "You're a great friend, Ame. But I don't think that's necessary. Besides, I have a cat allergy."

"But you love Trixie and she loves you!"

"That doesn't mean I can't have allergies."

"Well, I'll come get her and my stuff tomorrow." Now I'm feeling guilty for foisting my feline friend on my allergic friend.

"Okay. I'll probably be here all day. I'm calling in sick. I have that doctor's appointment in the afternoon."

"Do you want me to go with you?"

"That's sweet of you. But no."

"It might be kind of fun."

She laughs again. "Maybe some other time."

By the time I get off the phone, it is going on one. Henry is sound asleep, his arms sprawled out over his king-size bed. His body is smack in the middle of the sheets. What a strange man—a gentleman, a go-getter, a wild and sensitive lover. Yet still—he's not used to sharing. Perhaps, Dr. Freud, it is due to the fact that he is an only child raised by a doting-yet-aloof mother with no paternal influence.

But hell, Wendy is an only child and she's a sharer. It must be a guy thing.

I remember what he said when he asked me to move in—Wendy only has a one-bedroom while he has two. Maybe I should sleep in his second bedroom? Maybe that should be the deal? I use his second bedroom just until I get a job and a place of my own. And if things work out between us in the meantime, I forgo the search for a new apartment.

I grab my bag and lug it into the second bedroom, a sparsely decorated room (as if anything in Henry's house is even moderately decorated—it all looks like he ordered it right off the displays in furniture shops but left the geegaws behind—no pictures, no art, no whimsical window treatments.) A queen-size bed, matching teakwood dresser, chair. The closet is empty except for extra blankets on a shelf and a box with old sweaters and pants.

I'm exhausted. It's just as well I'm sleeping in here. Who knows what trouble I'd get into in Henry's bed? A gal has to sleep sometime.

The next day, Henry sends me flowers—a tasteful arrangement of yellow lilies with a card that says "Glad you decided to stay. All my love, Henry."

Yellow lilies mean "falsehood."

They might as well be the crystal ball I was hankering for. Now, instead of wondering about his other babes, I get to experience them up close and personal.

But let me back up and explain our living arrangements first.

The morning after our first night together as co-habitees, Henry wakes up, fixes a mean pot of coffee and heads off to work before I even know what day it is. When I finally awaken around nine, I splurge on a taxi to retrieve my things from Wendy's place and spend the morning talking about her plans.

She is dressed in a pink chenille bathrobe, her legs under her on her navy sofa, petting Trixie. I fix Wendy some breakfast—toast and coffee.

"You should get legal protection," I tell her.

"Why?" She sips at the coffee and nibbles halfheartedly on the toast. Her face is milky white and I suspect she was throwing up before I arrived.

"You never know with schmucks like Sam. He might decide down the road that he wants to be involved in junior's life after you've gone to the trouble of raising the little tyke."

"I wish you wouldn't call him that."

"A tyke?"

"No. A schmuck." She puts the half-eaten toast aside and wraps both hands around the mug. "If Sam's a schmuck, what does that make me? An idiot for falling for him?"

Yes! I want to scream. It's temporary idiocy, like temporary insanity. There's a cure! But it requires hard work and discipline—maybe I need to devise a flash-card system with photos of Sam on rectangles of stiff paper, and train Wendy to say "schmuck," "louse" or "jackass" as I hold up each one. That has to be the answer.

I keep these observations to myself. Instead, I say, "Okay, but if Sam isn't good to you, he wouldn't be good to your kid."

"Honey, I don't think I need to worry about Sam being anything to this kid. As far as he's concerned, it could be someone else's." She says it coldly with no hurt. Score one for Wendy.

"You mean…?"

"Yup. He asked me how he could be sure it was his."

"The…" Oops. Can't say that. But inwardly I shout it— the schmuck! The Czar of Schmucks!

"But when you were together," I say, redirecting my thoughts, "he never had any doubts, did he?" Huh! As if it matters.

"Not that I know of." She stretches out her long legs and yawns. "I don't care. I'm getting past it."

I know that's only partially true. I know she'll have moments of backsliding where she'll wish he would call and she'll be tempted to call him. Maybe it will happen when she hears the baby's heartbeat for the first time, or maybe it will come when she's lonely and afraid one night, or when some great-looking guy starts making eyes at her and she realizes that she'll have to tell him she's "with child" before she can get involved. Then she'll get all teary-eyed and just want to be loved and reach out for what she thought was love in the past.

"If you ever need to talk, don't hesitate to call me, Wen." I clear her plate away, wash the dishes in her sink, wipe down her counters and generally straighten her living room. Since I didn't really unpack when I "moved in" on Thursday, I only need to bring my suitcases to the foyer to "move out."

"You're a sweetheart, Ame. But you've got Henry now. Which, by the way, is fantastic." She leans on her elbow on the back of the sofa, looking into the hazy skyline. Heat has descended on the city as summer gets ready to roll in. It's mid-May but Baltimore will heat up and cool down this time of year like a broken thermostat.

"I don't know if I'd call it fantastic," I tell her, "but it's definitely convenient."

She gives me a good-natured scowl. "Henry is promising material. Don't let the past color the future."

"It's not like I expect all my boyfriends to die on me, you know," I say defensively.

"That's not what I mean. I know you still hurt—you'd be crazy if you didn't. Don't let that hurt keep you from appreciating something good, even if it's something different from what you had with Rick."

I pretend to busy myself checking the latches on my suitcase. "Call anytime if you need me, Wen. Middle of the night. Wee hours. Anytime."

She looks at me and smiles. "Thanks." Then she gets up and stretches with her arms above her head. Her robe falls open a hair, revealing her clingy satin spaghetti-strap nightie, one I'm sure she bought with Sam in mind. It shows off the outline of her abdomen. Wendy is going to be one of those pregnant women who glows. If I ever get pregnant, I'm sure I'll be one that bloats.

"I'll get dressed and drive you back," she offers. "You can't lug Trixie there in a taxi. Besides, I'd like to see Henry's place. It will be fun."

It does turn out to be fun. Henry's condo is nothing to

sneeze at and she's suitably impressed. When I drag my bags into the spare bedroom, though, she stands in the hallway with her mouth open and eyes wide.

"Why are you putting your stuff in here?" she asks.

"Because it will be neater this way."

"You mean he doesn't have room in his closet for your stuff?"

"No, I mean I'm not sure just where this relationship is going. He offered to take me in while I get on my feet. I thought that if I had my own room, it would be more like a business relationship."

Wendy laughs out loud, a quick bark of a laugh. Even though it's at my expense, I'm glad to hear it.

"Amy," she says as if she's talking to a child, "that has to be the silliest thing I ever heard. The man treats you well, is sympathetic, is unattached and has given you no reason whatsoever to suspect him of anything but good intentions—"

I snort but she disregards me and continues.

"Henry cares for you. It's nice. It's comfortable. It's sweet. Why can't you just accept that? It's pretty damn good."

I suppose after you've been with Sam the Schmuck even the smallest sign of affection can be interpreted in grand terms. Henry might care for me, but where on his "care" scale do I show up? Between his job and the sailboat he wants to own? Or am I even that high up on his "enjoy life" agenda?

"It's only been two weeks. I'm still getting to know him. I want to be cautious," I explain. "Come on, help me find a place for Trixie's litter box.

We wander around the condo and ultimately decide the litter box should go inside the door to the laundry. I had suggested inside Henry's closet but Wendy just rolled her eyes at that and moved on.

"You could really do some nice things with this place," she says, sitting at the kitchen table and looking around. "It's kind of empty and cold now."

"You want some cheese and crackers?" I ask, opening the refrigerator. That's about all Henry has in there—some French cheese, a quart of milk and a tomato.

"I should be going. Doctor's appointment at one."

"Do you want me to go with you?" I offer again.

Standing, she smiles. "Nope. I'll be okay. I'm getting used to the idea." She pulls her purse onto her shoulder and slides her sunglasses on her face. "I'll call you later and tell you how it goes."

"I'll be waiting. Don't forget—call anytime."

After she leaves, I sit at Henry's kitchen table, circling some want ads in Sunday's paper, and making a to-do list to aid my job-hunting strategies.

The condo development is quiet since everyone who lives in it probably works all day, and for a few moments I start to worry that I might miss some important news so I turn on CNN in the living room and watch an audience of folks give opinions on subjects they know little about.

Later I watch the *Baby Story* on TLC, and get all misty-eyed thinking of Wendy going through labor and delivery in about eight months' time. Finally, I half doze through *Trading Spaces* where some New York designer makes a mess of a clueless suburban couple's dining room, putting dried eggshells on the walls and plastic wrap on the ceiling. Hmm…maybe if I ever get mad at Henry I could do that to his dining room.

At five, I wander into the kitchen and put on a pot of coffee, wondering if I should get something for dinner or if Henry has plans for us.

By six, I'm on my fourth cup of coffee and I have an epiphany. I am in one of my cotton sundresses. It has a small floral print. The very kind of print you can imagine on what used to be called "housecoats"—the kind of robelike things our grandmothers used to wear around the house.

Yes, I have already become Henry's "little woman"! In less than twenty-four hours! And like the little woman, I wait. And wait and wait and wait. When he doesn't show up by eight, I walk to a nearby deli and grab a turkey sandwich, only eating half of it. My dry, angry throat can't swallow it easily.

Henry eventually appears; it's nearly nine o'clock and I'm feeling like my mother with a thousand resentful questions straining to pop out. Through gritted teeth I ask him if he's had anything to eat.

He tells me he had dinner with a prospective client and that he'd tried to call me but I wasn't in, and he goes to the fridge for some bottled water.

Then I ask who the client is. And he tells me "Diana Malvani." Ah, yes. Diana. One of the flower babes.

So as revenge, I tell him I thought it would be best to keep this move-in thing a businesslike arrangement.

"What do you mean?" he asks, staring at me over the water. He looks mighty fine tonight in a tired sort of way. His white shirt is wrinkled, his tie askew. He looks like he needs a hug. I restrain myself. It isn't hard.

"I don't think I should be a kept woman," I say, and add a little laugh to lighten the mood. It does not resonate, so I move on. "And we've hardly known each other, so I thought it would be best if I took over that spare bedroom."

I had planned on saying this in a "so there" kind of voice that would communicate instantly that if he expects a deeper relationship he should speak now or forever hold his peace.

But he says nothing, so I continue to babble on, improvising. Not a good thing with me. I get into trouble when I do this. Remembering how I wanted to help out around Gina's house to pay her back for room and board, I hear myself telling Henry that I will do things like "fix dinner, clean and grocery shop to earn my keep."

Why don't I just hang one of those decorative flags by the door while I'm at it—something with daisies and sunflowers embroidered on it, and oh yeah, maybe the message "Little woman and proud of it."

If I expect my offer to move into the spare bedroom to force him to his knees sobbing for me to sleep with him every night, I am sorely disappointed. In fact, I have miscalculated big time. And I should have known better. Henry Castle is a poker-faced lawyer. He's used to not letting people know how he feels. So no emotion registers on his wide sexy face except maybe—if his lip twitching upward a hair on the right side of his face is any indication—amusement.

"Okay," he says. He opens the freezer, doesn't see anything he wants, and closes it again.

"I have an account at Atlantic Food Mart," he announces. "You'll get back on your feet soon. Don't worry." He punches me in the arm like a buddy after a big win on the soccer field.

Thus ends our conversation. Henry heads to the bathroom and I head to "my" room. A few minutes later, I hear the television blaring in his room and I want to go watch it with him but don't want to be the first one to seek the other out.

Willpower is not my strong suit, though. I think of a question to ask him so I poke my face into his room.

"Why don't you make a grocery list and I'll go tomorrow. You're kind of low on things," I say, standing in the doorway. He's leaning back on his bed, legs crossed at the ankles, hands behind his head, his shirt unbuttoned.

"Sounds good."

"Whatcha watching?"

"Just flipping." He lands on an old *Law and Order*.

"I love that show." I drift into the room and sit next to him. He stays on that channel and we watch the show together and then we're in bed together and he's got his arm around me. Just call me "LW" for short.

The phone rings and I answer it, being careful to say "Castle residence." It's Wendy. The first thing she does is apologize for not calling earlier.

"I had to go to the drugstore after the doctor's, then I bought some groceries and came home and took a long nap," she says. She sounds happy. Not trying-to-make-the-best-of-it happy, but really happy.

When Henry realizes the call is for me, he gets up and goes into the kitchen.

"So, how did it go?" I ask.

"It was great," she says with excitement in her voice. "He told me everything looks good and he gave me some pamphlets to read and a prescription for vitamins. And while I was at the drugstore I bought this neat book on pregnancy and what to expect. I only have to go to the doctor's once a month until the end and then it will be every week. I'll have a sonogram next time and some other tests."

"Wow. That's wonderful." It really is. I'm not lying. I remember the baby show I watched that afternoon and how the women on it were so excited but surrounded by loved ones—including the father. Wendy won't have that.

"Do you want me to be your coach?" I ask. "You know—Lamaze?"

"I haven't even thought about that, but yeah, I was going to mention it. If it's not too much trouble."

"No trouble at all! It will be good practice for me. Gina wants to get pregnant, you know." But Gina has Fred and as soon as I say Gina's name, I realize that Wendy doesn't need to hear about a couple going through this together, and I realize that Wendy's probably thinking the same thing and I don't want to squelch her joy so I rack my brain trying to think of something else to say.

"Just let me know the schedule," I quickly add. "Since I'll probably still be out of work, I'm sure anything will be okay!" I mean this to sound self-deprecating but instead it comes off as self-pitying. Try again.

"You'll have to come over for dinner one night—with Henry and me." Ah, here I'm on safer ground—the turf of the "little woman." I'm beginning to wonder if I missed the name of this condo development and if "Stepford" is in the title; I'm beginning to get an itch to join a gardening club.

Wendy chats some more, actually reading a few passages from her pamphlets about what the baby's development is like during the first couple months. Her elation warms me. Shortly afterward I get off the phone and Henry returns to the room. My previous ire has evaporated.

"Everything okay with her?" he asks, coming back to bed.

"Yeah. Just great, in fact. She's doing really, really well."

He puts his arm around me again and we watch some more TV, like an old married couple with time-tested habits. And I don't go back to "my" room. Instead, I stay with him all night. Like sleeping over, except I live in the same condo. So much for my business arrangement and safeguarding my heart.

chapter 15

Holly: Domestic happiness

It probably won't surprise you to know that I was never a "go-getter." While I found my work at the Gelman Agency very fulfilling, I didn't see myself working there indefinitely. The problem was, I wasn't sure where I saw myself working indefinitely. Right before my first Christmas with Rick, the Gelman Agency laid off some employees. I've never understood why companies wait until before the holidays to lay people off. It seems so Dickensian. As a junior staffer, I was afraid my name would be added to the list. Rick thought my worries were unfounded. And even if I was let go, he said, he'd support me until I found something else. Maybe it was the cozy holiday spirit, or the fact this was my first Christmas with him, but the prospect of being a Domestic Goddess started to appeal to me, and made me want to appear on that layoff list. When it was clear Gelman was keeping me, I was disappointed.

I am beginning to think this will be my "Summer of Henry."

Sometimes I sleep in "my" bed. Most of the time I sleep in Henry's. I keep my things in the spare room, though, which becomes a symbol, to me at least, of the fact that our lives are still separate, not blended in the way my life was with Rick's.

Maybe moving in with Henry generates good luck, though, because within two weeks I snag a job. I can hardly believe it. It was so easy I should have been suspicious right away, but I was in a state of blind euphoria, finally getting something I wanted and needed with little effort. I thought the tide had changed and my planets were aligned. I thought maybe Tess had gone on vacation.

Speaking of Tess, my new job entails driving past her apartment every day. In fact, it entails driving out to the country from whence I came. I used to drive into the city for a job. Now I do the opposite. Life is funny.

Here's how it happened—remember that college's PR opening I called about? In a panic about my future, I phone the college from the flower shop a week after moving in with Henry. Eureka! They are just getting ready to post the job, and the secretary very helpfully reads me the job description over the phone. Assistant public relations director is the title, and I begin to think that "assistant" is just my speed right now as I jump back into the real employment pool. I burble on about my credentials and the secretary is so impressed, she says, "You know, they want to fill this right away. Let me put you through to my boss." And before you can say "too good to be true," I have an interview scheduled for that afternoon.

I don't want to call Henry at work because I'm afraid I'll jinx it. But I need to borrow his car to get out to the college, so I end up calling him, anyway. I'm vague about why.

"I need to, uh, run some errands," I say.

"There's an extra set of keys in the top drawer of my dresser," he responds, not knowing that I already know that from my previous glance through his things. Then he tells me where he's parked in his firm's garage. His firm is only a few blocks away from his condo. He could walk to work, but he sometimes needs the car for "appointments." When he first explained that to me, I imagined him with some of his flower babes. But I can't think about that now. Note to self: worry about Henry's fidelity later.

Getting a car isn't my only problem. I have to get clothes, too. All I have now are leisure clothes—a sundress, khaki capris, shorts, a bathing suit. Oh, and my leopard-print thong. Not exactly job-interview material. My old business clothes are out of date—those I haven't given to Goodwill—and I packed the rest of them away when I moved.

I scramble to reach Wendy to see if I can borrow something, but don't get her until nearly an hour and a half before my appointment. So, I've resigned myself to stopping at a mall on the way out of the city and buying the first decent staid suit I see. I'm getting ready to trudge up to Henry's parking garage when the phone rings and it's Wendy, returning my three calls.

After I explain my predicament, she urges me to stick with plan B. "You don't have many office things anymore, right?" she asks. And I can tell she's distracted by work and probably doesn't want to have to meet me at her apartment so I can shop in her closet.

"Stop at Hecht's on the way out of town. I saw a great little summer suit in their window. Sage-green military-cut jacket."

And a military price tag, too, is my guess. Wendy doesn't look at price tags much.

But it's clear I'm not going to convince Wendy to help

me with plan A, so I reconcile myself to using my charge card, which is already approaching red alert.

"Call me and tell me what happens," she says before I rush off the phone.

Rushing is the word of the day. It takes me ten minutes longer to get to the parking garage than I'd figured, and an extra five to find the car because it isn't exactly where Henry said he'd parked it. Then, traffic is heavy on North Charles. (Need I tell you exactly where? Let's just say it's around the residence of a certain someone, a certain someone whose initials are T. W.)

And I find the sage-green suit at Hecht's, all right, but I can either buy it in a size 16 or a size 2, neither of which fits. With just a half hour to go and a twenty-minute drive still facing me, I hurriedly pick out a floral-print dress that looks like a Sunday-go-to-meeting frock worn in prairie country, and pair it with an unlined cotton tan jacket. Hey— they fit and I'm in a hurry.

I arrive at the college, sweating, so I reapply my makeup in the car, dropping my lipstick, which leaves a smudge on the second page of my résumé. "Oh, shit," I say out loud, just as a white-veiled nun walks by the car.

Smudged résumé in hand, I head into the administration building, a two-story white brick building with a huge cross painted above the front door.

The nun who passed me on the way in happens to be the college president, Sister Mary Altamont, whose white hair matches the color of her short veil. She gestures to a seat in her office, looks over my résumé silently, and does not acknowledge the fact that she heard me cursing in the parking lot. Hell—I mean, hey—maybe she even lets a vulgarity loose on occasion, right? Looking into her green eyes, I decide she doesn't.

"We're eager to fill the position as quickly as possible," she says, smiling at me. "We're an institution in a state of transition, you see, and we can't waste time. When I heard you called, it seemed like a gift from heaven."

I'm not used to thinking of myself as someone else's gift from heaven, but I smile back, hoping I remembered to brush my teeth before leaving the condo.

She tells me a little about the college and their "vision for the future," which sounds suspiciously like just staying afloat. Then she calls in Karen Armstrong, the director of public relations, so they can both talk to me before I head off to a private interview with Karen herself.

When Karen comes in the room, I almost laugh out loud. She's wearing the exact same dress I have on. But paired with a navy-blue jacket.

Tall and big-boned, with short brown hair and gray eyes, Karen is very serious. I'm not even sure she notices I have on the same dress. Heck, I'm not sure she sees me in the room. She sits in the chair next to me and asks Sister Mary if she had a chance to review the galleys on the fund-raising brochure.

"Not yet," Sister Mary says, smiling. I'm beginning to sense that Sister Mary smiles at everything. Earthquakes. Meteor showers. First-degree murder.

Speaking of murder, Karen's voice implies that's what she'd like to do. "If you don't look at it soon, we'll miss the deadline," Karen says testily. "And the whole program will be pushed back. It will be too late."

"Oh, dear," Sister Mary says, and starts rummaging around on her desk, obviously looking for the copy. "This is why we need to hire someone right away. Too much to do!" She finally finds what she's looking for, which seems to be the signal for Karen to stand.

"If you could get it back to me by three, I can work late—again—and get it to the printer on my way home." Karen turns to leave and I look at Sister Mary for some cue as to whether I should follow Karen to my private interview. Sister Mary smiles. That's good enough for me. Grabbing my purse, I stand and thank Sister Mary for her time, shake her hand and rush out to the anteroom to catch up with Ms. Armstrong.

She's standing in front of a secretary's desk, growling out orders about a newsletter's mistakes. The secretary says nothing but her eyes narrow incrementally with each lash of Karen's tongue until they're nothing but narrow slits. I swear the secretary's getting ready to growl back.

As soon as Karen moves away from the desk, I step forward.

"Sister Mary said we should talk," I say. Then I smile. Maybe this is the language.

Karen grimaces, then looks at her watch. "Okay. Come on in. I have about ten minutes."

After she ushers me into her office it's clear she doesn't want to spare five, let alone ten minutes on me. Her desk is piled high with papers and I recognize pre-press blue lines for several publications, paper samples, media directories and the college's catalog with Post-it notes sticking out of virtually every page. Her phone rings almost instantly and she spends half of our time together arguing with what is obviously a direct-mail consultant on why she won't use his services again and how he can take the college to court if he wants his full fee after bollixing up some recent job. When she hangs up, she smiles for the first time, a quick, satisfied grin, the kind favored by the evil stepmother after putting Snow White to sleep.

"That's what you get when you use the discount guys," she says as a way of explaining. "Shoddy work."

"Who was it?" I ask, trying to sound pleasantly curious.

She names a mail house I'm familiar with, one I used to work with from time to time and had no problems with.

"Benny Mancuso is the contact I used to work with there," I say in recognition. "He's great." When I see Karen's irritated face, it's clear she was talking to Benny and didn't think he was great at all.

"Uh," I say, clearing my throat, "of course, businesses change. Haven't done business with him in a couple years." Uh-oh, don't want to go there—to the couple-year drought in my career.

Instead, I launch into an explanation of my publications experience. She nods her head impatiently, doesn't ask a single question, then stands abruptly when I take a breath before going on.

"Well, thanks for coming by." She extends her hand for me to shake. "I'm sure we'll be talking to you soon."

Convinced I won't be hearing anything from them except perhaps a postcard telling me the position's been filled, I head back to the condo angry and dejected. Driving away from the campus, I have to screech to a halt when some students run in front of the car on the way to the tennis courts. I don't know if I want this job even if they want me.

When I get home, I'm discouraged and irritable. I grab the phone and call Henry to let him know where I left the car in the garage.

"Why didn't you just wait and come pick me up at six?" he asks, sounding amused.

"I thought you'd want to, you know, drive yourself," I say. Of course I'd thought of picking him up. But it seems like a big step, a familiarity I don't want to take without permission. Or maybe I was just afraid I'd see some of the Squires folks.

Then I tell him about the crazy interview, and he says it sounds like I'm better off without the job.

"Something will come along," he promises.

As soon as I put down the phone, it rings again and it's

Sister Mary offering me the job. I'm so flabbergasted that I ask her why it's all so sudden even before I thank her for the offer.

"We told you," she reiterates, the smile still in her voice. "We want to fill the position very quickly. No time to lose."

All of this should be ringing alarm bells loud and clear. But my alarm bells don't work from lack of use. They've been overridden by my internal PA system squawking out that I better get a job and quick or I'll be dependent on Henry, or homeless.

So when she says "no time to lose," the PA system starts echoing that and I'm asking her when I start.

"You can come in tomorrow and begin by filling out some paperwork." She doesn't ask if I can. She tells me I can. I don't argue. It's a job.

When I get off the phone, I don't know if going in tomorrow to fill out paperwork will mean I actually start work then or just, well, fill out papers.

But I can't worry about that. I have other things to worry about. Like a work wardrobe. I wonder if I can still borrow some things from Wendy. I try to reach her again to no avail. She's in a meeting. I try to reach Henry to tell him the good news but he's in a meeting, too. I call Gina to let her know and half expect her to be in a meeting, too, but she's there. We've only touched base briefly since I moved in with Henry, though, and it's clear she's stored up a bunch of questions, so she's more interested in my moving in than with the new job, and we spend most of the time talking about that.

"I've been thinking some more about you and Henry," she says. "It's just that it's kind of sudden. He must really like you."

"It's not like that," I say. "He's just doing me a favor because Wendy's allergic to cats."

"A guy doesn't ask you to move in to do you a favor," she says incredulously. "I'm amazed you were willing to commit to him so soon. You've been so tentative."

"I'm not committing to anything!" I protest. "I'm renting his spare room, that's all."

"Renting?"

"Yeah. Like a boarder." I am making this up on the instant but I like the way it sounds. The word *committing* had me scared there for an instant. Henry's not committing to anything. Not serial-flower-sender Henry. And I'm not going to be the first one to ante up my heart. Note to self: tell Henry you intend to pay him rent.

"Well, that sounds weird," she says. "He gets you to pay rent *and* have a relationship at the same time?" Translation: why should he buy the cow when you're paying him to take the milk?

"He's not getting me to do anything. I'm volunteering to do it. It's, well, neater this way. Like you said, we've hardly known each other." Unless you're calculating in love-affair time. Like dog years, remember?

"I don't know…"

"I thought you liked Henry."

"I do, I do," she says, ruminating. "I just don't want you setting the wrong tone." Translation: why should he buy the cow when he can make the cow dance to his tune, *and* pay him to take the milk?

"Well, I'll have to have you over—you and Fred—to dinner," I tell her. Yup—that should make her feel better. Seeing us together, the picture of domesticity. Ms. Cow and her friend. I see myself at the stove, an apron embroidered with Little Woman tied around my waist.

"No, me first. I said I'd have you and Henry over."

Then we start talking about food and what she's cooking for dinner (beef stroganoff with sugar snap peas and citrus salad.) By the time we get off the phone, she's said a total of two words about my new job—"that's great."

If I expect Henry to be more enthusiastic, I'm disappointed.

He comes home a little before seven, yelling up the stairs, "Honey, I'm home!" with a laugh in his voice. But when he comes into the kitchen where I'm drinking a reviving cup of tea, he looks at the cold stove as if he'd really expected me to be at it stirring a pot, dressed in that frilly apron with the embroidery.

"There's nothing in the fridge," I say.

He nods his head, then opens the door to make sure I'm telling the truth. "We can go out," he tells me. I half expect him to give me a little peck on the cheek.

"Yeah, I need to go out," I tell him. "I need to get some clothes." And I proceed to tell him the story of the job offer. While I do so, his eyes narrow and his brows come together.

"They offered you the job this afternoon?" he asks skeptically.

"You don't think I'm good enough?"

"It's not that. It usually takes longer. And let's face it— you've been working outside your field for a couple years. They must have candidates who are working in public relations already."

"I don't think they interviewed anyone else."

He raises his eyebrows and peers at me with wide eyes. "What kind of outfit is it?"

"A small liberal arts college in northern Baltimore County," I say. "Our Lady of the Glade College."

He laughs. "A college named after an air freshener?" He opens the fridge again and pulls out a water, unscrewing the cap with one movement of his fingers.

"It's not named after the air freshener, silly," I say, but of course I'd thought the same thing when I'd heard it. "And it's been around since 1943 or something. Started as a small all-girls teachers' college, then went co-ed in 1975. Only has an enrollment of twenty-five hundred."

"I don't think I've ever heard of them," he says, swigging back some water. "What's the student body like?"

"Uh, locals, mostly commuters. Some Pennsylvania students," I murmur, then change the subject. I don't want to delve too far into this topic. One of the things I learned about the college as I asked polite questions during my interview with Sister Mary was that the average SAT score of incoming freshmen is only a shade above what you get for just filling your name out right on the score sheet. But hey— they have to go somewhere, right? And maybe Our Lady of the Air Freshener College is the place where they can learn and live in peace.

"I need to go shopping for office clothes," I tell him. "And stop by Wendy's. She might lend me some stuff. I thought we could grab a bite while we're out."

"Sounds good to me."

While he changes, I try Wendy but she's not home yet, so I leave a message that I got the job, and that Henry and I might be by later, and I'll call her when we're on our way. If nothing else, this should keep her from having Sam over. I'm not convinced she's completely given him the boot.

Since no stores are open in the city at night, Henry drives us to a mall in the suburbs, but it's not one I'm familiar with. Away from my natural shopping habitat, I have trouble adjusting. I buy only a few outfits—a navy blue suit, which I immediately regret because it might make me look like a nun, and a herringbone jacket and camel slacks.

Shopping with Henry is a new experience, too, that makes me a wee bit uneasy. He's patient but opinionated. When I hold out a gray silk pantsuit, he wrinkles up his nose as if he's smelled something bad. "Too plain," he declares. Then

I remember that Tess wore gray silk to the law gala and I smile smugly to myself.

I top off our evening of credit-card max-out by buying a too-expensive white cotton blouse to complete my nun look, and a pair of burgundy loafers with tassels. We grab a slice of pizza in the food court, and I feel really comfortable with all this—sitting with Henry at one of the wrought-iron tables with shoppers to the left of us and shoppers to the right of us. I quickly banish the thought.

On the way back to the condo, I try Wendy on the cell phone. When she picks up, she's groggy. I've awakened her.

"It's only nine o'clock," I say by way of apology.

"I'm bushed."

"Then I guess this isn't a good time to stop by."

"Well…"

"I'll come by tomorrow. I'll stop by after work, okay?"

"Okay. You'll have to tell me about this job, kiddo. Congratulations. That's got to be a record."

It isn't until we arrive home that I realize I have not told Fred that I have a new job and won't even be pretending to work at the flower shop the next day! Sure, I told Gina, but I didn't specifically tell her to tell Fred. And besides, I should do that, not her. I should be professional.

As soon as we get home, I call Fred's office, knowing he won't be there. But I leave a cheery message on his voice mail about the PR job, telling him I'll be happy to stop by the shop on Saturdays for a while to keep things on track until it shuts down for good.

But of course I'm not back on track. And it doesn't take long for me to completely derail. My job sucks. Big time.

The morning of my first day starts inauspiciously with a coffee stain on my new white blouse and a spat with Henry. Hmm…maybe we are beginning to act like an old married couple, after all, jumping over the whole courtship and wedding ceremony to the annoying rows.

As I change my outfit, Henry pops his head in the door of the spare bedroom and tells me he needs to get going. I'm dropping him off at work so I can borrow his car. God knows how I'll get to work without it since I have to drive nearly forty minutes to get to the college.

"I'm almost ready," I say, dragging out the floral dress again. I don't have a clean blouse to wear with the suit or the skirt. When I appear in the hallway a few seconds later, Henry looks at me funny, but he can't put his finger on what's wrong. I don't tell him.

After we hit the road, he takes issue with my driving, which is a sensitive topic with me to begin with. He tells me what lane to get in and when, and he visibly cringes when I take a too-fast turn onto Charles and screech to a halt in front of his building.

He asks me to either pick him up or drop off the car by six. Then, before he gets out, he says, "You know, you should make sure this job is really worth it."

"Look, I'm sorry I need the car," I say, exasperated. Traffic is behind me, and I'm afraid I'll get stuck in a jam near Tess's and be late. "I'll go car-shopping this weekend, okay?"

"It's not about the car." His hand rests on the door handle. "You shouldn't be taking the first thing that comes along. It might not be up to your standards."

"What standards? My standards are I'm out of work and broke!" I look in the rearview and see a minivan careening around me. "Besides, I thought you'd be happy for me."

"I'm glad you found something so quickly. But if it turns out to be a bad fit, you're no better off than you were before. You could be worse off, in fact. Stuck in a bad job and no time to job hunt. At least at the flower shop you had flexibility—to job hunt."

"I have to get going."

"So do I. See ya." He smiles and leaves and I seethe all the way up Charles Street. Why didn't he say something last night? Why did he wait until the first day of my new job to rain on my parade?

But last night, after our shopping spree, we celebrated my new job in a different way. Shivers compete with my white-hot seething.

By the time I make my way to Our Lady of the Air Freshener, I'm in a foul mood, and not just because there was a detour around 3900 Charles because of road work. Here I landed a job back in my old field in the space of a few days and nobody seems to be celebrating with me. Gina's good wishes were perfunctory. Henry is skeptical. And Wendy was too tired to care. If they don't care, why should I?

Why should I care fast becomes my theme song. After I fill out the requisite papers in the Human Resources office, I head up to the communications suite to report for duty.

When I interviewed with Karen Armstrong, it was in her office, a modest-size room with an airy view of the campus. I assumed that my office would be a nice bright little room next to hers that had seemed unoccupied when I'd come in. But I was wrong. Boy, was I wrong.

Turns out that office really belongs to the PR secretary, Irene Slayson. While she gets the great view of rolling farmland and interstate, I get a far corner of a narrow closetlike room with a thin dirty window stuck high in the wall. My work space consists of an L-shaped desk. If I roll my chair back an inch too far, I'm jammed in the neck by the edge of a drafting table. If I roll it an inch too far to the left, my elbow smacks a long table spread with mass-mailing materials that volunteers handle almost every day.

An attractive woman in her late fifties, Irene shows me to my abode and helps me boot up the computer.

"I didn't know they were hiring anyone," she says, eyeing me as if I'm pulling a fast one on her. "That's a shocker."

Irene disappears and works all day on jobs for Karen, who doesn't put in an appearance until after lunch. She zooms past my closet with a quick glance in my direction but does not return to give me assignments. So I seek her out and suggest that I get started on the employee newsletter which I'd like to redesign. I spent all morning reading old issues and already know what I want to do to make it better. It won't take much.

She nods and grunts out an okay, then holds up her hand for me to wait while she rummages through piles of papers until she finds a couple folders.

"Here," she says, handing them to me. "This is information on upcoming events, things of interest. Do some press releases on them."

I head back to my office and see that other chickens have taken up roost there. Three silver-haired women in polyester pantsuits sit at the long table. When I come in, they smile brightly. The one nearest my computer speaks up.

"Are we supposed to finish labeling these?" She holds up an alumni magazine that is about six months old.

"Uh…"

"Or should we work on the annual campaign letter?" The one in the middle holds that up as well. I notice it is more recent than the magazine—only two months old.

"Well…"

"I thought we were supposed to do something new today," the third one says.

I plop my files down on my desk and search out Irene, but she has vanished. Irene seems to vanish fairly frequently. Karen's gone as well, so I return to the closet that I now share with three other women who smell of Jean Naté and Prince Matchabelli, and I tell them they should just do whatever they had been doing the last time they were in.

When I sit down and start to look at the press release file, they bombard me with other questions.

"Are you new here?"

"Did you go to school at the college?"

"Are you married?"

"I have a nephew who just moved into town."

It's a steady stream of chatter. When they aren't talking to me, they talk to one another. One has rheumatoid arthritis and is taking shark bone every night. Another has hemorrhoids and sticks with good ol' Preparation H, and the third is seeing her eye doctor about cataracts the next day.

I am certifiable by the end of the day. If I thought I was nuts before, this job will seal the deal. I get nothing accomplished. My office is a cell. And no one seems to care that I'm working there.

When I pick up Henry, however, I plaster a smile on my face and tell him the work is great, my boss is a dream, and I really like working on a college campus. At least the last part's true. We order in Chinese and I call Wendy and tell her I don't need to borrow any clothes. I'll make do with what I have. Hell, I might even wear the coffee-stained blouse tomorrow. No one will notice, I'm sure. I hit the sack at nine-thirty. A bad job can wear you out.

The next day is no better. But at least I start picking up a rhythm. The volunteers seem to appear in the afternoon, so I work feverishly in the morning in order to allow for the interruptions after lunch.

The work itself, by the way, is mind-numbing. At least at the flower shop, I had scads of free time to daydream and feel sorry for myself. Here, my time is occupied with tasks that sear every imaginative brain cell from my head.

I write press releases about the college's anniversary. I write newsletter stories about how our English department chair gave a talk at her local church on "Understanding the

Subjunctive." I ghost-write speeches for our president, Sister Mary Altamont, extolling the virtues of the college, scrupulously avoiding the fact that we're not attracting new students, that our current students are all kids who probably should be repeating high school, and how our outstanding loans are about to default and our fund-raising campaign has gone down the toilet because the development director quit in a huff the week before.

Which kind of explains why they hired me so quickly. I have to spend half my time writing fund-raising letters and grant proposals, something I've never done before. In one of her rare appearances in the office, Karen shows me how to use the boilerplate information on the college and tweak it for each new grant possibility.

I suspect Karen is job hunting. Once, when I go into her office, she's not there (no surprise) but her résumé is up on her computer screen. And I've overheard her scheduling an interview.

You see, another drawback of my office is that no one bothered to hook up a phone for me. The phone on my desk is a party line with Karen's. If she's on the line, I can't use it. And if I'm on the line, she just punches away at the keypad, ignoring my pleas to stop. I've picked up the phone a few times when she's been talking to Human Resources offices about job responsibilities.

Turns out Karen's not the only one looking. The day after I arrive, the admissions director leaves for a job in Kentucky. And the dean of students is scheduled to head for greener pastures in Louisiana by the end of the month. Those are just the ones who've made their plans public. According to Irene, the registrar is going to retire soon and the secretary to both the Athletics and Chaplain's offices will announce her intention to take maternity leave in a month when she starts showing.

I'm on a sinking ship. They must have mistakenly thought I was a life preserver when they hired me. Have I put on weight? I wonder. Note to self: don't wear white.

That Friday, Sister Mary steps into my closet and grills me about corporate communications strategies and it becomes clear that they think because I worked in the business world, I must have some amazing savvy, that I will be able to design a public relations program that creates an image of success that leads to success itself. They think I have some goddamned magic wand. She stares at me and says cryptically, "Well, you'll think of something" and smiles even more broadly. I feel like I'm in the *Lilies of the Field* movie.

I might be good, but I'm not that good. Nobody is. So I tactfully point out to Sister Mary that sending press releases out every day announcing even the smallest occurrence at the college won't save our butts. In fact, sending out too many releases of the type that we're sending—announcing personnel changes—telegraphs the very opposite message. She purses her lips together, nods, says "Hmm…" and leaves, nearly tripping over a stack of old alumni magazines.

The job leaves me bushed and irritable, but damned if I'll tell Henry that. He just figures it's PMS. Friday night, Fred calls me to ask if I'm going into the flower shop the next day as I "promised." Groaning, I say yes. So much for a languid weekend curled up with a good book or a good Henry. Or going car shopping. Henry frowns when I tell him.

"I'm going to have to have my car back eventually," he says as I drink herbal tea wrapped in my terry-cloth robe in the kitchen. He's annoyed with me to begin with because I don't want to go out tonight. I'm beat, I tell ya! I'd fall asleep at a movie, and yawn my way through an expensive dinner. I'm out like a light at ten while he watches tennis. No need to worry about that "owning the cow" business. Henry's getting no milk from me.

★ ★ ★

On Monday, the car situation for Henry begins to look up. The ship of Our Lady of the Air Freshener is headed for the iceberg with deadly precision.

Karen is leaving. I don't find this out, though, until right before I'm about to leave for the day. As Mrs. Kliegle, one of the volunteers, packs up her purse to vamoose, she looks at me over the top of her reading glasses and says, "Are you going to apply for the director's job now that Karen's gone?"

"Huh?"

"What an opportunity for you. You should take it," Mrs. Kliegle continues.

"Well, I…where exactly was it that Karen went?" Come to think of it, Karen didn't come in at all today.

"Skidmore. My grandson told me this weekend. He said it was in the employee newsletter."

After Kliegle leaves, I search out Irene, but she's as clueless as I am. I'd step into Sister Mary's office for a moment and ask her, but her door has been closed tight all day and her secretary has been transferring in a series of calls from bankers. I hear Sister Mary's voice now from behind the door saying things like "The end of the week? Well, we thought we'd have more time…."

So on Tuesday, I become acting director of public relations, a title that would look good on my résumé if I held it for more than four days, which I am not destined to do because on Wednesday, Sister Mary Altamont asks me into her office, quietly shuts the door and tells me she's going to need "every ounce of strength and wisdom" I have to give. She's not smiling any longer.

The college will not open for the coming academic year. Those bankers who called her were giving her the bad news on the financial situation. In a calm voice she explains how the college hasn't been able to keep up with the times, how a big gift from a deceased alumna was lost when heirs fought it and won in court, and how the college can barely meet payroll from week to week. By the time she's finished, I'm afraid she's going to start bawling. Her mouth is turned down into a sorry scowl, and her lips quiver along with her voice. I don't think I can handle a crying nun. It does not compute.

So I muster all my knowledge and energy and advise her on how to handle the announcement. Since Karen is gone, I have to arrange for a press conference, which we'll hold the very next day. Sister would have deferred, but if there's one thing I know it's bad news will find its way out faster than you can say "abandon ship." Better to make the announcement herself and control it than to have reporters nosing around *Sixty Minutes*-style if she delays.

I work overtime getting everything ready, and that night I tell Henry what the situation is. He doesn't say "I told you so," but he does raise his eyebrows, and then he tells me that maybe next time I'll wait for "something more suitable" to my skills, instead of "selling myself" too cheaply.

Huh! He's getting me for free! No, scratch that—I'd offered to share expenses. I'm paying him! Well, I won't be paying him for long.

Right after the press conference, which is a showcase for my media talents, by the way, Sister Mary Altamont calls me into her office again. She spends a quarter hour profusely thanking me for setting it all up so well, and I'm beginning to think this is a prelude to giving me a bonus when she tells me I'll be let go at the end of the week because they're only going to be using a skeleton crew as they shut down the college. Last in, first out.

Mrs. Kliegle and the other volunteers give me an Avon gold-toned cross necklace as a parting gift. Apparently, they knew I'd be leaving before I did.

When I come home bedraggled and depressed on Friday night, my arms full of press releases for my portfolio, Henry gives me a hug.

"Something will break for you soon," he says.

What does that mean? Ice will break so I can move forward? Or china will shatter on my head?

"Let's go out to eat," he says. "I'm too tired to cook. And you look beat, too."

We've eaten out or gotten carryout virtually every night since I began my job, but I don't protest. I wouldn't have the strength to scramble an egg tonight.

Later, I lie down on the bed in the spare room just to "rest my eyes a bit." When I awaken at three in the morning, a coverlet has been pulled over my shoulders and the lights are out. That Henry. Maybe he's not so bad.

chapter 16

Thornless rose: Early attachment

*Even before you make a commitment to a guy, he can sting.
On my fifth date with Rick, we both started talking about
earlier relationships. The fact that we could open up to each
other so quickly was a sign of how compatible we were, how
few games we were playing. It felt good to tell him about my
high school sweetheart (who dumped me after going off to college) and the ones I dated during my own undergraduate years,
including Ted Brinkley, a history major I actually considered
marrying for a while (not that he'd asked me). But when it
was Rick's turn to share and he told me about his law school
flame, Sally Chessman, it didn't feel so good. It pricked. That
was when I knew I was falling in love with him. And that
was the night we first made love—at my place, to the accom-
paniment of Tony Bennett on the CD player and the scent of
a rose-perfumed candle.*

Being jobless never felt so good.

In fact, after the Our Lady of the Air Freshener fiasco,

I've come to truly appreciate the up side of joblessness. Henry has his car to himself and I have, well, sleep. And I'm not *really* jobless because I can still work at the flower shop whenever I feel like it, selling off inventory—at least the silk flower arrangements—and closing the books, right? In fact, going into the flower shop is high on my priority list given how I've neglected it.

The down side is that blasted problem of having no income. I'm not even sure I can count on getting my paycheck from Our Lady, which Sister Mary told me should be mailed out "by the end of next week—hopefully." And Fred's client has put me on an "independent contractor" status, meaning I only get paid for the hours I work at the shop. I can hardly complain about that arrangement after my less-than-scrupulous attention to the store.

Henry makes it clear on Monday that he doesn't expect me to contribute to expenses until I "get back on my feet again." As much as I appreciate the offer, I don't enjoy feeling like a "kept woman." Oh, no, I'd much rather be the Little Woman who pays her keeper. Remember the cow?

"I'll cook," I say over breakfast. I'm still in my robe while Henry is pressed and combed, in a black pin-striped suit and blue shirt. Man he looks good. I run my fingers through my hair to neaten it. "No more carryout. It's the least I can do."

"Whatever," he says. But he gives me his Atlantic Food Mart card so I can buy groceries.

The first week of this new joblessness has me canceling Henry's cleaning service, scurrying around searching for dustballs, going to the market, cooking new gourmet recipes (some of which I get from Gina) and giving the want ads at least a cursory glance in the mornings, circling a few so that Henry will see the circles before he throws the newspaper in the recycling bin each night. Okay, and I send in a résumé from time to time as well.

When I call Fred on Monday to tell him I can put in a few more hours here and there, he tells me not to bother. The owner doesn't want to incur the expense and I did such a good job at the flower shop on Saturdays there's nothing left for me to do there. Translation: the owner thinks I'm a shirker and Fred agrees, but Gina convinced him to soften the blow.

So I settle into a new routine: one I'm familiar and comfortable with—drifting. Every morning, I go to the Atlantic Food Market five blocks away. Since I don't have a car, I can only shop for as much as I can carry at one time.

I go in the early morning because the June heat becomes absolutely unbearable by ten and the only people out are émigrés from Mars.

The Atlantic is one of those small city co-op deals where too few goods are crammed into too small a space and where gourmet foods squeeze out staples. You can't find Campbell's tomato soup but you can find five different varieties of imported hummus.

I'm sure if I asked where the toaster strudel is they'd start murmuring incantations and sprinkling me with Evian.

The help is leftover hippie and you need a membership card to buy goods. The whole idea, I gather as I pick out plum tomatoes and bulgur wheat, is to create a market that isn't a slave to corporate culture, that supports family farms and free-range chickens and the sixties politics of Ben & Jerry's ice cream. Note to Atlantic Market owners: Ben & Jerry's sold out to a multinational corp a few years ago.

One morning when the store is actually crowded, I overhear one of the multiple-pierced cashiers complaining about an odor in the store.

"You know, it smells like something I can't quite put my

finger on. It's like when I went to Disney World last year. That smell."

Uh, the smell of people, perhaps?

Anyway, I'm learning to cook this haute cuisine stuff and Henry actually compliments me a few times, telling me "this one's a keeper" as he points to his scraped-clean plate.

I don't know if it's the food or living with Henry, but my headaches have receded. The last time I had one, actually, was that day at the hospital.

If ever I come close to riding the headache wave, though, it's the nights when Henry is late. After a one-week hiatus where Henry was home virtually every evening by seven at the latest, he starts staying out late about three nights a week or so, and each time he says it's because of a meeting with a prospective client. Yes, he warned me that this would happen. When I was borrowing his car, he told me we'd have to work something out soon because he hoped to get back into some after-work meetings digging up new business. I just hadn't realized precisely what he'd meant by "digging up new business."

But I learn to cope. Oh, yes.

I manage to suppress my little-woman urges to throw rapid-fire questions at him on these occasions. In fact, I have developed an actual coping strategy. I watch television, regularly checking the window to see if he is arriving home. When I catch his car pulling in, I head for "my" room and pretend I'm asleep.

Henry is on to this game, though, and it backfires on me. Knowing I'm going to "punish" him by sleeping in my own bed on his late nights, he feels comfortable enough to actually bring one of the clients home with him the next Wednesday!

After I scurry off to my room when I hear his car, carefully turning out the light so he'll know I've been sleeping instead of obsessing about where he's been, I hear him talking to someone, and a woman's voice answers!

Yes, I press my ear up to the door—what do you think I am, nuts? And I hear the artificial laugh of a woman trying to impress a man with her good humor, and I hear Henry's suave deep voice, the one that says "you're safe with me, baby" when in reality you're not. I hear him putting ice in glasses. I hear them clinking the glasses together. I hear the ice tinkle as they hoist back the glasses.

Speaking of tinkle, that's exactly what I have to do, and since I have no bathroom in my room, I either wait it out or embarrass Henry.

Hmm…embarrassing Henry. Not a bad idea, especially since I don't hear anything at all now. No voices, no clinking, no tinkling.

I grab my robe and open the door, then slam it shut behind me as I head to the bathroom to my right.

When I come out again, Henry's standing at the end of the hallway, drink in hand.

"Ame, let me introduce you to somebody," he says with that twisted-lip grin.

So I mosey on out to the living room in my short blue terry robe with the moon and stars appliqués all over it and my hair a ratty mess, and even though I don't have green cold cream on my face, I'm sure they'll remember it there when they think of this night. I am greeted by an image of womanly loveliness, a red-haired version of Tess Wintergarten, all sleek styling and fast curves. She wears a skimpy taupe dress with spaghetti straps that might have been a negligee in a former lifetime.

"This is Joanna Wentworth," Henry says to me, gesturing with the hand that holds the drink. "And this is Amy Sheldon."

She does not extend a perfectly manicured hand and I

do not offer my stubby-nailed ones. We do the quick grin routine.

But Henry's grin is unambiguously mischievous. He turns to Joanna. "Well, I should be getting you home." Then back to me, "Hope we didn't wake you. You can go back to your bedroom now."

Go back to my bedroom. Notice he said go back to *my* bedroom. He's sending signals with that one. Signal to Joanna—Amy has her own bed and therefore we are not involved. Signal to Amy—I know what you're up to and I can play games, too.

I go back to my bed all right, and I toss and turn until midnight when Henry saunters in, whistling! As he passes my door, I open it.

"Oh, sorry. Didn't mean to wake you," he says, loosening his tie.

"What was that all about?" I seethe.

"What was what all about?"

"Joanna. Bringing her here."

"I needed to pick up some papers about the firm. Faster to stop here for them. She's a client. Getting a divorce. Her husband's a lawyer. Very tricky case. I told you I'd be doing more of this."

"She didn't look dressed for a business meeting." Maybe some kind of business.

"I met up with her at a fund-raising event. Hopkins Club." He'd asked me to go to that event with him, but I'd begged off, still fearful of running into the old Squires crew.

Hopkins, need I remind you, is where Sam teaches. Hopkins is the university that abuts Tess's neighborhood. Case closed.

"Why do you have to wine and dine all these women clients? Isn't it unprofessional?"

Henry's amused mood vanishes. "I've brought five new

clients into Squires in the past six months alone. They are already considering me for partner. And I've only been there two years."

I remember what he told me at the shore—how intensely he's worked all his life. Old habits die hard.

"But still…"

"When these women are going through a divorce, they like to speak to their lawyer confidentially. Alone."

"Well, why does all that confidential talking take so long?"

"She asked me in for a cup of coffee."

"A cup of coffee?" I sputter. "Will you send her flowers tomorrow thanking her for her incomparable cup of coffee?"

His lip twitches upward. "No. I've decided that's overkill." He yawns. "I'm tired. I have to get up early." His voice turns serious. "Let me remind you. You were the one who wanted the 'business relationship.' I'm just trying to play by your rules."

He closes the door behind him and I'm left standing in the hallway. Trixie, who had been observing this exchange, shoots down the hall toward the kitchen and her food dish. Thanks, Trix.

Play by my rules, huh? What the hell made him think I knew what I was talking about when I made those rules? What is he—crazy?

To make matters worse, when I tell Wendy about this to-do, she takes Henry's side. On the phone with her the next day, she repeats what he said.

"You were the one who moved into the spare bedroom," she says. "What did you expect him to think? You're un-willing to commit. Why should he?"

Has she been speaking with him, I wonder suspiciously, sharing "talking points," perhaps?

"But," I sputter, "bringing a woman home! That's, that's outrageous!"

"He said it was business," she counters. "Would he bring a date home to see you? I think not. I think Henry Castle knows something you don't want to admit."

Uh-oh. Dangerous road ahead. I don't say anything, but that doesn't stop her from continuing.

"You told him about Rick, right?" she asks.

"Uh, yeah, that I was engaged," I mumble.

"Well, he probably figures you're not over him yet. So he's being careful. Can you blame him?"

Of course I can blame him! And I do! Why should I have to be the first one to take a chance? Doesn't the accident qualify me for some kind of pass in that department? Some kind of immunity totem from this special challenge?

That Sunday, I have another argument with Henry. The Fourth of July is around the corner and Gina and Fred invite me and Henry over. Gina even invites Wendy, but she's headed to Connecticut for a long weekend. Her morning sickness is gone and she's experiencing that glow I predicted—a kind of serene shine and great complexion. She still hasn't told her parents, but she's laying the groundwork for the resolution of her problem.

She's taking lots of money from them now—in fact, they have started giving her a monthly allowance. The payback? She visits at least once a month with the promise to move to Connecticut in the fall. That's right—she's emigrating. She has a scheme worked out for how to handle the pregnancy and child part but more on that later.

When I tell Henry about my sister's invite, he is at first very interested.

We're watching television in his room and both in good spirits. Henry cooked tonight—lamb chops and mint jelly, baked potatoes and salad. And dessert was served in bed. It was me.

"Sounds good," he says after I give him the news on the

cookout at Gina's place. Then he frowns. "No, wait a minute. Can't do it. I have to work."

"Work on the Fourth? Who works on the Fourth except fireworks coordinators? It's unpatriotic." I gently jab him in the stomach, which makes him smile but doesn't dent his resolve.

"No can do. I'm driving to the Eastern Shore to meet with a client. It's the only time…"

"Henry, how many fucking clients' hands do you have to hold to get their business? Maybe I should become a client and then you'd spend more time with me!" Yup. I actually say this.

"We live together. That's a lot of time."

"Not when you're out a couple nights a week." I sulk. Where am I getting these lines? Out of a black-and-white movie? I look down to make sure I still have color. Yup. Blue robe.

"You need a job." He stands abruptly and heads for the kitchen. I follow him there.

"I had a job! You said it wasn't good enough for me. Besides, I do my part!"

He stands in front of the open fridge. "You sit at home all day and you don't have enough to think about." He pulls out a beer, thinks better of it, puts it back and grabs a water.

"I'm plenty busy. I send out résumés, I cook, I clean. I can't help it if no one wants to hire me!"

"You need a positive attitude." He swallows some water. "An employer can see a bad attitude coming a mile away. It can creep into your cover letters."

So what starts as an argument about Henry's working the Fourth turns into an argument about my lack of job-search skills.

"That job at the Air Freshener College is a good example of what I'm talking about," he continues. "You took that because you were desperate. You can't feel desperate. You have to feel confident. Maybe you should go to a career counselor."

"You're beginning to sound like Fred," I groan.

"So? Fred could be right. Something's not clicking. How long's it been—two, three months since you started looking?"

"Not if you count the job I just had," I protest, but Henry shakes his head.

"You're still not into it." He returns to the bedroom, flops on the bed and switches channels.

"I am, too!" I follow him and sit on the corner of the bed so he has to look at me if he wants to see the television. "I've sent out maybe fifty résumés in the past month. And only two—count 'em, two—people called me. One to tell me they knew my sister in high school and another because they mistook me for someone they did want to interview! Fred's right. It's like I've been out of work for two years. I can't help it if I had an accident. It's not my fault!" Now I'm in trouble. Mentioning that accident gets me weepy and before you can say "it was your fault" I'm really crying.

I'm dripping fat tears onto his black duvet. He scoots over and puts his arm around my shoulders. "Let me take a look at your résumé," he says after kissing my forehead. "Maybe I can help."

And he does help. He takes my résumé with him to work the next day and calls me at lunch to make a few suggestions. I should rewrite the flower shop job to make it sound as if I worked on full-scale marketing strategies instead of what I really did, which was just to, well, market the flowers in terms of selling them. I should punch up the ad agency material to more accurately reflect the full scope of responsibilities I handled. I should include the Air Freshener College job but make it sound as if I was brought on just to handle the "downsizing." And he also interrogates me about any award I ever won or had a hand in winning and tells me to put those on it, too.

"I'll put a few feelers out for you, *conchita,*" he says in his bedroom voice. "We'll find something. Don't worry."

By the time the Fourth rolls around, I've forgotten how miffed I was originally that he couldn't make my sister's party and I'm getting dangerously close to uttering the *L* word. Maybe it's a good thing he'll be gone for a few days.

chapter 17

Purple lilac: First emotions of love

A wall of lilac bushes enclosed a small portion of yard just outside the Squires's kitchen door, bringing to my mind the great Walt Whitman poem about Lincoln's death, "When Lilacs Last in the Dooryard Bloom'd." Rick and I met in March. In April, he invited me to "his place"—his parents' house. They were traveling, he told me, which suited me just fine since I wasn't ready to "meet the folks." Even at the front door, I could smell the lilacs' heady perfume. Perhaps we were both intoxicated by their scent that night. Sipping chardonnay in the cool evening, listening to Puccini, he reached over and squeezed my hand. "You're good for me, Amy," he said, a broad grin on his face. "I love you." The accident was in late April. And now lilacs make me think both of that first rush of requited love, as well as the finality of death, of Whitman's lines: "I mourned, and yet shall mourn with ever-returning spring."

My parents come to my sister's cookout, and everyone asks where Henry is, and when I explain he's away on business they all raise their eyebrows as if they're in some synchronized eyebrow-raising competition. I have no trouble interpreting their meaning. Hmm...away on business, eh? Tsk, tsk.

Fred grills teriyaki chicken and salmon, which Gina serves with roasted corn on the cob with rosemary butter, a fennel-pasta salad and homemade cheddar-herb rolls. For drinks there's iced green tea with fresh mint and wine spritzers with fresh strawberries.

Gina's dressed in a loose gauzy white dress and my mother and father come in red, white and blue. Blue shorts, white shirts, red baseball caps. I am not making this up.

It's a curiously sad affair because the Fourth of July is the type of holiday that is best celebrated with hordes of strangers—at parades or fireworks or symphony concerts that end with the William Tell Overture and live cannons shooting off.

Fourth festivities with small groups of people are like funerals with only one attendee. It makes you feel like you're the last one standing when the rest of the world has moved on.

To enhance this lonely feeling, Gina's neighborhood is quiet as a tomb. There's a faint smell of charcoal in the air so I know someone is out there, but they're well camouflaged behind pruned boxwoods. No children's voices cut the silence and I wonder if Gina would even be allowed to have a kid in this neighborhood. Maybe there's some covenant agreement all homeowners have to sign before moving in: children will be sent immediately to boarding school upon arrival on this earth.

Dad badgers Fred most of the afternoon about the stock market. I think Dad thinks that Fred has insider info that he won't reveal, and it makes Dad a little surly. Gina is careful not to serve him any wine. When Mom reminds Dad that Fred's an accountant, not a stockbroker, Dad growls at her.

"Arthur Andersen," he mutters at her like a curse.

When Gina goes to get the blueberry-strawberry-vanilla ice cream trifle for dessert, Mom pulls me aside to the corner of the patio away from Dad.

"I haven't told your father you moved in with that Henry," she says.

"Why not?"

"I don't think he'd be happy about it."

"Why not? I lived with Rick."

"You were marrying Rick."

"I didn't know that when he moved in with me!"

She just frowns, her mouth outlined by little pieces of corn. I point to her mouth and she wipes it off.

"You should be careful. Look at Wendy."

"How'd you hear about Wendy?" I look over at my sister, who is coming out of the house with a tray loaded with fancy dessert dishes and a trifle bowl. I'd just told Gina today about Wendy's pregnancy—a sort of makeup confidence for the fact that I don't tell her much about Henry (because there's not a lot to tell). So when I'd arrived and spent some time in the kitchen helping her get things ready, I'd spilled the beans about Wendy's situation.

"Get out!" Gina said, her mouth dropping open. "What's she going to do?"

"Keep the baby. There are lots of single mothers, you know."

Gina pursed her lips. Clearly, she didn't think much of that option. "How will she meet someone now?"

"Single mothers do remarry, you know." Or marry for the first time, in Wendy's case. "Hey, don't say anything to anyone. She doesn't want it getting back to her employer yet." Gina has friends who work in ad agencies.

"No problem."

Well, I now know that "no problem" in GinaSpeak means "Hah!" The quisling—she gave up Wendy's story this very afternoon.

"Henry's not married like Sam is," I point out to my mother. No, not married, just keeping all options open. Much better for me, don't you think?

"What does that have to do with it?"

"Sam—Wendy's boyfriend. He's married."

"Oh, my god! I didn't know. That's awful. What a schmuck."

So at last we find common ground. If Sam only knew how he brings families together while ripping his own apart.

Wendy, by the way, has completely broken off with the cad. She's even called Henry about legally keeping the baby away from him.

What prompted her to take this action was a moment of heart-ripping backsliding on her part. As I predicted, she'd reached for the phone to talk to him one night—the night after the day when she'd heard the baby's heartbeat for the first time. Yeah, she'd called me and gushed for nearly half an hour about it, but it's not the same thing as sharing it with the guy who actually helped start the heartbeat. So she'd called Sam and damn him, he came over to see her—probably just so he could see what it was like to make love to a pregnant woman. I'm sure that's what they did. At least she didn't have to worry about getting pregnant since she already was.

What she did need to worry about was getting nicked by his sharp-edged psyche. She could hardly speak when she called to tell me about it later that night, waking Henry up and forcing me out of his bed so I could whisper to her in a corner of "my" room. Poor Wendy assumed once again if Sam wanted to make love to her, he might be softening toward the baby and the divorce.

But he repeated his dogma: he'd never made any commitments to her, that he certainly couldn't be expected to leave his wife when Wendy was disregarding his wishes about the baby, and he was a local board member of Zero Population Growth to boot. His parting shot? His wife had finally snagged a job at a university prestigious enough for her many talents—Princeton—so they were going to buy a home together and give up the bicoastal commute. End of story.

I told Wendy to come on over and she spent the night with Henry and me.

Devastated as she is, Wendy has a plan she's been forming for some time. Here it is: She still hasn't told her parents about the baby; however, she has told them that she wants to take them up on their offer to fund a Grand Tour kind of trip. Surprise, surprise, it will coincide with the point in her pregnancy when she's showing. After a few months, she'll return to the States, have the baby, and then make up a story about adopting some friend's abandoned child after the friend passes away.

Yeah, it sounds batty, but Wendy can pull it off. Even if her parents figure it out, she knows them well enough to know they will accept the single-parent adoption more than they could ever accept her having a child out of wedlock.

Wendy mapped this all out for me right before she headed to Connecticut for the Fourth.

And here, boys and girls, is where my own dilemma comes in. Yes, there is a dilemma here, and not just the "what is Henry really thinking about us?" dilemma. Not just the "how can I get my parents to accept my current status as a live-in girlfriend" kind of dilemma. Not the "how can I stop thinking of what Fred looks like naked" kind of dilemma.

I take some trifle from my sister and sit looking away from Fred and out onto the newly mown lawn. It's steamy as a crab pot, and I'm wondering why sitting out in this tropical heat is supposed to make the day fun when any other day this hot and humid Gina and Fred would be serving us in their air-conditioned dining room.

No, my dilemma is this one: "Should I go to the Riviera with Wendy for a few months?" Wendy has already asked me if I want to go, and I still have my two thou in the bank, so it's not out of the question.

And therein lies the rub. Just what is the question? Or the myriad of questions that have yes and no answers?

Do I want to go with Wendy? Yes.

Do I want to spend two months on the Riviera? Yes!

Do I want to leave Henry for two months?

Uh-oh. Can't answer that one. Every time I think of leaving Henry, I get this sick feeling in my stomach because the questions I refuse to ask and answer are: Do I think Henry will want me when I return? Will he ask me to stay? Will he send flowers to other babes while I'm gone?

You fill in the blank.

I can, however, answer this question: will our relationship be over if he is unfaithful? Hell, yes.

After Mom and Dad leave, I help Gina clean up while Fred does some obsessive-compulsive thing with the grill, spraying down the racks with oven cleaner and hosing them off on the patio. As I watch the foamy water spill onto the lawn, I think that he won't need to call the weed-control chemical company this week.

"Too bad Henry couldn't come," Gina says, placing plates in the dishwasher. No paper plates here. Real china. "We'll have to have you two to dinner soon. We still haven't done that."

"Yeah. Well." I hand her the platter the chicken and fish were on, and she wipes it down in the sink.

"Maybe in a couple weeks," Gina says happily. "I'll make a standing rib roast and new potatoes."

"Henry loves good food."

"Well, take some home with you. I've got chicken left over. And salad and corn."

She makes a little doggie bag for me which I hold on my lap when Fred drives me home. Yup, Fred drives me home since I don't have a car. It makes me feel like a kid again, but in a bad way. We hardly speak on the way to Henry's condo, which I'm sure is because we're still thinking of the naked-Fred incident. Better to pretend we don't know each other.

Henry is due back tomorrow so I sit on his front steps watching the fireworks over the harbor with an empty heart, drinking a gin and tonic. Trixie meows up a storm by my feet and I rub her behind the ears, but even she doesn't make me feel better. Trixie likes it here. She gets to roam around outside and a couple neighbors have taken to her.

And she likes Henry so much I'm almost jealous. She saunters up to him regularly when he's home and brushes her tail against his legs. When he gets into bed, she leaps—I am not kidding, she leaps—up next to him and purrs so loudly it sounds like she's got a couple of screws loose in her head.

I'm alone. Everyone in his Stepford condo development must be out celebrating. Lots of empty places in the parking lot, and lots of dark windows in the two-story buildings facing the lots.

I hear the whine and blast and see the red bursts, the white flashes, the blue explosions. In the distance, I hear the muted sounds of patriotic songs. "My Country 'Tis of Thee," "America the Beautiful," "God Bless America" and "The Star-Spangled Banner," which has special meaning around these parts since it's where it was written.

The fireworks are photo-flash memories in the night sky when I stand to go in.

"Come on, Trix. Bedtime," I say, and she reluctantly follows. Maybe she's waiting for Henry, but he won't be home until tomorrow afternoon.

At a quarter to midnight, I hear the front door open. Heart thudding in my throat, I grab a heavy flashlight and creep into the living room.

Henry's there, looking tired.

"Electricity go out?" he asks when he sees my weapon.

"Uh, no. You weren't going to come home until tomorrow."

"I wrapped it up, so I thought I'd head back." He comes upstairs and grabs me to him. His Hilfiger cologne masks the scent of sweat. Sweat doesn't smell bad on Henry. It smells manly. After a wet kiss that turns my fear to desire, he looks me in the eye.

"I think I'm falling in love with you, *conchita*."

chapter 18

Carolina jasmine: Separation

The winter before the accident, Rick went on a business trip—some conference in North Carolina. He wasn't interested that much in the conference itself, he told me, but it would give him a chance to see some of his old law school buddies. Although he was a Princeton grad, he'd gone to law school at Duke, an experience he said he wouldn't have traded for the world. His law school days were among the happiest in his life. The week he was away was a particularly difficult one for me. A work project tanked when the client decided to pull out, and Gelman blamed me for the mess. And Mrs. Squires had invited me to dinner that week because Rick had just informed her he'd asked me to marry him. I felt abandoned and unsure, and couldn't wait for his return. It didn't help calm my nerves that he was difficult to reach while away—not often in his room until late, and impatient to get to conference events when I did *talk to him. Of course, I spent all my time on the phone complaining, so who could blame him if he wanted to rush off, right?*

If I have one talent, it is my ability to turn gold into dross.

After Henry's quasi-admission of love, do I wrap my arms around him and confess my own undying affection? Do I coyly bat my eyes and say, "Henry, I don't just *think* you're in love with me, I know it." Do I shed tears of joy and tell him, in a voice dripping with earnest sincerity, just how much it means to me that he made this confession and that I've longed to hear him say this and have been thinking a lot about it myself?

Or do I sneeze, and then say "Me, too?"

My heart might be bubbling over with happiness, but the guard dogs in front of it snarl and snap and say "Wait a minute, hold it, too fast, too soon, get a grip, you've only known him a couple months." They're talking dogs. Very precocious. So after I apologize for sneezing at this heady moment, I mumble my ditto and that's that.

Yes, I hungered for the *L* word. I wanted to hear him say it. I even wanted to say it myself. But he wasn't putting the *L* word in its proper location—smack in the middle of the *L phrase*—as in "I *L* you!" He was just kind of dancing around the edges of it. I wasn't going to dive in before him. No, sirree, bub. I still had that "fragile" tattoo to think about.

Later that night, we make love, and while we're lying together in postcoital bliss on his bed, I turn back into the Little Woman and pull something out of her toolbox—nagging. Nagging always makes men want to say the *L* phrase, doncha think?

"I really wish you could have come to Gina's today. They wondered where you were," I say.

"Did you have a good time?" He strokes my arm in the

blue light of the room. Is there anything so peaceful as a moonlit room after making love? Which is exactly why I need to shatter it. It's like a wide pane of perfect glass and a baseball.

"Not without you. Everyone asked about you."

"And you told them I had a business deal." He inhales sharply. Henry knows where this is going. He's smart, which is why I like him.

"I still can't believe you couldn't get out of it. It was a holiday."

He pulls his arm away. "No, I couldn't get out of it. And you knew that. The day is over. Why bug me about it now?"

"Because it was important to me—to have you meet my family."

"Why didn't you say so?"

"I told you about the barbecue last week."

"You didn't say it was important."

"It's the first time I've invited you to something with my family. You're a college graduate. You should get it."

Putting his hands behind his head, he shakes his head in disgust.

"Besides, if I'd asked you to change your meeting, would you have done it?" I persist.

"Maybe." He grabs his silk bathrobe and sits on the edge of the bed with his hands between his legs.

"Who was the meeting with, anyway?"

He tilts his head and glares at me. "Roberta Calvin. I'm handling her divorce."

"That's another thing. All your meetings are with women. Don't you have any male clients?"

"A few."

"Do you ever have late-night meetings with them?"

"Sometimes."

"And you send them flowers?"

He rolls his eyes and slaps his hand on the bed next to him. "Look, I am trying to build a career here. If that means I have to wine and dine a few ladies, and make them feel good about themselves after their louses of husbands have done them wrong, so be it. It's no big deal."

It *is* a big deal to me, I want to scream. Rick was a lawyer and he never got clients this way. Who gets clients this way?

"But you're leading them on. You're making them think that you, you…" What is he making them think? That he's available? I choke on the word. "That you're living alone." So there. Take that.

He exhales sharply. "You're living in my spare bedroom. And besides, I introduced you to Joanna Wentworth."

Well, he might as well have slapped me. Living in his spare bedroom, huh? That's all I am to him? Some temporary tenant who cooks and cleans while she tries to get on her feet again? Oh, I know, I know—Wendy pointed out that this spare-bedroom thing sends mixed signals. But if I could get a clear signal from Henry, maybe mine would unscramble as well.

The "I think I'm falling in love with you" doesn't mean anything compared to the "you're living in my spare bedroom."

Tears sting behind my lids and I blink fast. I storm out of the room—or I hope it's storming because I haven't quite mastered that—and I go into the "spare bedroom" and slam the door. If he hears it, I don't know. The television is already on.

I punch my pillow and cry myself to sleep. Stupid me. I'm the one who wanted the "tenant" situation. I'm the one who suggested I "earn my keep" by cooking and cleaning. I'm the one who set up this ridiculous 1950s throwback arrangement. Was I taking stupid pills or something? Is this another yet-to-be discovered side effect of those migraine tablets?

I'm so bummed by this squabble that I actually confide in Gina the next day when I call to thank her again for the barbecue.

"Well, why didn't you tell him how much it meant to you, honey?" she asks incredulously.

"Because I thought he knew."

"Men don't know anything unless we tell them a thousand times."

"That's a dumb excuse."

"Not many are like Rick, sweetie. Trust me. Even Fred is not, well, perfect."

Maybe one part of his body is, I think.

"Fred's pretty thoughtful," I volunteer. I'm taking up for Fred? Things are bad when I need to do that to make a point about Henry. "He gave you those antique garnet earrings you wanted for Christmas. That was very thoughtful. He knew what you wanted."

Gina laughs. "The only reason he knew was because I printed out five photos of the things and left them lying around the house beginning in November. You don't think Fred would come up with that idea on his own, do you?"

Pop. Bubble bursting. And here I thought Fred was as meticulous about gift giving as he is about grill cleaning.

I sigh. "Maybe I'll have to try that. I'll be lucky if he remembers my birthday." My birthday is in two weeks.

"You better get started. What do you want, anyway?"

"I don't know. A job."

"Besides that."

"Actually, I like those earrings and wouldn't mind having a pair like them." What I really want, however, is another kind of jewelry. A friendship ring or a going-steady ring.

Or an engagement ring.

Yes, I know. I'm hopeless. I really just want an engagement ring because I was engaged and I liked it and

I don't like unpredictability. Right? It's not because I love Henry. I can't really love Henry. I love Rick. I'm supposed to love Rick.

Oh, hell. We all know what's going on here. I can't love Henry. He might break my heart. And all the king's men won't be able to set it right if he does. It's that simple.

Gina tells me she'll help me "train" Henry and she's in such a good mood that I let her plot and plan.

This consists of taking five photos of her earrings, giving them to me the next day when she comes by for lunch, and telling me the best places to leave them so Henry will notice them.

"Leave one in his car!" she says as she's about to drive off. "Under the visor. It will fall down and hit him when he opens it."

I take Gina's advice and drop these photographic hints throughout the condo. I can't bring myself to do the visor thing, though. Too obvious. (Like the rest of this, isn't it?)

Wendy calls me the day before my birthday to tell me she thinks she's getting thick around the waist and to ask me if I've made up my mind about coming to Europe with her. I tell her I haven't decided but hope to make a decision soon. I want to see how the birthday goes, but I don't tell her that.

The birthday dawns with nothing special happening. No nice card on the kitchen table. No breakfast treat with a loving note tucked in the bakery bag. In fact, the only note Henry leaves me is one saying "Don't forget to pick up coffee." We're out.

My parents call and both get on to sing "Happy Birthday," promising to take me out to dinner or shopping, whichever I prefer.

After I get off the phone, I do some more résumé-sending, and I mope around most of the day. Yeah, I go to the market and get the coffee. I even buy myself a little birthday cake, figuring Henry won't do it for me.

I work myself into such a state that I actually break down and call him during the day and sneak into the conversation the fact that I'm looking forward to seeing Gina later in the week because I know she has a special birthday treat planned for me. Am I subtle or what?

"Oh?" he asks, and I can hear the gears turning. Birthday? When's her birthday?

So I throw him a bone, just to make him feel bad for forgetting the day. "Yeah, she couldn't come over today because of some appointment or something."

Now he knows today's the day. Still a chance to get those earrings, Hen. I've seen them in the window of the estate jewelry store on Charles Street.

When Henry comes home tonight, he is carrying a bouquet of striped carnations, which mean "refusal" but send a different signal to me—he picked them up quickly on his way home from some corner vendor. In his other hand is a small box that he sheepishly gives me. It is professionally wrapped in silver paper and matching ribbon artfully curled. No card accompanies it.

Although the box is too big for jewelry, I'm thinking that an estate jewelry store might really cushion their stuff with extra layers of cardboard and tissue, so I'm hopeful as I tear away the lid. When I finally do get it open, I couldn't be more surprised.

No earrings. A digital camera instead.

Henry grins from ear to ear, proud of himself. "You like it?"

"Uh-huh. It's great!" I say with phony cheer. Yeah, I know a digital camera is a nice gift. And any other time I'd be happy as all get out to receive one. But I was so sure Gina's technique had a chance, even with Henry originally forgetting what the day was.

"I figured you needed one because I saw those lousy photos you've left around—couldn't quite get the picture right." He picks up this camera and proceeds to demonstrate its superior focusing capability.

While I pretend to pay attention, my Inner Feminista is laughing hysterically. Henry got the hint all right, just the wrong one. Wait till I tell Gina.

He takes me out to dinner to a beautiful and wildly expensive restaurant near the water. While I appreciate the gesture, it's a French restaurant and I'm in the mood for Greek food. I would have preferred a less-extravagant place, a bistro or café. But I let Henry fete me in his way, and thus feel oddly unsatisfied after his gifts and gestures.

When I tell Gina about it the next day, she is ecstatic.

"He shows promise," she tells me.

"But he didn't even remember it was my birthday until I reminded him."

"Yeah, but he tried to think of what you would want."

"And completely missed the mark."

"Next time he'll do better."

Wendy forgot my birthday as well, but her I forgive. She has someone else on her mind, after all, and it's not the same thing.

Henry might have tried to make me happy on my birthday, but he continues to do the meetings several times a week which makes me unhappy, and I know he's sending flowers because I see his credit card bill one day when I'm dusting. It's on his dresser and the envelope accidentally falls to the floor, and when I pick it up, the bill magically slips out and unfolds in my hand. Five orders. Yellow roses each time.

As I finish cleaning that day, I feel lonely and hurt. No more flowers for me, but yellow roses galore for new babes he meets. Prospective clients, my ass. More like "backups if this thing with Amy goes south."

This sets up a silent battle of wills. Wendy thinks I should just ask him not to send flowers to these women if it bothers me so much. She thinks I should be honest with him and tell him I care about him and it hurts me to think he's using his seductive charm on other women when he should be saving it all for me. Well, she didn't say it in those exact words, but you get the point.

I, however, prefer a more nuanced approach. When I do the grocery shopping now, I'm always sure to buy several things I know he can't stand—coffee ice cream, anchovies, frozen pizza. The message should be clear, right? You send flowers to babes, I buy stuff you don't like. Except for an occasional wide-eyed look in the fridge, he doesn't say a word.

The good news is that I get some job interviews at last.

I give up on the cover letter and start using the press-release-as-cover-letter for every inquiry I make and it's paying off.

I interview for a museum job and for public relations director at a local Catholic college that, unlike Our Lady of the Air Freshener, has a good reputation and a promising future.

The museum interview is a peach. They love me. I love them.

They give the job to an "internal candidate."

At least it's quick. I get that rejection letter in a week.

The college interview is less chipper. First, I'm interviewed by the Human Resources director, an older woman with boyish white hair who is dressed in a navy-blue suit. Since it's a Catholic college, I can't figure out if she's a nun. At least Sister Mary Altamont wore a veil to let you know she wasn't a civilian. (I'm going to burn my own navy suit after this experience, by the way.)

Not knowing if this woman is a nun throws me off kilter for the whole interview and I feel like I answer all her questions too cautiously, afraid I'm going to say something sacrilegious. She probably thinks I'm hiding something.

As careful as I am in her interview, I'm three sheets to the wind in the interview with the actual VP under whom the PR director works. This fellow, Brian Ripton, is just a little older than I am, cheerful, outgoing, with an iron-fisted handshake. He makes me feel so comfortable that by the end of the forty-minute session I've told him why I don't like coconut and how long it took me to recover after Rick's death. Note to self: do not leave prospective employers with the impression that they should ask for your release papers.

Needless to say, I don't get that job.

By the beginning of August, I have four more interviews, three of which offer the position to a "well-qualified" candidate while they "wish me well" in my job search. One snooty trade organization veep sends me a form rejection (after no interview) with a hastily scrawled note on the bottom: "I would advise you to lose the press release gimmick. It's unprofessional and sends the wrong message."

Maybe to you, buster, but it gets me in the door at a half dozen other places, and obviously acts as a screening device for me. If you don't like the press release, I probably won't like you.

Whenever I schedule an interview, I okay it with Henry so I can borrow his car. On those days, I drop him at the office first thing in the morning and pick him up at six or later. I like those days because I know I'll be able to count on him not scheduling any after-work appointments.

After all my effort, one prospect finally shows promise—a job with a city nonprofit, a tutoring program for kids in bad schools. The pay's not great but the job appeals to the idealist in me and, unlike the Our Lady of the Air Freshener job, it would be a good first step back into the nine-to-five world. The interview goes well and they ask to keep the samples of my work I bring with me, so they can show them to the board subcommittee that will ultimately sign off on the decision. When I leave their office, I'm about as positive as I can be that I've landed the position.

It's a Friday and I'm euphoric. I stand in the sunshine on Howard Street, smelling the city perfumes of fried food and smoke and pollution and garbage, and I love it. I get this job and I can walk to work. I get this job and I can be human again, instead of this needy bundle of worry I've become.

And this job is in the bag. I can feel it in my bones.

Wendy's been pressuring me about the trip to France and I'm thinking that if I get this job, maybe what I'll do is go over with her for two weeks and then come back and start work and start over.

Even start over with Henry, too. I'm tired of playing cat and mouse. Gina's right. Wendy's right. If I want something, I should come out and say what I want. And what I want is a serious relationship, maybe one that will lead to commitment. If I'm back on my feet again, I can have that talk with Henry, and know I can move out if it doesn't go well. In fact, maybe I should move out, anyway, so we can really start over.

On the walk back to the condo, I buy a bottle of champagne as well as some pimento-stuffed olives (Henry hates these), and pick up carryout pizza (Henry likes that).

Knowing I want this job, Henry had told me to call him to let him know how the interview went, so I do and am put through right away. After I prattle on about every detail of the session, including what I read into my interviewer's body language, Henry gives me a pep talk on how a positive attitude probably made the difference, and what great news this is, and what a great gal I am. Then he proceeds to splash bad news on me.

"I'll be late tonight."

Uh-oh. Late? Client meeting on a Friday night? Who has business meetings on a Friday night?

"Oh, darn. I wanted to celebrate. I bought some champagne. And pizza from Denitis."

"Well, hold that thought. I need to meet with someone about settling her parents' estate."

Okay, rewind. Her? As in "female client?" *Henry!*

"Can't you do it next week?"

"She's going out of town next week."

"What about the week after?"

"She won't be back until the end of September."

"What if I meet you at your office after the meeting and we can go out together?"

"I'm not meeting her here."

Major lump in dry throat. Not meeting her there? This is the first time since we've been together that Henry has missed a Friday night with me. He might take the prospective clients out other nights of the week, but Fridays are for us. Bottle of wine over dinner, quiet conversation, maybe rent a DVD and end up in bed. Occasionally, we go out. But mostly, we stay in.

"Uh…where are you meeting her?"

"A bistro near her place. Benedict's."

A wolf howls and wind shakes the house.

Or at least it feels that way to me. Benedict's is a new French restaurant near Charles Street and University Parkway. Tess Wintergarten is the client.

"Why don't you bring her here?" I improvise. "I could make dinner."

He is silent for a moment, then finds his excuse. "I don't want anything long and drawn out, *conchita*. I'll meet her, take care of business, then come home."

I'm left wondering if I'm the one he doesn't want to have anything long and drawn out with.

"Well, don't rush on my account," I snap. "I might go visit Wendy and celebrate with her." I get off the phone after an abrupt goodbye and feel like he hung up on me.

Who knows if he's seen Tess in the past? He's never revealed to me the names of the babes who've received the flowers. For all I know, Tess could be a regular on his "wine and dine and send flowers to" list. Speaking of flowers, except for my first week with him and my birthday (which I don't count since he obviously forgot about it), Henry has not so much as dropped a petal on me since we've been living together.

Within a few seconds of setting the phone down, it rings. Elation! It must be Henry calling me back to say he's changed his plans.

But it's Wendy, a near-hysterical Wendy. She's sobbing so hard I can only make out that she's in trouble and would like to see me.

I grab my bottle of champagne and head outside. Forget about city smells making me happy. It's blistering hot and humid—a lovely combination that leaves you breathless and limp within a matter of seconds. Wendy's apartment is a looooooonnnnnng walk away. To hell with that. I get to Pratt Street and splurge on a taxi. I'll be flush soon once I get that job. Within moments I am deposited in front of Wendy's high-rise near the Basilica.

By the time I buzz her apartment, I'm sure she's had some fresh run-in with Sam and I'm all prepared to give her a severe talking-to that will once and for all curtail these Sam urges. I have a list of things to say, some of them hurtful, some of them even untrue, but I'm prepared to fight to the death. The death of this Sam thing, that is. Cruel to be kind, that's my battle cry.

Upstairs, she lets me in and I start in immediately.

"You've got to stop this," I tell her, standing in the foyer, looking disgustedly at the crumpled tissue in her hand.

"What?"

"Stop seeing Sam."

"Fuck you, Amy!" she cries. "I'm not seeing Sam! I'm having a miscarriage." She storms back to her living room and plops on the sofa.

I want to slap myself. I want to inflict physical pain in a public place so that she can witness my humiliation. How could I be so dumb, so heartless? My own troubles evaporate compared to hers. I follow her into the living room and sit next to her.

"I'm so sorry. I thought…" I thought she was still an idiot. Instead, she's merely experiencing a tragedy. I'm the idiot.

"He couldn't find a heartbeat," she sobs into her tissue.

"Oh, my God, sweetie." I hug her then.

"It was strong every other time. He even felt it early."

I remember her telling me this.

"So when he didn't hear it today he gave me a sonogram right away." She gulps in air between sobs.

"And?" And I think I know what comes after that "and." I grow cold.

"And he says he thinks the fetus died." She bawls full force—messy, sucking, hiccupping cries of grief and I can do nothing to staunch the flow except to hold her and murmur "Oh, honey" over and over again mixed with "I'm so sorry." And mentally, I'm bludgeoning myself for compounding her grief by hurling accusations about Sam at her as soon as she opened the door.

After she gains control, I get her a glass of water and new tissues. "What are you supposed to do?"

"He told me to go home and rest and to come in on Monday, unless I have contractions in which case I should go to the hospital."

"Okay. So you wait until Monday. I can stay with you. At

least you're not having contractions, right? There still could be a chance."

Slowly she shakes her head back and forth.

"You're having contractions?" My voice rises. "Now?"

She nods. "They started as soon as I got home. I think the internal examination might have triggered them."

"We need to call the doctor! Get you to the hospital."

"That's why I called you."

"Have you called the doctor?"

"Yes."

"And what did he say?"

"He said what I told you—meet him at the hospital."

"Where are your keys? I'll drive."

After she tells me what she needs, I finish packing her bag and grab her keys. Then I help her downstairs with my arm under her arms holding her up. By now, the contractions are stronger and she's punchy from the pain, moaning and then laughing hysterically at how "bad it hurts." She seems surprised by the pain, as if her body's playing a bad joke on her.

I drive wildly up Charles Street, past Tess's house without even caring, and into the county. Wendy's doctor is at Greater Baltimore Medical Center, and by the time we hit the entrance to the hospital she's taken her seat belt off and is balled up on the floor of the front seat in wrenching agony. It's no longer funny and I'm afraid.

Just like my sister did with me a couple months ago, I pull into a handicapped spot near the door and get an attendant to help me get Wendy into the E.R. Her doctor, a man named Eric Bernstein, has already told them to expect her so she's whisked into a cubicle while I go move the car.

Everything is happening in a rush with no time to think so I'm dulled to pain. I hope Wendy feels the same way now. When I get back from the parking lot, nurses are already prepping her to go to a room. In addition to cramping, she's bleeding now—profusely. The nurses give each other know-ing looks that tell me they don't like this. I follow Wendy up to a room and sit by her side while the nurses do the hun-dred little jobs to connect a patient to the hospital's life force. Tubes here, monitors there, pills down the hatch.

The pills and the IV make the pain wane, so Wendy's main problem now seems to be the bleeding. After waiting a half hour in the room, I get restless and seek out a nurse at the brightly lit nurses' station.

"Isn't Dr. Bernstein supposed to be here?" I ask.

"He's on his way, hon," she says.

Back in the room, Wendy dozes. The room is dim and gray and I spend the time sucking in the air-conditioning and looking out a fogged window over the verdant hills of Towson. Towson, with its neat upscale houses and shopping malls and preppy schools. I console myself by imagining happy families in some of those homes, kids going out on weekend dates and parents settling down to watch TV with their bowls of microwaved popcorn. And then I start think-ing of my own Friday night ritual with Henry, which was ruined tonight by his "business meeting" with Tess. Sure, it would have been ruined, anyway, by Wendy's call. But that's a real emergency. Henry's meeting with Tess is not.

Why did I ever hook up with him? Since the moment I met him in the flower shop, I should have known that he wasn't good for me. And he's the one who's given me the key. He said I had to be confident. How can I be confident living with a man who uses his sex appeal to get clients?

"What time is it?" Wendy murmurs.

"After eight," I turn and tell her. Standing by her bed, I decide to grab her lucid moments and work with them. "I should call your parents."

"No," she says groggily. "Don't. It's only a miscarriage."

Only a miscarriage. Yup. Only an atom bomb to your heart.

"Where's the doctor?" she asks.

"They said he's on his way in." But I'm pissed he's not here and I search out the nurses again. A sweet-looking uniformed girl, who looks about sixteen, is writing something on a chart at her station.

"I'm with Wendy Jackson," I tell her. "They told us Dr. Bernstein was on his way in a half hour ago. Where's he coming in from—Kajeekistan?"

She titters. "Didn't anyone tell you? He had an emergency C-section just after he arrived. He'll see her as soon as he's done. It won't be long. I'll come check on your friend for you, though."

She follows me back to the room and goes through the routine—blood pressure, temp, pulse, bleeding.

"Hmm…you're losing a lot of blood here," she says to Wendy, whose eyes are only half open. "I'll see what we can do," she offers before mysteriously disappearing.

We don't see her for another half hour, during which time I go insane and Wendy has to go to the bathroom. I help her hobble to the little rest room a few feet away, and I wonder if I should call her parents regardless of what she says. What if something happens to her? They'd want to be here, right? They'd hold me responsible if they weren't here and something happens.

Something *is* happening. Turning around, I see the little-nurse-that-could rushing through the door and throwing open the bathroom door. Crumpled on the floor is Wendy. She's fainted! She must have hit the emergency button before blacking out.

"Call a nurse!" the sixteen-year-old shouts at me as she kneels down and feels Wendy's pulse.

A nurse? What is she—chopped liver? But I do as she says and run to the nurses' station. Incredibly, it's empty. Frantically, I look up and down the hallway. I spot a woman in what looks like a uniform. I can't tell nowadays—they all wear different things. White pants and colorful smocks. Who do they think they are—kindergarten teachers? What's the matter with the old white get-up and funky hat? If they opt for the kindergarten garb, they should at least have to wear badges that say "NURSE" in huge black letters!

"You have to help me!" I blurt at her. "Wendy Jackson in 304. She's fainted."

The woman looks at me quizzically, then turns into a nearby room. A few seconds later, a doctor in scrubs comes out with a clipboard in his hand. Because of the shower cap on his head, thick glasses covering his eyes and bushy mustache over his mouth, I'm left with the impression that this is Dr. Quackenbush from a Groucho Marx movie. I want to scream. But he appears unperturbed and takes his time following me to Wendy's room.

So this is Dr. Bernstein. Wendy can't even get a doctor who breaks a sweat to care for her. Maybe she and I *should* give up men and become lesbian lovers.

Once in the room, he asks the nurse a few questions. Wendy's rousing now and is appropriately confused.

"It's okay. You just passed out," the nurse says. "Can you stand?"

I go to her and help the nurse bring her to her feet. The doctor has fetched another nurse who brings in a wheelchair. Apparently, he is not allowed to handle wheelchairs himself. In a few seconds, Wendy is back in bed, and a few seconds after that, a stretcher comes in and nurses help move her onto it. From *no action* we've gone to body-moving central—from the floor to the chair, from the chair to the bed, from the bed to the stretcher, hup, hup! The doctor talks to me in the hallway, obviously assuming I'm next of kin.

"We need to do a D & C," he explains. "She's lost a lot of blood but that's probably just because she was nearly at four months. I think if we keep her overnight we can get by without transfusing her." He smiles quickly and pats me on the arm.

"Thanks." Wendy is rolled out now, and I pat *her* on the arm.

"Everything's going to be fine, sweetie," I tell her. "Dr. Bernstein is here. They're taking you in now." She is too out of it to respond and just stares bleakly at the ceiling.

After she's gone, I stare after her, suddenly afraid. Maybe she misunderstood me and will misinterpret my comforting message to mean she's not losing the baby? I think of running after her but stop myself. What would I say? "By the way, Wen, you *are* losing this baby. I meant to say you're fine even though the baby isn't."

Spent, confused, sad and even angry, I reenter her room and sit down in the chair by the empty bed. And I cry.

Oh, it's not the sobbing, gulping tears Wendy was justly entitled to. After all, what do I have to cry about? A ruined Friday night? Henry and Tess's escapades? They pale in comparison to losing a baby.

I cry because she's better off losing the baby, and when she wakes up she'll realize it and cry, too. She was denied the uninhibited joy of finding out she was pregnant, and now she'll be denied the complete cathartic grief of losing it. Other feelings will intrude.

All of these sad roads lead back to Sam. If he had been true to her, she could have been happy about having the baby and sad about losing it. Now the situation is curiously reversed. That damned Sam. He's a monster.

In a fit of anger I grab the phone by her bed, pull out the phone book and look up Sam's number. I punch in the numbers so hard I miss one and get a wrong answer. Then I try again and he's not home but his voice mail message kicks in. "Professor Sam Terrill here. Leave a message." Only prize-winning assholes leave their title in their voice mail message. *Professor* Terrill?

"This is Amy, Wendy's friend, you little shithead. Wendy's had a miscarriage. So you're off the hook, bastard." And I slam the phone down for good measure. And it feels so, so good that I cry again. I use up five tissues, I'm feeling so good.

And then I call Henry. At least Henry isn't like Sam. At least he does some nice things, right? He came to see me when I was in the hospital. He encouraged my job hunt. He pulled a coverlet over me when I fell asleep early one night. He's not married.

At least I don't think he's married. How would I know? Just because he told me? And what does it matter—if he's willing to lead other women on just to get their business? Maybe he's leading me on, too.

I don't know, I don't know, I don't know. I shake my head. I'll have to think about that tomorrow, Scarlett. Fiddle-dee-dee. Tomorrow's another day. Tonight, I just need a friend. Henry's "quick bite" with Tess, the She-Devil, should be over by now.

"Hello?" he answers on the third ring, just one before it kicks into voice mail.

"Henry, it's Amy."

"Where are you?" he asks, and his voice sounds kind of odd. Mine is trembling and I plunge forward and tell him the whole ugly story about Wendy.

"How is she?" he asks. I can't put my finger on it, but there is something strange about his voice. He doesn't seem concerned about me at all.

"Pretty weak. And unhappy. You can imagine. She's in the O.R. right now." I don't care anymore why I was angry at him. I want to tell him that it was stupid of me to set up the whole spare-bedroom scenario. I want to tell him I won't be the "little woman" anymore and I think I'm falling in love with him, too, but I don't want to be hurt again. I want to say all these things because I'm tired of wondering if I'm loved, and maybe if I start acting like I am, it will all fall neatly into place.

"I want to stay and wait until she comes out of the operating room. I..." Go ahead, say it. You can do it. "I would like it if you could wait with me."

It doesn't sound like my voice, at least not the voice I've become accustomed to using over the past two years. This voice is slower and a little tremulous. This is my heart's voice, unadorned at last.

In the background, I can hear a woman. Tess. "Darling, something wrong?"

My face flames with hurt and anger. "That's okay," I manage to croak out, and hang up.

chapter 19

Judas tree: Betrayal

I have an antipathy to Southern women. Maybe because I was under the illusion that I was one, being born south of the Mason-Dixon line, and it was a rude awakening when I went to college at the University of Richmond to find out that I didn't really qualify for that club. The Southern girls I met there were so much more confident, and so sure of their own feminine wiles. They were a perfect blend of both coquetry and feminism, the very balance I can't seem to find in my own life. And it always seemed whenever my eyes lit on a boy I might want to go out with, some postmodernist belle would get there before me, stealing him right out from under my eyes. I began to feel like a traitor on enemy soil, a Yankee (even though I wasn't officially one) on Rebel ground. Rick's old flame was a Southern girl.

But, of course, it's not okay. Henry not only did go out with Tess. He brought her back to our place! Yes, *our* place! I live there, too, right? And since I'm not there to act as a natural check on his impulses, who knows what was going on or about to go on?

As I think of what's happened to Wendy, of Sam's hard heart, of my own heartbreak with Rick, I realize that this little bump in the road—Henry—was probably inevitable. Years from now, I'll look back and think, yeah, that was pretty foolish getting involved with someone like Henry Castle right after getting over Rick, but I had to start somewhere, and look at me now all alive and whole and well.

I don't feel well. I feel sick to my stomach. I haven't eaten anything since before noon, so I wipe my eyes and ask a nurse where to get something.

"The cafeteria's closed, but there are some vending machines," she says, and gives me directions.

The hospital's confusing so I almost get lost on my way back after buying a PayDay candy bar and a Dr. Pepper. I manage to eat about half the candy and drink all the soda when they return Wendy to the room around midnight.

Everything went well, Dr. Bernstein assures me, standing outside her door as they wheel her in, and she should be capable of bearing children in the future.

"These things are a mixed blessing," he says, his surgical mask falling below his small chin. "It's usually nature's way of taking care of a fetus when there's something wrong with it. Something that doesn't make it viable."

"When can she go home?" I ask.

"I'll see how she's doing in the morning. If her blood volume goes back up and she's feeling okay, I can discharge her by tomorrow afternoon. She'll need to take it easy for a few weeks, I'd say. Is there someone who can help out around the house?"

"I can do it."

He heads off to see another patient and I head into the

dim room to see Wendy. She's just barely out of the anesthesia and glad the pain is gone and everything has reached some conclusion. She smiles weakly when I tell her I'm there, then whispers, "You should go home. I'll be fine."

Go home? Where's that? I might as well pitch up here in the hospital. Who wants to walk in on Tess and Henry? Walking in on Gina and Fred was bad enough.

Just as I sit down by her bed, Henry walks out of my angry thoughts and into the room. I shoot him a dark look that says he's not earning any brownie points by showing up now.

"I came as soon as I could," he says, standing by her bed. "How is she?"

"She's doing okay. I told you that on the phone. You didn't need to come." I don't look at him. "Wouldn't want to take you away from your important clients."

"You said you wanted me to come," he hisses back.

"Well, that was before I found out you were otherwise engaged." Still I do not look at him.

A nurse comes into the room, asks me cheerily how the "patient is doing" and I resist the urge to tell her that she's the one who should be telling me that. She takes Wendy's pulse, checks her IV and wakes her up so she can take her temperature. Everything must be okay because she leaves without a word and with no furrowed brows or grimacing lips.

"We were having a nightcap," he says through gritted teeth. "That's all. I thought you might want to meet her."

I remember that "having a nightcap" is how Henry and I landed in bed for the first time.

"Hmm," I say under my breath. He knew I was going to Wendy's. He knew I'd be out.

"I didn't know you were out when I brought her there," he says, as if reading my mind.

"Oh, that makes it all better, then," I whisper, "the fact that you wanted to rub my nose in it."

He offers no rebuttal. If he refuses to take the stand I can only infer he's guilty, right?

"I was just going to leave, anyway," I say, and stand. I grab my purse. "You can stay if you want." I bend over and tell Wendy I'm leaving. She murmurs an acknowledgment. "I'll be back tomorrow," I tell her.

I resolutely refuse to look at Henry as I leave the room. He catches up with me and we silently ride the elevator together. Then we silently walk out to the parking lot together.

Even though it's dark, the air is warm as a hothouse's interior. It swamps me when I open the door after the sterile chill of the hospital air-conditioning.

At Wendy's car, I unlock the driver's door and start to get in, but Henry stops me from closing it.

"Why didn't you tell me Rick Squires was your fiancé?" he asks fiercely.

My heart races. "What?"

"You blindsided me, dammit. This afternoon, after I talked to you, Calvin Squires stops in my office. He asks me what I'm up to. I tell him I'm going to see a client. He asks who. I tell him. He says he knows her and she's quite a beauty. And I say that I have a girlfriend, and oh, by the way, she's looking for a job, does he know of any openings. He asks who you are and I give him your name."

My gut twists. I can visualize the scene. Straight and tall Squires, with a long face capped by lush graying hair, always looking frail, as if a strong wind could blow him down.

"What did he say?" I whisper, even though we are out of the "quiet" zone.

"He said, 'I'm afraid I can't help you,' and walked away. Another secretary overheard. So she told me."

"About Rick and me and the accident."

"Yes."

"But you must have known. I mean, you work there. Where he worked." My eyes sting and I blink fast.

"Jesus Christ, Amy! You know what those people are like. They don't talk about anything but business. I had no idea…"

No idea that his current girlfriend might hold him back? It's unclear, and he shakes his head back and forth in an angry sort of way that doesn't clarify. And I feel like saying I'm sorry.

But dammit, I'm so tired of feeling sorry. I've spent two years being sorry. Henry should be sorry. Sam should be sorry. Rick should be sorry. Even Dr. Bernstein should be sorry. I wipe my face with the back of my hand.

"I get the picture. You wouldn't have gone out with me if you'd known." I pull the door away from him and slam it shut, then roll down the window to get rid of the stifling heat.

"I didn't say that," he says.

"You don't need to. I told you—I get the picture." I turn the engine on. "At least now I know. Better than waiting like Wendy did for Sam."

Henry lets out a snort of derision. "Right. I'm just like Sam. All men are like Sam." He bobs his head up and down in disgust. "Sam sure as hell made you one suspicious bitch toward men. Guilty until proven…"

His voice is raised and a security guard steps out of the hospital door and looks our way.

Henry shoots him a look and then a grimace back at me, and it occurs in my mind that we might end our relationship the same way we began it—with a uniformed man trying to save me from the "raging Latino."

He lowers his voice and steps closer. "How do you expect anybody to love you if you keep secrets like this?" His voice is thin and angry.

"I wasn't keeping anything from you, dammit. It just never

came up." And then, searching for a parallel, I hurl my own accusations. "You never talk about your other relationships. Why should I?"

"I told you—I didn't have any other 'relationships.' Nothing serious. Not until you, " he insists. "I don't mix business with pleasure. Can't you get that through your head? You're the one I really—"

"Don't!" I interrupt. So what if he cares about me? Fine way he has of showing it—bringing Tess and Joanna and whomever to his condo.

"Besides, you should have told me Rick Squires had been your fiancé when you told me about the accident." Henry rocks back on his heels and stares into the distance, shaking his head. "You should have seen Squires. He looked like he'd seen a ghost."

A switch turns on in my brain sending white-hot fury coursing through my veins. Henry blames me for how bad Squires feels?!

"Squires?!" I cry. It explodes out of me like a volcano. I'm tired of feeling guilty. "If it makes it any easier, you can tell him his son wasn't my fiancé. At least not when he died. *He'd broken up with me that night!*"

Tears choke my voice. I've told Henry something no one else knows. Not Wendy, not Gina, not my mother, not even good ol' Dr. Waylon Freud. Rick had broken our engagement the night of the accident.

In a strained voice, on the Baltimore-Washington Expressway just north of the Dorset exit, Rick had explained that he wasn't sure we should get married after all. He felt rushed and unsure. He needed some breathing room.

Breathing room? I could hardly breathe myself when he told me! My heart beat fast, nothing seemed real. Fear had gripped my gut. My soon-to-be-husband was asking for a divorce.

And while he spoke, my mind and heart grabbed for any life preserver within reach—maybe he just needs some reassurance, I thought, maybe he just needs to stay with his folks for a few days, or take a trip, or not see me from now until the wedding, or, or, or…

Or maybe he needed some other woman.

Sally was her name, Sally Chessman, the woman he'd dated in law school, the one serious relationship he'd had before he and I connected. He'd really been on the rebound, you see, when he met me, and it wasn't all settled yet but he hadn't been aware of that, not until he ran into Sally recently at that conference in North Carolina and found out she was joining a law firm in D.C., and the spark was still there, Ame, he couldn't deny it, and he knew it would hurt like hell and the last thing he wanted to do was hurt me because I was such a great person, and…

And I couldn't bear to hear him say the inevitable—that I'd meet someone else who deserved me. Panic rose in my throat as I silently screamed, don't say that, Rick, please don't say that. Because I wouldn't meet someone who deserved me if he didn't fit the bill. He deserved me! And I deserved him! Didn't I?

"I'm sorry, Ame, I really am," he'd said, "but I can't go on living like this."

And in a few moments, in a blinding, screeching crash, he had stopped living altogether.

When I awoke the next day and my sister broke the news to me that he was dead, I didn't believe her. Of course, I didn't say it at first. I listened to her, I saw her mouth moving. I heard the words "Rick didn't make it, honey," and I fell asleep, muffled by drugs and pain, so sure that God wouldn't take him and leave me with no recourse, no second chance to prove I was right for him and Sally wasn't, that he'd just been suffering from prewedding jitters, that everything would be okay again if I just got enough sleep.

When the news sank in, my reaction changed to "so, there, take that, you heartbreaker!" Because I'd been hurt so badly, not by the accident, but by Rick. And it was awful, but I felt, at first, that he'd gotten what he deserved, and when I cried, they were tears of vengeance and wrath, not sorrow. They were sobs of retribution and anger, followed by silent, steady tears of guilt for feeling that way, as if the accident really had been my fault because, for a fleeting moment, I was glad he was dead. Cause and effect.

The memory strangles me. For a moment, I can't speak. I stare at the wheel while tears cascade down my face.

"What?" Henry asks, confused.

"You heard me. He broke up with me." Not looking at Henry, I continue softly. "What do you want from me, Henry? An apology? Well, okay, I'm sorry—I'm sorry I was ever engaged to Rick Squires. And I'm sorry that he was killed in an accident. And I'm sorry I was driving. And most of all, I'm sorry I ever met you."

"Amy…" he interrupts, but I don't let him.

"Have as many women over as you like. Send them all flowers! Tell Squires you threw me out once you saw how bad it made him feel!"

As soon as I say it, relief washes over me. I knew our relationship would come to this eventually. Better to get it over with, right? And since this is a night of heartbreak all round, it's sort of like a two-for-one deal at the grocery store, a discount on grief.

"I'm going to Wendy's to get some things for her. I'll stay there. You don't want to keep Tess waiting," I say, and put the car in Reverse, cutting him off. He steps completely away and puts his hands in his pockets. I don't wave goodbye and neither does he.

chapter 20

Yellow rose: Jealousy or decrease of love

When I now examine my life with Rick through the magnifying glass of hindsight, the clues are obvious. I see the long nights at the office, the decreased lovemaking, the increased disinterest in my family and friends, all accumulating over time like evidence in a case. Remember the night Rick gave me roses because I was jealous of his new colleague? If only I had known then what those flowers signified. They were a peace offering, all right, but a peace offering for a war being fought on a battlefield unbeknownst to me—Rick's heart. Rick's affection for me had waned long before the night he broke the news that he wanted to stop the wedding. He was good at hiding his deepest thoughts, a skill he'd learned growing up in a quiet household. Thank God Henry never gave me yellow roses, or I'd have never gotten involved with him…but then again, maybe that wouldn't have been a bad thing. Not getting involved again, that is. The best summer of my life was when I wasn't involved with anyone, the summer of Sheila's pool.

So Henry now knows my secret. Rick didn't just die on me. He broke my heart first. Talk about two-for-one deals.

Rick and I had been at a dinner party in Potomac, a suburb of D.C. Some lawyer friend of his threw it and it was fun—glittering laughter, clinking glasses, expensive food served in a lavishly decorated McMansion. I felt like Cinderella that night. Poor girl makes good. Raised in the middle-class outskirts of Baltimore, I was rubbing shoulders with the upper-class of the D.C. legal circuit. I'd smiled so much that night, my face hurt.

But Rick had been quiet, which he attributed to a headache. However, he drank an awful lot, which I remember thinking was odd. Hard liquor, too, which he didn't usually go for. He was a fine-wine guy. But that night he'd had two Glenlivets, neat. And a couple more glasses of an Australian merlot. And even a glass of Courvoisier right before we hit the road, which is why I asked for the keys and offered to drive.

Little did I know he'd been screwing up his courage to break up with me. Poor fellow. He must have been elated to have me take the wheel. He knew I wouldn't be able to look at him too much when he plunged the dagger into my soul.

After I gained complete consciousness in the hospital, it quickly became clear he hadn't told anyone else about his intentions. Hell, he'd barely had the fortitude to tell me. And how could I tell anyone? They were all offering their condolences. So sorry to hear about your fiancé, dear. Rick was such a sweet boy, dear. We're just ripped up about your loss, dear.

What was I supposed to say? Wait, you're wrong, he wasn't sweet, and technically, he wasn't my fiancé any longer, but if you're sorry for my breakup, I'll take it?

No, better to keep it quiet, my own private humiliating pain. Better to remember only the good parts about Rick

Libby Malin

and think that he would have quickly changed his mind about the break. He would have laughed and hit his head and said, "wow, was that ever a dumb idea, huh, honey? Sally was never right for me," as soon as his hangover passed. That's what I told myself anyway.

Now I tell myself that what I will miss most about Henry is the sex. On Saturday, I awaken early, feeling like *I* have a hangover. Every footfall outside Wendy's apartment makes me think it's an early-riser floral deliveryman, bringing me a nice little raspberry bush (remorse) from Henry. Or even a small but elegant bunch of pine (pity). One of those miniature trees would do just fine—the kind that look like they belong in a bonsai garden.

No delivery comes.

The weather cooperates with my mood and Saturday is gray and misty. I don't think I or Wendy could have taken one of those in-your-face happy days with blue skies and sun screaming "up with people" stuff at us.

He doesn't call. While I bump around Wendy's apartment, I keep thinking back to our conversation in the parking lot and replaying it. Not once did he say anything remotely re-sembling consolation or comfort. Instead, he had been more concerned about how my not telling him had embarrassed him at work.

What a guy. I had him pegged from the beginning, didn't I? He might not be a schmuck like Sam, but he's a schmuck-in-training. Give him a few years and he'll be cheating on his wife like the best of them. Or at least breaking up with me.

Ouch. Cheating on his wife. The thought of Henry with some snazzy bride sends a twinge of hurt through me that zaps the anger away. It's just because I don't want him to be happy, right? I want him to suffer. Like me.

And I am suffering. I'm having boyfriend-withdrawal,

made worse by the fact that my best friend is in the hospital so I don't have her shoulder to cry on. And if I'm honest, her shoulder isn't going to be available for some time after what she's just been through.

What did I do before I had a boyfriend? How did I fill the time? Oh, that's right—self-pity. Hmm…and that's what I'm doing now, engaging in self-pity. Funny how it feels different.

Since I woke up early—well, I kind of didn't really sleep much at all—I spend the time cleaning Wendy's apartment for two hours until it's a decent time to go visit her. I change her sheets and straighten her dresser. I empty her hamper and wash her clothes in the basement laundry. I even manage to bake some brownies—from scratch, not from some box mix—which I arrange on an Italian pottery dish she has in the back of her cabinet. Looking at its festive colors makes me sad. It's a recent purchase—the tag is still glued to the bottom—and my guess is she picked it up one afternoon when hope was still in her heart about Sam.

At last, I head to the hospital, stopping in the lobby gift shop to pick up some flowers and a balloon. But all they have are bouquets of carnations, roses or daises. I opt for the daises, which mean "innocence."

When I walk into her room, Wendy's pushing a fork at some breakfast. Or at least that's what I think is on her tray. Maybe it's really Play-Doh or some arts-and-crafts paste for therapy.

She smiles when she sees me, but it's a phony smile that doesn't take long to crack. Her lips are chapped and her eyes have large circles under them. Still, she has a classic beauty, like a figure from a medieval painting, all white skin and feathery hair. How could any man pass her up?

"Thought these would cheer you," I say as I look around for a vase. Finding none, I stand holding them out to her.

"Those are lovely. What do they mean?"

"Uh…happiness is over the horizon," I make up. Just then a nurse comes in the room and admires the flowers as well while she checks Wendy's blood pressure and temperature.

"I can get you a vase for those," she offers.

But Wendy, who has a thermometer sticking out of her mouth, shakes her head. When it's removed, she says, "I'll be going home today. It's probably not worth it."

"So soon?" I ask, looking at the nurse.

"As soon as Dr. Bernstein discharges her. And he should be by any minute. He had a delivery this morning." The nurse leaves the room, blithely unaware of the dart she's thrown at Wendy's psyche.

There's no point in hiding it, so I tell Wendy about Henry and me breaking up. In a strange way, I figure it might make her feel better to know that someone else is hurting, too. She listens with creased brows, then bites her lower lip.

"I'm sorry to hear that." But her voice is less sympathetic than resigned. As if she's given up on expecting good things from men. "If you need a place to stay, you can crash with me."

"Just temporarily," I say, and she smiles. Temporarily has been going on for several months now with me.

"You know, Ame, why don't you come to Europe," she says after I sit in the chair next to the bed.

"You're not still thinking of going. What for? You need to recover!"

"I can recover over there as much as I can over here. And I can't face my parents just yet. I need a breather. I was really looking forward to the trip." Her eyes get watery. She'd looked forward to other things, too. "Besides, you still have your passport, right?"

My passport—Rick and I were going to Greece for our honeymoon.

"I have to find a job, Wen. I might even have one. I did a

terrific interview yester—last week." I don't want to mention yesterday. Maybe it will just go away, be wiped off the calendars.

She lets out a long sigh and doesn't look at me. "You can look for a job when you get back. It's not like anyone's been beating down your door."

I'm surprised at her cruel bluntness, but I ascribe it to her pain. We spend an hour watching television together, just news, and then some cooking shows, but she dozes most of the time. Dr. Bernstein doesn't show up and when I go ask the nurse where he is, she tells me quite merrily that he had another birth and "this one is just popping out!" She laughs while she says it. I feel like punching her.

When I see that Wendy is still asleep, I decide to spend the time grocery shopping at a nearby Giant superstore, so I tell the nurse to let Wendy know I'll be back.

Hooray for corporate supermarkets. This one not only has tomato soup, it carries toaster strudel, Pillsbury cinnamon buns, and Marie Callendar's chocolate cream pie.

Back in the hospital, Wendy's lunch arrives before Dr. Bernstein. We wile away the hours complaining to each other about the Gelman Agency, retreading material we've discussed a thousand times. It feels good to talk about something familiar and relatively harmless. We don't discuss her miscarriage or Henry at all. But both of us are wounded souls who need to recuperate.

Finally, after two, Dr. Bernstein comes in and I almost don't recognize him without the shower cap. He is nearly bald and what hair he does have is shaved close to the scalp. He looks oddly vulnerable. He's pleased with all her vital signs but urges her to take it easy when she gets home.

"You lost a lot of blood, Mrs. Jackson," he says to her, momentarily slipping and thinking she's married. "But you'll bounce back. Did the nurses go over with you all the things to look for?"

Wendy nods yes, but he goes over them, anyway—how to tell if something untoward is happening, when to make her follow-up appointment, how many weeks to wait before having sex. No problem there.

After he leaves, I help Wendy into a Laura Ashley-type dress, the only thing I could find in her closet that would be loose and comfortable. When she sees it, she laughs ironically, but doesn't protest as I slip it over her head and knot the ties in the back. I even attach the balloon to her wheelchair when we roll her out to the car. It says "Going home!"

At her apartment, I help her to bed and fix some dinner. Nothing fancy. Meat loaf and potatoes and green beans. Comfort food. I serve the brownies for dessert. She doesn't eat much or say much and later when I check on her in her bedroom, I see a pile of bunched-up tissues in the trash can next to her bed. Poor Wendy.

I spend Saturday night watching television alone in her living room and wondering what Henry is doing. And I start planning how to get my stuff and looking forward to the call I'll have to make to retrieve it. This and my lack of sleep from the night before have me conked out before ten. I fall asleep in my clothes and don't wake up until two in the morning. Then I panic, not remembering where I am, trying to figure out why Henry's not here and why he dumped me on this lumpy sofa.

Slowly, it comes back to me. He didn't dump me anywhere. I dumped him. A preemptive dump. My heart stops thudding, my breath slows down. Fear recedes, replaced by that dull after-breakup ache. I wonder how long it will last. I check on Wendy, who is sleeping soundly, and I go back to sleep myself. No use changing. I don't have anything to change into anyway.

On Sunday, I borrow some clothes from Wendy and fix a big Sunday dinner of pork roast and mashed potatoes and corn. After dinner, we eat pie, and Wendy gets up to clear the table.

"Sit back down," I tell her. "The doctor said rest."

"I'm feeling better," she says. "Besides, you can't play nursemaid forever."

After she puts things in the sink, I take over while she sits at the little table.

"If I get the okay, I can still go to France in September," she says, looking at me intently. "And I'd really like you to go with me, Ame. You'd be doing me a favor."

I shrug my shoulders. "I haven't ruled it out. I just need to…" I need to talk to Henry. "I need to check on a few things," I say.

"If you take a break now, you can look for a job when you get back," she says. "I'll help you. I'll send out letters for you and everything. It's not like I'll be doing much else."

"You'll go back to work. And my guess is you'll be run down for a while."

"I might not go back to work right away." The way she says it, I feel like she's holding out.

"Are you thinking of quitting?" I ask, placing a pot in the dish drainer.

"It's something I've been thinking about," she says defensively.

"What would you do?"

"Stay with my parents for a while. I was going to do that anyway. After the baby." Her voice trembles.

"But you go crazy when you're with them." And without a baby as a buffer, she'll be a lunatic before you can say "Mommy dearest."

Now she shrugs, with irritation. "They're not so bad." She stands, stretches and yawns. "If you want to get a good airfare, you should try to decide in a week or two. But I really hope you decide to go. It would mean a lot to me." She shuffles off to her bedroom and closes the door. My guess is she's taking her crying jag now. Sort of like taking a pill or a dose of medicine. She needs it to recover as much as any pharmaceutical on the market.

As I finish the pots, I feel guilty (for not being a good friend and jumping at the chance to go with her), anxious (that I'd get a job offer right before we took off) and sad (Henry) all at the same time. But mostly sad.

Henry. Do I wish he would call? You bet I do. I yearn for him to call. I dream of it. I hear him saying, "*Conchita,* I'm sorry. You suffered a great loss two years ago and I had no right to consider anyone's feelings but your own when it came to the accident. Please come back."

I would even be happy to hear him call and say simply, "Hey. What's up?"

In fact, all I can think of Sunday night is Henry. I want him to call me now so I don't have to call him first, and I do need to call him. I want to ask him to take care of Trixie, at least until I find a new place to live, because Wendy's allergic to her. I start to look forward to calling him, so I concoct games to keep myself from placing too much emphasis on it. I hoped he would call me—surely he must be wondering when I'll get my stuff. But as I drape the towel through the refrigerator door handle, I have an awful simmer-inducing thought. What if he just throws my stuff on the sidewalk in front of his condo?

Naw. I don't see it. There's probably some sort of covenant rule against it.

Disappointed that the phone isn't ringing, I make plans to talk to him on Monday. He'll be at work, and he can never talk long at work. Business setting for a businesslike call, right? He won't possibly be able to interpret my calling him as needing him.

But when Monday rolls around, I can hardly keep myself from rushing Wendy through breakfast so she'll hop in the shower and I can have the phone in privacy.

At eight-fifty-five, I have my chance. While the steady hum of spraying water comes from the bathroom, I grab the cordless and punch in the Squires number, asking for Henry in a low, conspiratorial voice. I'm put through to his secretary, then hit a roadblock.

"He's not in this morning. Can I take a message?"

For a brief, exhilarating moment, I imagine Henry so tormented over our breakup that he couldn't drag himself into the office, and I'm ashamed to admit that this scenario makes me very, very happy.

"No message," I say, "I'll try later."

As soon as I disconnect, I try his condo. He's there, and answers immediately in a gruff, almost angry voice.

"It's Amy," I say, very straightforward. "I just called your office and they said you were home."

"Yeah. Waiting for the damned plumber to show up," he says quickly. "Broken pipe in the bathroom."

Broken pipe in the bathroom? And when did that happen—as soon as Tess stepped over the threshold, perhaps?

"I need to get my stuff."

"Okay."

Just "okay?" I plough forward. "And I was wondering if you'd keep Trixie for a while. She seems to like you more than me." That sounds funny. As if I'm saying she likes him more than I like him. Maybe that is what I'm trying to say. "Wendy's allergic to cats."

"All right."

He doesn't say anything else, and I hear his doorbell ring, so I quickly squeeze in that I'll probably stop by either today or tomorrow for my stuff. "Bye!" I yell into the receiver, rushing to get off before he tells me he has to go.

A very unsatisfying call. In between each word, I'd really wanted to hear him say he didn't want me to go. Very simple. Not a declaration of love or undying commitment. Just that he doesn't want me to go.

And that's when it becomes crystal clear to me why I wouldn't commit right away to Wendy's invitation to accompany her to France. It's because I was secretly hoping Henry will ask me to stay, and I would stay if he asked me.

Damn, I want that in-ground pool. I wish Wendy's apartment house had one. I feel like diving into something cold that shocks and penetrates. Something that surrounds me with its protective transparent layers through which I can watch but not feel.

As luck would have it, I don't get over to Henry's condo until Wednesday. Because she's not supposed to drive for a week, Wendy asks me to run some errands for her on Monday, and on Tuesday I take her to get her hair cut because she's looking so blue I'm desperate to find something to cheer her.

I've been borrowing Wendy's clothes for four days, washing them quickly in the evening so I don't need to intrude too far into her wardrobe. This is growing thin. I want my stuff.

When I drive up to the condo on Wednesday, I can't help it—I want the pipes to still be broken and Henry to still be there. Maybe I'll break them myself and call him at the office to let him know? Nope. He'd probably just ask me to hang around until the plumber comes.

I tell myself I want to see him because I haven't yet felt a real sense of "closure." That was a word Dr. Waylon Freud used a lot. He used to talk about the importance of finding "closure" with Rick's passing. Except when he said it the first time, with his Southern drawl and funny inflections, I thought he was saying I needed "clothes, sure," and for a full quarter hour I'd reddened and felt angry and humiliated all at once that this grief counselor, who was supposed to be helping me, was insulting my wardrobe. Even after I figured out my mistake, I still felt embarrassed, and kept my hands glued to the spot on my gray slacks where a faded grease stain was barely visible.

When I think of getting "closure" with Henry, though, I zero in on one scenario. It's where Henry kneels at my feet while I look into a Gone-With-the-Wind blue-and-pink sky, and he rests his head on my calico skirt saying he hurts like hell now that I'm gone, and that he really does love me and what was he thinking not to come out and say it, and would I please stay, please, oh please, oh please.

Or maybe that's Rick I see on his knees.

Henry's not home and the condo smells like bacon. In the kitchen, I see the frying pan in the dish drainer, along with his morning mug. Everything neat and clean, probably even neater and cleaner than when I was the Little Woman.

After I gather my stuff together, I decide to give the place one quick once-over to make sure I'm not leaving anything behind. So I go through all of Henry's things. But I come up with nothing. No coffee ice cream in the freezer. No herbal shampoos in the shower. Not even a stray hair in a different shade. Or a dropped petal from a flower arrangement.

I figure I'll spend a lot of time patting Trixie and having a heart-to-heart about not getting too emotionally attached to Henry, but she hardly gives me a passing glance and heads for her cat-food dish in the kitchen with a diffident purr. No reason to linger. I lug my suitcase to the front door where I'm greeted by the UPS man delivering a thick envelope for me.

In the foyer I excitedly rip it open—but hell, it's a rejection letter from the tutoring program! I didn't get the job. Good thing I didn't celebrate last Friday, huh? Boy would I feel foolish now.

They've sent all my work samples back, which was nice of them, but not enough to soften the blow. "We were very impressed with your skills and attitude but hired another person whose qualifications more closely suit our needs," the letter says. Who knows what happened—another internal candidate? Someone who walked in off the street after my interview?

Note to all employers: do not use UPS for rejection letters. UPS is the Christmas gift man, the catalog-order man, the special present from Great Aunt Susy man. It's cruel to set up the expectation that something cool is arriving by the man in brown only to have him drop a little cloud of gloom in your lap.

Rejected, cross and still sad, I head back to Wendy's. It's been a red-letter day. Moving out of my boyfriend's condo and losing out on a good job prospect all in one afternoon. And Tess is nowhere to be seen.

Wendy's reading a magazine in the living room when I return. She's looking better—the color's returned to her cheeks, and her new haircut frames her face and shows off her eyes.

"Henry called," she says after I drag my suitcase over the threshold.

My heart races.

"He left a message. Your sister called him looking for you, and he just told her he'd give you the message."

Thud. That's my racing heart hitting the ground.

"Thanks," I say. I don't ask her how he sounded or if he said anything else. I suspect if he'd been sobbing or had blurted out he couldn't live without me she would have passed it along as well.

When I don't make a move for the phone right away, she puts her magazine aside. "I was going to take a nap." She smiles. And she follows through by heading for her bedroom. Man, but her apartment is small. I have to do something soon. I can't stay here. Maybe I need to head back to Gina's.

Feeling suddenly tired, I call Gina. She answers on the third ring, and when she hears my voice, she doesn't even ask me how I've been or why she couldn't find me at the condo. She launches into her news immediately. And what news it is.

"I'm pregnant!" she shrieks into the phone. I look over my shoulder to make sure Wendy couldn't have overheard. This wouldn't necessarily brighten her day.

"Wow! That's fantastic," I whisper. "When did you find out?"

"This morning. Just got back from the doctor's a little while ago. I almost told Henry when I called him looking for you. But I wanted to tell you first. After Fred, that is." She sounds hysterical with joy.

"How's Fred taking it?" I ask tentatively.

"What? He's *thrilled!* And why are you whispering? Are you at Henry's office or something?"

No, I'm just in the apartment of a woman who recently suffered a miscarriage. And I don't want to tell said woman about Gina's pregnancy. And I don't want to tell Gina about said woman's miscarriage. Bad karma. So instead, I tell Gina about my break-up.

"Oh, damn. That's too bad," she says, and I get the impression she's impatient with my bad news and eager to get back to her good news. "You'll find someone else. You've just started dating again, after all, Ame. It would have been awfully lucky if you'd found Mr. Right on your first time out." And to think—just a few months ago she was telling me how awfully lucky I was to have found Henry so early in the game.

"Oh, and I never had him over for dinner," she says, as if that's the important thing and not the shattered pieces of my heart.

I tell Gina I'm going to France with Wendy now that I don't have any more job prospects. I haven't even told Wendy this. Hell, I haven't even told myself. Note to subconscious: tell yourself important things before blurting them out to others.

"Whoa—you're going to France? When did this happen?"

I explain how Wendy's been planning this "vacation" for quite a while and she wants somebody to go with her.

"She broke up with her boyfriend, too," I say.

"Oh, that's too bad," she says. "But I have to say that a woman who dates a married man doesn't rank very high on my list."

I wonder if suffering a miscarriage will place Wendy higher on the list.

"Where will you get the money?" Gina asks me. "For the trip?"

"I just need the airfare and some expenses. Wendy's parents rented a place for her. I've got a little money saved."

"Maybe you should keep it, though. You know—for a rainy day."

A rainy day? I'm in a deluge with no land in sight. My rainy-day money isn't going to do me any good on my lonesome little ark. Better to use it up and have some fun.

"Well, Wendy doesn't want to go alone. I'd be like her traveling companion."

Gina grills me a little more on the trip, then goes on and on about the baby, telling me pretty much all the same things Wendy told me when she got excited about the prospect of becoming a mother—when she'd hear the first heartbeat, what to expect during pregnancy, whether she'd try to go the natural route with childbirth. Except with Gina, there's no dark cloud—an absent adulterer father—in the background. It's blue skies all the way. Damn, it feels good.

When I get off the phone, Wendy wanders into the living room. Despite my effort to talk low, she's overheard—at least the part about me going to France. Smiling broadly, she grabs a magazine as if that's why she came back out.

"This trip will be like high school," she says, even though we didn't go to high school together. "It will be so much fun! Wait till you see the place we'll be staying in. Close to the beach, with a little terrace, and even an in-ground pool!"

Did she say in-ground pool? Why didn't she tell me this earlier? It's kismet. No more wishy-washy wondering. Destiny calls. Who am I to question it?

chapter 21

Cypress: Mourning, death, despair

The Mediterranean was supposed to be my honeymoon destination with Rick. White sand, blue water, tall cypress trees swaying in the late-day breezes. His parents sent me a thank-you-for-your-sympathy note after I sent them flowers and a sympathy card filled with incoherent ramblings. I don't know what flowers I sent—Gina ordered them for me. Their note was more a transmittal slip than an outpouring of gratitude. "Thank you for your kind thoughts at this difficult time," it read in embossed script, and was signed "Emily Squires." No words of comfort or healing for me. Had Sally gone to the funeral, or sent flowers, or stopped by their house? What had they written to her? When I was well enough to start handling my own affairs again, I was wounded afresh by my telephone bills. In sterile black ink on blue paper was the tale of my heartbreak. At least one call a month to a North Carolina number. Starting the month after Rick returned from the conference near Duke. He always took care of the phone bills while

I handled gas and electric and we split the rent. Sally, I realized, could well have been more a part of the Squires's lives than I ever was. He had known Sally for three years, she was part of their "crowd," whereas I had been an outsider, and we'd been together for a little over a year. Not only was my future with Rick destroyed by the accident, my past was demolished as well.

In the next two weeks, Wendy perks up. Instead of moping around every day, she's on the phone with a travel agent and her mother planning out every aspect of this six-week sojourn. As soon as the doctor gives Wendy the thumbs-up, she goes out shopping, buying a completely new travel wardrobe, and graciously showering me with hand-me-downs she doesn't want any longer.

Having started the summer with a nearly empty closet, I am now awash in clothes. I have the items my sister bought for me when I first moved out of my country home. I have the items I bought myself before starting my ill-fated job at the College of Our Lady of the Air Freshener. And now I have designer castoffs from Wendy. Soon there won't be any more room for us in her apartment. The clothes will have taken over.

Which is another reason it's a good thing we'll be leaving soon. Although we manage to stay out of each other's way as best we can, Wendy's flat is just too damned tight. On one particularly difficult night all I want to do is either talk with Henry or be alone and brood about him, but I have to sit and artificially smile while Wendy giggles her way through sitcom reruns. I'm ready to move back in with Gina if only for the few remaining days before we leave.

But I stay, hanging on with my fingernails, not calling Henry and trying not to think of my future. But damn, it hurts. It hurts more than I figured it would. I miss Henry and I keep feeling like I'm on a temporary leave, taking care of a good friend, and I'll be back and he'll be waiting. But in my dark moments, I know he won't be.

Planning a trip to France is a decent consolation prize, a lot better than the other one I've concocted, which is imagining that Henry tries to call me but loses his nerve and hangs up before it rings through.

A few days before we are to depart, Wendy has a surprise for me.

"I never got you a birthday gift," she says one night after dinner, and hands me an envelope. I'm embarrassed. Is she giving me cash? I know I'm strapped, but this is a little mortifying—taking money from your friends. When I open up the envelope, inside is a handmade sublet lease for her apartment for six months. In the blank where the rent is supposed to go, she's filled in "zero."

"You can stay here when we get back," she says, "since I'll be heading to Connecticut." Wendy is going to re-enter the vortex of her old world. Her mother is already talking to her about an eligible young doctor she wants her to meet.

"Wen, this is too much," I protest.

"Don't be silly. I'm just paying you back, that's all."

Paying me back for what? Being a derelict friend? I didn't save her from Sam.

But this feels right, too. At last, at last, I'll have somewhere to hang my hat while I get back on my feet. Yeah, I know— isn't that what I was supposed to be doing these last couple years? I'm a slow learner.

My desire for Henry has faded to a constant, dull ache. Try as I might, I have trouble making the anger come back. Every time I think of our confrontation in the parking lot now, I think of him telling me I was his only serious relationship. And I think about how he questioned me about my fiancé before he knew it was Rick. Maybe Wendy was right—he wanted to know if I was over Rick before committing himself. But I was over Rick, right? Just because I didn't tell Henry Rick's name doesn't mean anything—right?

It was all about the sex with Henry. The great sex. That's all. Nothing more. Please, God, make it all about the sex. I can deal with that.

My ache for Henry intensifies this evening. Wendy goes to bed early, and I sit in the blue light of the waning day in this waning season. Outside the air is catching the whiff of crispness that fall promises, and it's hard not to think about how just a few weeks ago I daydreamed of spending autumn with Henry. Yes, I did. I might not have admitted it to myself, but I did. I saw us taking drives into the country to see the turning leaves. I saw us picking apples together at an orchard near where I used to live. I saw us giving out trick-or-treat candy to neighborhood kids. Both of them.

Dammit, I'm not going to be able to give into temptation for six more weeks, and probably by then I'll be over it. I cave and call him. I figure I need to tell him I'm going because what if something happens to Trixie and he needs to reach me.

It's nearly ten o'clock at night and it sounds like I've awakened him.

"Amy Sheldon here," I say.

"Hi." His voice brightens. "What's up?"

"I just wanted you to know I'll be leaving tomorrow." Leaving tomorrow? I've already left him. "Leaving the country," I add in a hurry. "I'm going to France with Wendy."

"Doesn't Wendy have to rest?" he asks. Don't ask about Wendy, my inner voice screams. Ask about me.

Uh-oh. My inner voice is back. I'm not leaving a moment too soon.

"She got checked out and the doc says it's okay as long as she doesn't over do it."

"How can you go to France? I thought you didn't have any money."

"I have a little saved. I'll use it all up."

"What about a passport?"

"I have one from when Rick and I were together. We were going to go to Greece for our honeymoon." Oddly, it feels good to be able to talk about Rick to Henry. I hadn't realized how Rick's ghost had come between us until now.

His questions make me wonder if this is his way of saying he doesn't want me to go, which sets up a desire in me to hear him say that very thing, and by the end of our short conversation, I'm pressing the phone deep into my ear as if listening closely enough will allow me to make out secret coded messages that say, "Don't go. I'll miss you." I'm not able to pick anything up through the static of our conversation, though, so we will have to hang up. Then I remember why I called, or at least the reason I used to let myself call.

"Uh, about Trixie. I thought I'd give you my number in France. In case something happens to Trixie."

He asks me to wait while he gets some paper and a pen, and when he comes back I rattle off the number of the cottage Wendy's rented.

"We'll be there the last four weeks. We're traveling the first two."

"Sounds like fun."

"Yeah. I think it will be. I've only been to Europe once before. A school trip. Senior year of high school. We went to London." And I proceed to tell him all about my senior trip. Every detail, even down to how Heather Pakoskyzc threw up on the plane. I'm pathetic. All I want is this nice warm feeling back. Henry and me.

"I heard from Gina," I say breathlessly after silence passes between us. "She's pregnant."

"Really? That's great. Tell her I said congratulations."

"Yeah, it *is* great," I say, and we both know what I mean. She can be happy about it but Wendy couldn't. "She said Fred's happy as a clam, too."

"That's nice."

We've exhausted the things we can say without hurting each other, so I reluctantly get ready to hang up.

"Sounds like a great opportunity for you," Henry says before I offer my farewells. "I've been to Europe only once, too. During college. I'd like to go again."

"Yeah, it'll be great. I need the break."

He doesn't say anything else, and now I'm really thinking he wants to tell me to stay but he can't possibly do that when he's just said it's such a great opportunity for me because that would be selfish, right? He's really being selfless by not saying it. So we're stuck in this awful quicksand of competing good wishes.

"Thanks, Henry," I say at last. "For putting me up."

"The pleasure was mine, *conchita*."

Henry doesn't send flowers before we leave, but Sam does. They arrive in the morning before we head to the airport. A bouquet of tiny white rosebuds. I wonder why he waited so long, but then again, it was probably at the bottom of his to-do list, right after "seduce young coed" or "betray wife." The card says, "Sorry to hear of your hospitalization. Sam." He might as well have said, "Glory, hallelujah! Thank God the baby's gone!"

Buds of a white rose mean "heart ignorant of love."

Wendy does not ask me what they mean. She's about to throw them away when I suggest she give them to her neighbor, an elderly woman who rarely gets out. So we leave them on her doormat with a cheery note.

Although Wendy's still tired, she's happy to be leaving.

Like me, she's leaving lots of "stuff" behind, shaking it into the wind like a dirty dust mop. After my confession to Henry about Rick, I feel free to tell others. So in the days before my departure, I let Gina know of my humiliation at Rick's hands. Gina's reaction was silence followed by "I never wanted to say anything, honey, but Rick always seemed a little insincere to me." Good ol' Gina. I know I can count on her to spare me the pain of telling Mom and Dad.

Wendy's heartache is too fresh, though, to burden her with mine. I'll tell her later.

To hell with my past. Onward and upward.

chapter 22

Hyssop: Cleansing

I started hankering for an in-ground pool almost from the moment I came out of my drug-induced daze after the accident. Being stuck in a hospital bed with tubes in your arms and beeping machines by your head makes you want to dive into something cool and wet where sounds are muffled and images are blurred and yet you still feel curiously alive under it all. Recuperating at my sister's house, I would sit sweating in her living room, staring at her neat little backyard, thinking how it was the perfect size for a pool, and how if I dived in, my casts would dissolve and my limbs would be free, sort of the way Franklin Roosevelt would feel whole again once he was in some warm spring water somewhere.

    I was in the hospital for two weeks, then in a rehab center for four, and finally landed at Gina's house for the rest of my recovery that summer. Mom and Dad wanted to take me back to their place, but retreating to my parents' home seemed like an ignominious defeat I could not face. The first week out *of rehab, Gina took me to Rick's grave where I leaned on crutches and squinted in the sun while she placed jonquils on the site. They mean "I desire a return of affection," but I didn't know that at the time. At her home, she pampered and babied me, fed me, and even washed me. I couldn't take baths with the casts on, and this restriction most of all made me want a pool all to myself, some place protected and cool where I could swim and swim and be safe, and where my tears would mingle with the shimmering blue and no one would know why I was crying.*

On the airplane to France, I have to take a sedative. It's one of Wendy's, prescribed by her doctor in case she needs help "getting rest."

I thought I'd get a migraine. Instead, I get this overwhelming sense of claustrophobia. The walls are closing in on me. People surround me. I can't breathe. Wendy gives me one of her pills.

Within ten minutes I'm asleep and I manage to miss the meal they serve as well as the whole flight experience, which is okay by me. The lack of food, though, means when we land I do have a migraine but I can't take one of my magic pills because I'm afraid it will get together with the sedative and either kill me or do something worse—like make hair grow on my chest.

I don't know if it's the sedative or what but I have one of those strange dreams on the flight that seems so real that I feel like I actually experienced it, and am confused when I wake up.

I dream I'm back in my old bedroom in my parents' house waiting for a date to show up. It's dark and I stand at my window looking up the hill searching for the lights to his car. Ours is a quiet street so each car that comes down the hill makes me feel expectant and exuberant, thinking it must be his. It's a happy feeling, waiting at that window, knowing I'll have some fun and then be able to come home to my purple-skirted bed and be taken care of and loved.

And when I wake up, I want nothing more than to be back in that room.

I told you it was a strange dream. The thought of staying with my parents usually sends shivers up my spine.

When we land in France, the air is warm and close, which surprises me because I guess I expected it to be sweet and balmy since it's so far away from humid Baltimore.

We're booked into a first-rate hotel in Paris and on the taxi drive into the city, my problems with Henry and Rick flash before my eyes. That's because Parisian cabbies have a death wish. I think they aim for pedestrians. Note to self: do not walk in Paris.

Even my migraine can't dull the splendor of this city, though, and as soon as we check into our gold-and-red rooms, I decide to risk hair on my chest and take a magic pill.

With the headache receding, we both do some preliminary sightseeing, just kind of aimlessly wandering streets while we pinch ourselves to remind us that we're really here. Wendy was right. This *is* like a high school senior graduation trip. All pleasure and no guilt. I could get used to it.

For the first week, we see all the usual haunts in Paris and its environs—Notre Dame, the Eiffel Tower, Montmartre, Napoléon's Tomb, the Louvre, and some modern art museums. We take day trips to Versailles and Fontainebleau and I dream of Marie Antoinette and the Scarlet Pimpernel.

I buy cheap beads at an outdoor market and we end up eating two meals a day because we splurge on late and fattening breakfasts of croissants or pastries, then find cafés in the evening where we sip Cointreau and eat small portions of more fattening food.

By the end of the second week, I'm homesick for American flavors, so we head on over to the Champs Elysée and stop in at the McDonald's there. Parisians might thrill to the heroic arches at the end of this grand boulevard, but it's the golden arches that tug at my heartstrings.

Finally, we pack up and head for the "cottage" by the Riviera, taking trains and traveling through some areas that are fun to see but not worth stopping at.

As we travel, Wendy reverts to the culture of her heritage—wealthy, pampered and dependent on fashion. She starts reading *Vogue* again—except she doesn't really read it since it's in French. She just looks at the photos and comments on various items. She speaks curtly and loudly to porters, taxi drivers and vendors. Now I'm eager to get to the Riviera, where we'll pretty much be on our own. I'm beginning to fear she'll start an international incident.

Since her French is nonexistent, this means she experiences lots of frustrating moments with eye-rolling on her part and sneering on their part. I try to step in when I can, dusting off my high school French. A surprising amount comes back to me and my proudest moment is when a couple in Fontainebleau ask me for directions and I manage to spout them out in perfect French, only to hear the man say "damn" with an English accent. They'd mistaken me for a native.

The cottage turns out to be a mini-villa that instantly makes me think this is the kind of place where Zelda and F. Scott Fitzgerald lived before they descended into alcoholism and lunacy. Set up on a ridge overlooking the Mediterranean, it has stucco walls and a red-tiled roof, lots of rooms, a walled terrace, and—drumroll, please—an in-ground pool.

At last, I have arrived at Mecca.

Or have I? The pool is not huge—no Olympic-size number, just some modest for-my-personal-use thing that the owner had installed. Just the kind of pool I'd envisioned in my pool-dreaming days. Private. Cool. Silent. It glistens and beckons in the sunlight like a jewel wrapped up just for me.

And you know what? After baptizing myself in its depths a few times, I find I prefer the beach. The pool is lonely and still. The beach, on the other hand, is filled with interesting characters and the sounds of people enjoying themselves even though it's September.

Isn't life funny? Here I'd spent a couple years hankering after an in-ground pool and when I finally get one—or at least the exclusive use of one—I find it's not to my liking.

The few times I use it, I find myself thinking of Rick. But now those thoughts are not gossamer-coated memories of love or even painful examinations of the clues to his disaffection. They're flashes of small things I didn't like about him. Like the fact that he was a little snobbish. I'm sure he once feigned a stomachache to avoid having dinner with my parents. And he had an annoying habit of folding only his clothes after we did laundry together and leaving mine in a heap on the bed. And when he proposed to me, it hadn't been over a romantic candle-lit dinner at an expensive restaurant. It had been after we'd laughed uproariously over a stupid joke, and he'd looked at me, his eyes bright with glee, and said, "We should get married." And, you know, Rick was kind of awkward in bed, like an overgrown boy, quick and needy.

And, except for the yellow roses, he never once gave me flowers.

What a surprise—he wasn't perfect. Don't get me wrong—he wasn't an ogre either. He just wasn't like…

Well, he wasn't like Henry. I know, I know—Henry's not perfect either. But as I sit poolside, I realize that Henry's pretty good. Henry is, as Gina described him, "a catch." And I can't see Gina describing Henry as "a little insincere." If anything, Henry's sincerity is both fault and asset.

He won't be trifled with, something I didn't realize while I was with him.

He hadn't brought Joanna Wentworth and Tess Wintergarten to the condo to seduce them. He'd brought them there to prod me. Tell me you're over your former loves whoever they might be, he was saying, and I see only you. Just tell me, goddammit.

Okay, so maybe this technique was lacking in—ahem— the sweet milk of human kindness. Maybe I have a right to be irritated at his blunt approach. But I wasn't giving him much to work with, now was I? He kept his heart safely locked away all right, but he had offered me the key and I had refused to open the safe.

The whole flower-sending routine was a sham. He wasn't bedding those babes. He was merely drumming up business, just like he told me. He didn't mix business with pleasure, and taking them out was obviously not pleasurable, whereas being with me was.

Since coming to France, I've replayed my last scene in the parking lot with Henry more than a dozen times. I keep struggling to remember our precise words because rekindling the anger and hurt assures me I was justified in walking away. But here's the problem—the exact words are lost in a fog of dull ache and emotional confusion. I wonder if my lack of clarity is due to a desire to block out the things I wish I hadn't said.

At some point, though, I realize my befuddlement is actually due to a desire to block out the things *Henry* hadn't said. You see, I'd heard in my mind's ear Henry telling me goodbye-get-lost a hundred different ways since I met him. It was only natural that some version of those words would seep into the memory of our big fight.

But he never said those words. Not in the parking lot. Not ever.

The first time I realized he hadn't said them was when I was lying on a beach staring into glistening water, going over the argument for the fourteenth time. When I figured out he hadn't uttered that phrase, I felt like turning to the bronzed body next to me and apologizing.

That parking lot confrontation was our first really big argument. It didn't have to end with a breakup. It could have ended with a glorious reconciliation followed by a Deeper Understanding.

But I had become proactive, anticipating next steps. I was so sure, at the outset of the relationship, that the ending had already been written somewhere in the skies. Bring it on, I'd shouted to the heavens. Amy Sheldon can take it. She's done it before. She'll do it again. Lose a guy. Move on.

Henry is what he is. What you see is what you get. Except I didn't get him, did I? No, I let him get away. Didn't I say I had a knack for turning gold into dross?

After the pool loses its charm, I find myself skirting its landscaped sides and heading to the beach each day where I watch French families and French men (and some watch me) frolic in the drenching late-summer sun. Sometimes Wendy goes with me but she likes to bring her cell phone and often talks to her mother, who is fast becoming her best buddy. I read, book after book. Old favorites and new thrillers. Before long, I'm brown as a berry and feeling like a girl again at the end of summer vacation when going back to school doesn't sound so bad after all. I'm restless.

Not that it's a bad life. In fact, I highly recommend it.

Our daily routine consists of awakening around ten, eating fresh bread and strong coffee at a local café, changing into our swimsuits and sitting on the beach. Around three, we head for the cottage to nap, then we plan dinner. Going to the market and fixing it takes a couple of hours, then we sip wine on a cool terrace and talk about the future. Sometimes we go to a concert or sometimes we shop in the afternoon or write letters. I keep in touch with Gina every few days to see how she's faring, which is stupendous, all systems go.

By this time, I am comfortable enough to share Gina's pregnancy news with Wendy, and she's feeling better enough to show some genuine happiness, even asking me about her due date and doctor. Not Bernstein, thank God, but some woman named Preston.

I still haven't told Gina about Wendy's miscarriage, but I figure by the time I get back Gina should be past the danger stage of the pregnancy and I'll mention the news to her then. I'm actually looking forward to going back now. I'll be able to spend some time with Gina, shopping for baby clothes with her, then retreating to Wendy's old apartment, so I don't need to worry about running into Fred naked.

I start plotting out a new job-hunt strategy. I will go to a career counselor and maybe even an employment agency and I'll do "informational interviews" with any PR director I can think of. And if that doesn't work, maybe I'll go back to school.

As we sit on the beach every day in our cool sunglasses and oil-slicked bodies, I realize I'm starting to feel optimistic again. Somewhere in the last two years, those nerve endings must have been cut. Now they're rejuvenating. Maybe *this* is a side effect of the magic pills.

The only thing missing from this paradise is Henry. Do I miss him? You betcha. Especially now that I've begun to realize that he wasn't so bad, and he wasn't unfaithful, and he was…well, he was probably in love with me, and he would have told me outright if I hadn't been so sure he was going to hurt me. And I constantly wonder if it's too late.

A week before we're slated to come home, Gina calls again—on a Sunday—because Mom and Dad are over for an end-of-season barbecue. I sit in my sunny bedroom with its deep blue coverlet on the bed and pine furniture and gauzy curtains blowing in the late-day breeze. They all get on the phone, one after another, even Fred, who sounds crazy-happy, the kind of primitive happy a man can get when he likes the idea of getting a woman pregnant. My mother's faraway voice almost makes me want to cry for some stupid reason.

As soon as I get off the phone, it rings again. And I'm thinking it's Gina with something she forgot to tell me or Wendy's mother who sometimes calls on Sundays at the cottage instead of on the cell phone.

But instead, it's someone whom I don't expect to hear from. It's Henry.

When he hears my voice, he says, kind of formally, "Amy, Henry Castle here," as if I have an address book filled with Henrys.

"Hi there," I say shyly, and my heart starts to race in anticipation, because just the sound of his voice dredges up those old want-to feelings—I want to hear him saying things he's never said, and I want to say some things myself that I'm still afraid to say. "Everything okay with Trixie?"

"Huh? Oh, yeah," he says. "Look, I tried to call you yesterday."

"We went to a casino."

"Well, I had a message on my voice mail Friday for you. A Brian Ripton says he wants to talk to you about some new position opening up."

Ripton, Ripton—the veep at the good college who interviewed me, the one to whom I spilled my life story.

"Did he leave a number?" I frantically look for a pen and give up when Henry starts giving me the number. I grab a lipstick and write it on the mirror. "Thanks."

"Sounds promising," he says, in a way that suggests he doesn't want to get off the phone.

"How are you doing?" I ask, sitting on the edge of the bed.

"Pretty good."

I can't resist. "Any new clients?"

I swear I hear him smiling. "Nothing out of the ordinary."

And I want to ask if he's happy or if he aches a little for me the way I do for him, and if he thinks we could give it a try again or if it's better to let it go and oh, by the way, do you still have women to your condo and when you said you thought you were falling in love with me, did that mean you did eventually fall in love with me but I was too blind and dumb to notice?

Instead, I ask, "Send any flowers lately?"

And incredibly, he says, "No."

So we talk for another twenty minutes. I tell him who Ripton is and he speculates about that job.

"I hear they're expanding," he says of the college. "You must have impressed him if he remembers you."

"Oh, yeah, I'm sure I left an impression."

"If you call him back from France, he'll be doubly impressed."

"I can only hope."

"Let me know if you need any help," he offers. "I think you left your résumé on my computer."

"Yeah. I'll call you if I need something. I'll be home in a couple weeks anyway."

"Where you going to stay?"

"Wendy's. She's letting me sublet her place."

"That's nice. Back in the city again, eh?"

"I like the city."

"Me, too."

"Well, I'll call you if I need something," I say, waiting for him to say something significant, to send some signal.

"Right."

When I tell Wendy about the call I funnel all my enthusiasm into reporting that I have a really good job prospect and hardly say a word about the conversation with Henry.

Wendy sits on the terrace looking at a magazine and idly tapping her fingers on the wrought-iron table. She's all in black today—black shorts and tank top, black sandals, black scarf around her hat. Come to think of it, she's beginning to remind me of a blond version of Tess. This is creepy.

"So you can call that guy when you get back! Sounds like you might have a job," she says with appropriate delight.

"No, I was going to call tomorrow."

"You're kidding. From here?"

"We have a phone."

"But you're on vacation."

Uh-oh, she *is* becoming Tess Wintergarten—rich, spoiled, out of touch with the workaday world.

"I think I need to jump on this lead while it's hot," I say. Then I switch topics. "What do you want to do for dinner? We have some leftover chicken."

"We could go out," she says.

Going out is not good for my pocketbook right now. Despite the fact that the major expenses of this trip are covered, Wendy's propensity to do things in the most expensive way possible has meant my little pile of cash has dwindled significantly.

As if reading my mind, she offers, "My treat."

"Okay."

Later, we head to a nearby café where we order shrimp in garlic and provençal vegetables. We drink too much wine and Wendy insists on buying an entire Cointreau-soaked cake to keep at the cottage.

By the time we carry it up the hill to our abode, it has

jostled around in its box and is mashed almost beyond recognition.

In the kitchen, she opens the box. "Mmm," she says, licking her finger, which she has sluiced through some frosting. "The French do know how to cook. When I get married, I'm getting a French cook."

Wendy's desire to get married has reached obsessive proportions. Her mother keeps her abreast of the eligible bachelor population of Hartford and my guess is Wendy has a score sheet hidden among her lingerie.

Later that night, we sit on the terrace eating cake and drinking brandy, and it's nearly ten o'clock but the sky is a royal blue lit by a bright moon.

"Here's to a better next year," I say raising my glass to hers.

"Hip hip," she says in return. "To finding another Rick."

For some reason, I don't feel like drinking to that toast.

"Henry," she says confidentially, "was no Rick."

No, I silently answer. He wasn't. Thank God for that. And I tell her, at last, about Rick's desire to call off the wedding.

Without missing a beat, she says, "The schmuck… Damn them, they're all schmucks!" and she gushes for a half hour about how hard it must have been on me, and peppers me with questions about his family, and whether anyone else knew, and we talk long into the night.

After she heads to bed, I change into my bathing suit and dive into the silent pool for one last lonely swim.

The next day I wait until early afternoon to call Brian Ripton, calculating that he will just be arriving in his office by then. And when I tell him I'm phoning from France, he is suitably impressed. The college has decided to expand their public relations office, he tells me, and divide into a publications department and a public relations department. They want someone to head up the publications department, though, who has PR experience—not a graphic designer but someone used to working with graphic designers. Remembering my background at the ad agency and how well our interview went, he wonders if I'm interested in the job.

It's all I can do to keep from screaming hysterically. Am I interested in the job? Am I…

"Yes," I say smoothly. "Very interested."

"I'll call Human Resources and get the ball rolling. We have to post it first, of course."

Of course. For internal candidates. Damn. It seemed so close. So close.

No, dammit. I won't let it get away. Not like I let Henry get away.

"Mr. Ripton, why don't I fly in tomorrow and we can talk about it?"

"I'd hate for you to cut your vacation short."

"It's just about over anyway. And I'm very, very interested in this position…" And then I go into a spiel about the college and how much I liked it there when I interviewed and what I saw in their current publications that could be improved and how I'd go about doing that using their current resources, and by the time I'm done I'm sure someone else has taken over my body because it doesn't sound like me anymore.

No, it does sound like me. The old me. Optimistic. Goal-oriented.

When I finish, Ripton says he looks forward to talking to me and I know if I manage to get to him in the next forty-eight hours I can probably bypass Human Resources. He's a VP, after all, and he can tell them who he wants. After all, if Sister Mary Altamont could do it, surely he can.

"I'm going home," I announce to Wendy when she wanders into my room after lunch. Already, I start throwing things into my suitcases.

"Why?"

"That job—it looks like it's coming through for me."

"Oh." She pouts. "It can't wait? I was thinking we could rent a car and drive to Monaco at the end of the week."

"Sorry, Wen. This is a big chance for me." I open my wallet and am disappointed to see that I'm lower on cash than I thought. I ended up tipping the waiter the night before when Wendy didn't have a small-enough bill. I don't think it would be politic of me to ask for the money back, even though it was her idea to go out. It's a good thing I'm leaving. Too much friendship can be expensive.

Zipping my suitcase shut, I turn to her. "I called and I can catch an evening flight. If I hurry, I can be at the airport in time." There's a small airport nearby that connects to larger hubs. From there, I'll zoom home. It will take every single last cent I have to do it. When I concocted this plan in the five minutes after I got off the phone with Brian Ripton, I figured I'd borrow money from Wendy to make it home.

But now, looking at her mouth twisted into a frown and her leg twitching angrily in front of her, I realize that Wendy is no longer the kind, generous woman who invited me on this trip as a way of thanking me for helping her. Wendy is now…her mother's daughter. She wants what she wants when she wants it. And she wants me to stay. Better not to ask for money. I'll make do. I have a few bucks left on my credit card limit.

"Well, whatever…" she says, and leaves.

After tucking my passport into my purse and my sunglasses on my nose, I call for a taxi to meet me at the bottom of the hill. I've noticed they charge an exorbitant amount more to come up to the cottage. Then I find Wendy in the kitchen and give her a big hug, which seems to melt the crust she's formed and makes her return to her old self, at least for the moments we say goodbye.

"Hey, it's been great fun, Ame," she says, sniffling. "Don't know what I would have done without you."

"Well, you go get 'em, tiger," I say. "I expect a wedding invitation in the mail by Christmas."

"I'll be working on it."

Excited, I tramp down the hill and wait, and end up cutting so close to the bone with my expenses that I have exactly two dollars and twenty-three cents in my purse when I finally board a jet home. I didn't even have enough money to buy myself dinner at the airport, consequently I get on the plane with a splitting headache and no pills. I used up my last one a week ago.

I settle into a seat and listen to two college grads nearby giggling and chattering for hours about how great their two weeks in Paris were and how funny it is that the roast beef dinners they're serving on the plane taste like chocolate. I don't have the heart or the stomach to tell them that the roast beef has Grand Marnier in it, which is a liqueur used in some French chocolates.

The smell of the stuff nearly does me in and I have to head for the can twice during the trip, but nothing comes up. I try to think of other things. The whole random-thought thing: images of pools, myself diving in, coolness, slickness surrounding me, a feeling of weightlessness. By this time I realize I haven't made any arrangements for an airport pickup, and I don't have enough money for a cab or an airport-to-city limo or anything. I can't think about that. All I can think about is my headache.

Hours later—or is it decades—the plane bumps and rocks its way through heavy cloud cover on its way into BWI. I alternate between prayers to stay alive and prayers to not vomit on those nicely dressed girls next to me.

When I head down the narrow walkway into the airport, I look for a phone. I don't know what time it is, only that it's light outside. I'm still on European time.

No answer at Gina's. What the hell—I call Henry. I try his office and punch in his extension after the electronic directory comes on. No receptionist, no secretary. He answers the phone himself—he's there!

"You said to call if I needed anything."

He recognizes my voice instantly. "I did."

"Well, I need a ride from the airport."

"When?"

"Right now."

He laughs. "I'll be glad to come get you." He tells me where he'll meet me and that he'll be there in about a half hour.

After getting off the phone, I have just enough money to afford a Coke. With it, I sink onto a black-cushioned bench in the waiting area where Henry said he'd meet me, and swallow about half the Coke while I find a Motrin bottle on the bottom of my bag. Only three left, but they'll have to do. I'll get my magic pills refilled in the morning.

Maybe I'm dehydrated, because the Coke starts to revive me. Or maybe it's the Motrin. Or maybe it's being home again. Or maybe, or maybe…

Maybe it's the sight of Henry, ten minutes late, rushing down the walkway with a big grin on his face. And his heart on his sleeve.

Funny how I never noticed it there before.

In his hand is a huge bouquet of flowers. Tulips. Garish red tulips. Declaration of love. And I know he knows what they mean.

"Welcome home, *conchita,*" he says and swallows me up in a big, fat kiss.

On sale November 2005

Hardly Working
by Betsy Burke

Lessons on how to catch a snooze, a fab deal on eBay and a new boyfriend— all on company time.

PR chick Dinah Nichols and the rest of the gang at Green World International have never taken themselves or their work too seriously—until now. When head office takes notice, Dinah has to spin her PR magic and work hard to make this "hardly working" crew shine.

Available wherever trade paperbacks are sold.

RED DRESS
INK
TM

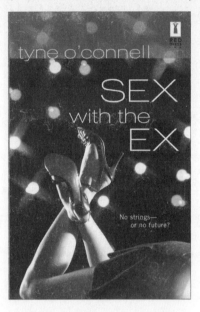